Hippocrates and

The Hobgoblin

~ The Child of Mürindür ~

A Novel By

C.S. Colvin

Illustrations By

F. Introne

Published by Pondering Corporis 2018

Printed in the United States of America

First Printing, 2018

ISBN 978-0-578-42721-8

Dedication

This book is dedicated to my friends, family, and patients that we could not save, for the ones that we thankfully did, and for all the others that we hope to salvage along Life's bridge. To my wife and family, thank you for helping me find my way home at a time that I did not think it possible. For my children, remember these three things:

1). Neither the mind nor memories therein define your existence.

2). The world is far more beautiful as seen through the eyes of imagination.

3). The heart never forgets.

Luxatio aeternum

Author's Note

Life is a precipice. It hurts at times to balance, bare and precariously, on the rugged rock. It demands forbearance and fortitude. For many lost souls, it's far easier to stare into the Abyss below. There's a solace there, an anticipated practicality colored in absolute, where the fog and fatigue of an ubiquitous unknown fades to the ebon glow of certainty. It is seductively effortless to fall. For those suffocating amongst the living, it seems serene; no further need for strength, or struggle, hapless breath, or agony, but through even the darkest of times, heed that siren's temptation. It is merely a façade, a fleeting relief from whatever burden you bear, but for those left behind, your legacy becomes ugly, fetid, and flawed until nothing-recognizable remains. Therefore, hold fast upon that rock even if for but a moment, each time you tempt your fate. The terrain was never meant to break you, merely strengthen what lies within. - csc

Table of Contents

Hippocrates and

The Hobgoblin

~ The Child of Mürindür ~

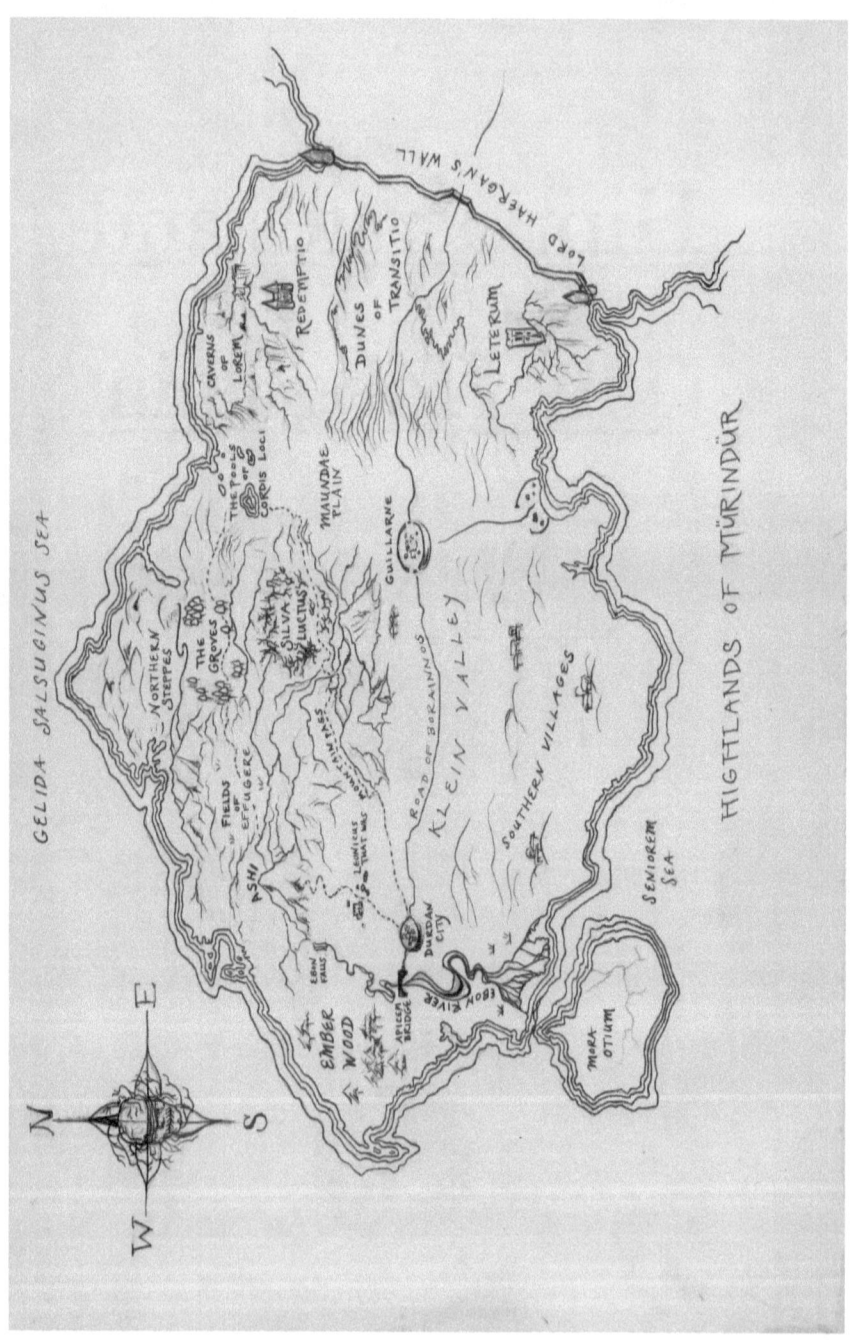

Chapter 1: A Dream

A white-oak fan twirled the tepid bedroom air, as Time slipped into a slumber, and the world slowed. The restless man in the sheets below, however, fought fervently the nightmares roiling about in his mind, while sounds of the bustling city mumbled and slurred. In an archaic anchor realm far from our own, at the feet of an eternal prison, imbued gates buckled from their hinges, and the forces of a relentless rage surged forth. As the last hero fell in the caustic ambush, a somber, sacrificial presence took flight from the fissured mortar of the walls. Bound no longer, it traveled as a slipstream across the cosmos, past the stars, toward something quite predestined. More than a thought or memory, it was a remnant of something long lost. Drifting through the ceiling vent above, the ethereal mist settled. It glided, gilded, quietly into the nares of the exhausted physician. It burned and disappeared.

Creed choked, coughed, and sat up quickly as if to spit. He looked about, and rubbed his face briskly in a disoriented fashion as his chest heaved and ached. Thinking it was heartburn, he shuffled to the fridge in the nearby kitchen, and garnered a gallon of milk. The carton was half empty when a cluttered bang and rustle crashed about his backyard. A recent neighborhood watch reported four burglaries this month, so with the flip of a light switch, Creed peered into the small yard of brown grass and empty flower pots. Something blue and luminescent skirted along the fence line. He blinked and it was gone, but curiosity led him into the grass. Barefoot and tired, Creed noted nothing out of the ordinary beyond a broken pot and something akin to bird tracks in the potting soil. Mere feet away, a Raven peered at him from a fence post, shrouded in a faint white smoke. With a squawk, it took flight, and was consumed in the moonlight.

§

The following afternoon surpassed him once again in a brilliant debacle of poor commuter planning. Lack of sleep contributed to a mid-day nap, an inadvertent alarm silenced, and now he was at the mercy of five o'clock traffic in the metropolis.
"Come on! Use the goddamn turn signal, jackass!"
Creed laid into the horn, and the nearby driver bellowed something unintelligible with the middle finger. Foo Fighters' "Walk" was screaming at him through the speakers, the rain was relentless, and the dashboard clock was annoyingly accurate. It was a quarter past five in the afternoon, and this would be the third shift for a month he was late. He ran the badge across the parking garage sensor repeatedly until the barrier rose, and he pulled quickly into the corner spot. Grabbed his coat and stethoscope, forgot his lunch in the jeep, and hurried into the stairwell. He hadn't met with his director yet, but it wouldn't be long. It was painfully obvious when you ran late to an ER shift… repeatedly.
He snuck in via the back hallway past pre-op, around the elevators, and through the doors next to room "25". Nurse Chandler wasn't amused.

"Dr. Huntly, he's been waiting for you for thirty minutes. There are fifteen charts in the rack." She motioned with her head around the corner.

"Who? Rainard?"

"No. Luckily for you, Dr. Rainard is upstairs with admin to discuss Joint Commission. Dr. Tarney is pretty angry. He's been waiting to turn over two people with workups pending, and you forgot tonight was his anniversary. Creed, you look like shit." Nurse Chandler had a way with words. Blunt. Factual.

"I'm not sleeping, and when I sleep it's when I shouldn't be," he replied.

"Did you shower?"

"Yes of course I did. You think I like wallowing in the crap particles down here?"

"I have no idea, but you better get over to the front side in a hurry. Tarney's wife called up here, and when he got off the phone it looked like he needed a new pair of pants from the ass-chewing he got."

Creed ran past the counter racks of the nurses' station, grabbed a few charts, and logged into his computer. He glanced up to see Tarney staring him down, coldly.

"Glad you could make it, Huntly."

"Sorry, Jim... I just..."

"Whatever, man. Mallory just called me, and I have 45 minutes to make it all the way across town to get ready for our dinner. We talked about this last week."

"Jim...listen, I..."

"No. Look, we all feel bad. Every single one of us, but it's been a year now, and we're just watching you turn into this screw-up. This hospital is a beat down, and we're all burnt. If you need a break, then take one, but we can't keep waiting on you to get your life…" Creed could see the anger on his face.

"Enough. I get it. I'm sorry. I've been talking to someone. Just started last week. Ran late from the appointment. It won't happen again."

"You're talking to someone now?" Tarney, asked.

"Yeah."

"That's good man. Who is it?"

"I'd rather keep it quiet. Just don't want to make a big deal out of it," Creed replied.

"Fine. I won't say anything. You're not drinking, are you?"

"I don't drink anymore. You know that."

"What's that smell?"

"What smell?" Creed turned, and realized his long white coat smelled like a liquor store dumpster. He dug in his pockets, and the small, hand-held sanitizer bottle had leaked in the heat of his jeep. His coat was a slimy alcohol swab.

"Fantastic."

"Listen, I gotta go. Bed eighteen is an old guy with smelly urine and soaked diapers. He's a little altered, and low-grade temp with a history of dementia. Waiting on labs, but then he should come in for an admission assuming the head CT is normal. Bed twenty-two is a vaginal bleeder with fibroids, and I was just checking her blood tests, but couldn't find a nurse to do a pelvic exam. She's screaming and acts like she's dying, so I ordered an ultrasound also. I'm sure she's fine, but if you could check, that would be great." Tarney smirked as he gathered his things.

"Tell Mallory I said, Hi, and I'm sorry."

"She knows. None of us see you anymore outside of the hospital, Creed. We should get together sometime. Even if it's just for a sports event or something."

"Yeah I'll let you know. Have fun."

"Well hopefully my wife won't be livid all night. Seriously, if you need to talk…"

"I'm making it man. One day at a time. Get out of here before you make me feel worse." Creed nodded as he cleared his throat, turning to the desktop, and reviewing the department tracking board.

There is a rhyme and reason to a tertiary ER. It's an intersection of humanity and happenstance. Decisions run amok countered by conscience and medical endeavors. Dark but somewhat justified, emergency medicine in Creed's mind served as an ironic thwarting of Darwin's theory. Most of his time and energy was spent on people making bad decisions, and what little reconciliation he could offer. He didn't do this job because of the mounds of mistakes in the waiting room, however. He didn't enjoy pelvic exams or medication refills. He didn't enjoy debating the need for antibiotics with overzealous soccer moms. He lived in the pit, this pit, waiting for the people that truly needed him… the patients suffering the worst moments imaginable in an effort to hopefully reverse the near-death… the almost tragic.

The Emergency Department was chaotic as usual for a Friday afternoon, and the paramedics were lined up at the ambulance bay entry. Patients leaned against the wall holding emesis basins while nurses and techs scrambled to turn over beds with new sheets and gowns. It was a machine. Flu, strep, pneumonia, strokes, heart attacks, psychotics, drug addicts, and gunshot wounds moved from the city streets through the halls of Mercy like refugees on a conveyor belt.

He looked at the tracking board, and planned out his strategy for the shift. Who is the most ill, who could he get out quickly, and what procedures likely needed to be done. He made his way to the first exam room when Dr. Rainard walked up to him. Dread. Sheer dread.

"Hello, Creed."

"Dr. Rainard," Creed acknowledged.

"Please, when are you going to start calling me Paul?"

"I guess when I don't feel like I'm constantly on the verge of being called into your office."

"That's mostly up to you, you know that, right?" Rainard was always one for the rhetorical.

"Yes."

"You got a few minutes?" the director asked.

"Of course," Creed nodded.

"We can just talk over here." They made their way to the hall corner.

"Listen, your late arrivals on shift have to stop today. Period. End of discussion. The whole group is getting irritated with you. I understand you were half an hour late today?"

"Yes."

"I think everyone has naturally given you some significant space, as have I, but you still have a job to do, and professionalism is of the utmost importance."

"I understand," Creed acknowledged.

"Do you? We've had this discussion multiple times, and I'm sorry to say that this has to serve as your final warning. I'm going to write this up as a formal counseling session, and we're going to outline a performance improvement plan."

"I see. Sounds fantastic." Creed fidgeted with his stethoscope as he looked at his boots.

"Fantastic? Really?"

"I'm sorry. None of it is intentional. I hope you know that. I love working here which is why I stayed after residency. I love the people. I still love medicine. I just need some more time to figure stuff out," Creed explained.

"Your time is up. You need to start seeing a counselor."

"I'm fine."

"No, you're not. Nothing is fine. You may take excellent care of patients, but your life needs to be more than that. Your job needs to be more than that as well. Part of your performance plan is to attend a weekly counseling session. I have someone I want you to see."

"I don't think HR would approve of mandatory psych sessions, and I'm…"

"I don't care about HR, Creed. I'm worried about you, and where I may find you in six months. You haven't been the same since you lost Jessie, and I feel I have to do everything I can to get you back on track. You have a gift, and a promising career, and no one blames you for struggling, but in the end, we have to expect everyone to perform to a certain standard. Your charts are often 30-40 in the hole. You've had a couple of patient complaints this month as well."

"They were drug seekers."

"That may be, but you need to start addressing everything, or you're going to need to find a new place to work. I'm sorry, and I feel horrible for saying that, but it's time. I need you to pick yourself up again, and the department needs you to get your stuff together. Understand?" The tone was more paternalistic than nihilistic.

"Yeah," Creed replied. At 6'3", he stood a good six inches over Rainard, and yet felt as if he were five years old again. Creed's long dark hair hung over his brow, and slightly obscured his hazel eyes. He was angry, and felt cornered, but he didn't want to disappoint his director. Rainard was in his early fifties, and had been at the institution longer than Creed had been an adult. He was well respected, and known to be invested in his colleagues. His nickname with the nursing staff was "Papa Bear". There wasn't an easy way to say 'no' to him. Rainard handed Creed the counselor's business card, looked up at him, and placed his hand on his shoulder.

"The first session is always the most difficult. I made an appointment for you on Monday at 10 a.m."

"I work Monday."

"I'm taking your shift, so you can do this."

"Yeah but I...." Creed protested.

"You're working 18 shifts this month. I think taking this shift off your shoulders is reasonable."

"Fine. I'll be there on Monday."

There was a noise up front in the waiting room. A bunch of bodies ran through the doorway. He could hear the screaming. A mother ran into triage and tossed her limp, gray, infant into the nurse's arms.

"Dr. Huntly! Dr. Huntly! We need you in Room One now!!"

Creed looked up to see the little mass crumpled in the nurse's hands as she ran to the large resuscitation bay.

Damn, he thought.

"Good luck, Creed. Someone else needs you." Creed looked at him, and turned toward the exam room as Rainard walked down the hallway back to his office.

"Ok. Get the baby on the monitor. Call respiratory. Let's hit the 'Code Blue' button. Genie, get an IV and assign some people for compressions. Do we have a pulse?" he asked out loud. Creed felt along the soft infant arm. Nothing. He felt for the femoral artery. Nothing.

"Start compressions. Get the mom in here." Personnel came in from everywhere.

"Code Blue" was a common occurrence in the department, but babies were always different. It's unnatural and wholly unfair to see such innocence truncated abruptly. The stress was palpable, and everyone wanted to help in some way. These were the moments that always served as the crucible of a physician's mettle. Creed's voice and heart rate slowed. His speech pattern became methodical like a metronome of commands.

Slow and steady, keep the beat. Keep everyone moving.

He took a short history from the distraught mother. No known trauma. Normal birth. No sick contacts. No recent doctor visits. No fevers.

"No, doctor. She was just fine yesterday," the woman explained.

"Are there new people in the home?" Creed asked.

"Yes, my boyfriend." Fontanelle was soft. The charge nurse gave Creed a concerned look.

Bruising on the neck.

"Where's the boyfriend?" Creed asked.

"We were giving her a bath, and I left to get the fresh towels out of the dryer. She's been real colicky lately, and I heard her crying, so I decided to make some formula, and warm it up for her. I went upstairs, and she wasn't breathing. My boyfriend was giving her mouth to mouth. After we called 911, he went to his mother's house to get the car, but now he won't answer his phone."

Check the pupils.

"Pupils are fixed and dilated guys. Keep going. Give another dose of Epinephrine. What we got? Pulse check."

No pulse.

"Keep doing compressions. I have nothing on the monitor. Please continue bagging." Three more rounds of CPR and epinephrine took place over 15 minutes.

Why do they always kill the kids?

"Pulse check," Creed exclaimed.

Come on. Come on. Do something. Anything. You don't.... wait. What's that? Yes!

"I have a pulse! Monitor shows sinus tachycardia at 160. Let's get the chest x-ray and go!" While they waited for the x-ray tech, Creed placed a breathing tube down the infant's throat to help her breathe. As he did so, copious amounts of water and blood came up from her lungs.

He drowned her. That piece of shit.

"Ma'am, I think your boyfriend needs to come up here. I have a few questions for him."

When he looked up though, she was gone. No one could find her. The infant was all alone besides the caregivers in the room. Creed notified the police officer in the hallway about his findings. The search for the mother and boyfriend began. Meanwhile, the nurses packed the baby up for CT. They had done this three times already this week.

No time to waste. Creed was notified that four more ambulances were en route with victims of a five-vehicle collision at highway speed. He could hear the screaming from the ambulance bay doors. "My leg! My leg! Oh God!"

Paramedics were holding the patient down while keeping pressure on the wound with gauze and the tourniquet they placed. The patient's left leg had been severed mid-thigh. Apparently, he had been trapped within the engine block and steering wheel. They brought the leg in as well, but it was mangled with fragments of bone jutting through the flesh.

"This is a 24-year-old male who T-boned a mini-van at high speed. Two vehicles hit his vehicle from behind. We have two IV's, and his current blood pressure is 95/50. No medical history. He's been drinking, and admitted to cocaine use."

"My leg!!! Oh my God!!!" The man screamed as Creed shook his head, looking at the bloody mess before him.

"We need trauma down here, and let them know we have three more rolling into rooms. Get the blood going on the rapid infuser, and let's give him some TXA," he said as he finished his exam, "and a brief bedside ultrasound for internal bleeding."

The Trauma team arrived and started barking orders as usual. Luckily, Creed didn't have to deal with the team, just the staff trauma surgeon, Flannigan. They had known each other since residency, and both stayed at Mercy along with their girlfriends at the time. They occasionally met up at parties, but for the last year, ever since Jessie died, Creed just worked. Continuously. Weekend shifts, holidays, nights. Whichever shifts people wanted to give up. He hadn't seen Flannigan in anything other than some ED crisis. It was good to see him now.

"Marcus, this guy's pressure is dropping and he has free fluid in the belly. Obviously, his leg is gone, and Ortho needs to get involved. Giving him 4 units of blood now. Spine seems good. I haven't done any scans. He is piss drunk, but needs the OR."

"Yeah looks like it. Give him some Ancef, and we'll tube him upstairs. Anesthesia already has the room ready. I hear there's three others?"

"Yeah been in here with this one. No idea what's waiting for us in the department."

"Well," Flannigan said with a smirk as he ran his fingers through his curly red hair, "I haven't pulled an all-nighter in the OR since last week. Might as well get the coffee brewing. Gonna be a long one."

"I'll let you know what I find out," Creed assured. They nodded at each other, albeit the subtle awkwardness was still there. Nothing needed to be said. Nothing could be said.

The end of the shift came quicker than expected, and he finished up his charts around 2 am. Creed saw a total of 40 patients, although now their faces were a blur. His body was exhausted with small muscles twitching here and there in his feet, but his mind was still rolling 100 miles per hour. He walked out to the dim lit parking garage, and turned the ignition. It was so quiet besides the hum of his Jeep. He hated it when the hospital sounds were gone. They helped distract him, but now there were no beeps or alarms. No order requests. No bed rails falling anymore. Just eerily and vacuously quiet. It was times like these that he would pretend he had more work to do, or go back into the hospital to "look over some things", but he knew he needed to go.

The ride home was solemn. There wasn't a car anywhere to be seen. It was as if he had the world to himself if even but a brief moment. A few miles later, he slowly pulled into the driveway of his three-bedroom home, and turned the jeep off. Quiet again. It had to be close to 4 a.m. by now. He was feeling tired which was a start. Didn't even bother to shower at this point. Walked past Jessie's hobby room, the first closed door in the hallway, and lumbered toward his king-sized bed. The soft glow of the aquarium and the gentle grind of the water filter eased him into the sheets. He clicked on his oscillating fan for some more white noise.

It was a December night uncharacteristically warm so late in the year. The fan turned, and the air conditioner hummed, but Creed still sweat through his sheets. His insomnia was relentless despite his efforts, but he knew once his mind was able to disconnect from the day, the dreams would be worth it.

Shortly after the death of his fiancée, his nightmares had given way to someone else, another woman. She was familiar and kind, and although it was never a guarantee, he hoped to see her again tonight. He needed to. When she would visit, her presence settled him, and he felt it was enough to carry him through the day. He rolled to his side, semi-conscious. His mind churned. The ER shifts were blending together. Faces of strangers suffering from their myriad of disorders and injuries. Frustrated, he looked at the pill bottle on the nightstand next to the mineral water. He hated the need for those things, but within seconds, he swallowed three tablets, beckoning some semblance of rest. He tried to picture the elk in the meadow of his mind, and the shimmering water of the thousand pools.

Breathe. Just Breathe.

§

The amber-shag bull Elk lumbered through the felled aspen and evergreens. His antlers hung low within the fog as he foraged, but occasionally the ivory tips of his blackened main beams rose nearly as high as his shrill bugle. The cascades of sound reverberated down the mountainside.

Creed felt the wind across his face, and breathed deeply. It was clean. Pine was in the air. Willows and birch trees embraced the evening's glow as the moon scattered its fingertips through the forest boughs, and anchored a glowing spring of light near the water's edge. The woman was there. Creed smiled, and a calm was felt. She stood patiently waiting, beautiful and tall. Legs interlaced, her slender figure was silhouetted beneath the silk gown and light. Some of her facial features were hidden, and yet again she was so familiar. High cheekbones, flaxen hair, and smiling eyes welcomed him.

"Good evening, kind sir," the woman said playfully. Her voice, soothing, hypnotic.

"Hello again," Creed replied.

"You look tired, my love."

"I am." He shrugged. He felt for his pockets, but the linen pants he wore had none.

"Why so …"

"Melancholy?" Creed asked.

"I was going to say timid," she replied, reaching for him. Creed looked around, lost in a way, but comfortable as if he were home.

"We meet here like a hidden secret, but I don't know your name."

"Oh, but you do, my love."

"I feel like I should. Every night, well most nights, you're waiting for me. Your name is somewhere in my mind. It's Heavenly I suspect."

"Almost."

"Aren't you afraid of being here… out here alone at night?" he asked her.

"Why would I be?" she questioned.

"Well for starters there are wolves, bears, and some kind of tracks near the water's edge I've never seen before." As Creed studied the tracks, the large cloven hoof marks in the mud bristled his skin. The woman moved to ease his mind, so she smiled and offered her hand as he walked towards her. Creed tried to brush her hair aside, but she demurred, and held his hand tight instead. He found the mystery intriguing.

"Let me help you rest," she said, as he leaned forward. He reached for her waist, and let his gentle grasp slip slowly to her hip. She cradled his head, and kissed him.

They settled onto the soft tawny grass. It was as they had done so a thousand times. He was bigger than her, and yet she held him closely as if he weighed nothing. He felt peace, and tranquility, but most of all he felt loved. Creed couldn't remember who he was or what he did, but he felt as if he knew her as long as he had ever known existence. The small bump beneath her gown had grown. He felt the baby move as he placed his hand over her belly, and smiled. She laughed, gently.

"Don't get him all excited. Every time you're near him, he kicks and bucks endlessly. I suspect he's ever much the troublemaker as his father."

"I can't wait to meet him," Creed chuckled. "When will that be you think?"

"It won't be long my love. You've forgotten so much as you always do, but when it's time, you'll arrive. Everything will come back to you as before. Your home and your family will be here. We'll be together again soon, and many of our…" there was a loud snap of a tree limb nearby.

The tranquil moment was over. Creed sat up abruptly, and reached for something, anything as a weapon, but there was nothing but cold air across his feet. She stood as well, and readied herself. He looked at her, but she was calm and unafraid. Creed could feel his stomach churn. Something was off entirely. The sounds came and went.

"What is it?" Creed asked warily.

"Shhhhh… my love."

"We need to go," Creed insisted. He reached out as thoughts of her being harmed burned his mind's eye.

"Not yet. Wait," she replied.

"I don't want to lose you…" Another limb snapped beneath a heavy pace. Creed grabbed her hand, and pulled her toward him. She placed her hands upon his chest.

"I'm never far from you, my love. Rest and we'll see each other soon. No matter how many lives you traverse, remember this, the heart never forgets." There was a flash, she was gone, and he was alone once again. The mountainside faded slowly as the ground drained itself from his bearings. After a few moments, he was within a void. Quiet. Cold. Nothing.

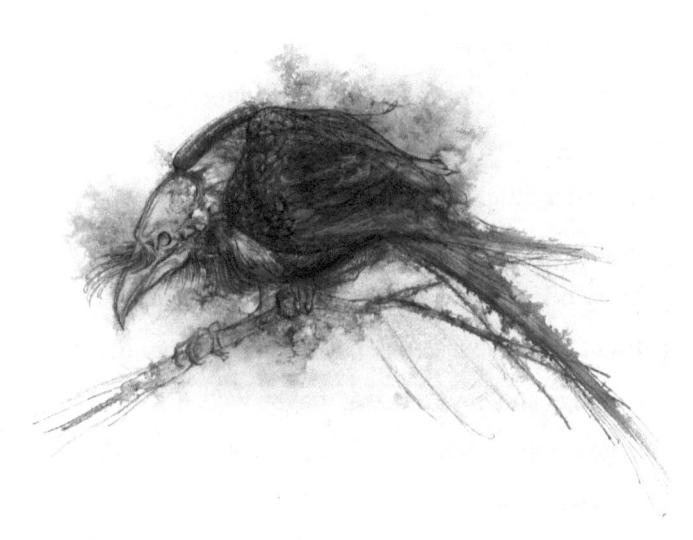

Chapter 2: A Conversation

Sunday arrived, and he had the day off. Creed finally got some decent sleep, and by mid-afternoon, he was awake, sipping coffee alone. The Austrian cuckoo clock on the kitchen wall rolled its gears with a gentle tick, tick, tick as the bronze pinecone counterweights stretched for the floor. The winter's grey was spilling around the window blinds, so he cracked them just a little. A cold-weather front had blown in overnight. The wind whistled about haphazardly as he touched the frosty pane.

A day off was more a burden than a relief. He didn't want to go outside. No close friends to speak of, not anymore. He could go to the Village and have a pizza, maybe walk a ways around the college campus. Not sure if the museums were open. The flower garden was solemn for winter. What to do? He felt more amiss within his home than without, and had contemplated selling it. He felt uneasy every time he passed Jessie's room. Her ghost seemed to hover there.

He thought about the local sports bar, just for the noise and energy of a Sunday football game on the big TVs. The bar was too tempting though; it would be too easy to have 'just one drink'. After Jessie had passed, Creed knew one thing. He wasn't going to break. He wasn't going to quit like she did, and he had managed enough patients with enough mistakes to know alcohol at that moment would become an 'oft too easy escape…', a rabbit hole to absenteeism. It would be too convenient, and he felt too undone, too conflicted to allow something so certain into his life, so avoidance was necessary. Since the home wasn't where he wished to be, Creed dressed and set out to walk the nearby university campus.

The trees were wistful as willowy as they were. Occasionally the wind would nip his eyes, and he'd blink. He had walked the track hundreds of times. His thighs and back were too tired to run again today. The walk was nice, but it didn't slow his mind. He had no plans for the holidays considering he was an only child, and his parents had passed away. The world was so big yet seemed like an infinitesimally small confine of memories and space in time. How does one move forward? He had been in survival mode for so long that he forgot what it felt like to laugh, to live. He was alone, and nothing made it more evident than his continued trek across the track.

The Fine Arts Museum wasn't far away, and he saw a banner strung up high on a lamppost advertising the Monet Water Lilies series. It was a touring exhibit for the next eight weeks, and who knows when he'd have another chance at something so beautiful. He loved Monet, and the ideal blend of water and introspect was something he felt akin, so naturally a day at the museum was now the agenda. Though the day turned toward the lower temperatures, it would be worth the effort. *Not much further anyway*, he thought.

He walked inside the doors, and greeted an elderly gentleman. He paid and ventured past the front counter. The Monet exhibit was to his left, but first he smelled the coffee. The small shop had freshly brewed some Columbian roast, and he felt nothing would suit the art tour better than a tall cup. The aromatic warmth relaxed his chilled hands, and he headed down the long hall of inspiration. Although it was quiet on the auditory front, it was an explosion of visual volumes. The lines and light in each piece took minutes to appreciate. He was in no hurry, and the occasional new patron admission would break the otherwise singular sound of feet across the freshly waxed floors.

I wish I could paint like this. I should have been an artist. Imagine molding the world through my perspective, he thought.

He smelled a fresh waft of lavender.

"I'm sorry to bother you, but where did you get that coffee?" Her accent sounded foreign, but he couldn't place it. He looked to his left thinking she had approached him from the start of the hall, and felt sheepish when he realized she was to his right. He turned again awkwardly, startled that someone would reach into his meditative moment, and started to speak.

"It's just to the right of the..." Her eyes and voice were strangely familiar.

"I feel like I know you from somewhere. Do you work at Mercy?" She smiled, and shook her head.

"No."

"I'm sorry. I could have sworn we've met. I'm pretty awful with names, but I generally never forget a face. A patient's family member perhaps, or...."

Her azure gaze was striking behind the cat eye, black-rim glasses. Her hair was a vibrant strawberry blonde pulled high into an updo with some wisps wound errantly down her temples. Creed had somehow become a simpleton in less than three seconds.

"Well it's always good not to have a forgetful face," as she smiled, "Where did you say the coffee was?"

That voice....

"Yes, ma'am just to the right of where you came in. They just made a fresh batch."

Say something you idiot, she's making eye contact and conversation.

He couldn't. He'd forgotten how. All he could do was stand there, trying not to look stupid, as his mouth searched for something beyond the sudden overwhelming dryness.

"Enjoy the Monets," she encouraged, as she turned toward the coffee shop. Her ivory, woven duster, dark jeans, and over-the-knee boots made him stare a little too long, long enough for her to turn and acknowledge him.

She has dimples.

He cleared his throat, and turned away.

Creed returned to his art revival, studying each brush stroke as he wondered what sounds and weather swirled about Monet when he massaged his palette. He stopped at one beautiful image of a high arching Japanese bridge cast across the pond. What a beautiful metaphor he contemplated.

An origin, an arch, and a destination. Much like Life I suppose.

He stared at the light strokes on the far end of the bridge when suddenly they wavered. It was subtle, but for a moment he felt he saw a woman in the distant grass. She seemed to smile. It was mesmerizing.

"Ever wondered why he chose that bridge?" The woman in her woven duster asked, with coffee in hand.

"Yes," startled, Creed chuckled. "I've wondered many times. I was just thinking what if there was no bridge. How would that change its meaning? It's almost as if since there is a bridge, we have to cross it otherwise what's the point?" He looked at the painting once more, and the mystery woman in the distance was gone.

"Wow. I just liked the pretty colors." She expressed her impress in playful intonation. There were her dimples again.

"I never did catch your name," Creed noted. Now he was composed; granted he had to look away when he asked otherwise he might begin to fumble.

"I'm not supposed to talk to strangers."

"I did help you find coffee," Creed joked.

"True. Do you see anything else you like in the painting?" Her left eyebrow raised slightly.

"I like the bridge. I can picture myself walking to the middle of it, and looking down into the reflection of the pond. Staring into the water, I imagine my face and expressions would be distorted, an alternate reality with the ripples. Without the bridge, I don't think we could have that unique perspective, a challenge to our status quo." He looked at her, and his face felt warm. "I can remember my parents had this small wooden bridge over their dry creek. I used to pretend I could travel in time from one island to the next while grumpy old trolls lived under the bridge. I guess I had a pretty active imagination." He was sincere and trying to ignore the impasse of introductions, but she simply smiled again.

"You do have an old soul." She sipped slowly on her coffee as he looked at her. Creed knew he'd somehow seen her before, but where? College? Medical school? Hospital? Charity banquet?

"Yeah, I suppose I do. You sure we haven't met?"

"Not in this lifetime." She looked at the painting and sighed.

"Heh." Now he smiled. "Yeah if I had a past life, I'm not sure I would have jumped head first into this one. Probably would have just stayed where I was at."

"Naturally. If we had a choice, why would anyone want to jump into uncertainty?"

"Morbid curiosity?" he replied.

She laughed. There was a gentle joyfulness in it. He looked at his watch. It was getting close to 6 p.m., the museum would close soon, and he still needed to get groceries. It was going to be another long week ahead. He also had that counseling session tomorrow at 10, and Rainard would be expecting him to make it. He didn't want to leave, but it was time.

"Well, it was a pleasure meeting you. Hope you enjoy the coffee and water lilies." Creed turned toward the door.

"Pleasure meeting you." She took another sip from her coffee looking up at him through her lashes.

"Well," *Do I shake her hand? Do I wave?* "Have a good day." He turned and left the art gallery somewhat stupefied, walking into the crisp air, and retraced his steps to the university's parking lot.

Home again, and the house was quiet as ever. He put the groceries away, and considered dinner, but somehow wasn't hungry. The hum of the aquarium became slightly louder when he raised the lid to feed his four fish. The fish, however, did have an appetite, and nipped at the water's surface as they each swallowed the orange and yellow flakes. He wanted a bigger aquarium, but considering he couldn't even keep up with his own laundry, it was unwise. He threw a load of scrubs into the washing machine, and ran it, not knowing what he'd wear tomorrow to meet the counselor. If he dressed as though for an interview, she'd think he

31

was odd and obsessive. If he wore a T-shirt and jeans, she'd likely consider him insincere and inconsiderate. He hated the idea of being analyzed. What to do? Maybe he'd get the flu tonight, or develop appendicitis. He didn't want this meeting to happen. He had a hard-enough time sorting through the things in his mind let alone allowing someone else to wander inside as well. She'd probably ask about his childhood and his parents. No doubt she'd ask about work, and of course the obvious, Jessie.

§

It was 9:50 a.m., and he sat in the waiting room of the counselor's office. Three other adults, one man and two women, sat quietly reading magazines. No one talked. It was odd, but understandable.

Who wants to talk about why they're here?

He wondered if other people were forced to come here by their bosses also. They seemed normal. Regular clothes. No one smelled like vomit or cigarette smoke like so many of his patients. He was wearing his gray Polo pullover and blue jeans with a pair of old brown Lucchese Caiman-tail boots. He clasped his hands as if waiting for a surprise while his mind kept jumping from one topic to the next, never long enough to focus on anything of substance. "Mr. Huntly?" The lady was short with white hair and reading glasses, which hung delicately from her white pearl chain. She was wearing a holiday cardigan sweater over her white blouse and long beige skirt. She had worn, brown flats with the thread slightly tufted along the toes, a big white smile, and a strong southern accent. He got up, and walked to the open door.

"Very nice to meet you Mr. Huntly. I'm Sheila Ceres. Just head on back to the third door on your right."

"As in the Greek Goddess Ceres?"

"I think you mean Roman, and not quite. Horrible story really, but a nice way to explain the seasons. Not that we get much of those in Texas."

They walked down the hall, he went through the door first, and found the seat nearest the office window. She sat behind the mahogany desk surrounded by psychology textbooks and family pictures. The brass desk placard read Mrs. Sheila Ceres, LPC.

"How are you doing today?"

"Fine."

"In what way?"

"In a fine kind of way."

"I see. Well, when Paul called me, and asked if I had any openings, I didn't really. He asked if I could make some room for you, and I did. He seems pretty concerned about you."

"Yes, he does." Creed was curt.

"It doesn't matter how concerned he may be if you aren't willing to be here. As I'm sure you already know, if you aren't willing to talk with me about why you're here, then we can't really plan on getting anywhere with our time. Paul told me some about what's happened in your life this past year."

"Most people I work around know what happened. I just choose not to talk about it."

"Why is that you suppose?" Mrs. Ceres leaned forward in her chair.

"I'm not sure how to say anything to anyone in order to make them feel less awkward with the conversation." Creed moved his feet slightly pigeon-toed as he glanced quickly out the window. His nails scraped slowly over his palm callouses.

"Paul mentioned that you seemed more withdrawn…. short…. a little agitated, and I can see why. You prefer to keep this part of your life separate from work. I suspect that gets more difficult with each passing day. Especially with what you do."

"Maybe," Creed huffed.

"I'm not trying to make you angry, Dr. Huntly."

"Look, I don't know what to say here. I don't want to waste your time, and I definitely don't want you to think I'm being rude. I don't have people I can talk to, and we just met, so this is all a bit new and abrasive to me. I don't know where to start, and it's hard enough to think about any of it let alone say anything out loud." There was silence for a minute or so.

"What happened last year? Let's start with that," Ceres stated.

"My fiancée died in a motor vehicle accident," he replied.

"Accident?" she asked.

"Why? What did you hear?"

"Paul mentioned that she died in a car wreck."

"She…." he took a long deep breath, "She…. ummm." His voice was feeling strained slightly. He picked one callous off completely. It stung a little.

"They said she committed suicide. It was a long few weeks afterward, a fog really. I didn't see it myself, and I didn't want to. The medical examiner ruled it a suicide based on her journal and the evidence on scene."

"What evidence?"

Creed cleared his throat. It was getting unusually tight.

"She drove off the bridge into the ravine below. No tire marks, which suggested she didn't hit her brakes. It was the middle of the afternoon, and she had slept the night before. No drugs or alcohol. No prior medical history besides severe depression." He thought about her moments when the sadness was so suffocating, she couldn't get out of bed, and he had to cover for her at the hospital. He'd tell her residency director that she was ill, but would never say why. Most days she was happy it seemed, but when the bad days came, they thundered hard and fast. The memories were leaking through the cracks in his mental quarantine.

"Everything happened so quickly that day. I was working a shift, and they brought in this traumatic arrest: twenty-seven-year-old female in a single motor vehicle collision. She was tubed when I walked into the room with the trauma team," his voice trailed, "they were doing CPR, and her hands shook each time they did a compression.... just lifeless."

He hadn't looked at those mental images in months. Tears started rolling down his face. He could taste their saltiness, and tried to wipe them on his pullover. The containment was breached.

"I'm sorry," he mumbled with a raspy voice.

"Don't be sorry," Ceres said reassuringly.

"I'm sorry for crying. I'm stronger than this."

"It has nothing to do with strength."

"For me it does." He paused and gathered himself.

"There was blood everywhere, and her face was unrecognizable. I was surprised the medics even got the tube. We cut her clothes, and rolled her over. I saw the broken angel wing tattoos on her back. I just... just froze." He could still hear the loud voices, and the chaos swirling around him. The nurses had looked at him with disbelief not understanding what he was trying to rapidly process.

"That's when Marcus Flannigan came into the room, and I told him it was Jessie. I didn't do anything. No orders. No procedures. I just stood there." He felt he should have done something, anything even if it were to just hold her hand.

"Her parents requested a closed casket, and had pictures of her everywhere in the church. The place was packed. Standing room only. I got up to speak. I don't remember much of what I said besides 'Lord hear our prayers.' Over and over again, but it didn't matter. None of my prayers mattered that night in the hospital chapel either. She was gone, and it was because she wanted to be."

"When did all this happen?" Ceres asked.

"December 19th last year. It's coming up on the one-year anniversary," he replied.

"I'm sorry."

"Don't be sorry. She did this to herself and everyone around her. It was selfish, and stupid, and meaningless. She had the best therapists. I made sure she took her meds. She took great care of patients, and halfway through her intern year she realized she wanted to be a cardiologist. She had a purpose, but it was all pointless."

"Are you angry with her?"

"I hate her." His tears were cascading uncontrollably, but his voice was resolute.

"That's pretty strong, Creed."

"It's real."

"It's normal for those left behind with suicide to feel anger towards the deceased…"

"No. I'm angry, and it's okay. It's been my strength. That rage… that unmitigated rage has kept me warm all these months. That rage forces me to get out of bed every day, and fight. It's that rage that keeps me moving forward. Sympathy, kindness, and love… all of that…. that, that crap… none of that worked. Rage… rage is my answer to apathy and self-pity."

"I see. Creed, rage is a powerful, powerful force, but it is terribly blinding and its warmth is short-lived. Tends to cut you off from wanting to have relationships, from living your life in peace. If you ever do try to reach out to anyone, that anger will only hurt those you wish to be close to. It will cripple the ones you love. Maybe over time you will find a way to forgive her."

"I don't see the point in trying," Creed replied.

"Well then, maybe for your own sake, if you can't forgive her, you can find a way to forgive yourself."

Creed contemplated everything. He had little left to say.

"I can see today was tough. Let's work on scheduling something for next week," Mrs. Ceres directed.

"I have my schedule on my phone. I need to see…"

"Nope it's already been arranged for next Monday at 10:00 am. Your shift will be covered. Next month you can start blocking off this time."

"Well… I don't think."

"I think it would be good for you to process our session today, and not worry about work. Over time, the sessions will lessen in intensity." Her tone was assuredly confident and absolute.

"Ok then. Thank you, and I guess I'll see you next week." His head was pounding at this point, and his throat was dry.

"Yes sir. It was a pleasure meeting with you today, Creed. I look forward to it."

Chapter 3: A Confrontation

He stirred on the couch the next day, having woken up from a dream with the ethereal woman again, and this time it seemed to last much longer. They had talked and laughed for the most part. He rubbed on her stomach, and felt the baby move. He felt so connected to her and their unborn child. The air was rich with smells of lavender and honeysuckle, and this time nothing interrupted their visit.

It seemed too real to be his imagination, but there he was awake and naked now in his living room with the alarm sounding off on his cell phone. He had an evening shift, and after showering and a close shave, he got dressed in his navy-blue scrubs. Poured his coffee into a thermos, and began the slow migration through traffic.

The shift flowed as averagely as they often do. Nothing heroic but the continued mounds of the wanton, worried-well piling up in the waiting room. Mentally, it was minimal, but spiritually the patients seemed to suck the life out of him. The mundane ambulatory nature of it all was the antithesis of the blood pumping adrenaline surge he enjoyed. Today felt more like an urgent care clinic instead of an Emergency Department. He kept up with most of his charts, and continued signing prescriptions for antibiotics and pain meds always willing to give the benefit of the doubt if someone appeared to be suffering. He generally displayed a fair degree of compassion for people in pain, all except for one... H.S.

H.S. (Howard Shillings) was a well-known fixture of things gone wrong. He had high blood pressure and poorly controlled diabetes as well as fibromyalgia, chronic back pain, and a mix of alcoholism, cirrhosis, and drug addiction. He could be sick, or he could be ornery, but rarely was he necessary. He would often come into the department three or four times a week. Some of the docs gave him pain meds for a few days, and fewer still would send him out empty-handed. It was easier to give him a dozen pills if it made him go away faster. One can only fight and argue and get belittled so much in a single shift by malevolent patients, so it was human nature to acquiesce if from nothing more but sheer exhaustion. Not for Creed, however. Creed saw this as a direct affront to his practice… to the very purpose of Emergency Departments everywhere.

"H.S. is here," one of the new nurses mentioned in passing.

"Fantastic." Creed made his rarely seen eye-roll.

"Please pick up his chart. The other doc will just give him a week's worth of Norco."

"Yeah I got this. I just saw him a few days ago." Creed grabbed the chart and headed over to exam room 15. He knocked on the door, and opened it.

"Hello Mr. Shillings…" his tone was quite steeped in faux sincerity.

"Dr. Huntly," Shillings grimaced his half dozen remaining brown teeth.

"What is it today, sir?" Creed asked.

"My back is killing me, and I missed my pain clinic appointment yesterday."

"Yes… because you were here in the ED during your appointment."

"Well I was hurtin' then too."

"You seem to always be 'hurtin' Mr. Shillings."

"Most days."

"Ok then. Let's examine you." Creed pulled off his stethoscope to listen to the patient's lungs.

"I'm hurting too bad for you to examine me. Can you give me something for pain first?" H.S. held his hand up.

"Nope," Creed replied.

"Look, Doc. I had a rough night. Just give me something for pain, and you can decide what you wanna do next."

"How about you let me examine you, and then I will still get to decide what I 'wanna' do next."

"Well now you're pissing me off!"

"Oh??"

"Now you're just being a smart ass. I want another doctor!"

"Not happenin', Cap'n."

"I! Want! A! New! Doctor! Now! Jackass!!!"

"Security? Yvonne, get security for me please. It looks like it's time for Mr. Shillings to go."

"You can't kick me out! I have medical problems. Now I'm getting chest pain!"

"Luckily your last heart cath was normal six weeks ago, Mr. Shillings. You can't manipulate me into drugging you up again." Creed stood there defiantly with his arms crossed.

"You listen here, you little pissant. I'm not leaving until I get some goddamn pain meds!"

H.S. stood up and clinched his fists and teeth. He seemed to rock back and forth in his torn canvas sneakers. Something frightening flickered in his eyes, something peculiar and otherworldly. There appeared to be hazy black smoke for sockets. It was brief, and

Creed almost missed it. He squinted slightly to look at Mr. Shilling's eyes again. *What was that?* He shone a light into Shilling's eyes. They appeared normal albeit the pupils were small as always from the opiates.

"How's your vision today, Mr. Shillings?" Creed asked.

"Wouldn't you like to know? I see things now. I've seen you."

"Ok. Is that a threat?" Two security guards grabbed H.S. and started pulling him out of the exam room down the hall. H.S. turned around one last time and shouted at Creed emphatically.

"You have no idea what I will do to you! Just wait! Your day's comin'! Hippocratic oath my ass! You're no Hippocrates!"

"Alright Mr. Shillings let's go." The in-house off duty police officer knew H.S. well. He grabbed his arm, and off he went. H.S. was gone, but Creed felt particularly incensed.

"What a prick," he muttered. The nurse asked him if he was worried.

"Nah. He's a brittle, burned-out piece of garbage. I get death threats all the time by guys twice his size. He must be really feening for some 'candy' at this point." Creed washed his hands, and looked at the hospital exit one last time.

Bizarre.

A few hours passed, and it was now 11:45 p.m. when he normally would have peaked with patients. At this point he had twelve, and the night had just begun. The Universe was heavy-handed. His mind drifted again to the year before, but he focused on the lab results and plans for discharging the next few patients. At this pace, he'd see fifty before the shift was over. Multiple patients were languishing in hall beds with psychiatric problems. Many of them were suicidal; some were moderately depressed while others were clearly psychotic. It put a significant strain on the ER staff since each patient required a bedside sitter. Although it bogged down the flow of the department, the patients were in no condition to be left alone or sent home even though everyone's instincts were to find a way to "get them out of here."

No one liked staring at the mentally ill for hours on end. It was easier to ignore them, or walk away, avoiding eye contact at all costs. Creed couldn't ignore them, however, and he needed to find a way to transfer them to a mental health facility. He planned to update some of the family members after talking with case management, so he left the Red pod, and headed to the family conference rooms. Many of his patients would waste days in a holding area pending psychiatric transfer. How would he explain this to the families? How do you objectively describe to someone that their loved one is no longer capable of making good decisions, their minds were broken, and now they would have to go away, incarcerated for being ill.

He turned the corner into the main hallway, and looked up to see unmitigated fear. Fear in all its variations of scrub colors. Five people frozen, looking at what stood before them. H.S. was in the hall, and held a gun to the charge nurse's temple. Creed stopped quickly, and the rubber on the bottom of his Keen hiking boots squeaked obnoxiously. H.S. turned his gaze from the charge nurse to his adversary. Creed at first felt unsure of what to do next, but then he became angry. He could feel his pulse racing, and imagined his hands around Shillings' bony neck.

"H.S. put the goddamn gun down," Creed ordered.

"Hello, Doc." His voice was raspy and dull.

"Mr. Shillings put down the gun. She didn't do anything to you."

"She laughs at me. They all do."

"No one is laughing at you. Put the gun down."

"No!"

"Right. Ok. Security?" He looked everywhere, but security was nowhere to be found. They were all tied up with the mentally ill. It was a handful of nurses, techs, and Creed standing between H.S. and the unsuspecting department of patients.

"What do you need Mr. Shillings? Are you in pain?" Creed's bargaining was obtuse, but an attempt nonetheless.

"Always."

"I can get you something for pain."

"Not here for that today, Doc."

"Why are you here?"

Keep him talking. Don't let him shoot Marjorie. Keep him talking. Give him space. Keep your hands open.

"You know why, Doc."

"No, I don't," Creed replied.

"You like your dreams, Doc?"

"What?"

"I have dreams too, but not as pretty as yours. She's awfully, pretty isn't she?"

"Mr. Shillings we all dream."

"No. Some of us never wake up. Some of us walk around in this godforsaken nightmare. Day in and day out with no end in sight." The off-duty police officer walked up behind Creed.

"Mr. Shillings, put down your weapon!" the officer said as he pulled his gun, and aimed the red laser onto H.S.'s chest. The officer seemed calm, but Creed could see his pupils getting bigger, and a slight tremor in his upper lip.

"Mr. Shillings, please". Creed extended his hands, "listen to the officer. Put the gun down. You're sick. We need to help you, so let's calm down, and lay the gun on the ground. We'll get you into a room, and get you the help you need."

"I need to sleep," H.S. replied.

"Me too."

"I haven't slept in months."

"Me neither. Now come on Shillings, we can help you get some sleep. Just listen to the police officer, and put the gun down."

"It isn't fair."

"What isn't fair, Mr. Shillings?" Creed asked.

"That some of us will never be more than this… this trash you see."

"I don't see trash."

"Ha! You look at me and want to walk the other way. You see me now? You see this gun? Now! Now you see me!"

Shillings slowly changed into something dark. His eyes flickered behind a strand of smoke. Creed was the only one who seemed to notice.

"I do see you, Mr. Shillings."

"I see you, Creed Huntly."

"Okay. Okay then. You see me. I see you…let's…"

"Mr. Shillings, this is the last time! I will use force! Put the gun down now, or I will shoot. Put it down!"

The officer was clearly focused on one option only at this point. The security guards arrived, and stood behind the police officer. H.S had managed to create a bottleneck, and only people coming down from the upstairs elevators could approach him from behind. There were a few seconds where Creed could hear everyone breathing. The sounds drifted.

H.S. was strung out. His face sunken and gray. Long wiry hair made him look like a homicidal Halloween effigy. His body odor was ripe and sour as his sweat drenched the white t-shirt beneath his windbreaker. He shuffled his feet, and turned his shoulders to square up with Creed. The fury in his eyes oscillated like heat waves. His brow furrowed, and Creed could detect the semblance of a grin.

"Mr. Shillings don't do it. Just put it down. Listen to the officer."

"Do you hear that, Doc?"

"Hear what?" Creed asked.

"The whispers."

"No. No, I don't hear any whispers."

"It's like a thousand mumbling bees in my head. The words don't make sense. They can't speak, but they do."

"Do you hear voices, Mr. Shillings?"

"They can't speak because their mouths are sewn, so everything is angry and mumbled. They have something to say. All of them do, but I can't understand. I see them in my nightmares." Shillings took a deep breath, and smiled. "It's almost over. The voices will stop. I'll finally get some goddamn sleep."

Shillings' eyes and mouth were gone, blurred in some kind of macabre mask. Creed blinked to reconcile what couldn't be happening, and he opened his mouth to speak, but no sound, just a blinding muzzle flash. Creed heard a thousand whispers, rumbling through his mind. Then silence

Chapter 4: A Transition

Smoke and mist roiled about the tree and shrub brush roots, with Creed's hand barely visible over the brim of the crater. His fingers began to fidget, and he eventually sat up disoriented, with a pounding headache. Everything was heavy and slow. He could smell the scent of fresh toiled dirt and new ash in the air. The ground was spongy and warm, but as the icy Highland breeze wafted from above, his skin tightened with goose bumps. He looked up to see an occasional snowflake drift through the broken limbs of the forest canopy. It appeared he had fallen, naked, from above. The sky was getting darker as all its colors faded to tones of orange and yellow with the sunset. Creed had no bearings on his whereabouts, but through small breaks in the surrounding woods he could see other mountain slopes. He was not at home anymore.

The throbbing of his scalp subsided over a few minutes, and he recalled the flash from Shillings. Was he shot? Was he dead? Was he dreaming? None of it made any sense. He knew, however, that he needed to find shelter, and hopefully the means to start a fire of some sort. The temperature was dropping quickly. He walked out of the crater, and milled about gathering limbs and kindling. He sought a small cave or indentation in the rock around him, but despite his efforts, there was no meaningful way to hide from the cold. Creed stacked the limbs he'd gathered side by side for a lean-to of sorts resting firmly against a large, felled pine trunk. A rustling of leaves broke his concentration.

What was that?

He felt the ground move slightly, and then smelled heavy, musky breath. Creed stood up and found a sharp rock by his feet, pulling it from some shrub roots, and held it like a long cleaver. His heart was pounding, and his feet began to sweat.

"AHHHHHHH!"

He screamed, hoping to frighten whatever or whomever was approaching. The shadows of branches from the nearby trees were too high for him to reach and climb to safety. He couldn't see the trail before him. He felt fear, and worked to breathe through the pounding in his chest. Then he heard a voice.

"Easy friend." Someone spoke to him from above with a thick Scottish accent. Creed looked up to see a large silhouette. Something fell to his feet.

"Who are you?"

"A friend. Take the rope. You won't remember much as it is, but trust me and take the rope."

"I'm not picking up anything. Where am I?" Creed asked as he slowly stepped back into the crater.

"You're in Mürindür, in the Ember Wood to be specific. I'm here to get you home. I watched you fall from the sky as the Welfalon so often do, but I managed to steer your soul to the mountainside away from the desert. It took my mammoth Bog and I a bit of time to get up here, and to be honest, I'm happy we found you before nightfall. Things tend to get contentious in the dark," the stranger said.

"Bog? Mürindür? Welfalon?"

"We can talk more about it later, but for now, I need you to take this rope, and climb up here. There are creatures about you'd likely not prefer to see." As if on cue, the bowels of the woods grumbled. Feral bellies bellowed out to one another. It was feeding time, and packs of various carnivores were forming up, the stranger explained. The melody of the nighttime chorus was imposing.

A few animals made way to the crater brim. There was scarcely enough light to make out their hairy short bodies, and large pink eyes. They lacked ears, but had gargantuan arms with thick nails. They appeared to be built for tree dwelling. They also appeared to be hungry. Creed looked at them briefly. One reached for his leg, and Creed raised his rock to threaten a strike. The animal didn't take kindly to the gesture, and instead opened its mouth to reveal a series of razor teeth as it hissed.

"Seriously! I don't care what you are, but I'm leaving, alive! I'm not hesitating for one second! If you come any closer, I'll bash your face in!" Leaves rubbed themselves loudly in the distance, and Creed turned his head. He couldn't see anything but shadows. He looked back toward the stranger's voice, and readied his rock.

"You will do nothing of the sort," the stranger informed him. "Those Skeetlings will eat you alive, and in the time it took for you to scream, there'd be nothing left but bones. You need to trust me. Those creatures you see before you won't wait much longer, and there are larger things, more horrific things that wake, and begin to roam as we speak. I'm here to get you to safety, to get you to her."

"Her, who?"

"Take my hand." The stranger walked down Bog's shoulder, and offered assistance.

"No. I need... I need to go. I need to find my way somehow, back home. Just going to head this way." Creed turned to his right, climbing over a burnt tree. He stumbled, hitting his face against the charred bark. There was a sound before him as he hesitated on his hands and knees. The Skeetlings were hungry, and a bit too curious. They clicked and chattered to one another, calculating an attack on the two-legged piece of meat.

"AHHHHHH! What are those? What the hell are they?"

"Skeetlings. They eat smaller animals, but it appears tonight they feel a little ambitious. Grab the rope before they make you the first of many meals tonight."

"I've got to find a way."

Creed backed up slowly, there was a sound of padded feet once more, and when he glanced quickly, he saw them encroaching upon what little space he had remaining. He twisted to his left, and was about to unknowingly sprint off an unseen cliffside.

The stranger didn't have time to convince Creed of anything more, and he grew impatient. He could smell the stench of sulfur in the distance, and knew if they didn't leave soon, survival would be unlikely. The stranger tapped his mammoth on the scalp, and its long trunk wrapped tightly around Creed's waist hoisting him skyward so suddenly, he dropped the rock.

"STOP!!! STOP!! PUT ME DOWN!"

The muscular trunk obliged, and dropped him a little harder than necessary onto a cold, wooden bench. The stranger climbed into the front seat, reins in hand, as the Skeetlings daringly came closer. The mammoth snorted a retort, and they backed away. Creed stood up, but fell into the bench again as the mammoth turned sharply to head back down the mountain trail. Everything was dark, and the slight sway of the seats made Creed quite sick especially since his head still felt so heavy. He needed to focus on something, so he looked through the tree branches and caught the moon on a wayward glance. He turned to it, and focused on the white sphere. His head was spinning, and everything went dark.

§

Creed woke on his side to the crackling of a small orange fire along a tree line of an open field. He could see a large beast sitting on a log across from the smoke and heat. It didn't look human, but it was hooded and sat upright like a man. It had the mannerisms of a large ape, but it methodically swirled a large mead horn, and periodically drank from it with froth remnants on a long brown, braided beard. It didn't speak. Not at first. Creed looked down at his chest, and saw he was now wearing a heavy white tunic and a pair of black pants made of wool with cloth ties around the waist. He wore brown leather boots with scuffed brass buckles just below the knee and ankle. There was a plate of torn, toasted bread at his feet. Creed sat up realizing he was hungry, and ate the toast slowly. It was still warm, and had small bits of dates and dried berries of some sort. It was remarkably well flavored considering this surely was another one of his dreams. He looked around for some means of egress, but the bread was so good he thought he might have seconds.

"This is pretty amazing," Creed noted.

"Thank you," the stranger replied.

It was peculiar to be out there in the dark as the winter wind brushed the flame tips of the fire, but it started to feel like he was camping. Creed's mind wandered off for a bit to the time he went to Estes Park in Colorado alone. He got lost for two days, and had never been happier. He quickly came back to his new reality, and looked about. Surely, if the stranger had wished him harm, he would have done something by now. Creed began to relax, and took another bite of the bread.

"I can't see your face. Do you have a name?"

"My name is Ojin," the stranger replied.

"Hah. No, really?"

"Really."

"That's a weird name," Creed replied.

"It's a family name."

"Okay. Well, my name is Creed. It's a pleasure to meet you."

"Creed is it? You've gone by many names in the past, but for now we will call you this," Ojin affirmed.

Creed rolled his eyes a bit, but the conversation was easy enough. His head was clearing as his nose detected heavy hints of lavender and perfumed mountain laurels. Everything was so foreign, so bizarre. He looked to the sky again, and realized two moons opposed each other on the distant horizon when before he had only seen one. He forcibly blinked two and then three times, but the moons remained, one red and one white.

"What do you call this bread?"

"What would you call it?" Ojin asked.

"Well it has fruit and stuff, so I'm sure you gave it a name. I will call it Fruit bread."

"It comes from a language you may not understand anymore. It's called Festorbius. We serve this bread to family and friends generally during holidays or special feasts. Takes a few days to make because the bread rises so slowly."

"Nice. Nice, and original." The tunic was itchy. It was bound closely to his body by a high riding woven belt tied into a knot.

"Not trying to be ungrateful, but do you happen to have a shirt I can wear under this thing? It's pretty itchy."

"Here, take this." Ojin threw a white linen shirt in Creed's direction.

"Thank you." Creed untied the belt, took off the tunic, and realized how sore he was everywhere. His shoulders were burning. His neck cracked when he turned to his right. The shirt felt nice, and he donned the tunic again foregoing the belt. He sat back onto the log he had woken next to, and finished the remaining bread. Now he was thirsty.

"Have anything to drink?"

"Yes." A thud landed beside Creed's feet. He uncorked the leather flask, and smelled the mead. It was tempting, but the worst thing he could do now was become further disoriented. He threw it back.

"Sorry, I don't drink alcohol anymore." Ojin squinted through the fire, and shook his head. Creed could see his displeasure.

"Here". Thud. Another flask. This one smelled like green tea.

"What do you call this?"

"Mebum."

"Thank you." He took a long swig of the Mebum flask, and was shocked at how sweet and refreshing whatever it was… was. It reminded him of cold watery honey without the sticky aftertaste. He re-corked the flask, and started to gather his thoughts.

"Ojin?"

"Yes?"

"Am I dreaming?" Creed wondered.

"No."

"It feels like a dream. Where am I again?"

"Mürindür," Ojin replied.

"Where is Mürindür?"

"It's another world."

"Another world?" Creed asked.

"Yes," Ojin affirmed.

"That explains the two moons. So, I am dreaming."

"No." Ojin sounded as if he were losing patience.

"I'm on another planet, and you're telling me I'm not dreaming."

"It's a world, not a planet," Ojin insisted.

"Ok. What's the difference?"

"A world is comprised of a people, life, and purpose. A planet can simply be a cold rock."

"Why am I here? Am I dead? If I'm not dreaming, then I must be dead." Creed just couldn't seem to comprehend anything, although he was trying. It seemed as if something were wrong with his mind.

"You're not dead… not yet anyways."

"Well that's foreboding," Creed mumbled.

"You need rest," Ojin grumbled.

"Are you mad? You seem mad."

"I'm worried."

"Huh. Interesting. You're worried? I'm talking to an ape-man in another world, and you're worried?" Creed animated to the air with his hands.

"You don't remember anything? Not a single moment?" Ojin asked.

"I've never been here before. There's nothing to remember," Creed argued.

"You have been here many times. We have served together many times."

"Am I supposed to know you?"

54

"This is a shame, and now, of all the moments we've truly needed you to recover quickly, you arrive with amnesia. This most recent life must surely have scarred you."

"You don't know anything about me." Creed stood up.

"I know many things," Ojin replied.

"This is so cryptic."

"Sit down. Tomorrow will be long, and we need rest." There was a loud snort in the camp.

"What was that?" Creed squinted toward the dark moving mound a few yards away.

"That's Bog. Do you remember anything about him?"

"Who's Bog?"

"He's a mammoth."

"Heh… yeah… Mammoth. Like an elephant or more like a big horse?"

"Mammoth."

Bog stood slowly until he completely blocked the stars from Creed's view. Ojin and Bog walked toward the fire, and the flames grew in exaltation. Creed could see their features in lit accents of shadows. His eyes widened. Ojin stood well over seven feet tall, and his fat, tufted tail, whisking shy of the ground, was scarcely hidden by his large woolen cloak, and his thick hairy shanks. Ojin wore a dark colored kilt of browns and greens, and an open leather vest with a tan linen shirt beneath. The mouthpiece of a pipe stood out from his chest pocket. Ojin's tusks were yellowed ivory, grown clearly over his upper lip, and the cloak hood nested in a crooked fashion, atop his pointy ears and errant light brown fur. An aged face with bristled brows, and small round glasses framed his deep-set orange eyes. His beard was twisted in two separate braids woven with gray. Ojin leaned onto his knurled oak staff, with hands embraced, clasping a jade orb embedded within the dark iron bindings of the wood. The jade churned like a storm beneath his hands.

Bog appeared to be a mammoth male in his prime, twenty-foot-tall at the shoulder, and covered in muscle and a chocolate brown wooly hide. Burs and broken twigs were trapped within the long hairs of his broad legs. The beast had a steel breastplate with flank and belly armor chained to a two-bench saddle on his back. Sharpened morning stars jutted from the end of his tusks. Bog smelled like a wet dog. Ojin snapped his fingers and the battle saddle fell to the ground like a turned cart full of pots and pans. Bog took in a big deep breath. Creed simply stared at the tusks of Ojin and the mammoth as they towered over him. He scrambled back across the log and into the tall grass.

"Dear lord!" Creed exclaimed.

"Don't be so dramatic."

"Right… does he eat meat?" Creed asked.

"You mean humans?" Ojin teased.

"We can start with that."

"No. He eats everything but meat."

"Ok. Cool. Good deal. Does he bite?"

"No, but he does have a temper. He didn't have a nap today. You know how he likes to nap."

"Right. Okay."

"He wants to sleep, so we should sleep. Sit down," Ojin urged.

"Sounds good. Wow. He's huge! You're huge! What are you supposed to be?" Ojin appeared dismayed as his tail twitched impatiently. Creed's speech seemed to slur a bit when he spoke.

"I am a hobgoblin," Ojin said with authority.

"I thought you were little mischievous imps in stories."

"No. Imps are vile. Hobgoblins are something entirely different."

"Like Ogres?"

"No. Ogres are horrific! They hate hobgoblins. We hate Ogres."

"Hobgoblin. Hobgoblin. I'm trying to think if I've ever seen one in stories or a movie. This has to be a dream."

"I'm afraid it's not," Ojin affirmed.

"How many of you are there?"

"Legions in the beginning, but now only a few thousand left. We live a long, long time, but like all things the Endüerduul calls us too."

"What is that glowing orb thing?"

"That's my staff. All hobgoblin druids have one once they clear the crucible. It is bound to me, and I to it."

"A hobgoblin and a mammoth. What in the world? Never saw this coming." Creed belched repeatedly. "Ojin, I feel weird. What was in that Mebum?" The fire began to spin in Creed's eyes. He staggered, and fumbled to steady himself. Ojin walked closer.

"Just nectar and glacier water. Why?"

"I feel dizzy. Not good. I feel sick. I think I'm going to…" Creed leaned over the log and heaved repeatedly. He couldn't tell if he or the ground was swirling, but he held onto that rotten log desperately. His mouth was sour. It didn't take long to notice a pool of vomit slowly draining into the grass. Creed caught glimpses of worms in the firelight.

"What the hell is that?" He threw up again. Flies and maggots tumbled in the vomitus.

"That's what I thought," Ojin snorted. The hobgoblin waved his hands and the entire collection of liquid mess floated into the air, flies, worms, and all, and held it over the tips of the flames until it was nothing but ash.

"Bumble Worms and Fugue Flies. Nasty. Vile."

"Flies?" Creed questioned.

"Someone didn't want you to be here. They didn't want you to be found."

"I *don't* want to be here!" Creed confirmed.

"What was your last memory before waking up in that hole on the mountain?"

"I was in the hospital. One of our patients was pointing a gun at me. I was trying to get him to stop. Then the gun went off."

"Anything else?" Ojin asked.

"There was a loud humming sound, and whispering people, but I couldn't understand what they were saying. It sounded intense, but I couldn't make out the words."

"*Caedere*. Naturally."

"What?"

"Caedere are the soldiers of Death. Cursed souls. Tormented. I knew they were crossing, but had no idea they were being this bold." Ojin was more animated, and began to pace as he wrung his hands.

"In what way?"

"A Caedere attacked you, and tried to deliver you to Leterum, but in case that failed they filled your stomach with Fugue Flies to disorient you. Induce confusion. The Bumble worms ruin coordination and balance, so you would be less likely to run away when they hunted you." Ojin spit into the grass as his stubby hobgoblin ears twitched in frustration.

"Uhhh…" Creed wiped his mouth only to vomit again. His stomach was finally empty.

"We need to close camp and move tonight. We can't wait until dawn." Bog let out a moan, and bellowed his discontent. "I know my friend, but we must get to the city. We need to send a message." Ojin snuffed out the fire with the remaining mead, and with a thrust of his palm, motioned the armor onto Bog once more.

"That can't be true. I was in the hospital one minute, and then the forest the next."

"There is always a moment briefly in death when Time actually ceases to exist, where you are held by the Ostiarius, the gatekeeper, any time you jump from the mortal realm to here. He assesses you, and determines if you may proceed. A Caedere had to have met you in the Ostiarius Chamber."

"What do you mean jumped?"

"We'll talk about that later."

"Oh man." Creed burped uncomfortably.

"Do you remember anything? A large Cyclops with four arms and a trident with glass everywhere?"

"No! I think I would remember that!" Creed followed Ojin about with his hands on his head in disbelief.

"How did they get to you so fast? They can't bend Time. They just can't," Ojin protested. At that moment, Creed looked up, and he could feel the wind move wildly about.

"The man… the man that you were fighting with… did you look into his eyes?" Ojin whispered hurriedly as he repacked everything and threw it onto the travel bench. His back was turned to Creed when he heard a distant sound.

"Yes. His eyes disappeared," Creed replied. Ojin bowed his head and shook it.

"Caedere on Earth. This is profoundly disconcerting."

"I don't understand."

"How did that happen? How could this happen? Something is wrong. I thought we had more time."

"Time for what?" Creed asked.

"Climb on Bog's back now," Ojin directed.

"What?"

"Now!" There was a rapid fluttering of wings headed their way. Ojin raised his arms, and spun around, casting a spell to hide their presence.

"Shhhhh! Get down. Don't make a sound."

Creed nodded and kneeled beside Bog's hindquarters. He stared and made out a large flock of winged rogues in the moonlight. They churned in a circle, slowly at first then more erratically until some of them landed in the grass, and on top of the rotten log. A dozen black-feathered birds hopped around the fire, and squawked and cackled in the ash. Their galling voices heralded news to an unseen master. They fluttered about the camp long enough for Creed's feet to go numb in his stance, and for Bog to slowly kneel to the ground. Ojin stood motionless, mindful of unwelcomed sounds and sights. They waited a little longer within the safety of the spell, and suddenly without provocation, the largest bird spread his wings, and took to the sky. The flock followed, and as they flew further away, a sense of calm came over the small band.

"Ravens," the hobgoblin whispered.

"They were looking for us?"

"Yes."

"They seemed focused," Creed noted.

"They hear one voice. They were a scouting party. They found a camp, but likely no idea it was our camp. You are being hunted my friend. From now on, do not speak. We will ride to Durdan southeast of the Ember Wood. A man named Ryval runs a small blacksmith shop there, and we can sleep in one of his horse stalls. I am a good friend of the Lord of Durdan, and he will grant us safe anonymity. No one else knows you are here yet, but Leterum knows you've crossed. He just doesn't know where you landed."

"Leterum?"

"Death eternal. He walks this realm, as do you and I. We have much to discuss. I'll explain it to you along the way. Put this on."

He handed Creed a merlot colored hooded cloak. They mounted Bog, and turned into the tall grass, making their way to Durdan City. The creatures of the night were stirring, and the watchful eyes of the Ravens would not rest. Sleep would have to wait.

Chapter 5: Mürindür

Sounds echoed across the midnight landscape while shadows feigned retreat, dancing in the distance. Ojin held the reins and looked incessantly for some locale betrayal, an ambush, or a wayward Raven. Though they traveled in the open, the spell, or the *Penumbra* as Ojin described it, cloaked them and muffled sound. It was a curious spell indeed. Lanterns on the posts of the wooden bench flickered softly, and yet their light never once would leave the confines of their dome. It did very little to assist in visualizing the road, however, since light never left the Penumbra, it merely reflected back into their eyes. Bog was able to see well enough, and Creed had asked Ojin twice before to leave the lanterns on. It settled him somehow.

Boredom crept in as the journey continued. Creed occasionally would ask a question when he observed an animal from the safety of his bench seat. For hours they traveled, and with little else to do, it was entertaining to learn the fauna of Mürindür. He felt it must be similar to a safari. Ojin would describe what he could while being mindful of his voice. Nocturnal beasts like Walburdors (pig snouted wolverines with webbed feet) and Gnarlgurgons (tree climbing lizards the size of goats) scurried about the tall grasses and aspens, eating small rodents and ground Squail (a Highland, pheasant species with glowing fore-feathers). Creed learned Criconeums (eight-legged toads with oblong jawlines) preferred swallowing their prey whole as opposed to the wingless Feltcrane (stork-like birds with silvery scales and serrated talons), which enjoyed skewering its food, alive, repeatedly as if a sewing machine until it was pulverized as jelly. The native species of this strange world, fascinated Creed, albeit gruesome to a degree. He worried what the horrible creatures were that Ojin mentioned beforehand, but it didn't help to think of those calamities now.

Creed noticed even in the dark how varied the foliage was along their trail. Thick oak trunks were intermingled with moss-covered limbs of skinny birch and alder trees. As the road wound slowly down the mountainside, the branches ebbed and flowed, near and far. It was rhythmic, and beguiling as the low-tide waves of an ocean. Bog was slowing, and as the land started to level, he stopped.

"Come now, Bog. We can't stay here. We still have a little ways to go," the hobgoblin encouraged. Bog grunted at Ojin.

"We've been at it for a few hours. I can sympathize. My backside is numb," Creed concurred.

"We need to keep moving. Once daylight breaks, we'll be safe and asleep within the walls. It's not much further. Let's go, Bog." The hairy trunk came back like a whip and knocked the hood off of Ojin's head. His ears stiffened in annoyance.

"Truly... you test me at times." Ojin was none too pleased. When Creed saw him grimace, his tusks flattened his upper lip. It almost appeared that he was pouting.

"After all I've done for you. We've traveled further in the past. This is nothing in comparison. Find the will, and let's get to the city."

"He's tired. I'm tired. You're tired." Creed felt the relevance in the mammoth's fatigue.

"Doesn't matter. It would be folly to camp here on the road when we're so close."

"It matters when exhaustion leads to injury. He's our only means of transportation, so if he passes out or breaks something we're done."

"Bog has gone many days without rest in the past. He knows what's at stake, and why we need to press on. Rest isn't a luxury we can afford right now. If we rest, and we are found, we fail."

Ojin snapped the reins once more, and Bog begrudgingly moved onward; his large hairy mammoth feet drug slowly through the dust and briar.

"That's a lot of pressure," commented, Creed.

"Ha! You have no idea."

"Well that's true. I have no idea. None. Zero," Creed sarcastically replied.

"That much we agree on," Ojin confirmed.

"Ok then, so tell me about Mürindür. Tell me why I'm here."

"It is complicated."

"Try me."

"You are part of a very significant change for Mürindür. The Endüerduul has foreseen it."

"What does that mean for me?"

"It means you and your love will soon have a child. This child means everything to us."

"The woman in my dreams?"

"Yes." Ojin chuckled. "I knew she would visit you. She often would when her mother wasn't looking."

"So, she is real? What is her name?"

"Celeste, your bride-to-be. She is the Princess, mother of your unborn child, and the daughter of Serena, Queen of Mürindür."

"Celeste. What a beautiful name." Creed pondered this all for a moment while Ojin waited.

"The two of you will bring the only human child ever born into the world of Mürindür. Our worlds have long been separate, magical bounds make it difficult to cross, to mix. When the Cataclysm took place, all magical beings, beasts, and lands were forced in a mass exodus to leave Earth and come home to Mürindür. We don't know what this child's birth could do, so we must ask for the Endüerduul's blessing. If the blessing is attained, it is a promise for balance. A hope placed upon your shoulders to make right what has gone unchecked for so long. Leterum does not wish for that to happen. He's worked too hard to make this world his own."

"I take it he and Serena don't get along?"

"No. The entire Highland region is split along their battle lines and strategic boundaries." Ojin motioned all around as Bog continued forward. Creed looked into the night sky.

"Why two moons?"

"They are not moons, but the Endüerduul and the Undüavalle."

"You've lost me."

"The Endüerduul is the resting place for those that serve the Lux, the good, the light of the world. The Undüavalle is reserved for those that serve the will of Leterum and his confined brother, Acrom. Their resting place will be one of torment at the feet of Acrom for eternity."

"Right there in the sky? Paradise and damnation?" Creed asked.

"Yes. They are a constant reminder of the balance, and balance is vital for everything. For now, we have lost ground, and the balance has been found forfeit." Bog came to a sudden stop again.

"Bog!", but before he could continue, Ojin looked over the mammoth's large head, and saw the terrain. Trees had been crushed, and with others, the bark was shorn mid-height in a series of columns. The hobgoblin eyed the markings. Many of them were scorched sporadically. Ash blew about the roots. The mud was moist and cracked along the drainage ditches as if the event took place days before. Wagon wheels and broken spears littered the ground. No bodies to be found. Sulfur wafted in a yellow fog obscuring the means forward. Bog began to breathe faster, and looked about anxiously. He took a few steps back as if to rise up on his hindquarters. The smells were all too familiar. Tufts of hair littered the fields. Large prints in the crushed grass heralded an ominous presence.

"Easy, Bog. They're gone. Easy now." Ojin stroked the mammoth's fur, and dismissed the stench with a wave of his broad furry hand. A brisk breeze blew from their backs, and the path was visible once again. They continued around a bend until the trees parted slightly, and revealed a distant bridge.

The hobgoblin looked ahead and described the dark and turbulent River Ebon as the Apicem Bridge stretched before them. Creed leaned forward in his seat, peering just to the right of Ojin's broad shoulders. The bridge was an impressive sight to behold. Hand hewn and historic in appearance. Even hundreds of yards away, Creed could see the six, one-hundred-foot-tall Centurion statues sculpted of core pillars mined from the Cerulean Mountains. Three Centurions stood on either side of the bridge, anchored deep into the bedrock, each holding a spear in their riverside fist, and in the other, lit oil lanterns hung high above the thoroughfare from thick, rusted chains. Blocks of chopped stone were embedded over arched iron beams to form the roadway of the architectural wonder. The Centurions faced the Mountains with their backs to the city as the lanterns cast an eerie glow onto the serpentine river.

As they ventured closer and ultimately approached the entrance of the bridge, Ojin explained to Creed how the structure could hold over four thousand men, eighty abreast, in a phalanx. Countless battles had been held on this colossus construct. Ogres and hobgoblins, trolls and men, mammoths and catapults, boulders and flame have painted legends onto those very stones.

They marched forty yards along the incline of the structure, but then a rumble, and a crack could be heard behind them. Creed turned quickly, and saw nothing. Although the bridge had stood for thousands of years, tonight it felt uncertain. The pillars were steady but insincere. Bog treaded as lightly as he could, moving further toward the city gates, as the cold mountain air whistled beyond the muffled turbulence of the water below. Creed looked on either side of the bridge at the River Ebon. The crested whitecaps splashed and sprayed as they hurried south. Ojin told him that once someone fell into its black depths, the River Ebon claimed them for eternity. Creed wondered how many souls had fallen prey to its current.

The River Ebon cut a broad, deep swath in the rock of the Highlands, and created the natural border between the mountain wilds of the Ember Wood, and the broad rolling hills and plateaus of Klein Valley. The river's origins were Ebon Falls formed by the tributaries of the endless mountain streams, and it wound through the region until it fed the briny estuaries of the Seniorem Sea. The granite banks were as glass and they seemingly moved reflectively in unison with the water. As they traversed the road stones, Creed looked up at the statues, and felt the dry heat of the lanterns. Chips and cracks were seen throughout the bridge, but none were too critical; simply wrinkles in time and mementos for aged warriors. At the bridge's pinnacle, Creed looked down river, and witnessed small torches moving about. It appeared to be forty or so men walking single file through the woods. He could hear the barks and whines of the dogs. It was a patrol.

The Klein grass wisped about in the night air as they walked across the bridge and made the slow descent toward Durdan City's cobblestones. Even in the dark, Creed could see the numerous buildings perched within the confines of the walls. Golden orbs of light were spaced about the sentry lookout posts, and could be seen for miles in the valley below. A large iron gate within a stone arch greeted them, the quartz within the rockwork glimmered in the moonlight, and Ojin shouted within the shroud of the Penumbra.

"Open the gate!" he bellowed.

Soldiers moved about. The metal clanging of their gear was distant.

"Who goes there?"

"A humble hobgoblin seeking refuge." Creed noticed Ojin's tail whisking back and forth across the bench as if he were a predatory cat anxiously waiting to pounce.

"Show yourself."

"I am traveling under the auspices of anonymity, and I wish to meet with Lord Perrindor. I have news from the Ember Wood."

"What news?"

"The kind I wish to speak in private."

"You can speak with us or you can turn yourself around, Master Hobgoblin!"

"Let me speak with Perrindor, or I'll find a place to put you," Ojin warned.

"Not bloody likely! You can be Ogre fodder for all I care! Be gone!"

Ojin lifted his thick furry fingers from the reins, and the unsuspecting soldier's feet left the ground. Once he reached a few feet in the air, Ojin made him float just over the wall. Enough to encourage some gentle diplomacy.

"Ahhhhhhhhh! Please, please...."

"Open the gate, kind sir," Ojin requested once more. Creed could hear rustling above.

"Ojin! Ojin, Is that you?" another voice shouted.

"Perrindor?" Ojin asked.

"Put the kid down you overgrown hothead. I'll open the gate." The soldier landed precisely where he once stood. The chains rattled over the metal cogs, and the iron-gate opened slowly and deliberately. Ojin and Creed ducked beneath the bottom spikes as Bog crossed the threshold. Perrindor hurried down the stairs and squinted in the torch lit streets to see them, but all he could make out was blurred buildings through some prism.

"Ojin?"

"Yes. Meet me at the blacksmith shop."

"It's been moved. Head to the Keep, and I'll let you in through the west corridor into the Hall and Commons."

"I had hoped to avoid notice. Word travels fast," Ojin cautioned.

"I will clear the path. No one will know."

"Well enough."

Perrindor mounted his horse, and with four other men, raced back to the Keep atop the hill. The weary travelers felt some relief in knowing that they made it safely within the walls before the sun rose when the skies would be filled with dark ambitions. Bog moved forward ever so slowly so as not to bump or crush any of the nearby soldiers. Twice, Ojin had to ask them to step aside and make way. It would be simpler to tell them a mammoth was coming through, but there would be little wonder as to whom rode the mammoth, and what business a hobgoblin had in Durdan at this hour.

They traveled slowly upward to the Durdan Keep at the center of town, winding through the market place and single bedroom homes. Doors were locked and windows shuttered. Not a soul was found along the cobblestones. Oil lamps stationed about the building corners created halos of light within the shadows. They passed the place where the blacksmith shop once stood, but was now an ashen sinkhole. Black timber stood where the barn had once sheltered animals and blacksmith wares. The corrals where the cattle and sheep were often worked had become chalky, gray stumps, scarcely high enough to contain the mice that scurried about searching for grain. The Durdan Temple and its looming bell tower were spared, but the main academy, which served as the primary means of education in the city was scarred in ruins and ash as well. Coals littered the alleyways. Thankfully, the remainder of the inner city seemed intact. Creed looked back while the gate lowered mechanistically to the ground. The most damage seemed a mere hundred yards into the city, a woeful wedge of war.

Chickens scurried about the roads along with the occasional goat. Creed could hear the mooing of cows in the distance. A curious creature built similarly to the llama stood in a side alley, staring at Creed as they passed. It had a large black stripe of fur like a mohawk, running from its head to its rump. The hair fibers had tips of glowing white light, subtle, but when glanced at briefly from the side it appeared to be a floating luminescent eel of some sort. Two large udders hung heavily beneath its belly, and when it saw Creed it stopped chewing its cud, and guffawed. The sound was a cross between a donkey and a bullfrog. The mammal had no problem seeing through the Penumbra spell. It worried Creed a bit, so he asked Ojin.

"Ojin, what is that thing there in the shadows?"

"Ah. That my friend is a Xinquat, and it appears to have taken an interest in you."

"Can it see me?"

"Yes. Don't fret. It's rather docile really, and from its milk we make phenomenal cheeses and cream. They can see what others cannot, but thankfully it does so quietly."

"Not too quietly as it would seem."

"No, but now *we* need to be," Ojin admonished.

"Ojin," Creed whispered dryly.

"Shhhhh... don't speak."

"What happened here?" Ojin pulled Bog to a stop.

"You need to be quiet. Ears are everywhere. Once we get to the Keep, we can talk." Ojin grumbled under his breath. Creed sat back and looked about. He felt a thousand years and miles from his home. What he wouldn't do to find his dream siren, and hold her close. He hoped she wasn't far.

The city seemed to be a refuge, a refined bastion of sorts. No doubt the statues on the bridge served as symbols, defiant toward the inhabitants of the Ember Wood and what lie beyond it. Walls made labyrinths of pathways between homes and shops alike as they moved further within the city. The buildings bore older scrags and scars, certainly earned over the centuries. Interspersed throughout the districts, great watchtowers stood draped in thick orange vines with wine-red leaves seen waving gently in the upward beams of the tower lamps. Elegant and brutal the towers stood, for within their arched stone windows they bore sharpened harpoons steadied at specific points along the distant perimeter wall. Creed wondered what could be so enormous as to necessitate an iron projectile as big as Bog.

As they neared the Keep, brown stucco buildings encircled an open lawn before its gates. The road turned from dark stone to dry white remains. Statues of former Durdan leaders stood at the ready, lining the Keep's path, and seemingly escorted them along the crushed lye and bone road. Beneath each statue, skulls with hardened tusks had been pressed together through mortar and time. The skull piles stood six feet high at the statue bases, and Creed looked down upon them with curiosity.

Once within the gates of the Keep, they walked west of the main entrance, and there stood Perrindor with two sentries and a smile on his face before a gargantuan extension of the castle. It appeared to have been built for giants. One could have stacked three Bogs, one on top of another, before they touched the apex of the doorway. As they strode closer to the entry, the sentries instinctively stepped back. Their leader stood still. Perrindor was a modest man, six foot, and hair past his ears. He had grey in his short beard, and a scar across his right cheek just missing his eye. His voice was coarse and robust. He motioned them through the high archway into the darkness.

"Ah hah! I knew you were in that blurry ball somewhere, friend. Let me see your face."

"Let us inside, and I will let down the Penumbra," Ojin said. "I need your guards outside the door."

"But why? We're two days past an Ogre siege. They brought their catapults and firestones. The whole place is on alert."

"Trust me. I need discretion." Ojin insisted.

"Men, outside. Guard the door. I will leave the lock undone for now."

The two broad-shouldered brutes nodded, and stood outside while Perrindor released an iron lever, which slowly, via a complex system of pulleys and chains, closed the vaulted doors behind the mammoth. Ojin let down the Penumbra, and he snapped his fingers again. The sconces along the castle's interior walls lit simultaneously within the Hall and Commons, bringing the barren haven to life.

It was a long-arched rock hall, which emptied into a vacuous room, spacious enough to hold a dozen mammoths comfortably. Further on, two smaller hallways split like the branches of a "Y". The floor of the main room sat at the bottom of a ten-story tower with competing spiral staircases winding upwards as a double helix to lofts and shelves of books. Beds were scattered about above and below. There was a musty smell in the air like wet fur. Weapons were secured along the walls, and the armory was down the hall to the left while a large makeshift forge, anvils, hammers, crafts, and dull orange coals were to the right. Banquet tables sprawled out before them at the end of the great hall. As the flames grew, the entire room filled with warmth, as did Perrindor's face. He couldn't quite hide his astonished look.

"Ojin! Bog! It's been ages! Welcome back to Durdan! Used to be the two of you at my table every new moon, but with what's been going on everything seems to be out of the ordinary. I understand you've been in the Ember Wood for some time now. Anything new?"

"Many things. The mountains grow restless with what lies underneath. I fear there is much more to the recent events we've witnessed." Creed sat up a little more, and made the bench creak. Perrindor walked a little closer, and gasped.

"And... wait. You've brought someone else I see! By the Endüerduul! Is that who I think it is? It can't be!"

"Yes, my friend. He entered this evening."

Creed and Ojin stepped down from Bog's back, and Bog rolled slowly to his side. He had enough excitement for now, and wished to sleep. Ojin motioned his hands again in an "s" shaped pattern, and the armor fell to the ground. He patted Bog's thick fur, and could feel the beast breathe deeply. His overgrown child was spent. Bog was snoring within minutes. Perrindor embraced Ojin slapping him on his thick back, and then went to embrace Creed. Creed stumbled away awkwardly.

"Hippocrates! My friend! It's been too long!" Perrindor exclaimed.

"I don't..." Creed couldn't recall. He put his hands up.

"Ok. Ok. My apologies. It's too early. I always forget. You've leapt so many times, I'm sure you're weary. It probably all becomes a jumbled mess at some point. You need rest, and then it will all come back my friend!" Perrindor turned to Ojin with a raised brow.

"It's taking him longer this time, Perrindor. They fed him Fugue Flies."

"Who?"

"Caedere most likely."

"When?" Perrindor asked.

"When he leapt. Not sure where."

"Impossible."

"They're crossing already. Something has changed."

"This may explain the Ogre raid. They were bolder than usual. Outmanned ten to one, and they didn't hesitate. They attacked a few hours after dusk, and it took an entire evening of volleys and skirmishes before they crossed back over the River Ebon."

"Did you see Caedere or Lord Leterum?"

"No, but at one point I saw the Titan Ignis."

"Ignis?"

"For a moment. His crown of smoke rose above the treetops. He smashed the bridge with his mace, and took a step forward as if to leap into our city. The bridge is intact, but our engineers will need time to mend the braces."

"How could we be this far behind? How is Ignis awoken? How is he free?" Ojin asked.

"No idea, dear friend. Many things have escalated quickly. You've been here. Have you not seen the aggression?"

"Yes, but I have been traversing the realm these last few months searching for answers. I've entered the Ember Wood many times recently, but I'm surprised I didn't come across the Ogres sooner." Ojin rubbed his aching head and sighed. His tail brushed the floor in fatigue.

"I fear they have planned each attack with some strategy not evident to me. They achieve very little beyond our wrath and damnation. Any terrain they obtain, they relinquish within days to attack somewhere else. It seems random. Purposefully," Perrindor explained.

"That much is true. Leterum is calculating. Probing. He does nothing without a purpose."

"We cannot know the Universe's plan in all of this, but we can eat and celebrate your visit tonight! It does my heart great good to see your face once more. I see Bog has taken to the floor as usual. Nowhere else he could stretch out like that but the Hall and Commons! I have beds over here for the two of you. Wine? Roast?"

"No. No. Thank you. We need rest, but only for a few hours. I feel that we have lost too much time, and we have far to travel." Ojin raised his palm politely.

"Understood. Hippocrates, I have fresh clothes for a man your size over here, and a little more useful than those rags. Chain mail is over there by the new blacksmith shop. The last one took a fire boulder right down the middle. Ryval barely got out alive." Creed walked toward the blacksmith pit, and gathered the chain mail. He went behind the nearby wall in order to change into his new clothes. He listened intently as Ojin and Perrindor discussed everything that had transpired.

"How did you repeal the attack?" Ojin asked.

"Serena sent an army of her Bellatorum. Their numbers have dwindled as of late. Last I heard Serena had pulled many back to her and the Redemptio Keep. Much of the Highlands go unchecked," Perrindor explained.

Ojin slowly turned his staff as the jade orb swirled like a green snow flurry in his hands.

"There are rumors that something now threatens even the immortals."

"Well I suppose so. She only sent fifty archers and pikesmen to drive the Ogres back. Ignis disappeared when they arrived. When morning broke, we found nothing but footprints and broken weapons. I lost many men that night." Perrindor stared at the ground.

"I saw the devastation on our way down," Ojin noted.

"Honestly, Ojin, it felt like more of a diversion. It was half-hearted." Perrindor animated with his hands.

"Diversion for what I wonder?"

"Not sure. My patrols haven't seen anything before or after. There is word from the scouts that small skirmish squads have been probing the southern villages. Pillaging as they go."

"Emboldened," Ojin acknowledged.

"Yes."

"They're searching or taunting?" Ojin asked.

"Perhaps both. I suspect they're baiting the Queen and Princess."

"Serena and Celeste are too smart for that, and that would be too simple. We need to get to the Capital of Guillarne in three days' time." Bog stirred, and snored loudly. It was enough to startle Perrindor. He looked at Ojin and then Creed, shaking his head.

"That's ambitious my friend. Ravens are everywhere."

"It's necessary." Ojin insisted.

"Why not bring them here?"

"That isn't the plan. We cannot miss that window. If the child is born before the Endüerduul accepts him in his mother's womb, it could be disastrous."

"Understood. You will need help."

"I had hoped to keep the band small. The Penumbra can only hold so many."

"You just need one man. You know him well. Xaris."

"I thought he would be with Serena? Why is he here?" asked, Ojin.

"He joined me once the raids began. The Queen insisted despite my resistance."

"And the Princess?" When Ojin asked this, Creed peaked around the corner. He wondered if she were safe as well.

"They travel together as always with their Bellatorum. Their whereabouts remain unknown. I swear to it."

"Where is Xaris now?" Ojin asked.

"He's following up on some scouting reports. I will let him know you are here. He will join us once he's finished and you have rested." Perrindor patted Ojin's shoulder.

"Well enough."

They looked at Creed. He tossed his old rags to the side of some nearby wine barrels.

"Honestly, Ojin, you could have found him some better clothes."

"They worked well enough for the trip here, Perrindor," Ojin replied.

"Hah! This man needs armor, and his spear! For the gods, this is truly a blessing! The Great Hippocrates in my Keep! You don't need many more men once he's on his feet!"

"You've confused me with someone else I'm afraid." Creed looked at the jubilant man, but couldn't recover a single memory or thought that helped him remember.

"Just time, my friend, all in due time. This is Durdan, the great bastion of the Western Highlands! You are safe here and very much welcome. Rest. I will get you at mid-day. The sun has almost risen. You need your sleep. Much to discuss!" Perrindor slapped

Ojin on the back with vigor, and bounded outside the vault doors whistling as Creed watched the doors close once more.

"That was weird," Creed muttered.

"He's a good man. Eccentric at times, but he enjoys what he does. He protects the city, and after all these years, he still does quite well. Serena owes him a great deal for holding this part of Mürindür secure."

"The city looks pretty beat up."

"The City of Durdan has withstood thousands of years of direct assaults. The Ember Wood is home to creatures you've never seen in the light, and they along with the Ogres, trolls, and now a titan have always attempted to tear down its walls. Yet to this day, Durdan stands, one end facing the wild, and the other with an eye on the Capital of Guillarne far to the East. If Durdan ever fell, the Capital would likely not have the means to sustain attacks on all fronts. If the Capital falls, the Highlands would be lost. It is said that Durdan alone keeps the beasts of Hell at bay. For me, I have seen many things in this city. Some good and some horrific, but the people are the truest and most resilient beings you will ever meet."

"And yet, you don't seem to trust any of them."

"I trust a few, but believe me when I say this, there are eyes everywhere. Leterum can be very convincing especially when he sets his mind on something, and for now we must limit the number in our circle."

"He called me Hippocrates."

"Yes." Ojin nodded.

"Is that who I am in this world?" Creed asked.

"You have been many men on Earth, but as Hippocrates you became a legend in Mürindür. That is who we know you to be."

"Hippocrates was an old man."

"He was a young man before he was an old man." Ojin winked.

"I mean he was the grandfather of medicine. All of his stories were as a scholar, an elder. How was I that man? How is that man a warrior?"

"When I first met you on Earth, you were a young Hippocrates. You had fervor for disease and decay. You even believed there was a way to defeat Death himself. You studied the sciences and politics. You were well versed on philosophy and history. You also enjoyed combat, perhaps too much at times under the mentoring of the hoplites. You moved quickly. Fiercely. Legend has it you were a descendent of Hercules. Some said they thought you to be Ares on Earth."

"Ironic."

"Indeed. I was there the day you threw down your spear in Spartolos, and ran to the aid of your countrymen. Under arrows and assault, you saved many lives that day and the days after, tending to their wounds."

"You would think I would remember that."

"One would. Men followed you and your exploits. You dedicated yourself to the healing arts for which you are still remembered. Many years later when you died on Earth, you came here." Ojin smiled.

"As an old man?" Creed asked.

"You arrived as your true self. The man you thought yourself to be. You landed in the Dunes of Transitio. The Caedere came to harvest the wandering souls, the Vagus, but you took up a spear. Something inside you pushed you to battle. As everyone else gathered the Welfalon souls and fled to the safety of Redemptio, you stood your ground, alone and unwavering. Unaware of where you were or why, you defended those that others had chosen to ignore, to abandon. The Bellatorum were impressed. They came to your aid, the Caedere were defeated, and the Vagus were taken to Redemptio as well. That was just the beginning. Battle after battle, campaign after campaign, you helped Serena and her Bellatorum across the lands, and as a reward, were offered a rare honor."

"Such as?"

"It will take time for you to remember. I hope sooner than later. Until then, none of what I tell you will make sense. We should rest." Ojin turned to ready his bed linens.

"I don't understand how people know me, and I can't remember a single damn thing about this place. It's infuriating. How did he know who I am by looking at me? I don't even look like Hippocrates. Is this who I really am?" Creed motioned to his chest.

"Yes. This is who you are. The hair, the height, and the wrinkles may change, but the eyes have always been the same." Ojin smiled as his ears twitched.

"I don't know how I am going to remember."

"I don't either. Every time before, you would wake up and in a matter of hours you were nearly yourself again granted it would be days before you gained your strength. You need to sleep. We can discuss this later."

"I want to discuss this now." Creed squared up his shoulders.

"Please. A few hours won't change anything, and may help you recover well enough to remember." Ojin had his hands up, open and assuring.

"Am I Hippocrates?" Creed asked again.

"Yes."

"How do I go back, to my old life? Things made sense yesterday. Today everything is a nightmare. Can I go back now? Back to Earth?"

"No."

"How do I go back?"

"You leap."

"How do I leap? I want to leap now!" Creed started to ready himself.

"That's not how it works," Ojin explained.

"Tell me how it works!!"

"Lower your voice," Ojin sternly addressed Creed. The hobgoblin's eyes were aglow. This frustrated Creed even further.

"Tell me!" Creed yelled.

"You complete your purpose. You finish your trials."

"And?"

"The Endüerduul opens two portals. One will take you into the Endüerduul. Please, we can wait to discuss this."

"Explain to me exactly how to get the hell out of here. I want my life back. I want to be back on Earth."

"You were miserable there," Ojin said pointedly.

"How would you know?"

"I know. All that matters now is that you are here, and we have been waiting for you. It will make sense very soon."

"There are two portals. I get to choose once I'm done with whatever it is you people have me here to do?"

"In a way, yes. It's complicated."

"Where does the other portal take you?" Creed asked.

"The other will take you back to Earth, but it is different for you."

"How so?"

"We are tired. Let this wait a few hours. Please," Ojin beseeched his friend.

"Tell me now!"

Ojin sighed. He walked slowly to the bed and sat down as it creaked, rubbed his itchy scalp, and his heavy hands flattened his ears, sliding back towards his neck. He unfastened his cloak, as his rough, bare-feet arched, toes tip-tapping with hesitation.

"In these very fields upon which this city was built, you were chosen by the Lux Bellatorum, the warriors of Serena and servants of the Lux. They chose you as a Luxatio, a forever fragmented, dislocated piece of light. A soul that would return again and again, and yet never remains."

"Luxatio?"

"You took an oath. You chose to give up the Endüerduul, willingly, forever committed to return to Earth to serve your fellow man, to inspire, to innovate, to transform humanity one earthly life at a time. When you return to Mürindür, you serve the Lux until it is time to go back. This is why Perrindor knows you. This is why no one else can know you are here. This is why the Caedere attacked you on Earth where you would be defenseless, and why they seek you out even now." Creed was perplexed with angst.

"How many of us are there?" There was a creak outside the doors, and Ojin's right ear turned ninety degrees to listen for unwanted guests as he continued.

"A few hundred, but some are unaccounted for."

"I can't ever go to the Endüerduul?"

"No."

"Never?" Creed asked again.

"Never. It is the price you pay for the role you have assumed."

"Why would I do such a thing? Was I confused like I am now? Did they take advantage of me? How could I possibly give up an eternity of peace for an eternity of struggle and death?"

"It isn't as bad as you think. It is an honor. You were chosen. You were awake, and happy to take the oath. You have many lives you are responsible for, and you are a leader amongst men. Luxatio are the men and women who have molded history. Artists, pacifists, musicians, philosophers, physicians, scientists, politicians, warriors all of whom you remember from history books, played their part willingly as well. They return here, and do the same until it is time to help mankind once more."

"They were just people in those books."

"No. They were more than that. They became more than a thought or an ideal. They showed humanity the way. They sacrificed themselves, so that the world would grow and evolve to something worthwhile."

"The world is a horrible place. Death. Famine. War. Poverty," Creed detailed.

"Yes. It is all those things, and yet why do people carry on? Why through all the ancient civilizations up to the present did people dare to dream?"

"They didn't know any better. That's what humans do. They hope and remain ignorantly optimistic."

Creed kicked at his tunic on the floor, and stared at the doors to the great hall. He wanted to leave and run away. He wanted to find a way home.

"Hope is not ignorance, my friend. Hope is the current of fortitude within your heart when all else seems lost and forfeit."

"I can't ever undo the oath? Give it up? Start over?"

"I'm afraid not." Ojin lowered his head for a moment. Creed paced slowly.

"I'll never see my parents?"

"Unlikely."

"So, they're up there." Creed pointed to the sky.

"Yes," Ojin affirmed.

"And I can't go?"

"No, my friend. I am truly sorry. This is why the Luxatio are revered in Mürindür. They have sacrificed an eternity of peace. There is more…"

"What more do I need to hear? I'm trapped in an oath I don't remember. I feel isolated. I feel abandoned. I am… I won't ever… see… anyone?" Creed threw an empty goblet across the hall. The metal clang continued even as it rolled from their sight.

"Ok. That's enough! We don't need to discuss this anymore! I am sorry. We have to prepare for the new day. Rest. I'll get you some wine." Ojin attempted to placate him, but Creed wasn't having any of it.

"I don't want wine!" Creed screamed.

"We both need to rest. You were clamoring for sleep back on the road, so now you can sleep!"

"How can I sleep? I don't want to be here!" Creed became angrier. His eyes welled up with tears. His breathing increased as he clinched his fists. He felt warm all over as if he were within an oven. Ojin stood up from the bed and approached him cautiously with his hands raised. He had set his staff aside on the bed, but now turned to look at it as if it were needed. The jade orb was aglow.

"Easy. Easy. Breathe. Breathe slowly." Ojin's robes began to move in the waves of heat emanating from Creed.

"I can't ever… won't ever… see anyone again? Never? It isn't fair! I don't want to be here! I don't want to ever come back! I want to rest! I want all of this to be over! NOW!"

Creed paced about the floor. He kicked a nearby wooden stool, and smoke laced its legs as it tumbled. The flames in the Hall and Commons' lanterns grew higher in pulsating bursts, lapping the stone arches with black spit. The tears were streaming down Creed's face. He hated every bit of where he was. When the tears hit the floor, they dissipated into steam. Bog began to stir as his trunk lifted from the ground.

"Hippocrates, please. I told you. You aren't ready for any of this. Sleep. We all need some sleep. We can…" Ojin stepped closer for a moment, but stopped quickly.

"I AM NOT HIPPOCRATES!!"

Creed stared angrily at Ojin. He appeared to stare through him at something far away. The air rumbled uncontrollably. The lanterns began to melt as molten metal trickled down the walls like water, and the stone cracked from the intense heat. The coals in the blacksmith forge grew white hot causing one of the flat bit tongs to fold in half, falling to the stone floor in a liquid heap. An incendiary wind rose swiftly around Creed, fluttering pages of the books high above him in the lofts, as bed sheets and linens flew locked within a cyclone of arid rage.

"CREED! ENOUGH!" Ojin shouted, but Creed couldn't hear him. Painful uncontrolled images beat upon his brain like hail.

The heat and light were blinding. Ojin shaded his eyes, and raised his left hand. He couldn't focus, and his breath was fleeting. He tried to focus on casting a spell, but the air was too overwhelming to take in. The beds rattled, and the foundation quaked as Creed began to float inches from the ground. The Keep would surely be destroyed if nothing more were done to extinguish Creed's rage. Ojin knelt, and crawled across the hot stone floor toward his jade staff. Suddenly, a large wallop from Bog's trunk caught Creed clean across the nape of his neck. He flew into the wall, falling to the ground unconscious. The heat dissipated, and the lanterns slowly dimmed.

Chapter 6: Ojin's Preparations

Ojin awoke to a gentle hand on his shoulder, and he sat up briskly. It was Perrindor. The hobgoblin looked to see Creed still asleep on the nearby table on which he had placed him, and noticed a small swollen area, purple and angry, above Creed's right eye. Perrindor spoke.

"Rest well, Ojin?"

"Yes. What time is it?"

"It's afternoon." Perrindor and another man eclipsed the daylight.

"We need to get ready. You let us sleep too long." Ojin rolled slowly from his pine wood bed. The poor furniture crackled in relief. He reached for his vest and cloak.

"You rested as you should have. We have been busy packing and preparing all morning. Your friend over there appeared to have a rough time though." He motioned to Creed.

"He lost control," Ojin replied.

"In what way?"

"Something he's never done. Something I've never seen. Not in a man anyways. Much like someone else we know," the hobgoblin explained.

"Ohh?" Perrindor looked about. He saw the black scars along the columns, scattered books, and linens across the Hall and Commons. He walked over to the forge, and picked up a disheveled, twisted tong now cold as the floor. Many of the books had been burned.

"Fire?" Perrindor asked.

"Yes."

"That's not good. It's difficult to control. Impossible to foresee." Perrindor looked worried.

"Yes," Ojin agreed.

"He's never done this before?"

"Not to this extent. I taught him flame gathering eons ago to start fires and light torches, but nothing like this. This is something entirely foreign to me," Ojin explained.

"Curious. First Ignis and now this."

"Indeed."

"Have you heard from her?" Perrindor set down the tongs into the smelter.

"Serena?" Ojin asked.

"Yes."

"Not in some time. She needs to see him. Maybe she will know what happened."

"Should we wake him?" Perrindor asked.

"I suppose. Honestly, not sure what we will find. Maybe we should prepare for the road, and wake him once we've left the Keep. I don't want him blowing the whole place up." Ojin looked over his friend as he sipped a glass of water.

"Agreed. My men are still trying to clean up the city from Ignis. No need to dash it all out of impatience. I had hoped to speak with him again as Hippocrates. I still owe him my life."

A solemn man of Moorish ancestry walked up behind Perrindor. He stood nearly as tall as Ojin with two gladius blades across his back, cinched within a cracked leather scabbard. He wore a thick leather tunic vest, black linens made of dyed wool, and a dagger on the left side of his belt. His boots, gauntlets, and greaves were old, but the buckles appeared polished against the blacked-out clothing.

His hair was pulled back tightly with twine. He too had a scar, but across his neck extending onto his right shoulder. He had deformed, cauliflower scarred ears, and one looked as if some of it had been bitten off. His beard was cinched in two places, hanging low and heavy as a Lion's Head medallion with silver chain lay flat across his chest. Ojin looked him over. Reading his eyes. His intent. The man was built for war. They smiled.

"Xaris, it's been a long time." They greeted one another with a brisk embrace.

"I've been scouting the skirmishes throughout the lower townships."

"Really? Why not the Bellatorum? I thought you to be with the Queen."

"I was as always, but she insisted once they went into hiding. We felt it would give me an opportunity to report more to her while waiting for the two of you. I thought we had more time," Xaris replied.

"So did I." Ojin nodded.

"The Caedere have been pushing westward from the desert, aggressively. Relentlessly. The Capital troops have broken through twice to aid the Redemptio Keep on the other side. The roads have been stricken with plague and despair," Xaris explained.

"Is Redemptio cut off?"

"Lately, no, but it is day to day. The Guillarne Guard protects the supply lines, and has been evacuating the new souls in the day. It's all they can do to keep the corridor safe," Xaris replied.

"And the Lux Bellatorum?" Ojin asked.

"Everywhere. The battles are continuous, and they are spread thin. Where the Guard is needed, they respond. Where man suffers, they respond even less. Between the Ogre raids and the Caedere, there is little rest for anyone." Xaris stood with his hands on his hips.

"Why battle for new souls?" Ojin asked.

"They aren't looking for new souls, Ojin.," Perrindor said. "The Caedere are searching for someone else." He paused, and crossed his arms. All three looked to Creed.

"They're looking for him." Perrindor motioned with his head toward the table.

"If the Lux could have pulled him sooner without the Caedere knowing, or if we could have just had more time before he arrived…" Ojin felt defeated now that he knew what lay before them. Perrindor, always the optimist, shore up his beastly friend. He patted Ojin on the back through the robes and fur.

"Yes, but who knows why the Lux didn't, my friend. Sooner or later it was destined to happen, but none of that matters now. The fact is, you are here, the both of you. We will help in any way that we can. We have fresh horses if you wish to leave Bog. He will be well fed, and cared for closely." With that, Bog raised his head and yawned. His trunk started to sniff Xaris and nuzzled his neck. This was a welcomed and familiar smelling family member.

"Ha, ha, Bog. Long time my friend. You didn't seem too sociable this morning. We have fruit and fresh Nelumbo blossoms, your favorite. They're as pink and succulent as ever. Plucked from the nearby lake this morning." Xaris buried his face into Bog's cheek. Ojin shook his head.

"I think we'll need him although it may help to have horses for you and Creed."

"Creed?" Xaris looked upon their unconscious friend.

"He isn't himself as you can see by looking around, Xaris. We haven't had this much damage since the Iceland Cretans came to visit. Ojin said it was fire." Perrindor looked about once more with raised brows.

"In all the years that I've known him, he's never done this. Does the Princess know?" Xaris asked, appearing troubled. Ojin knew how much Xaris detested the magical unknown.

"No. As I told Perrindor, we will speak with the Queen first. She will know why and how this came to be." Ojin patted Xaris on the shoulder and turned to gather his things. Perrindor kicked a charred goblet across the hall. Xaris walked toward Creed, leaning over the table and studying him further. He touched the dry blood on the lacquered wood.

"Perhaps he is possessed, Ojin. Sick."

"He isn't possessed, Xaris. He is tired and confused. Before you go casting doubt on this man, remember what he is meant for and for whom he is meant for."

"That's exactly what worries me. She needs to know." Xaris stared at Ojin.

"She will know when it's time, and that's the last we will talk of it. Am I clear?" Ojin asked.

"Understood." Xaris turned and walked away. Perrindor patted him on the back.

"Well enough then. We'll give you two horses. Our strongest. We will also fit you with food, clothing, weapons, and a spear for our friend. Xaris, when Hippocrates, I mean, Creed, wakes, you may need to give him a refresher. You remember his style."

"Quite well. I was there at the Battle of Leonicus. He held the ground for two days until the Lux could bring reinforcements. He seemed calm… almost in a trance back then." Xaris looked about the Hall. "This does not seem to be the Luxata I witnessed that day. When he is ready, we will knock the dust off him, and sharpen his edge."

"Xaris, Perrindor, do you know of a way not on the Road of Borainnos? The Caedere will be flying Ravens along its fields and waterways."

"There is a small valley with a honeycomb of caves. We used it to get here."

"Where?" Ojin asked cautiously. There were many places he did not wish to venture. Perrindor rolled a map out on the nearby banquet table, and pointed to a dark line, which stretched miles above Durdan toward a great mountain. Ojin was quite dismayed.

"Ashi," Perrindor said sincerely.

"Are you sure? No one travels that road. I haven't ventured that way in over a hundred years. Intentionally. What about the mountain pass?" He looked flatly at Perrindor's face.

"No. Ashi is the best way my friend. You easily flit about through space as a hobgoblin, but the rest of us mortals have navigated its secrets for quite some time. It's been the safest way to acquire the high ground. You needn't be worried about what walks the earth or below it. You should concern yourself with what owns the air. The caves will be your best bet." Perrindor cleared his throat.

Ojin turned away and clasped his hands behind his back. He paced in half circles. He stooped slowly because his back was stiff, and threw his hood and cape over his shoulders. He clasped a gold disk upon his chest to bind the cloak's seams, and rubbed the smooth emblem of the owl on the bracket piece. It reminded him of home. He thought about the horrors of Leonicus, and the loss he suffered on the roads nearby. It wasn't something he wished to revive in his heart.

"It's a maze, Perrindor. Men have gone mad in its depths," Ojin said about the Ashi tales.

"Xaris knows the way my friend," Perrindor assured him.

"Any movement along the Ashi Pass? Surely there are Caedere patrols," he asked.

"No. My men and I arrived hours before you this evening. There was nothing when we scouted the path," Xaris affirmed.

"Ojin, it is the best way. It heads north, and then turns due east far enough to get you into the southern edge of the Groves all while remaining unseen, notwithstanding the Fields of Effugere of course."

"We were to meet at the Pools of Cordis Loci. We would still need to head south a few miles. Are you sure the mountain pass is not an option?" Ojin persisted on finding another path to their destination.

"No," as Xaris ran his finger across the map, "The Silva Luctus lies in the valley below the pass. The trees are restless, and something new torments them. They would likely cry out to Leterum if we were discovered."

"Has Leterum been seen in the skies?" Ojin asked.

"No. He has stayed within his Keep for a fortnight. There are whispers of something powerful within his domain, but we have no eyes."

"So, we head northward into certain doom, blindly, to gain our salvation," Ojin mumbled with worry.

"True my friend, but it will be with Honor. The Endüerduul will be pleased." Perrindor grinned.

"Perhaps," Ojin whispered.

Ojin gathered his other things while Xaris went outside and loaded the horses with rations. Bog ate fully of the Nelumbo blossoms, and appeared content. Ojin snapped his fingers, and the armor and the war bench found their place on Bog's thick body. The armor appeared more snug than usual, so Ojin loosened the cinch until room had been made for the full belly, and then walked to the stone table. He looked upon Creed with empathy, knowing his friend was suffering from something yet understood. He lifted Creed, and carried him as a child up the mammoth's shoulder to the bench upon Bog's back. He tucked a bundle of clothing beneath his head, draped his body in blankets, and dressed his scalp with some cold oleander salve. Once everything had been gathered, he walked Bog down the hall, out into the light, and looked upon the City of Durdan below.

It truly was a beauty to behold. People were walking about the old streets, selling wares, greeting one another, and carrying on about their day. If one could merely forget where they were, and the war outside the walls, it would appear to be as any other bustling pedestrian mountain waypoint. Durdan was comforting even if for but a moment as Ojin contemplated the road ahead. The mammoth stood while Xaris tied the horses in a long chain to the flank hooks on Bog's armor. The group ventured onto the open lawn of the Keep, and Creed's limp, unconscious body twitched within some nightmare he could not escape. His breathing was labored, so Bog reached back with his trunk to check on his passenger, softly brushing his bruised forehead. Creed coughed harshly, and shifted. He rolled over to a better position, and remained asleep.

Once outside, Xaris climbed upon his stippled stallion, Nos, and fastened a long sword behind the cantle. He adjusted in the seat, and cupped the saddle horn. His bow and arrows remained bound and sheathed before his knees. As he placed his boots within the stirrups, he witnessed his men gathering. Nothing formal. No salutes. They stood at attention, quietly.

Ojin knew Xaris to be a legend in his own right. The Highland troops regarded him as a battle savvy warrior, and one in whom Serena cast a great deal of trust. When he ventured to Durdan to lead the counter raids to the Ogre ambushes, the men looked to him immediately. His understanding of the terrain, and unmitigated fury when his swords were drawn, brought fear to the hearts of those who opposed him and the Queen. Xaris acknowledged the soldiers with a gentle bow of his head, and pulled his cloak over fully. Sparing his beard, his features were obscured.

Ojin held Bog's reins and looked into the soldiers' faces as he stood at the east entry. The citizens below were oblivious, but these warriors had seen what waits for them at night in the wild. They knew the Caedere patrols were relentless. Little did they know, however, that a desperate secret lay hidden within the pile of blankets high above in Bog's bench.

Ojin climbed atop Bog, and made way slowly past the battalion. He wished he could allay their fears, but in reality, it was highly likely Durdan would be attacked again, and this time without their guardian. The city had been hit hard on this last assault, but if they could remain steadfast, the time bought would assuredly grant this small band the opportunity it needed to escape and regroup. Ojin looked back upon the great Keep, and waved briefly to Perrindor. His face was somber, but Perrindor managed to work out a small smile before turning, and directing the repairs and tasks for the day. He looked at Ojin once more, and held his hand high then turned into the doorway. The doors slammed shut with a thud, and punctuated the constant vigilance of the city.

Far below, on the main street, Ojin caught a glimpse of clothing and baskets held on high. He stared a little longer, and realized it was hundreds of weary refugees. Some rode in horse-drawn carts with barrels of water and crates of food. Amongst them, on horseback, a handful of the Guillarne Guard kept a watchful eye. The refugees were on foot, dusty, and undoubtedly fearful of their exodus. This worried Ojin although he knew why they were here. The Queen could no longer guarantee their safety within the walls of the Capital of Guillarne, which could only mean they were expecting a siege of some sort. To lose the Capital, would be detrimental to their cause, and likely a death stroke to the whole of the Highland plains. He hoped it was merely a precaution and nothing more.

As they ventured across the lawn and through a small street, Bog approached the city's northern black gates. They were far less ornamental than the ones that faced the bridge westward. Ojin cast the Penumbra, and looked upward past the city walls to cliffs cast in shadow. Ashi was a great looming mountain, but the Ashi Pass was a trail of trial all on its own with no greater obstacle than the ruined city of Leonicus. The Highland spirits walked those grounds, and they would willfully depose their whereabouts to an eager Leterum. Although the sky remained empty for now, the need for discretion was paramount. He wondered if they could make it so easily into the mountain without discovery. Ojin looked back once more upon Creed wishing him to recover quickly. If they were to make it through the Ashi Pass, it would require everyone's wit and will. He needed his friend to return. He needed Hippocrates.

Chapter 7: The Ashi Pass

With the Road of Borainnos fleeting eastwardly, the small crew traveled north along the Ashi Pass. Creed awoke to the gentle rocking of his seat, cold and disoriented, realizing he had little to cover himself with. There was a blanket on the bottom of the bench's footrest, so he leaned and grabbed it for warmth while his head throbbed. His fingers gingerly palpated a swollen mound above his eye. Blinking repeatedly in the cold to wash away the tears, his vision cleared, and he could see they'd been traveling for some time through unrecognizable terrain.

The road was overgrown with olive underbrush and timber, at times creeping invasively across the thoroughfare. Where the briar failed to grow, the ground was armored in limestone and flint rock. There was scarcely any wildlife to note beside the random ground squirrel or lost squail. Ojin sat in front of him, and apparently hadn't noticed Creed was awake, so when the passenger tapped the driver's shoulder, the hobgoblin nearly jumped out of his seat. "Good lord, man! You should warn people before you go tapping them out of a deep thought!" He swiped at Creed with his tail.

"Sorry. Wanted you to know I'm not dead."

"That's a relief," Ojin curtly replied.

"I suppose. Where are we?" Creed asked.

"We are moving northward along the Ashi Pass in hopes of finding an alternate route to your bride."

"She's up here?" Creed asked.

"No. Celeste and Serena will meet us in a special place called the Pools of Cordis Loci. It is there that we will wed the two of you, and ask for the Endüerduul's blessing."

"How far is that?"

"Likely another day or two away by ground." Ojin coughed, and cleared his throat.

"I guess we're going over a mountain then, judging by the incline."

"Actually, we go up in order to go down. The entrance to a complex cavern system is mid-way up the slope. Once we enter it, we will proceed through the caves toward the other side. That's where we will walk out into the Fields of Effugere toward the Pools. That is where Celeste will be waiting for you," Ojin explained.

"Anything we need to worry about up here?"

"Everything, so stay still and quiet. We have a ways to go."

Creed bundled the blanket tighter around himself. He looked over Ojin's left shoulder, and saw a large soldier dressed in black, riding a stippled horse. The man didn't turn to look at him, but somehow his posture seemed familiar. The swords across his back clearly meant business, and Creed wondered why anyone else would choose to come with them. He shrugged off the question, and instead began counting the number of mountain peaks west of them along the horizon. He counted thirty-seven.

They marched for hours upwards through scattered islets of vegetative debris amongst a patchwork of Klein grass. Durdan had become a small circle of lights below. The horses' heads bobbed up and down with each steep yard. The group was quiet aside from the hoof beats. Occasionally an iron shoe would click loudly on the rocks, and Ojin would wince. Though the Penumbra could deflect light and muffle sound like a distant room, he explained, anything or anyone paying close attention could hear the rocks and metal if nearby. Fortunately, there were no settlements for the living along this road, and for good reason.

"We are approaching an old city named Leonicus. Do you remember it?" Ojin asked.

"Not really. Some of this seems like a dream, and the rest seems foreign."

"Nothing living, lives here. It is a vile ground steeped in death and fear. Keep your eyes open."

Ogre ruins slept beneath blankets of drab moss and briar. Decrepit pillars leaned as tombstones. Foundations cracked and split from the egress of civilization. No one wished to rest or labor above this soil that bore witness to so much atrocity. As the band traveled further onto the grounds, Creed saw a broken stone arch, which read "Leonicus".

The sign triggered violent flashes in his mind of weapons clanging against one another as blood spilled under a mid-day sun. He could hear the barked commands of unit leaders, and the screams of the fallen. He saw himself bloodied with a long golden spear in his hands, and he remembered the fear in an Ogre officer's eyes. As the spear met its mark, Creed blinked. He was back to the present, and looked upon rows and rows of oval stones polished with inscriptions to the right of the trail. Creed wondered how many bones lay within the confines of those markers, and as he looked about, thousands upon thousands seemed more like a possibility.

They made good progress despite the slow, steady incline.
Surprisingly, Bog was quiet, and didn't complain. Ojin steadily
held his gaze forward with an occasional turnabout in his seat to
determine ambush opportunities and routes for escape. Fortunately,
there were no walls, just trees and broken stone, but the lore and air
made Creed uneasy. Nightmares he scarcely remembered traipsed
the shadows, but in the pit of his stomach he knew this was a
wretched place. They were a day's ride from Durdan City now, so
reinforcements were not an option, according to Ojin, and Creed
hoped they would push through. The hobgoblin, however, stopped
the caravan.

"Xaris, we will rest here tonight."

"Bad idea, Ojin. This is too open, and we should continue forward
to the outcroppings of rock ahead. Everything before us is dark and
unholy. We will only feed what waits for us."

"I agree, Xaris, which is why this *should* be the place. No one
comes here. Patrols avoid it when they can, and Leterum will look
to the cliffs tonight because he assumes, we will seek shelter. We
can have Bog prop stones into a structure, and rest beneath the
Penumbra."

"I don't like it. We don't know what lurks about. My men and I
made sure to pass through quickly before. If we are found, we will
not survive." Creed leaned out from behind Ojin.

"I'd have to agree, honestly. Doesn't feel right." He waved at
Xaris, but the warrior merely nodded.

"If we walk into Leterum's patrols, no one will survive." Ojin
stated pointedly. Xaris scowled as Ojin stroked his beard. Creed
could sense the impasse. Xaris looked back up the mountain slope,
and cleared his throat.

"Let me scout ahead first. Maybe then the Ashi Pass will declare itself."

"Fair enough. Please lower us down, Bog. Creed, let's build a barricade." Bog lifted Ojin up and placed him on the ground, and then wrapped his trunk around Creed, carefully smelling him in the process. Bog hesitated for a moment.

"Bog, he's fine," Ojin assured his friend. "What he did back there was an anomaly. He won't hurt you."

The mammoth grunted in a begrudged fashion, and finally ferried him gently beside a jagged rock of granite. Creed tried to pat his trunk slowly, but Bog withdrew and began moving boulders, setting them in a pile nearby. Xaris made his way up the mountain, and soon he was swallowed up within the darkness. Ojin tied the horses to a nearby oak tree, and rummaged through mounds of limestone and granite remnants. Creed rubbed his sore scalp as images of fire consumed his mind.

"What happened in Durdan?"

"What do you remember?" Ojin asked.

"I was angry, very angry," Creed recalled.

"Yes, you were."

"Did I catch on fire?" Creed asked.

"Sort of, and I've never seen anything like it."

"Am I sick, Ojin?"

"I don't believe so."

"Well then why would something like that happen?"

"I honestly don't know. For now, help me move these stones into a makeshift wall."

Creed walked about collecting rocks, lifted what he could, and within an hour, they had a stone shelter, albeit too small for Bog.

The mammoth would have to sleep outside the front entry, but it was a clear night, and to the outsider, there was nothing to see but the brilliant stars. Creed's breath was a frosted mist when he exhaled, and he shivered uncontrollably despite his layers of clothes. Ojin started a small fire within the confines of their respite and the cloak of the Penumbra. The warmth was welcomed with open hands. Creed noticed that neither Bog nor Ojin were bothered by the cold. Naturally, their thick fur made a perfect complement to mountain travel. In the moment, Creed wished he were covered in fur.

Ojin rummaged through some leather bags near Bog, and threw a bundle of blankets at Creed's feet while he hung a small kettle of hot water over the flames to make a stew. Creed wrapped himself in the blankets, and watched Ojin sprinkle herbs and salt into the kettle with his thick fingers. The hobgoblin dropped shallots, garlic shavings, and a beef bone into the medley. It wasn't long before the air was bathed in soothing smells. It reminded Creed of an Italian restaurant he visited weeks beforehand.

Two hours passed with no sign of Xaris. The warrior was wise and weathered, but with the state of current affairs, anything was possible as the realm heaved and burped foul demons, and if they lost him, it would be best for them to turn around, explained Ojin. "Xaris is our guide through the Ashi. If he doesn't come back soon, we will need to make a decision on whether to proceed, or head back to Durdan. I haven't traveled the Ashi in many years, and with the trolls constantly mining its depths, we would almost certainly get lost."

"If we head back, then what?"

"We will have lost a day of travel, and would likely need to find a new means to get to the Queen. The baby will arrive soon, and I hate to lose more time. There is a spell we use here called the Fuga. We can envision a location, and then fly to it within the confines of the magic. I would have taken us through the Fuga to Serena and Celeste, but it would almost certainly draw the attention of Leterum and his army. If we wish to travel secretly, ground is our only means." Just then, Creed heard a rustling in the leaves. He was hopeful it would be Xaris, but when Ojin stood and looked over the wall, the hobgoblin's heart sank.

"*Yulprost*. Stay very still," Ojin instructed.

"What's a Yulprost?" Creed whispered.

"Wandering spirits that are drawn to fear. They feed off it, and they are as quick as the wind."

"Maybe we should put out the fire?"

"The Penumbra hides the light and smells, but Yulprost don't sense elements of the concrete, living world. They sense souls."

Creed stood slowly to catch a glimpse of the Yulprost. Dozens of the creatures milled about the ruins searching for sustenance. They walked hunched over smelling the ground, or stretched on their hindquarter claws, sampling the air with their narrow snouts. Long undulating tentacles wove incessantly beneath their short torso cloaks.

"I witnessed a man stumble and then ultimately get devoured by a pack of Yulprost one night over the walls of an old village. They ate like a swarm, and nothing remained but a few bones. The Yulprost graze about the soil of bloodlust terrain, and some say it's because of death in the ground, but others suspect it has more to do with the fearful residue left behind when things don't die well."

105

Tonight, there appeared to be no pattern to their searching, which suggested to Creed they were unaware of the new inhabitants in their ruins.

"I need a diversion, something to scuttle them down the mountainside," Ojin proclaimed. He thought for a moment, conjured up a goat, and projected the white animal bleating and running down the trail back toward the city. The Yulprost watched with faint interest, hesitated, but did not appear to be convinced. A Yul looked quickly to something stirring a few yards away. Twigs snapped, and a series of haunting howls burst from the tree line in the distance.

A pack of wolves took the bait, and they burst from the brush to chase the illusionary livestock. One young wolf looked back briefly, and caught a glimpse of the eerily quiet spirit scavengers. Little did the wolves know they had now become the prey. The Yulprost descended eagerly down the slope, and hunters and hunted alike disappeared beyond Creed's sight. Ojin sighed and looked at Bog. He had slept through the whole thing.

"Lazy beast." Bog snored lightly. Creed and Ojin sat down to sip on their stew, but they didn't have much time to enjoy it.

There was a tumble of small rocks and pebbles, and then a faint whistle. Ojin's ears perked up, pivoting to the left. Creed heard footsteps with something tumbling and grunting along. He peered into the darkness, and caught a flash of moonlight on a sword's hilt. It was Xaris.

"Ojin, let down your shield. I can't find you." The hobgoblin waived his hand, and all became visible again.

"Quick, get in! The Yulprost are roaming the woods. They could come back any minute." Xaris came forward, nearly tripping over Bog's trunk.

"The shield is effective, Ojin. Couldn't find any hint of you."

"I wish it was a shield, but blinding the senses is well enough."

Something struggled in the dark on a rope.

"What have you there?" asked, Ojin.

"A scout. Found him a mile up near the rocks. I nearly passed him before I saw his hand flapping."

"Flapping?"

"Yes. Not a very good scout."

Bog stood up suddenly. He paced and grunted, knocking over part of the rock perimeter, and nearly the stone hut as well. He was clearly agitated and raised his front leg. Ojin could smell something too. The bristly hair on his back rose sharply as warm white plumes of angst spilled from his nostrils. His eyes grew in preparation, and he readied his staff. Xaris stepped back and put his hand on his dagger. He was worried Bog might trample them all.

"Hold it. Hold it. Bog steady! Ojin, calm him!"

"WHAT DID YOU FIND? WHAT DID YOU BRING TO OUR CAMP?" Ojin bellowed.

"This." He pulled on the rope, and the creature fell forward. It was green, brutish, and just shy of five feet. On its knees, it stared at the fire, and began to moan and cry, though his mouth was covered in a tight cloth tied behind his stubby curled ears. The creature's hands kept rubbing the air with its wrists bent inward as they too were bound.

"An Ogre?" Ojin snorted with disgust.

"Yes, an Ogre scout. He appeared to have been waiting for something or someone. I found him with these." Xaris threw a small crossbow and a handful of bolts to the ground.

"Impossible! No one knows we're here. Were there others?"

"No."

"Was he able to signal anyone?" Ojin was agitated with his questioning.

"I don't believe so. He hadn't even drawn the string on his bow, and his bolts were still bundled a few feet from him. He sat crouched and trembled."

"You should have killed him! There will be others. They may have followed you."

"There were no others. He was alone. No fire, just bird bones around his feet. Once I tied him up and covered his mouth, we waited for half an hour. No movement. No sound. He was alone."

"He needs to go. I don't care where or how, but we cannot bring him with us," Ojin insisted.

"We should interrogate him. Find where the nearest camp is, and move past it," Xaris countered.

"No. Kill him, or I will let Bog." Ojin motioned to his friend. The mammoth was tense and ready. Xaris was unyielding although it would be unwise to wrangle an angry Bog.

"It would be a waste, Ojin. We haven't made it far, and if you wish to complete this journey alive, I suggest you heed my advice. He may prove to be worth something should we need leverage."

"Xaris! I don't need to remind you of the history of my people and Ogres! My family! My home!"

"No, you don't, and neither do I!" Xaris took a deep breath and sighed. "We can keep him bound, throw him on the bench, and

keep going. We need time to figure out what he may know. We kill him, and we have to hide the body not knowing what awaits us."
Xaris took his hand away from his weapon.

"Killing him is simpler. No risk. We know our way, and can take our chances," Ojin explained.

"That's foolish Ojin! Don't let your hatred blind you. You're wiser than that. He's been abandoned. He's weak, and hasn't likely been with his tribe for quite some time now. I consider him an asset."

"He is twitching. He might be ill or possessed. This very moment someone or something could be staring at us through his eyes."

Ojin leaned in cautiously to see the Ogre's pupils. The prisoner's eyes merely watered.

"He's not possessed. His eyes are not clouded. I think he's touched. Slow witted. Dumb," Xaris explained.

"Does it speak?" Ojin paced about the fire, his staff at the ready. This was all too readily convenient.

"I don't know, honestly. I didn't feel like giving him the chance, Ojin."

"Well?"

"You heard him! Speak!" Xaris tugged on the rope for compliance. The creature moaned and cried behind the gag. His fingers were twitching rapidly. The Ogre bit his lower lip as his stubby broken tusks reached for his cheeks. The tears were streaming, and he was rocking incessantly. Finally giving up, the Ogre fell to his side, sobbing. Bog put his foot down, and began sniffing the Ogre, head to toe, over and over again repeatedly as if questioning the smell was necessary.

"Speak!" Xaris pulled his dagger and cut the cloth loose from his head. It fell to the ground, but the Ogre could only muster a moan.

"He's holding something back. Maybe if you threaten him," Ojin encouraged.

"It won't work. Just stop it. Stop!" Creed said, as he walked out to the group. He knelt down to be eye level with the Ogre, and took in a deep breath. The Ogre smelled like fresh rain on clay. Earthy. Plain. Creed tried to look him in the eye but the Ogre gazed down, and struggled to raise his nervous hands above his ears, as if he were to be struck.

"You should untie him. He isn't a threat."

"What?" Xaris questioned.

"He isn't possessed, spellbound, dumb or slow, or trying to trick any of us. I've had patients like him. He may not be human, but the condition is the same. He's scared. We're overwhelming him. Just untie him." Creed opened his hand as if to request a tool to do it himself.

"Of course, he's scared. He's outnumbered! They're all cowards. They fight in groups killing and pillaging as they go. Get them alone, and they cower." Ojin spat on the ground in disgust.

"Untie him, Xaris. Now." Creed stood with clenched fists.

"No! You can't even remember the history of our lands let alone your name. Sit down," Xaris admonished.

"Let him go. Cut the rope and let him go, or I'll do it myself."

"Not bloody likely." Xaris gripped the rope tighter while Bog kept sniffing the Ogre.

"Who is this guy?" Creed asked Ojin as he pointed to the soldier.

"I told you. This is Xaris the Commander of the Durdan Army. He volunteered to be our guide. You have known each other for many years, and although you likely will doubt me when I say this, the two of you are actually pretty good friends."

110

"Does he take orders?" Creed asked.

"Watch your tone, Hippocrates. Friend or not, I will still knock some sense into you even if you are …" Xaris grit his teeth.

"Are what? What am I?"

"Broken," Xaris said.

"Broken? You want to see how broken?"

"You wouldn't last five seconds with me in an arena. Sit!" Xaris crouched into a ready stance.

"Who's running this circus, Ojin?" Creed asked as he continued to stare Xaris down.

"I am, and Xaris has our best intentions in mind even if I disagree with what he's brought into our camp. Let's all take a moment, and calm down. Sit. Let's eat our stew. We can tie the Ogre to the horse tree until we figure out a solution. Xaris, you should probably cover his mouth again."

"No. Let him go." Creed stepped closer to Xaris.

"You dimwit. Get away before I put you in your place!"

"Xaris! Enough!" Ojin shouted.

"I'm not afraid of you, Xaris. Something tells me it won't end as you suspect it will."

"Would you like to have a go, Hippocrates?" Xaris stepped closer to him.

"Fine by me." Creed now stood between the Ogre and his challenger.

"Have at it then!" Xaris brandished his dagger.

"Enough! Tie the Ogre up, Xaris. Sit down, Creed! Every beast from Ridgeline to Durdan can hear you. We might as well all just light the fires and call down Leterum himself!"

"Ojin, tell pighead to sheath his knife."

"You sheath it, boy!"

The campfire pulsated as it grew under Creed's anger, and the tension was clearly palpable. Xaris took a step back to lunge, but before he could move further, Bog whipped his legs with his trunk, and Xaris fell to the ground, his dagger flailing into the dirt. He lost the Ogre rope, and jumped to his feet with his hands on his swords. Everyone stared at one another, but the Ogre dared not move.

Ojin motioned sternly at Bog with his hands in the air, but the mammoth shrugged and went back to sniffing the prisoner. Creed glared angrily at Xaris, and imagined what it would feel like crushing his throat within his hands, but after a moment he looked down, and took a deep breath. The campfire wilted to a normal intensity as well. Creed knelt and took the rope off the Ogre's neck, and cut away the remaining bindings with a flint rock. He went to touch his head, but the Ogre ducked away fearfully.

"If we release him, he will find others, and we'll have no chance. You will have killed us all, Hippocrates," Xaris admonished as he sheathed his swords.

"That's why *you* should have killed him, Xaris." Ojin turned to the fire, and sat on a log he had pulled up earlier. Nothing was going as planned, and the odyssey was nearly dead before it had begun. Creed turned to both open-handed.

"How about we give him some space? Warm him by the fire? Feed him? Maybe then we'll learn a little more. I don't think he talks from the look of it. Assuming it's a he, but maybe he can point to things, or draw us something in the dirt." Although obviously afraid, the Ogre's rocking had slowed, and his hands spun occasionally, touching his face and ears.

Bog's snout leaned in to take another whiff, and inadvertently the Ogre's hand brushed against his fur. The mammoth pulled his trunk back quickly, as did the Ogre with his hand. As Bog tried to smell him once more, the Ogre's fingers clasped the fur assuredly, and let the hairs tickle his fingertips. Bog was hesitant, but permissive. The Ogre turned his face into the trunk, and buried his forehead in the bristled tufts, playing with the fur, until the rocking stopped all together. Bog was frozen. He dared not move. Creed smiled.

Ojin looked on beleaguered as he emptied the cold leftovers, and served hot stew in three burl wood bowls, contemplated for a moment, and then made a fourth. Irritated, Xaris dusted himself, and went to check on his horse. Creed sat down, seasoned steam wafting in his face, and motioned for the Ogre to sit beside him. The Ogre was too busy with the mammoth fur to notice, however. Within moments, he was asleep on Bog's trunk, and although Bog appeared petrified, he did not disturb the Ogre. Creed looked down upon the green creature, and in the firelight, he saw the lashings, and the charred brands. He noticed that Bog too had been scarred and burned. Small patches of hairless skin on the mammoth's underbelly served as testaments to some prior brush with brutality, so there stood Bog, and there lay the Ogre, seemingly kindred victims of cruelty. Creed took a sip of the stew.

"This is good, Ojin."

"Thank you. How are you feeling?"

"Better," Creed replied.

"You know, Xaris is one of our greatest allies. You owe him more than you could ever repay."

"I vaguely remember something about him, but that something didn't feel right. I acted upon that. I'm sorry, but torturing another living being has never been acceptable to me."

"Yes, but this is different. This Ogre could easily ruin everything," Ojin explained.

"I don't think so. I feel it in my gut."

"Your gut is empty. Have more stew, then we can talk."

"Ojin, when I was out, I dreamed I was in France during the Black Plague. How is that possible?"

"One of your prior lives my friend. You were, in fact, there. I remember you telling me about it. Thousands upon thousands of dead. It had been centuries since I last visited the region of Bordeaux, and from your tales I felt it likely best I not return. Leterum made an aggressive move back then, one in which I suspect lead us to where we are today. He took a third of Europe with one swipe of his sickle."

"Then there was another dream, Ojin. People called it The Battle of the White Mountain. It was bloody. Brutal. Nothing to do with religion, and everything to do with power." Creed paused with a small amount of broth at his lips, and set the bowl back down. The images of dead bodies on pikes stole his appetite.

"Yes. That was a sad, sad time, my friend. Religion has often been wielded violently throughout history. Your memories are coming back, Creed. These are not just dreams. These are all the lives you've led on Earth between your visits here."

"I couldn't change the outcomes, Ojin. The lives lost. There was so much death. I knew what we know today, but I had no tools. No medicines."

"You have always been a healer, but science needed time. Do you remember this place now? This world?"

"Things are more familiar. You are very familiar. I remember Bog. I remember, vaguely, battles I was involved in here. The images are distant and disconnected."

"Yes, but you are waking! It shouldn't be long before you remember it all." Ojin slapped his knee, appearing pleased.

"When I caught everything on fire at the Keep, how did it stop?"

"Bog."

"Bog seems to stop a lot of things. Except for that green thing over there." Creed chuckled.

"It's an Ogre, a very small one. Typically, they outstand me by a full foot."

"Bog looks like he's going to have a stroke," Creed observed.

"He was tortured when I found him, a small calf, the runt of his mother's birth. The Ogres value strength over everything else. They despise weakness. They have long trained the war mammoths from wild herds on the tundra, but treated Bog like a plaything. Target practice. They would fire up their swords and pikes, and poke him until he bled, and cried himself to sleep. I found him in a camp when on patrol with the Guillarne Guard. We had been tracking the Ogre army for days. I watched as they laughed and made him tremble. When we ambushed them, I cut the bindings on his cage, and carried him away with me. We made sure every last Ogre was dead." Ojin spit into the campfire. "I lit their bodies on fire, and watched their ash blow. Once he healed, he began to trust me, and we've been together ever since."

"I'm sorry." Creed glanced at Bog once more. "He's so big and overwhelming. I never would have thought."

"No one does. Truth is he outweighs and looms over all other war mammoths now. If he had stayed with the Ogres, he would have been their alpha. The irony."

"Should I move the Ogre then?"

"Not sure. We need to keep him quiet. No telling what lies out there in the dark."

Just then, a Raven landed next to Ojin on the log. Ojin and Creed looked at one other, and back at the bird. The Raven stared at them. Beady prying eyes roved quickly about the camp. Hesitation. Ojin knew what this meant. He had forgotten the Penumbra.

"Quick!" he yelled.

The Raven opened his mouth, and started his shrill cry when a dagger flew past the hobgoblin, and the bird's head fell from its body. The air was turbulent, and the band was in imminent danger. Ravens landed all about, and it was too late. Xaris drew his bow and fired repeatedly with his arrows while other birds flew in circles above. Ojin cast a spell to the night sky like an explosion of sound, which slowed their wings, forcing some to fall unconscious into the dirt. Bog moved and the little Ogre tumbled, but with his trunk he was able to grab a half dozen birds, and smashed them into the rocks. Feathers fluttered about without purpose. Creed swung his hands at a few. They came close enough to be able to peck his eyes out, and some tried. He managed to grab one by its chest, and pulled its head off quickly. The black feet of the decapitated spy twitched rhythmically in his hands. Ojin thumped the ground with his staff, and the remaining birds fell in a daze. He stomped them with his feet as did Bog while Xaris finished off the wounded with his blades. Black bodies littered their camp. A short flutter was heard, and against the red moon, a Raven was seen a hundred feet in the air. Its shrill cry echoed.

"Xaris!" Ojin screamed pointing at the Raven.

"I'm trying!" He launched two arrows back to back, but missed. The Raven was getting away.

THWACK!

The bird fell lifeless. No sound. The air was dead. All of them stood still, fearful of the noise their rapid hearts made. Pebbles tumbled as a pair of feet made their way to the fire. There stood the Ogre with the dead bird in hand, and a black bolt through its body. He tossed it onto the ground. The Ogre had killed the bird with his crossbow.

"Impossible." Ojin stared in disbelief.

"That explains the pile of bones by his feet. Apparently, he's quite the hunter," Xaris said, cleaning the blood from his face.

"Xaris. Creed. Sit. Bog, squeeze in." Ojin cast the Penumbra around them all, and threw the bird carcasses in the fire.

The flames burst into greens and blues with each cast. Everyone grew quiet. Creed sipped on his stew looking above into the ether. Xaris slowly sharpened his dagger. The Ogre sat on his heels, and stared at the fire as his hands searched for comfort. Bog draped his trunk over the Ogre's shoulders, and the fingers found their place. Soon enough even Bog grew weary. He lowered his head, and struggled to keep his haunches tucked in tightly. The Ogre's fingers strummed the fur like a harp while Xaris stared at him.

"Why does he do that?" the warrior asked.

"He's stimming." Creed answered.

"What?"

"It's soothing for him. Settles his mind."

"What?" Ojin echoed.

"He was born this way. He can't help it. Not one bit of it. Kids back home get diagnosed early, and often require years of therapy and work just to be able to survive. He likely has difficulty with loud noises, crowds, and chaotic situations. Can't speak, but clearly can focus and hit a flying bird with a crossbow. There's probably a whole lot going on behind those eyes right now that we just can't see, but regardless of what you think, he's not stupid."

"That's what concerns me. There is definitely a great deal going on behind those eyes," Ojin scoffed as he broke out his long pipe. He dipped his hands into a pouch within his fuzzy, brown woolen vest. From his left chest pocket, he pulled a pinch of sweet-smelling tobacco, and packed the brown shavings into the bowl. He lit the pipe, and puffed two large rings into the air.

"He's here alone. He's smaller than his kind. He can't relate to the world the way you and I can. You see the scars. He isn't one of them, Ojin. It's amazing he survived at all," Creed argued.

"You seem impressed," Ojin said.

"Well why not? It would be nearly impossible for any of us to live out here alone, and yet here he is. Who knows for how long, and yet here he is. Still standing. He's a survivor."

"We can't trust him. He could simply be lost. His tribe might not be far behind. We should leave, and set up camp elsewhere." Xaris appeared uneasy with the lackadaisical mood of the camp, sharpening his dagger across a whetstone. Creed suspected he wanted to pack it all up and leave.

"How long do you think we have before more Ravens come?" Creed asked Ojin.

"There are likely more on their way. If we run now, we may be running into a trap."

"So, we just sit here and wait?" asked, Xaris with the steel grinding slowly across the grit.

"The bodies are gone. The Penumbra is up. Yes, we wait. Hidden. Silent."

"Last time we hurried, and left the camp for the city when the Ravens came."

"Last time, Creed, we needed to meet with Perrindor immediately. I had planned to talk with Serena then, but when you... overreacted, it left my mind entirely. This time is a time for caution and patience. They will arrive, and we will escape once they leave," Ojin explained.

"So, do they just keep flying around Mürindür? Looking for people? Looking for me?" Creed stood and searched for some more comfortable footwear. Ojin nodded.

"The Ravens scout the lands for Leterum. They give him word of what lies beyond his Keep. They attack the lost ones, the Vagus, in the Dunes of Transitio, and pluck out their eyes. They do the same throughout the lands. Then the Caedere come with their vultures. They tie down the victims, and sew their mouths shut, forbidding them to speak. Once Leterum arrives on his chimera of indigo and smoke, he does the rest. He baptizes them in the dunes beneath fire and molten sand. Then nothing but despair." Ojin cleared his throat as Xaris sheathed his dagger, and stood to ready his horse.

"Has anyone ever tried to help the Vagus?" Creed asked Xaris.

"Sometimes. Legend has it you did once." Xaris stared at Creed looking for any hint of recollection, but Creed had none. "If you believe in legends that is. I'm not so certain I do anymore." Xaris walked out of the Penumbra into the open air.

Ojin finished the remaining embers of his pipe, wafting aromatic rings into the night sky. Creed fidgeted as Xaris kept pacing about, and it didn't appear that any rest would be obtained at this point. Ojin thought for a few minutes, and looked about the mountain. Nothing seemed to be coming for them despite their concerns, so he cleared his throat.

"I suppose we can talk about packing and moving onward if you…" Creed and Xaris rolled everything up, and Creed dumped the stew onto the rocks. The broth trickled down the slope through the cracks of old foundations. Xaris had Nos by the reins, and looked at Ojin.

"Let's go then."

Ojin took a deep breath, and raked his itchy shins with his fingernails. His kilt came down just at the knees, leaving a nice gap for a scratch.

"Very well. Let's continue heading upward. I hope that it's worth the risk, Xaris." The hobgoblin stood, and he and Bog deconstructed the camp, slowly lowering the stones to lessen the sound. Ojin gathered the few things he had unpacked for the meal. He snapped his fingers, and Bog's battle saddle rose and secured itself on the mammoth once more. Ojin kept stepping around the Ogre who remained oblivious, staring into the fire. The former hostage drew into the dirt with his fingers. Once Bog was loaded up, Ojin walked over to the fire to extinguish it as Creed prepared to climb into the bench seat.

"What's that?" He huffed at the scribbles in the dirt. Creed walked over to see.

"PAX."

"Yes, I see that, Creed, but what does it mean?" The Ogre rubbed the back of his hand over his smooth scalp. He wrote it again, and again each time rubbing his scalp.

"I think that's his name," Creed said.

"Rubbish. That's no Ogre name," Ojin replied.

"Exactly. He doesn't think he's an Ogre. He probably named himself. Pax is it?" The Ogre stood. He still wouldn't make eye contact.

"Regardless, we need to figure out what to do with him," Ojin reminded everyone.

"Well I assumed he's coming with us." Creed motioned to Bog.

"We take him, and figure it out as we go?" Xaris asked Ojin.

"And should he signal them? Cry out?" Ojin questioned.

"Then it ends. Right there," Xaris assured.

"He won't. He could have let the Raven fly, but he didn't. Doesn't know us, but he helped. He won't give away our position. I can feel it." Creed nodded at the curious Pax.

"Now you have feelings?" Ojin asked with doubt.

"One. I've got one feeling. We keep the Ogre. Come on Pax. Get on up there, big guy." Pax shied away.

"Come on. You can sit next to me, and not that grizzly bear over there." Ojin raised his brow.

"A nap, and now you make jokes?"

"What? He's not oblivious. He can tell you don't like him." Creed stated.

"I don't," Ojin affirmed.

"Ok then. Come on Pax, climb up Bog, and take a seat." Pax still wouldn't budge.

"Can I get a hand, Bog?" asked Creed.

Bog grabbed Pax around the waist, and hoisted him into the second row. Pax nervously paced, knees bent, back and forth along the bench, so Bog brushed his shoulder with his trunk, and nudged him to one side, patting his chest twice. Pax settled, and sat still as Creed climbed up after him, handing him his crossbow and quiver of bolts. Ojin sat upright in the front seat once more. The caravan was safely hidden beneath the Penumbra, and they continued onward towards the rock cliffs

Chapter 8: Ambush

As they marched slowly uphill, the wind whirled about once more, and another flock of Ravens flew quickly down near the camp behind them, clawing the dirt, and calling out to one another. Without much direction, some of the birds rose, and erratically circled the group. Ojin held the reins, and they came to a stop sixty yards away. The Ravens widened their flight path in concentric routes seeking the source of noise from before. Creed felt an urge to run with the persistent flock refusing to migrate, but despite the pounding in his chest, he tried to put on a brave face for Pax. Nos paced left to right, but an assured pat from Xaris quietened him down. A moment passed, and the flock regrouped, flying southward toward the valley. It was a wave of anger gone as quickly as it had come. Ojin sighed.

"That was close. They know something is up at this point, but they don't know what. I wouldn't be surprised if they brought more with them in an hour," Ojin worried.

"Then we best make good time," Xaris assured. Bog moved forward, and the group continued on their path, hoping to reach safety before too long. Creed had held onto a bowl from Ojin's kettle dinner, and although it cooled somewhat, he offered it to Pax, thinking it may calm the Ogre.

"Here's some stew. Pretty good actually. Try it." He held it next to Pax's face, but the Ogre didn't appear interested.

"Ok. Let me set it right here then. We're rocking a bit, so be careful. Try it when you're ready." Pax smelled it, and licked his lips. Once Creed moved away, the Ogre picked the bowl up, and gently sipped the flavored broth. Within minutes, the bowl was barren. Pax held onto it staring at its emptiness until Creed took it from his hand, and the Ogre began rubbing the lacquered finish of the wooden bench, burping a few times. Creed chuckled.

After a few more miles, the silent fatigue was upon them once more, and although Creed was well rested, the others needed sleep. Even the horses' hooves were dragging across the grit. Three hours further from their first camp, Xaris stopped, and whispered to Ojin. "This is good. There are some trees over there. We can lie up beneath the outcroppings ahead. No fire this time. We'll bundle for warmth, and you keep your shield up."

"Good enough. Bog, let's settle down here against the rocks." The group moved beneath the granite shelf, and not a word was spoken. Pax curled up beside Bog, and Xaris leaned his back against the mountain. The horses remained tied to Bog's harness, and Xaris simply looped his reins to his belt. Creed whispered quickly.

"I'll keep watch."

"Are you sure?" asked, Ojin.

"Yes. I'm good. Head isn't foggy anymore, and I've had rest. No different than a night shift back home."

"Good. Wake us at daybreak. We shouldn't be but a few hundred yards from the entrance to the mines."

"Couldn't just take a road, could we?"

"All *you've* seen is Ravens. What I fear are the vultures. The Caedere have moved further west than they ever have before. We don't have the means to stop them."

"How does anyone stop them?"

"Serena's Bellatorum."

"Got any of those around?"

"No. Unfortunately."

"Where do we find them?"

"They show up when they can, responding to those most in need. While you slept, I discovered they were fighting all over the realm. Skirmishes continue to break out, and the Bellatorum are all that stand between us and the beasts of the Undüavalle."

"So, what do we do if something walks up?" Creed wondered.

"We kill it quickly. If we can't kill it, we run."

"Good plan."

"Wake me when its time." Ojin rolled over. Creed sat for a moment, and cleared his throat.

"Ojin?"

Ojin stirred and grumbled.

"Yes?"

"Does she miss me?"

"Who?"

"Celeste. Does she miss me?"

"Yes. She always misses you when you're gone."

"I'm worried." Creed said.

"About?"

"What it will feel like when we see each other."

"Why worry about something like that? You two have known each other for millennia."

"Yes, but this feels different. We're having a baby, and I can't even remember how she smells. I can't picture her face right now."

"When you see her, it will all come back. It always does," Ojin assured him.

"Well, what if…"

"Stop. You worry too much. Now be quiet. Keep an eye out. We just need an hour or two of rest, and then we'll keep going."

"But…"

"Shhh." Ojin rolled over, and pulled his cloak atop his head.

The silence was sudden, and Creed sat there alone. He looked up to see the two moons. They seemed larger than before, and judging by their height, he assumed it was well past midnight, assuming Time even functioned here at all. He looked about the makeshift camp, a grizzled warrior, the furry giant mammoth, an Ogre, and a hobgoblin. *What in the world?* In a matter of hours, he went from normalcy to Mürindür.

Creed sat there trying to imagine Celeste's face, and how the baby felt in his hands when he dreamed. He pictured the brief moments they had with one another beside the water's edge, and wondered if he could uncover more images if he concentrated hard enough. He took a deep breath, and closed his eyes, but instead of his bride, a myriad of old experiences flooded his mind. There were mummification moments in an Egyptian desert, and images of him managing fevers in the midst of a Baltic storm upon a Viking warship. He could smell the field amputations during the French Revolution, and easily remembered the fear of mustard gas in The Great World War.

The images kept unfurling. At times so fast, they seemed to have just happened. He would look up and see the moons again, knowing he hadn't left the mountainside. He tried to reconcile everything, but each time he acquiesced. There was no explaining any of this unless he was willing to just accept everything Ojin told him, and yet, he felt unwelcomed, and unfamiliar in his own body. He was a visitor in some vessel far past his understanding. He felt more as Creed than anyone else, and for him Hippocrates was a ruse. But there they all were, magical beasts and a burly, breathing fossil.

Creed stood up to stretch his legs. He couldn't see behind their perch, but looking forward, he witnessed a dark valley below. No light, but from the moons. The trees had lost most of their leaves in their silhouette except for the furs. He watched for Ravens and vultures, but the night sky was vacant. Wind whistled. A distant stream burbled and spit.

He looked over Xaris. A rough appearing man indeed. Creed wasn't sure what issues the soldier had with him, but when the morning came, he would try to make amends. If he were to survive whatever excursion they had now found themselves upon, it would require more humility than hubris. He watched Ojin breathing. The hobgoblin's ears would twitch while he dreamed, like a horse's when flies were too eager, and his large furry feet stuck out from beneath his cloak. His toenails were thick and yellow, which reminded Creed of patients from the nursing home. Creed noticed that Pax would kick his legs periodically, but he lay like a child beside his newfound friend. Bog's trunk apparently served as quite the blanket. The mammoth's chest heaved and fell with each breath, as he lay recumbent onto the mountain cradle.

Despite the curious nature of the Penumbra, and its ability to blunt the wind, it didn't do much to block the cold. Creed threw on a dark woolen cloak, and pulled the hood over tight. He walked over to the horses, and brushed their necks, caressing their soft crinkly noses as the short whiskers passed through his fingers. While brushing them, he wondered about the Penumbra, and searched for a border or margin, but there wasn't any. He reached forward with his hands, and eventually realized if he walked far enough, his hands became blurry like passing through a waterfall. *That must be it.*

He passed his hand back and forth slowly, careful should he witness something overhead. Standing outside the Penumbra, one would see fingertips appearing and disappearing like some parlor trick. *Fascinating*, he thought.

Creed sat back down beside Ojin, and looked at his hands. He had no weapons. The Ravens could have plucked his eyes had he been alone. The idea was unsettling. If only he could figure out how to use the fire from Durdan, then he would have the means to defend himself. He vaguely remembered a time with Ojin in a cold cave somewhere in Mürindür years ago. It was his first lesson in flame gathering.

"Flame gathering is like harvesting ripe fruit. It's there for the taking. Remember now, it feeds off of raw emotion, and at times can get out of control. Today we only need enough to light these twigs."
"Just light the twigs?"
"Yes."
"With what?"
"Picture something exciting."
"Hmm. Well I haven't seen her in a few days…"
"No. Not that exciting. Pick something smaller. More mild. Fire is a direct reflection of your intensity."

"Ok. How about fishing?"

"Good enough." It took multiple attempts as it would for any novice. He stared at the twigs and thought about fishing. He studied the grain in the dry sticks. He watched for something in the curled, cracked leaves. He got impatient. He took a deep breath, and closed his eyes. This time he pictured his love, her eyes, soft lips, and the small of her back.

BOOM!

The blast of heat was so intense it singed his knuckle hair. He opened his eyes as Ojin snuffed the glowing curls on his chest and beard, hurriedly. The twigs were nothing more than orange embers, and the surrounding dirt was soot.

"What did you envision?" Ojin asked him.

"Her. Bathing."

"Naturally."

"Yes. Naturally."

Creed smiled at the memory. That's when the idea came. He stood up with everyone sleeping, and went to gather twigs. There were a few lying about which would suit his purpose. He bundled them together, and placed them in a small hole within the soil. He sat cross-legged in front of the pile, and searched for memories. Creed tried to picture Celeste's face, but it was errant in his mind as if it were a mental rabbit hiding in the briar. He tried to remember his dreams over the last few months, but they too were distant. As he relaxed though, he caught a fleeting mental glimpse of her smile, and focused on her lips. It was slow at first, but his fingers felt some warmth. He could smell smoke. He opened his eyes and looked down to see a singular flame dancing slowly beneath the pile. He watched it grow gently, moving from one twig to another until the small campfire was in unison. He was rather amused with himself not to mention slightly astonished. The heat felt nice, and he rubbed his hands slowly like a rotisserie over the yellow tips of light. Creed heard something snap in the trees nearby. He jumped, startled, and immediately snuffed out the flames. The cold returned.

Creed walked to the margin of the Penumbra, and there was another snap. A small rock rolled before him stopping just inches from his boots, and when he looked up, a heavy sickness settled in his stomach. The moonlight revealed the ambulatory nightmares.

Three dark figures lumbered forward from the trees upon thick caprine legs with cloven hooves, yet they walked upright, slightly hunched at the shoulders. They stood eight-foot-tall with ashen wings, the tips crumbling only to form again and again. Bloodied, black robes roiled about their bodies. Their leathered flesh was cracked and seething as their hands writhed. One stood a mere lunge from Creed, and arched its back high to smell the air through the hole in its mid-face.

Creed glimpsed the creature in all its horrid glory. Long white hair fell across the scalp and shoulders with a smoke facade pulled across sunken eye sockets. The creature's face was taut, stretched too thinly over bone, and the lips were sewn shut with a long stitch of brown sinew. The beast bellowed and grunted, then the whispers came, and the creatures unsheathed crescent blades the shape of sickles from their backs, each of them searching, whispering, stepping. Creed felt a firm hand on his back.

"Shhhhh. Caedere. Don't move." Xaris slowly unsheathed his blades, and watched the hunters through the Penumbra.

Nine more Caedere emerged from the shadows of the mountain. They were deliberate in their search each taking a path down toward the valley, moving slowly away from the camp. One of them fluttered ten feet from the ground, gliding in the air down the mountainside, and fell to the rocks with a thud. The ground shook Creed's boots. He took a step back, but was stopped by another hand. It was Ojin.

"We need to walk slowly back to Bog, and wait. If we run now, we will die," Ojin whispered. The air rustled the forest floor leaves as vultures from above hovered and descended all around. Many perched on tree limbs squawking to one another. The Caedere walked slowly then stopped. They turned in unison to look up the path seemingly right at Creed.

"They know we're here," Xaris whispered. He lowered his stance.

This is impossible, Creed thought.

"It's a hunting party with one focus. We won't make it uphill in time, Ojin." Xaris stepped closer to the Penumbra edge. Creed felt uneasy inside, and his face began to flush and sweat. Steam wafted about his neck. Ojin grabbed Creed by the meat of his arm.

"Get back to Bog. If we fall, you must run to the Ashi. You can lose them in the mines."

"I can't. There has to be another way. I'll get lost," Creed protested.

"These Caedere sense something. We can't run from them, and the two of us would scarcely contain one Caedere. We will hold them as long as we can, but you have to make it back to Celeste. Your child must not be lost, or else we've fought for nothing."

"Give me a weapon then. I *have* nothing." Ojin looked to Xaris, and the warrior nodded. He moved quickly to Nos, and unsheathed the long sword from the saddle. He walked to Creed, and handed it to him.

"Keep the blade high. This is a long sword, not one of those spears you like to use so much. Its weight is best wielded when held high." Creed took the sword, and clasped it firmly with both hands. He held the blade above his head, and waited for the impending command.

The Caedere moved quickly up the path hissing and crackling. They spread out in a semi-circle. Swords drawn. They moved toward the group like the pack of wolves from the ruins of Leonicus. The vultures were excited, and their wings flapped in anticipation, then, a shrill high-pitched cry. Creed knew this sound. It began every one of his dreams. The ground trembled. "Quick! To the rocks!" Ojin commanded.

The three struggled to run toward the boulders where Bog and Pax now stood, awake and fearful. Dirt and pebbles fell all around them. The vultures were disturbed from their roost and took to the air to keep watch. The Caedere charged, and Creed looked up. A beast leapt from the rock shelf above, and fell before him, tall and robust. Its head arched as if to taste the moons, and its horns framed the sky. It bugled once more. The steam from its breath rose high. The Caedere stumbled, and the mountainside shuttered.

Suddenly hundreds of bull elk charged relentlessly over the rocks down the mountain, and through the Caedere. The thousand hoof beats roared like thunder crashing through the dark figures. The Caedere angrily swiped at the animals, wounding some, but they were easily overwhelmed. One by one, Caedere fell beneath the stampede. One of the hunters hung up across the main beams of an elder bull, and was thrashed about repeatedly until it fell down a ravine. Some leaped briefly into the air, but their clipped ashen wings couldn't hold their weight for long, and they fell further down the terrain. Within minutes, the elk cleared the path, and the Caedere were gone. The last of the bulls trotted past, and the dust hung heavy in the air. Creed breathed a sigh of relief, and turned toward Ojin.

"We made it." He felt the ground crash behind him. Creed turned back, and two Caedere stood seething with bloodlust. Creed was frozen. Ojin screamed.

"Run!" It was too late. Creed couldn't run. His legs were rigid with adrenaline.

The Caedere to his left struck first, and Creed barely parried the attack before the second beast managed to kick him in the chest. He fell hard into the rock, and dropped the sword. The first Caedere struck again, but Xaris jumped in front of Creed, and caught the Caedere blade with his two swords, scissoring the Caedere's metal. Ojin struck the beast in the stomach with his staff, but caught a misdirected blade strike across his back. Fortunately, it was broad side, and merely knocked the wind out of him. Creed stood, and dove for the second Caedere's legs. They tumbled down the path as Ojin screamed.

Creed tussled with the dark being as they rolled over rock and broken timber only to crash into a gray tree stump wider than them both. The Caedere was stunned, and its sword had fallen in the fray. Creed was the first to stand, and grabbed a large flint rock with jagged edges. Before the Caedere could lean forward from the stump, Creed caught it across the face shearing the flesh as a rotten peel. The Caedere grabbed Creed by the ribs, and dug its fetid fingers into his chest, but Creed didn't slow in his relentless attack.

He pummeled the Caedere's face, brutally, over and over, like mincing a large melon. The bones cracked and sheared under the violent beating until the Caedere no longer moved, and its body lay limp upon the stump like carrion beside the road. Creed was heaving from pain and breathlessness, but he loomed over the remains, still alive and scared. Ojin was the first to reach him as Creed held the rock in the air, preparing for one last strike.

"Are you okay?" Ojin asked.

"I think so," Creed replied. They looked over the creature, and Ojin placed his hand on Creed's shoulder. Creed threw the rock to the ground.

"I suppose you didn't need a sword after all."

"I wasn't going to let him take me. Not here. Not like this. Those things are monstrous." Creed looked up the mountainside, and saw Xaris cleaning his blades.

"Yes, they are. The children of Leterum never rest. We made quick work of that demon, however. We were lucky. We'll need to get moving once more. We must hide the bodies quickly. The vultures will be back, and the other Caedere won't be far behind," Ojin explained.

Creed pulled on the coarse hairy hindquarters of the lifeless Caedere. The body fell from the stump into the soil like a heavy sack, and the two friends pulled the carcass a few yards into the broken tree line. They went up the slope, and helped Xaris do the same. All three joined Bog and Pax, and shared a drink of cold water from Ojin's flask. Nos and the other horses had somehow stayed close to Bog, and none of their supplies were missing.

"Why do you think they attacked us, Ojin?" Xaris asked.

"I have no idea. They could clearly sense something. Their vultures looked right at us, as did they. Creed, what happened?"

"I'm not sure, but I am certain it was likely my fault. I walked to stay awake, and stood at the periphery of the Penumbra. I sat back down, and I was cold. I felt if I could just warm my hands it would take the edge off, so I tried to…"

"You tried to start a fire?" Xaris questioned with a frustrated tone.

"I remembered something you taught me a long time ago, Ojin, and I tried it. Surprisingly, it worked. I didn't think it would. I don't know how it could, but it did. I focused, and suddenly there were small flames in my hand."

"The stupidity of it all! My god, Ojin! He nearly got us killed!" Xaris was irate.

"It wasn't the flame, Xaris. The Penumbra could easily hide that. It was his ability to draw on the substance in the air. They sensed the magic and nothing more." Ojin held his hands up toward Xaris as if to prepare for a charge.

"It doesn't matter, Ojin! We've scarcely begun, and the very man we are trying to protect welcomed the demons to our doorstep! Get him under control, or I will have to!" Xaris spat on the ground, and stormed off to tend to Nos.

"I didn't think it would happen. Truly." Creed tried to placate the group.

"You mustn't attempt flame gathering of any sort without me. Is that understood?" Ojin instructed.

"Fine."

"You aren't fully awake, and I'm more concerned with your temperament than anything else. We will work on this, but make no mistake. Leterum likely knows you are here now, and we have run out of time. These Caedere will burn in Acrom's hands before they let you escape again. We need to move to the caverns, now." Ojin turned, and patted Xaris on the back. The two walked off, talking as Xaris threw his hands into the air with angered animation. Creed took a deep breath and sighed. He looked at the two moons, and then down the gravelly slopes. He just wanted to go home.

Chapter 9: The Ashi

They moved in a rushed fashion, once more along the trail, ever mindful of the darkness that was coming for them. Creed chose to walk since the incline was so steep, but his thighs burned. His lungs were cold from his quickened breath, and he hoped they would find their mountain destination soon. A half hour later, they stood before the once gated entrance of the great Ashi. Runes had been carved over the arch of stone, now draped in ivy and vines. Creed stared at the symbols for a moment when Ojin interjected.

"It was a warning carved by the first keepers of the Ashi. Men once lived here, and they feared the beasts outside. 'Death will come for those who will it. The Ashi will consume them all.' Rather ominous wouldn't you say?"

"Quite," Creed replied.

"The Ashi has many things that make it mysterious and dangerous, but we hope to avoid them all as we quickly make it through. Once we are on the other side, it won't be long before you and Celeste are reunited once again." Ojin patted Creed's back assuredly.

"Ojin, we need to get inside. The wind is disturbed once more. The Ravens are coming." Xaris nodded down the mountainside. Tree limbs were bending in the distance.

"Inside. Everyone please go inside. Let's get going." Bog huffed as Pax picked at the bench seat. They made their way in first followed by Xaris, Ojin, and finally Creed. He kept staring at the trees waiting to see another Caedere emerge from the shadows, but nothing came. The woods were seemingly barren for now.

The caverns were quiet, and not nearly as cold. Creed could feel the chill slowly ebb, but noticed the ground was soft and sticky like the shallow remnants of a porridge bowl. As he looked around, Creed noticed paintings and long passages of ancient texts across the walls. Running his fingers along the dry, stained rock, he wondered how many lifetimes ago this wall became a canvas. Ojin gathered them deeper into the caverns, and struck a small fire on the ground with a tap of his staff. He took limbs and pieces of dried wood out of his vest pockets, and piled them over the naked flame. Soon the wood took on the heat, and Ojin addressed everyone.

"I plan to reach out to Queen Serena. Everyone please be quiet, and we will keep this brief. When I do this, it won't be long before something or someone can sense it, and it could jeopardize their location as well as ours. I will speak, and then we will head through the Ashi. Understood?"

Creed was worried about their location.

"Shouldn't we go further into the mines? It won't take much for those things to tumble in here and find us."

"They won't follow us in here," Xaris explained.

"Why?" Creed asked.

"Their birds can't fly here." Xaris pointed upward. Creed looked and saw the ceiling crawling.

"What are those?"

"Düobii."

The creatures hissed and scaled the rocks with ease, nimble for their large size. With a reptilian head on either end, they moved back and forth in a linear fashion. They skittered about on six legs as their large ,revealed crooked canine teeth, protruding when they hissed. The teeth glowed in the firelight, and each head had a row of black-ink eyes, like a spider, as they scanned their domain. A bat flew quickly past, and a large Düoba lurched for the food. One head bit hard on the cavern ceiling stalactite, while the other struck the prey quickly. The Düoba hung there swaying slowly as a trapeze artist, and the head with a mouthful of bat made quick with its meal. Once it was done, its body curled back to the ceiling, and scurried into the shadows. There were dozens of them moving about. Bog looked upwards and paced as Pax ducked nervously to hide.

"They rarely leave the cave ceilings. The soil is poisonous for them," Xaris attempted to reassure everyone. Creed could see droppings and fluid coming from above. It was Düobii excrement, Xaris explained.

"Their waste mixes with the salts on the ground, and burns their flesh when they're exposed to it. You should be fine as long as we don't get too close to the ceiling." Bog stared at Xaris with big brown eyes.

"You're ok my friend. Little too big for their tastes I suspect." Xaris patted Bog on the leg.

"You said their birds can't fly here. The Caedere need their vultures and Ravens?" Creed wondered.

"Although they see through Leterum's veil, it's as if through a fog. The Ravens and vultures give them instantaneous sight and senses. They are inextricably linked," Ojin replied, stirring the wood.

"Ironic since the birds were the ones responsible for stealing their sight in the first place," said Xaris as he took Nos by the reins and walked him away from the fire.

"Yes. Ironic indeed to ever wholly rely on those who seek you harm. The Caedere truly are cursed."

Ojin opened his hand, and whispered. After he repeated the incantation three times, he closed his fist. A green ball of air burst into the center of the flame, and it grew until the small campfire was a flickering emerald hue. An image appeared slowly then came into focus. A woman of long red hair, braided with strands of gray, stood before them. She wore a hooded white cloak and a wide silver chain around her waist. Xaris and Ojin bowed their heads in respect. Creed backed away a little further, unsure of what to expect. The woman pulled back her hood and spoke.

"Ojin? What happened? Has something gone wrong?" the lady asked.

"Serena, the Caedere are north of Durdan. We came across them near the ruins of Leonicus. It was a small patrol, but they realized they wanted something in our vicinity."

"They have been relentless. The barriers that once held the realm safe from Leterum have broken. The Caedere are no longer contained in any region of Mürindür, and roam wherever they choose. The Undüavalle is untethered, and it is all that we can do to manage the chaos," she explained.

"How did it become untethered?" Ojin asked.

"Leterum has taken down the centurions at the Undüavalle Gate. The gate and prison columns have been breached, and we know not what has managed to escape. Acrom is still imprisoned, but his minions have likely found their way to Mürindür." Serena motioned with her hands.

"Impossible." Ojin closed his eyes in disbelief.

"I've come to understand nothing is impossible anymore. They've gained momentum, and all that Leterum wishes to conquer has become his domain. Acrom grows as well. The two, once they rejoin on the battlefield, will become insurmountable. Why do you wish to seek us out? You know he will sense this soon." Serena looked behind her, and then at Ojin once more.

"We will not make it to the Pools of Cordis Loci, Serena. We've traveled only a brief distance, and nearly lost everything. We're in the Ashi now. Can you meet us in the Fields of Effugere?" Ojin pleaded.

"We will try. We give up much to leave the Pools. This has become our inner sanctum. There are reports of dark sacrifices outside the Groves. We are strongest here."

"I know of no other way," Ojin replied sadly.

"It is dangerous to choose the Ashi. You know this," Serena said pointedly.

"Yes. We felt that it would be, and…" Ojin couldn't finish as Xaris interjected.

"My Queen, Perrindor and I felt it the only way. Ravens scour the lands. We have already annihilated one flock and been chased by another. We wouldn't have made it five miles out of Durdan had we taken the road east to the Capital of Guillarne. With the Ashi, we don't worry about the skies. I've traveled this path many times, and I can assure you, we will make it out the other end."

"I understand, but you must know the Undüavalle will birth the darkness into Ashi's depths if it hasn't already. I visited the Gates, and the guardian souls imbued within its very stone have vanished. It is likely demons run throughout the mines as we speak, unchecked and hungry. Be wary, and be ready." Serena looked at Xaris sternly.

"We don't plan on being here long my Queen. My men and I made it through quickly unscathed a day ago. We saw no sign of Acrom's forces," Xaris assured her.

"Yes, but now you have something Leterum and Acrom both want. Is he there with you?" Serena asked.

"Yes. Creed, step forward." Ojin motioned, and Creed walked up to stand beside him. The woman looked him up and down, and smiled.

"Our mighty Hippocrates. We knew this day would come, but for you it was far too soon. I'm sorry that you have come home to such a mess. We have found ourselves defending everything, and have little time or resources to launch an offensive attack. Creed is it?"

"Yes ma'am."

"I am Serena. Do you remember me?"

"Vaguely." Creed's mind reached for prior memories, and found scattered pieces of conversations.

"Creed, I know you must have many questions, and everything is likely a blur, but please trust in Ojin. He is my steward and confidant. We have weathered many storms here in Mürindür together. The coming days are crucial for our cause, and Leterum will do all that he can to stop us. Trust in us, and we will see each other soon."

"Yes ma'am." Creed nodded in return.

"There is someone who wishes to see you, my son, and I suspect you have missed her as well."

Another womanly figure stepped into the flame, and once she looked up, Creed's throat became tight. Her flowing flaxen curls draped her shoulders, and her azure gaze was once more hypnotic. It was the woman in his dreams. He had stared into those eyes for hundreds of years. The memories came in waves crashing down upon his consciousness. This woman he recognized. He smiled.

"Hello my love." She held her hands out to him. He reached for hers only to realize it was an illusion.

"Celeste?"

She smiled back at him.

"Yes. You remembered, my love."

"I'm trying. This is so weird. Everything is just bizarre. Things are so jumbled up in my mind, and I don't feel like myself anymore. I feel angry. I feel lost."

"You are Hippocrates. You are not a lost soul. You are not lost at all. You are my hero. My love. I have always been there for you when you have fallen, but I couldn't this time. Forgive me. Leterum is looking for us, and for our child. We couldn't risk it. I'm so sorry."

"I understand. I wish you were here," Creed replied.

"Me too. You look…"

"Tired?"

She smiled again.

"Yes. I worried about you."

"I don't understand what's happening to me. Something is stirring. Something I can't control."

"What do you feel?"

"Rage. Raw, epic, rage." Creed tried to put words to the emotion.

"From what?" Celeste asked.

"I don't know, but it's always there, and I can't make it go away."

"I'm so sorry I'm not with you. I can feel how troubled you are. We will see each other soon. Remember, as foreign as things may seem now, you are finally home. Mürindür is your home, and always has been. Please stay safe, and make it back to your family. Make it back to me, and our son. Xaris, please watch over him."

"I will, your Grace." Xaris bowed as Celeste looked at Creed, and stepped back for Serena to speak.

"Ojin, what do you sense in him?" the Queen asked.

"Well not much for now, but some things have changed indeed. I'd like to speak with you when we meet. He has somehow tapped into something beyond anything I understand from the past."

"He caught Durdan Keep on fire, my Queen," Xaris replied. Ojin stared at him, perplexed.

"Fire, Ojin? Interesting." The Queen raised her brow.

"Nothing out of the ordinary took place when he fell, but he did arrive with fugue flies and bumble worms. I can't imagine he was infused with anything else prior to that, however. I have no explanation for it, Serena."

"So many things have come to be without explanation, Ojin." Serena looked down for a brief moment. "The balance is broken, Undüavalle is free to cross into our realm, and I have come across beasts that Leterum himself could not harness. We are the last vestige between what has descended upon us and the very souls we wish to protect. This is a dire time for us all with significance I haven't seen since the Cataclysm. We had hoped to meet at the Capital of Guillarne, but when everything changed, we elected to find one another at the Pools. Now it appears those plans must change again. We give up safety to some degree by moving so much across the land, but if we lose you three, we have gained nothing but an end. Discretion is of the utmost importance." Serena spoke sincerely as she looked at Creed.

"Understood," Ojin assured.

"Each of you must… wait. Hmmm. Who is that? Is there a stranger among you, Ojin? I see you have a fourth." She motioned to Bog.

"Yes. We have another. Not by choice, but by happenstance and necessity," Ojin explained.

"Curious." She closed her eyes briefly. Then she felt the presence once more.

"An Ogre, Ojin? I am truly surprised."

"As am I." Ojin affirmed.

"Step forward child." Serena motioned to Pax. He climbed down from Bog, and walked toward the fire. The heat made him look away, but he didn't move.

"Do you have a name?" The Queen clasped her hands very much intrigued. Pax didn't make a sound. He stood pigeon-toed as his fingers danced back and forth across his thumbs. Serena waited patiently, and then closed her eyes. She smiled after a moment, and looked at him once more.

"Hello, Pax." Pax acknowledged her briefly with a sideway glance.

"Ojin, he may prove to be useful, so curious though. He doesn't look like much of an Ogre, does he? I'm sure they mistreated him quite horrifically. Do you trust him? Does he have a weapon?" Ojin nodded toward the crossbow on the bench.

"He's a good shot with that thing," Creed added, "he killed a Raven mid-flight, and Bog seems to have connected with him at some level. I suspect he has a good heart if for nothing more than a ringing endorsement from the mammoth." Ojin looked at Creed and frowned.

"Does he now?" Serena smiled. "Creed, your compassion has never waned. That in you I most admire. Nevertheless, remember whom we are up against. His cunning and cruelty knows no bounds. Leterum knows you are here now, and your death will be the first step towards his domination."

"Serena, how long before you plan to arrive?" Ojin put his hand on Creed's shoulder for reassurance.

"Give us the better part of the new day, Ojin. We will hurry. Although Celeste and I could meet you sooner, it appears each time our Bellatorum enact the Fuga, and fly about the realm, Leterum's beasts aren't far behind. We've traveled mostly by foot these past few days. Reach out to us once more before you leave the Ashi. We will know more then," Serena instructed.

"We will see you soon," Ojin promised.

"Celeste?" Creed asked.

"Yes?" the Princess replied.

"How is he doing?" Creed motioned to her belly.

"He's getting so big that I can barely sleep at night. When he moves though, I feel that you are with me. He is fine, my love. He acts as if he wishes to come soon, but I have assured him he needs to grow a little more. He misses you. I sense that as well. Remember who you are my love, your purpose, and your family. Please know that we will be together soon." She smiled, and the flames rose and collapsed into a pedestrian dance of reds and yellows once more. Creed felt hollow with heartache.

"*Cor numquam operae praebitae obliviscitur*," Ojin said.

"What does that mean?" Creed asked.

"*The heart never forgets*. Even after all these years, the two of you have always seemingly been one." Ojin smiled as he patted Creed

146

on the shoulder. Xaris looked away at the cave walls and dark passageways around them.

"She is so beautiful, even more so than in my dreams. All these feelings, memories, and events were just suddenly there. Images so vivid." Creed explained with his hands.

"Every time you crossed, she was there. Celeste knew intuitively where you would land. She would be the first image your eyes would see when you woke. She insisted on it. She loves you fiercely," Ojin explained.

Xaris cleared his throat and spoke.

"I was the royal family's bodyguard before I was asked to protect Durdan. She would watch you fall each time, and hurried in the chariots to your side. The three of us would gather you up, and bring you home. Once you were ready, the Queen would receive you, and held a banquet in your honor. When in Mürindür, the Princess would never leave your side, and she wept each time you left. I wondered how much her heart could truly take. It wasn't always rose petals and sunshine, Ojin." Xaris concluded with a heavy tone of admonition. Creed lowered his head in guilt, and was certain he would have never left her willingly.

"Xaris, they both suffered. It was never one-sided. He wept each time he went back as well," Ojin retorted.

"Yes, but he could at least forget momentarily. She was left with solitude each and every day."

"They chose one another, freely. It's important to remember that, Xaris," Ojin scolded the warrior.

"Surely, I wouldn't choose to leave her?" Creed asked.

"It wasn't a choice. It was your duty." Ojin patted Creed once more on the shoulder as Xaris opened a saddlebag, removing three pieces of petrified wood each two feet long. Creed stared at Xaris, sensing more to the animosity, but his mind, as hard as it tried, could not recollect a recent event. If they were allies, he felt it to be tenuous. "What are those?" he asked.

"These are torches of the Tree of Amaranth." Xaris held them at arm's length. "Ojin, would you mind?" The hobgoblin snapped his fingers, and the torches were lit. Xaris gave each member one to hold. Pax looked at Xaris with big eyes.

"Hadn't planned on you. Bog has lanterns. Climb on top of him." Pax looked nervously at the Düobii roaming the rocks.

"They won't attack you. They like the winged snacks mostly." Pax still didn't move. Bog let out a soft grunt, and tapped him on the chest, so the Ogre lifted his arms and was ferried to the benches once more. He knelt down for comfort.

"Xaris, do you know which path to take?" When Ojin held up his torch, the caverns appeared pocked with randomness. Creed saw chewed bones littered about.

"Yes. Look up. We follow the Düobii and the Düobii avoid blind tunnels. Make sure to keep your hands up. Few things more noxious than Düobii shat in your eyes," Xaris smirked as Ojin coughed from the pungent fumes. The small patrol made way, and headed toward a gaping cavernous mouth. The Ashi was waiting

Chapter 10: The Mines

Water trickled and echoed in the distance. With a turn of the torch, Creed could see crevasses open into nothingness. Crystals hung from all directions, some seemingly reflective as mirrors. As they ventured further, the temperature warmed, and the frigid air didn't grip the throat as much. The musk was dense, but beyond the smell, Creed felt the place to be quite beautiful as the torchlight bounced across walls and the occasional crystal. Yellow, green, and red stones sparkled on the cavern floor as he noticed less and less scat scattered about.

"Ground looks different," he said.

"Yes. The Düobii prefer colder air, and they avoid the other creatures deeper down. They still scurry through the Ashi, but to a lesser extent. If you look up, you'll see a few are still tracking us." Xaris motioned his head upward careful not to glance his eyes in that direction.

"No. That's ok. I'll take your word for it. What creatures deeper down?" Creed asked.

"*Xystrahs* are slimy gray slugs that spit their stomach juices on you, and then slurp up what remains. *Derenbloons* are wooly haired bats that can't fly far, but have bodies like a centipede, and their wings glow in the moonlight. They like to suck on anything with blood. Now, *Thackers* are truly salty beasts. They are built like honey badgers from my homeland, and have webbed feet to swim in the

Ashi waters. Thackers only have one eye that can see everything, they never blink, and their backs are covered in spiky crystals. They'd just as soon bite your leg off than look at you. Finally, you have your trolls, tons of trolls really. They have mined the Ashi for generations, and eat anything that moves." Xaris motioned his hands high above his head to simulate a troll's gargantuan status. "Trolls?" Creed chuckled at first. Ojin explained.

"Yes. There are two kinds of trolls. The giants stand as tall as two-story buildings, and the shorter ones we call *Spurgles*. They're the engineers that create the machines and tools to mine Mürindür. Ashi used to be one of the top producing mines in all the land. The Ashi trolls were obsessed with legends and the bounties of the rock. Always digging deeper even if it meant a certain demise."

"What happened?" Creed asked.

"The trolls mined the rock for what it brought them and their clans. With unique bounty, Ashi trolls gained notoriety and nobility. It was their way of ascending society. The last Troll King of Ashi was said to have discovered the great spear Ejiciam. This was the weapon used to cast Acrom into the Abyss. The Troll King of Ashi was murdered in his sleep by something unknown, and Ejiciam was lost. Once the king fell, the Ashi trolls fought amongst themselves for the spoils, the kingdom was ruined, and many escaped to start new mines. Some stayed behind to seek out Ejiciam with hopes of ruling the kingdom once more." Ojin looked about, cautiously.

"Did you see any trolls on your way down to Durdan, Xaris?" asked Creed.

"No, but you can hear them at times. They are far below us," Xaris replied.

"What else lives down here?" Creed looked around with his torch as he walked.

"Not sure. Men don't generally explore the Ashi. There are drunken stories in camps at night, nightmares and exaggerations most likely. Hardly worthy of record." Xaris cleared his throat.

"Ojin, you seem quiet," Creed noticed.

"My mind is a little preoccupied." Ojin rolled a smooth stone in his fingers.

"I'm sure it is. What are you thinking?"

"Get out of the Ashi as soon as we can."

"It doesn't sound too difficult. Haven't had any issues yet," Creed pointed out.

"Xaris is intentionally avoiding a few things," Ojin explained.

"As in?"

"Xaris, would you like to expand?"

"There are tales that a bridge to the Undüavalle Gates connects the Ashi. Something that has never been proven but creates fear just the same. If what Serena says is true, it is possible some demons may now be able to enter these caverns. I doubt it, but that's probably what Ojin is referring to."

"I thought the Moons were in the sky."

"Yes. They are, but they are connected in many ways seen and unseen to Mürindür," Ojin explained.

"Serena mentioned the Undüavalle was 'untethered'. What does that even mean?" Creed asked.

"Leading from our world to the Undüavalle is a common path, called the *Fata Uiam*, which ends at the Undüavalle Gates. It has somehow been disrupted. A band of centurions, immortals much like the statues of the Apicem Bridge, were tasked with guarding the Gates, preventing an unlikely break from the prison into Mürindür. She says those centurions are lost. I'm not sure how. This may explain the fire titan, Ignis, attacking Durdan. If there is a bridge from Undüavalle into the depths of the Ashi, we may not see the light of Day," Ojin warned.

"It's a myth my friend. The bound bridge may be faulty, but we do not know that it leads here. We marched this route days ago, and beyond defiled boots, we had nothing else to show of it. I suspect if demons ran amok, we would have seen them spilling out the mouth of Ashi." Xaris wagged his finger at Ojin hoping to minimize any concern.

"All the same. Let's hope they have not crossed. If the Undüavalle is truly unguarded at this point, then we must be aware of what comes. Serena didn't say what they were doing to contain it. We have to assume it hasn't been abandoned."

"Let us hope," nodded, Xaris.

A sound wafted from below. *Ahhhhhhhhhhwhoooshhhhhh.* Followed by a clang of metal on stone. The sound continued once more, twice more, then repeatedly for a few minutes, and then a garbled growl. The caverns shook. For a moment, the ground felt unsteady, and Bog picked up the pace. Pax bobbled on the bench like a ball while everyone else trotted alongside the animals. The mountain stone rattled, and the walls flexed.

"ARRRRGGGHHHHHHH!!" Then another clang, and a grinding sound which made their feet vibrate.

"What was that, Ojin?" asked Creed.

"Steady. Bog, slow down." Ojin had his hand on the mammoth's hip, but it was no use. Bog started into a slow gallop with Pax swaying in the lantern light. The ground shook more. It was enough to weaken everyone's confidence.

"Are there earthquakes in Mürindür?" Creed looked about as the embedded gems gyrated. His sense of balance was thrown, making each step off-center and careless.

"No. No earthquakes." Ojin rose to a jog. Suddenly, boulders of crystals rolled past them as debris clouded the air.

"RUN!" Ojin screamed.

The Düobii were crashing from the rocks onto the earth. They hissed and scurried in pain, searching for walls to climb atop. Squawking dark objects flew briskly overhead. Xaris attempted to mount Nos, but the horse was having none of it, and raced to catch up with Bog. The entire group was in flight. Creed sprinted behind, but the horses' hooves flung dirt and muck into his face slowing him, and obscuring his vision. He ran into the side of a cavern wall, and fell to his hands and knees.

"BOG! STOP! GUYS! STOP." But everyone raced further ahead.

Bog's pace quickened into a full stride, and he disappeared into the darkness with a glowing halo of lanterns encircling Pax. Creed could barely make out the shadows of Xaris and Ojin as they too were showered in the ceiling's remains.

"WAIT!"

Creed stood only to stumble once more to his knees as the mountain trembled, and the groans and hollered epithets from below seemingly surrounded him. He could hear frantic screaming. The voices became louder the closer they were to him, and he blinked hard to see Xaris and Ojin offering their hands to pull him up.

"STAND! RUN!" Ojin encouraged, but there was a sudden shudder, and rocks split as timber. Creed hesitated for a moment, and their support gave way. All three fell into a dark, dank void.

§

Blistering cold water slapped Creed's face. His left arm was numb from the immersion as his body balanced precariously on a ledge. Fortunately, his torch still flickered, albeit meagerly. He pulled himself up, and blew gently on the flame. It grew again, and its warmth was welcomed as he noticed a dark mountain stream curving ahead. Crystals cast wavering rainbows along the walls with the torchlight. He set the torch down, and washed his face in the water, cleaning out his eyes with the heel of his palm until his vision was clear again. Beyond the percolating stream, there was no sound. Then a cough, and a grumble.

"Who's there?" Creed asked as he spun around to look. He held the torch high, and could see a large mass with hairy feet and thick gray soles. He recognized the yellow toenails.

"Ojin!" Creed ran to help him up, and was thankful he wasn't alone. Ojin sat slowly, and shook his head. Dust and pebbles tumbled from his hair, and he dug deeply with his thick fingers into his left ear. He pulled out a small rock, and flicked it into the stream.

"That was unfortunate," Ojin surmised as the rock plopped into the water.

"What happened?" Creed asked.

"The damn floor broke beneath us! Probably some witless troll pounding at a pillar!" Xaris was there too, and angrily flung a rock into the water.

"Quiet! They may be around us," Ojin warned.

"Someone, help me up. This rock is crushing me."

Creed walked toward Xaris' voice, and found him covered in broken rock slabs. His head was visible, and legs were exposed, but besides a free right hand, his upper body was trapped. Creed pushed hard, and managed to slide one of the slabs off to the side. Xaris took a deep breath and coughed. Slowly, Ojin walked over, limping, and together he and Creed lifted the remaining slabs off the warrior. Creed was the only one with a torch, so for a moment, they huddled together for warmth, and an opportunity to get their bearings.

"How far down do you think we are, Xaris?" Ojin asked.

"No idea."

"How do we get out of here?" Creed wondered.

"We follow the stream," Xaris explained.

"There's got to be another way. This water falls into darkness. We slip and we could drown."

"Xaris is right, Creed. We follow the stream. It will take us to the bottom of the mountain." Ojin rubbed his scalp.

"The rivers shouldn't be far. We're likely half a mile from the basin." Xaris etched out a small map in the dirt.

"Does all the water flow into the common rivers?" Ojin pointed to the crude picture.

"Yes. There are tunnels above and beneath the rivers, but eventually the water finds its way to the same outlet. The rivers fall like staircases, which spill into the *Lacus Atromento*. Once we make it to the lake, the road out will be easy." Xaris tapped the line leading away from the lake picture with his finger.

"Nothing seems to be easy," Creed complained. The ground above shuttered again, and rocks fell into the stream splashing them with frigid water.

"Damn trolls! They'll bring the whole forsaken place onto our heads. We need to move. Now!" Xaris looked at Creed, and reached for the torch.

"I got the torch, Xaris. I'll take point." Creed walked forward as the others followed along a narrow path, slick with water, lime, and algae. After a few feet, the trail descended quickly alongside what appeared to be a waterfall.

"Careful now. We won't likely find you should you fall," Ojin warned.

Creed looked at him and grimaced. For the first few steps, it seemed certain he would make it, until his boot slipped. Down he went, quickly falling to his right hip, hard. He slid into another corner of rock, and remained still. Sitting there for a moment as his lower back and hip throbbed from the pain, Creed looked to his left with the torchlight where he saw a path beneath the waterfall. He glanced back at Ojin and Xaris.

"There's a walkway!"

"Hold the light toward us, so we don't fall on our backsides like you." Creed stood wincing, and held the torch above his head. The other two managed to make it down what now appeared to be a twenty-foot slope of glistening rock. Once they were safely on the flat surface of the path, the three clambered across smooth stones set straight in a line, and came out the other side, staring into a short tunnel. Creed's hair reached the tunnel's ceiling, and Ojin had

156

to crouch just to follow. Although nothing touched them as they wound their way down, Creed felt squeezed by stale air as if he were caught within the fist of the great mountain.

As the trail ebbed and flowed, he sensed incapacitating dread. Creed's mind flitted haphazardly as a result, while errant flashes of prior lives dotted his senses. They were speeding emotions of experiences he hadn't ever known to be his. He stopped for a moment, engulfed in sadness. The heaviness was suffocating. Burnt flesh, agonizing screams, and persistent roars of detonated munitions pierced his reality. Creed covered his head and ears with his arms, but couldn't muffle the pain. Everything was spinning from his memories of the Somme Offensive. Then a whisper.

"Get up!"

"What?"

"Get up! Get up and quit being such a sack of shite!"

"Who's there?" He sat forward, looking around, and found nothing but dark slate and emptiness. He covered his ears and screamed. "Show yourself! Come on!"

"You lie there wallowing in your own pity like a pool of piss, yet you fail not yourself, but everyone around you!" Creed spun.

"I'm all alone here!"

"Look again, Leftenant!"

"I can't... I can't see anything." But as he turned, Creed witnessed hundreds of wounded British soldiers. Buildings were crumbling, and bodies, four-days dead, littered the streets.

"GET UP! THEY NEED YOU!"

Creed knelt down, and placed his hand on a soldier's gangrenous leg. The skin sloughed off in his grasp, blowing away as moth wings. He took his torch, and used it to cauterize the stump, and then a nearby bleeding flank wound in a man filled with shrapnel. The memory was bending. Hundreds of men through the ages lined the streets in different battledress. He hung IV antibiotics, and tightened tourniquets around the amputated limbs. He packed wounds with gauze, and debrided necrotic tissue. One of the soldiers with his head wrapped in bloody garments, stared at Creed through his dead eye.

"LOOK OUT!"

Creed blinked and the soldiers were gone. Ojin was shaking him forcibly while bent gingerly at the waist.

"Creed. Look out! There's a beast!"

Creed found himself face to face with a Thacker. It hissed with Creed's face so close he could smell the rotten fish still clinging to its teeth. They backed up slowly as the creature approached; its back crystals glowing. Creed didn't want to retreat, but couldn't go forward. It was an impasse.

"GO!" Ojin yelled. The Thacker hissed at him.

"GO ON! LEAVE!" shouted Xaris, but the Thacker came closer. Creed waved the torch to scare it, and the Thacker stood on its hind legs, then a brisk banter.

"Oy! I'm tellin' ya I saw me a light down here. A bright one!" a stranger's voice explained.

"Ya seein' gem glimmers again. Nuthin' down here."

"Wait and see. Shhh. I heard somethin'."

The sounds came from the falls, and Creed looked for movement. He turned back and the Thacker was gone. The footsteps were closer. The three shuffled, crouched, and hurried quickly down the tunnel. Creed's thighs were burning, and his breathing rapid. The strange voices became more distant as they navigated the endless maze until suddenly a waft of cold air hit his face with mist. The path opened over another large cavern with multiple waterfalls. Creed stopped so suddenly that Ojin and Xaris nearly bowled him over.

"It's a dead end," he said, exasperated.

"See if you can shuffle to the side as we did before," Ojin encouraged.

Creed moved his back to the ledge, and as he inched his way down to make room for the others, he looked about for an escape. He tried to extinguish the torch, but it wouldn't go out. He dipped it in water, and although dimmed, it would grow once more. He contemplated throwing it into the falls, but the darkness was unbearable.

"Ojin, what do we do?" The voices were getting louder.

"Can you see another trail?" Creed looked, and noticed shadowy steps in the light's glimmer. They were so steep that they appeared more as a leaning ladder than a stairway.

"I see steps. This trail ends here."

"Not good. Not good." Ojin shook his head.

"They're getting closer, so you better move. Get up those stairs. Now." Xaris pushed the group up their only option. Creed leaned into the rock so that his chest would slide over the stone. He pulled with one hand, and pushed with his tired legs. His hip continued to throb from the earlier fall. He continued one step at a time; methodically forcing himself to move an inch when moving seemed impossible. Before long, his right hand felt a flat threshold of a doorway, and he pulled himself through the frame. Creed turned to his friends.

"I found a doorway. Give me your hand."

Ojin reached for Creed, and crawled to the top. The large hobgoblin made way through the door as Creed helped Xaris to his feet as well. The voices they heard before were gone, and they had a chance to breathe. Creed rubbed his side, but was thankful they weren't trapped in the tunnel any longer.

"Creed, what happened back there?" asked, Ojin.

"What do you mean?"

"You stopped, and began mumbling to yourself. Something about bleeding and gangrene," Xaris noted. Creed noticed the warrior's leery stare.

"I don't know. It was fast like a bolt of nightmare. I was in a street of an old European township, and there were wounded everywhere. Death was everywhere. I felt I had been there, but nothing made any sense. I came around and saw that beast in front of me."

"That's one of the largest Thackers I've ever seen." said, Xaris.

"Is your mind right?" Ojin looked very concerned.

"It's good for now. What's happening to me?"

"You're still waking up. Your mind needs time to settle still. If you see something out of place, stop, and sit down. We'll make sure you don't get lost in your illusions." Creed felt unsettled that something so long ago was so real moments before. He didn't trust his mind either.

They continued to follow a well-worn path into an open cavern. Once they walked around a bend in the mountainside, they found themselves within a mining camp. Wooden shanties stood thirty-feet high with cots and straw-stuffed pillows. Mining hats were tucked beneath the cots, and ropes strung across the shanty roofs holding clothes large enough to be sails. Wooden clubs with iron nails and broken brackets lay beside each cot as well, should there be unwanted raiders.

Caged fire pits crackled throughout the settlement. There was a complex machine with pistons, cables, and a long conveyor belt. As it churned, bumped, and burped, the device sifted through rocks and grit dumped into the receptacle by a gigantic troll. He stood nearly twenty-foot-tall, and wore a tanned leather smock with wool shorts. Periodically, he would pick up gemstones, and toss them in a pile. Creed knelt down as Ojin whispered.

"That's a troll," he said.

"I figured as much," Creed replied.

"They aren't very smart, but they are truly violent. We need to find a way around this camp without being spotted." Ojin motioned to small spaces behind the tents pitched precariously on the cliff edge.

"Heh, heh, heh. Hello there."

A yellow-toothed, portly Spurgle with a brown bandana stared at Xaris. A second and third Spurgle gathered around them. They had come up from behind on the steps.

"I told ya somethin' was lurkin' about, Porsul."

"What's a Hue-man doing in the Ashi? Our Ashi." They each wore a lime-green lantern on their chests below their bandanas; the glow accentuated their oblong noses. Pick axes were slung over their shoulders like muskets.

"Gormul, last time we had Hue-man we cooked it for days. A feast it was. Feastin'. Feastin'. Loves me feastin'." The large Spurgle grinned.

"Hordul, I likes feastin' too. This one looks chewy. Last one was fat with drippin's."

"Ya. Made good gravy. We need some pork fat mixin' with this one." The three Spurgles tilted their heads.

"Two Hue-mans and a hobgoblin. We do have enough for a feastin'!" The leader, Porsul, drooled slightly at the thought. Creed interjected.

"We're lost, and we didn't mean to trespass. If you just let us walk away, we'll be out of your hair in a second." Creed smiled weakly. He noticed each Spurgle had loops of rope across their shoulders and back.

"This one talks too much, Porsul," Gormul observed.

"Yes, it does. This one talks way too much." Porsul agreed.

"Let's make a deal. You can have this torch, which apparently never goes out, not even in water, and you give me some of that rope around your shoulders. Even trade. We leave your Ashi, you get a never-ending torchlight, and we'll never have to see each other again."

"We'll take the torch, and boil you with it." They cackled with glee.

The Spurgles lunged at the three, but fell as Creed and the others turned quickly to run toward the cliffside. They ran right into the shins of the large troll who had quietly snuck up on them. He reached down, and picked all three up in his large hands before Xaris could unsheathe his swords. The giant smiled and made a little dance, turning them in the air as if he were playing with dolls. They were trapped.

"Oooooooohhhh. It smells like jelly! I likes jelly!" said the giant.

"Shut it. Take them to the kettle!" Porsul commanded.

The giant frowned, and walked the troupe to a large black cauldron in the center of the camp. The cooking apparatus stood steady on its three legs in the center of a bundle of kindling. Piles of pans and filthy food debris lay haphazardly to the side like a dump. There were bundles of dry trees stacked in a waffle pattern near a small bonfire, casting shadows and smoke upward to an undetectable ceiling. Half a dozen giant trolls sat hunched forward, and they began clanging their pick axes against their mining pans. They could smell the bounty.

"Look here you dumb oxes, we havin' a feastin'. None of ya get a taster 'til the stew is done!" Porsul was not very kind in his address.

The giant trolls stood and stomped the ground like a bass drum in protest. Porsul charged them and wagged his short, fat finger in the air. They quietly withdrew, and some of them licked their lips with anticipation. The giant troll captor threw the hapless crew into the cauldron, and their feet clanged the bottom. The brim was nearly three times the height of Ojin, and it did not appear there was a means to escape. The broad belly of the pot portended calamity.

"Ojin, cast a spell! Get us out of here with the Fuga!" Xaris paced back and forth pounding on the iron prison.

"I can't simply fly us somewhere without my staff. It doesn't work that way."

"Where is your staff?"

"Somewhere with Bog I suppose, assuming he's okay." Ojin patted the bottom of the cauldron. "At least the floor is still cold," he assured everyone.

"That likely won't last long I suspect," Xaris said as he stood with his hands on his hips staring at the opening above. They could hear yelling and chanting outside the cauldron.

"*Gornups! Gornups! Gornups!*" the trolls chanted in unison.

"No. No. No! No Gornups! We got no mullets, and we got no unips! We havin' Obs and Homs instead! Now sit down, and quit shakin' the dinner!" Porsul admonished.

"What's 'Obs and Homs', Ojin?" asked Creed.

"It's a rather ingenious stew of bones, rock salt, and herbs. Sometimes they toss a few potatoes and gourds in to add some texture. The mullets are curious stalks with frozen grubs burrowed inside, and if you cook those just right it adds a sweet taste at the end. Unips, however, are disgusting spider sacks of cattle carrion. I have no idea why anyone would want that. It reminds me of rotten haggis. I do, however, smell rosemary and tarragon, so I suspect they've planned this stew out quite well." Ojin nodded. Creed stared at him irritated.

"Maybe you can stop your food critique long enough to help us find a way out. Here, help me up." Creed motioned upwards.

"You won't reach it," Ojin replied.

"I'll jump. Come on." Ojin obliged, and squatted down for Creed to get onto his back and ultimately his shoulders. Ojin half squatted in preparation.

"On three, boost me up."

"Fine. Count fast. You're heavy."

"One, two, three go!" Ojin launched Creed into the air, and with a stroke of luck, Creed managed to gain a grip on a rusted out hollow of the brim. He hung there for a moment until he could swing his other hand over. He pulled slowly, and finally threw a foot up as well. He readjusted, and was now straddled across the top of the cauldron a few feet from the hook of the folded handle. Creed inched closely to the metal bar to hide from the watchful eyes of the Spurgles.

He looked about the camp. The giant trolls sat on their boulders, pouting. The Spurgles were preoccupied in the open kitchen preparing the meal. Although some aspects of the camp were obviously foul, the kitchen was well kept. Against the rock wall, there was a stone table, fifteen feet in length, organized by herbs, sauces, and spice. A rack of knives and metal cleavers were set in the middle. Beastly bunches of meat, salted and cured, hung on ropes behind the stone table while a few barrels of molasses and mead sat beneath it. Sacks of flour, sugar cane, and a crate full of brown eggs were to the side. There was a clucking of poultry in the nearby hen house.

The Spurgles directed two of the trolls to grab the tree trunks, and stack them under the cauldron. Despite Creed being right beneath their noses, the trolls didn't notice, and merely packed the trees as tightly as they could. They walked to the nearby waterfalls, and came back with leather teepees full of cavern water. Creed knew what was coming next. He looked down and whispered.

"They're coming with water. Hold your breath."

"Wait. What?" Ojin asked, but it was too late. The trolls emptied their tepees into the cauldron, and soon Ojin and Xaris were struggling to tread water in the icy bath. After a second round of the pounding deluge, the prisoners floated within six feet under the brim. Creed couldn't reach them, and there was no other means of escape. Ojin spit out a mouth full of water, and spoke through his soaked beard.

"We will drown here if you can't find a way to get us out!"

"I'm working on it. Hold on," Creed assured.

"There's nothing to hold on to!" Xaris shouted.

Creed saw the leader, Porsul, grab his torch and walk toward the cauldron. The Spurgle had an ill-intentioned grin under his nose. Creed had little choice at this point. He leapt from the cauldron brim and rolled to end up face to face with the would-be chef. The Spurgle laughed.

"Are we in a hurry to be my dinner, Hue-man?"

"It's time to go. I'll take that!" Creed lunged for the torch, but the Spurgle was surprisingly quick, and side-stepped the attempt. The commotion garnered the attention of the large trolls, and Porsul's friends. Two of the giants walked over to grab the mobile morsel and toss him into the pot, but between their ankles, Creed noticed an armory to the right of the shanties. There was a rack of artifacts and weapons, spoils of the deep mountain mining, with a hand-scribbled sign "Rusty Clangers" above the rack. Helms, shields, polearms, and blades of all kinds sat dull and dusty, but upright along a lengthy oak platform. It was merely a few yards away. He had a plan.

Chapter 11: The Past Comes Home

Creed dove to the giant's great toe, and kicked it hard beneath the nail, peeling it back with an awful tear. The troll was seething in an angered frenzy. Blood oozed around the nail bed as the giant stomped at him, repeatedly missing the target. Creed bounced, rolled, and sprinted toward the weapons. He grabbed a long sword at first. Another giant troll kicked at him, and Creed managed to bury the broadsword deep into its calf, but the flesh hung onto the weapon, and he couldn't withdraw it for another swipe. The troll fell back, and stumbled into a series of tents and other kin, forcing them all to teeter to and fro in disarray.

Some tents fell over the side of the cliff, as the smaller shanties leaned awkwardly as if a house of cards. Trolls tumbled, falling to their knees and backsides. Creed ran to the weapons rack, and took a curved scimitar in time to parry a knife thrust from Gormul. The fight lasted for but a moment as Creed struck downward, breaking the blade, and the mortally wounded Spurgle tumbled toward the bonfire lacking entrails and a functioning heart. Creed tossed the broken blade to the ground, and went to grab a spear when he saw Porsul make a run for the cauldron.

Porsul still held Creed's torch in his chubby hands when he made it to the base of timber below Ojin and Xaris. Creed took the spear, and with a short sprint, threw the weapon like a javelin toward the vile Spurgle. It missed its mark falling short at the feet of the chef, allowing Porsul to light the pile of dry trees, and within seconds the flame had spread beneath the entire pot. Smoke rose high above the camp as Ojin and Xaris began to yell, but the sounds faded in Creed's ear.

He felt something awaken within his chest, something fierce. It was frightening at first, but then he acquiesced. He took a series of deep breaths, and closed his eyes. Each time he inhaled, the flames of the camp grew, higher and higher as if he were the bellows of a smithy. The flames under the cauldron lapped over the iron brim, and the heat was sweltering. The fire pits, torches, and lanterns throughout, swelled in unison, as did the camp's bonfire, pushing the trolls back toward the kitchen. The lanterns about the remaining Spurgles' necks grew reckless, casting their faces aglow, aghast in molten green.

The air began to stir, and tufts of dirt tumbled about Creed. Along the sales rack of rusty, dusty clangers stood one item wrapped in muddy sediment and cloth. Beneath the ragged linen, the speckled metal appeared worn as if colored in a hot oil finish, and it was aflame. An array of blues, yellows, greens, and burnt bronze emerged from beneath the cotton fibers as they shriveled away in embers to reveal the fearsome end of a long, curved glaive. A second, opposing, crescent of metal curved halfway to its spine to form a recess within which a blue flame tumbled weightless. The glaive was chained to the rack, but not for long. The links bent and snapped with a sudden crash to the floor. The giant trolls stood shaken, pointing to the glowing relic, but their Spurgles had more pressing matters.

"Porsul, I can't get it off of me! It's burnin'. It's burnin' me!" Hordul gurgled.

"I know, Hordul! I know! It bites! It stings!" Porsul attested.

The Spurgles were running in circles clutching at the neck lanterns. Their hands were scalded as the chains branded their skin. The black cauldron flames rose as funnels high above, and now the giants were filling tents with water hoping to douse the chaos. They threw water on the cooking apparatus, and the steam from the warm iron hissed and crackled as the flames dimmed. Torrents of muddy soil slicked the camp, and soon the giants were falling face first in the turmoil.

The cauldron fell over from an errant troll leg, and tumbling water washed Gormul's remains over the edge. Porsul and Hordul flit about, and pounded their necks and chests, hoping to snuff out the blistering baubles. Creed opened his eyes, and glanced over at the glowing dirty glaive. It called to him. He ran for it, slid, and arose, clutching it in both hands. The glaive came alive and seemed to hum. He turned toward the cliffside, and noticed a tent had fallen as a bridge across a narrow crevasse. Creed ran toward the cauldron, hoping his friends were still alive, but as he did, a clawed hand ripped at his chain mail. Creed spun into it, and the Spurgle flesh was felled with a subtle, skillful stroke of the glaive, merely muscle memory. Porsul screamed in agony. "AWWWGRRRRHHHHHH!" His wrinkled hand fell into a shallow puddle.

Another troll's toe hairs caught on fire, and he leapt and swayed like a drunken ballet dancer. He stumbled past the bonfire, and grasped for the tilted handle of the cauldron, hoping it would slow his fall over the cliffside. The troll fell from sight, but not before pulling the iron sphere to the very edge where it teetered precariously. Creed raced to help his friends, knowing they could plunge into the rivers below at any moment.

"FILTHY HUE-MAN!" Porsul screamed, as spittle frothed his terse lips. With his remaining hand, he grabbed a bone cleaver, washed aside from the kitchen table, and charged. Creed stopped and pivoted, his stance widened. Porsul struck low forcing Creed to jump, and the Spurgle's backstroke nearly took his hamstring. Creed slid a half step back, and swung heavily downward. The glaive fell like an anvil though it felt light as a red oak staff. With a wet 'thwack', the assailant wobbled.

   Porsul's head rolled freely into the bonfire grimacing all the way as his body leaned to the side, slumped in an awkward stance, propped solely by his mining boots. The bone cleaver fell to the ground. Creed ran to the cauldron and looked inside. His friends lay somnolent.

"Ojin! Xaris! Get up! We have to move!" Ojin rolled over slowly, coughing. Xaris didn't move at all. Creed ran to his side, and rustled his chest and belly, trying to get a response. There was none. Creed checked for a pulse, and although present, it was faint. "Ojin! You good?"

"I'm not dead yet if that's what you mean." Ojin moved the long-wet hair of his head and beard to the side of his face so he could see.

"Xaris isn't breathing. We have to get moving. Those trolls aren't going to run around forever." Creed kneeled down over Xaris, and performed three rescue breaths on the warrior. He waited, and performed two more with subsequent pauses and pulse checks. The camp was burning all around them now with moats of ash and mudslides. The giants were struggling to escape, but each exit was blocked by flame. Creed looked up to see Hordul pointing at them, screaming.

"Ojin, we really have to go! Can you do anything?"

"I can disappear, but that won't do you two any good."

The trolls were headed their way. Creed gave two more breaths, and pumped repeatedly on Xaris' chest. Water sputtered from the downed man's mouth, and Xaris coughed and gasped. Creed rolled him to his side.

"Hold him here just like this. I need to get them away from you guys." Ojin looked behind Creed.

"They're not going to let you out alive."

"Fair enough."

Creed charged the oncoming crowd, but they stopped before he could strike, and the giants bellowed while shielding their faces. Someone was shooting them from afar. Creed looked to his right toward the teepee bridge, and saw a wonderful sight.

"Bog! Pax! Yes! Ojin, they found us! Look!" He pointed to the large mammoth across the chasm. Ojin followed his direction, and nodded. Pax was standing, loading his crossbow as quickly as his Ogre fingers could. Each of his volleys managed to embed within the giants' faces. One took a shot to the eye, and fell to his knees wailing in pain. Creed saw their window of escape was narrow and short lived.

"Ojin, let's go! Come on. I'll help you. Let's make it to the fallen tent." Ojin and Creed picked Xaris up around the waist and shoulders, and the three shuffled to the canvas bridge. The tent's center pole hung firmly from its anchor in the camp to the boulders next to Bog. They would have to balance for twenty yards on a log that was six foot wide. Creed turned to Xaris, and saw him looking about.

"Xaris, we're leaving. We need you to focus. Look at Bog and keep going straight."

"Let me get in front of him, Creed. Xaris, hold on to me." Ojin moved to the front, and stepped onto the beam. Xaris followed, still disoriented, and they moved in tandem slowly to their escape. Creed stayed behind for a moment.

"AHHHHHH! YOU NASTY HUE-MAN!" Hordul flung his hatchet at Creed, and the small axe brushed his shoulder, drawing blood. It careened off into the darkness below, splashing into the river.

The remaining Spurgle was relentless. He grabbed a broken spear next, and thrust toward Creed's chest. Creed swung the glaive to the side, and lunged twice, but missed both times. They circled one another as Creed heard distant cries. Smoke billowed about, and made it difficult to see. Creed's eyes watered, and he scarcely had time to wipe them when he felt the displaced air of the spearhead near his cheek. He rolled, and saw the shadow of Hordul side straddle to his left.

"Creed, the tent pole is on fire! The bridge is on fire!" Ojin screamed. Creed didn't have time to process what he heard, however, as Hordul continued his attacks. He knew he needed to finish this once and for all, but the Spurgle hid well within the dust and debris.

It's not worth it, he thought.

Creed saw an opportunity to run, and he took it. He sprinted toward the burning timber, and jumped a few feet forward. He walked heel to toe quickly across the bridge as fire lapped the wooden underbelly, and once halfway, he could see the lanterns atop Bog's bench. The air was clearing in the middle of the chasm. He began to push faster almost to a jog when he heard Ojin yell once more.

"Turn around! Turn around!" Creed stopped in time to see Hordul a few feet away. The Spurgle chased him as a rabid badger. Creed slipped, and fell to his back just as Hordul was within striking distance. He dared not let go of the glaive, barely clasping it with three fingers of his left hand. Hordul lunged for the kill.

THWACK!

Hordul's eyes locked onto Creed's. His face was a grim mask of finality. He stumbled back, and the spear fell from his hands. The Spurgle reached for the thick black bolt in the center of his chest, but his strength was gone, and all he could do was concede. Creed watched as the short terror tilted, and flipped slowly end over end illuminated by the bright green lantern about his neck. The river claimed yet another victim, and Creed breathed deeply.

"Move, Creed! Get across quickly!" Ojin yelled as the bridge fire grew, and Creed heard the sounds of wood splinter and crack. He forced himself to stand, and stumbled to the end of the beam where Ojin caught him as he fell. The camp portion of the timber was now consumed with orange embers and flame, and shortly the bridge was no more. Canvas, wood, and rope all fell leaving no means of escape for the remaining trolls. The expedition party, now reunited, watched from across the chasm as the camp survivors fought the flames and collapsing homes. Ojin helped Xaris climb atop Nos, and then made it onto his seat with Bog's reins in hand. Creed stood there for a moment, wondering what would have happened had any of it gone differently, but for now it mattered not. The caravan began the slow descent to the Ashi's cavern floor, and he followed behind on foot, weapon in hand.

Chapter 12: Lacus Atromento

They tracked the river for over an hour as it sped toward a series of waterfalls. The roaring, toiling currents split into nine corrals of stone fingerlets. It was beautiful to behold. The group came to a stop on the riverbank as they watched the white-water crests fall over into the depths below. A broad stone path wound down slowly to eventually run parallel with the current. Creed peered within the forest of shadows, hoping there was an exit soon. Xaris continued to cough and wheeze while Ojin wove his hand over the jade of his staff atop Bog. Droplets of water floated away in a mist. The hobgoblin's long hair was dried in the process, and it appeared to Creed, that the same was happening to the lungs of Xaris. Pax rubbed his forehead repeatedly while tapping his fingers on the bench rest. He seemed relaxed. Bog reached around with his trunk, and scratched a bald spot on his flank while the horses attached to his armor hooks patiently waited.

"Ojin, any idea how much further?" Creed wondered.

"No. Xaris?"

"We head down, and then it will be two to three hours more." Xaris coughed violently, and belched a full cup of water from his lungs.

"Are you okay?" Creed asked.

"Well enough. I've been working on that last bit of river water for the good part of an hour. Feel like I can breathe again." They all looked about at the expanse before them. The caverns loomed high above as the river snaked its way along the floor.

"We need to keep going. That troll escapade likely set us back a great deal, and we've taken quite a few breaks along the way. We can't afford for Serena and Celeste to wait for us in the open. Leterum won't hesitate to attack," Ojin warned.

"We still have a ways to go my friend. Let's get out of here first, and then we can worry about the fields. It isn't Leterum that you should worry about should he choose to fight with Serena. Soon enough, she will unleash five-thousand years of fury on this soil, and there isn't a soul on this world that could survive it." Xaris coughed again, leaning to the side of Nos to spit.

"Xaris, she restrains herself for many reasons, but all it would take is …" Ojin attempted to explain.

"It won't happen. Celeste and her child will not be harmed. I will see to that," Xaris replied. The warrior seemed to be coming around as Creed watched him sit upright. Xaris was strong indeed, but subdued it would seem since the cauldron episode.

"I'm sorry about what happened back there. I moved as fast as I could to get you out. The trolls were everywhere." Creed looked at Xaris as they made their way along the path.

"Next time you can give me a boost instead. I don't particularly enjoy drowning." Xaris spit again, and this time he groaned afterward. "How long do I have to keep coughing up my lungs?"

"Probably a few days, honestly. No telling what was in that river water," Creed explained.

"Once we get you to Serena, she will breathe life into you, and you will feel like a new man. All I can do is pull as much of it out of you as I can," Ojin assured him.

176

"I'd be happy to no longer be an old man, let alone a new man." Xaris grinned as he spat another remnant of froth. They continued down the path.

"Don't we all? I remember when I first learned of the Ashi. I was studying at the academy back home. I was very young and idealistic then. It seemed so exotic and surreal. The magic and the lore that spilled from its domain was enough to ignite the senses, and spur inspiration. Years later, I went on an expedition with some fellow hobgoblins, and a smattering of Serena's Bellatorum. Within a day, I and a single Bellator remained." Ojin stared forward as his body swayed from Bog's gait.

"What happened?" asked, Creed.

"We ran into an army of demons. Acrom had recently been imprisoned following the Cataclysm, and we were sent to round up his infantry. Truly, we were supposed to be a scouting mission, but with a masterly planned ambush, the bodies fell as ears of corn during harvest. I lost my best friend that day." Ojin cleared his throat a few times to suppress the memories.

"I'm sorry, Ojin," Creed replied.

"Me too. Creed, war is a terrible, terrible thing, and no matter how strong a certain side may be, there will always come a time when they find their faults upon the battlefield. Remember that in the upcoming days. Leterum will not let you merely waltz into the Pools with Celeste, but even he has weaknesses."

They soon found themselves below the Ashi falls, and the white noise became a distant roar. They marched along the main river now, following it until the faint rapids dissipated into a serene lake. Xaris dismounted into the soft gravel, attempting to muffle his cough.

"Lacus Atromento. It is said that the Ashi wept when Acrom escaped his first imprisonment, and innumerable souls were tormented. The water became the only means of peace for those who would be named victim beneath the demon lord's wrath," Ojin whispered with a lowered voice.

The Lacus Atromento stretched before them as a small ocean it would seem. Their lantern lights glimmered as trails along the water's surface. Bog came to a slow stop. Exhausted, the mammoth reached for a drink at the shoreline. Xaris grabbed his trunk.

"No, my friend. We don't disturb the lake. Never. Not much further, and we will find smaller spillways to fill our flasks. Here we simply look." Ojin stepped down from Bog, and stretched his legs. He was about to cast the Penumbra when he looked down, and saw a small ripple followed by another, and yet another.

"Xaris. Look." He pointed to the shoreline.

"Nothing lives in this lake," Xaris whispered.

"No. Nothing *living* does." Ojin peered along the lake's surface, but could not make out the ripples' origins.

"Ojin, get Bog and the Ogre away from the water, and head toward those rocks. I will scout the lakeshore, and be back within a few minutes," Xaris requested.

"I'm coming with you," Creed insisted.

"As am I," Ojin confirmed. Xaris shook his head.

"It's safer if I'm alone."

"You're sick. You cough or pass out, out there in the dark, we won't find you. We go as a team, or we don't go at all," Creed said defiantly. Xaris coughed into his sleeve again. He gave in.

"Fine. Fine. We can all go, but I will take point. We should all walk slowly around the lake. The ripples could easily be cavern water from above. I don't plan on staying long. We look, and if there is nothing to see, we head out of the Ashi. Agreed?" Ojin and Creed nodded.

Xaris led them slowly along the lake's edge as Creed noticed an increased frequency of small waves rolling over the pebbles. There was an earthen rise before them, and once they strode forward a few more yards, Creed could see a glimmer of light on what appeared to be an island in the middle of the lake. They stopped, and Bog, Nos, and the other two horses instinctively knelt down. Metal clanged with urgency, and the light seemed to move erratically. More ripples and more waves disturbed the shore.

Across the water, Creed could hear grunting in a language too unfamiliar. Sparks speckled the dark, the grinding of metal on whetstones, and the sound of bone on rock. He struggled to make sense of what he saw even though he knew something dark was before them if only he could remember what they were. They appeared to be large muscled demons with crimson-hides, Ovis horns and beastly legs with bare-bone hooves.

"Mael'deua. Hundreds of them. They are the soldiers of the Onyx Order, the infantry of Acrom himself," Xaris said. Ojin stared wide-eyed with disbelief.

"They've been imprisoned for thousands of years. How in the name of the Ether could they be free?" Ojin pondered.

"The worlds are untethered. We know this now. These beasts will spill onto the plain, and we won't be able to contain them." Xaris drew his swords.

"No." Ojin shook his head in defiance. "We can't take them all on. We need a plan, and a good one at that."

Creed stared at the beasts, and noticed they were all heavily armed as smoke rose from their bodies. To the right of the massive gathering, there was a hastily constructed stone altar. Candles flickered on the corners of the empty tabletop, illuminating urns and oil flasks. Creed wondered whom the altar was for, and what would be placed upon it.

"Why is there an altar?" Creed asked.

"Why is there ever an altar? They plan on performing some dark ritual for Acrom. It doesn't matter what or why. The dark magic involved is nothing we wish to see. We need to hold them here. They need to be stopped," Ojin replied.

"How did they get here?" Creed asked. Ojin pointed to a broken stone structure from whence the Mael'deua emerged. There were chains shorn from their rock anchors. A trap door from this world to the next had been violated, and from a depth unseen, the Mael'deua pulled their brethren out by hand, one after another.

"Well they can't fly and they can't swim, so how do you suppose they plan on getting off that island?" Xaris paced back and forth.

"I don't care to know, but it's our job to push them off. We can drown them in the lake if need be." Ojin motioned to the water.

"With what?" Xaris asked. Ojin looked at Bog. Bog wagged his trunk in protest.

"Not much from you, my friend. They cannot withstand the temptation. They are bred to bask in violence, so we give them violence." Bog stood up and paced about, as did Pax within the benches. Ojin had to stand beside the mammoth, and wrap his large hairy arms around the wooly warrior. "Be calm, friend. Know that we are able." Ojin patted Bog's ribs.

"Can we close it? Can we close that portal?" Creed asked.

"With what? The same rocks and chains they shattered?" Xaris appeared impatient as he berated Creed.

"Easy, Xaris. Easy. He asks a good question. No point in killing these Mael'deua if only more will appear. No. I will funnel water into the tunnel and freeze it."

"They will only melt it. They will be freed again," Xaris argued.

"No. This will be Haunsa Frost. It will always steal the heat, absorb it, and the ice will grow deeper into the island indefinitely. It will be a perpetual prison."

"How do we get them in there?" Creed looked to Ojin for a plan.

"You," Ojin replied.

"Me? Are you crazy?"

"Stand over there. Xaris, Bog you too. Pax, if you must." The four members were not too keen on the idea. The waters were deep, and the enemy was numerous. Creed did not wish to swim to them only to get slaughtered.

"Now, Xaris climb atop Bog, and draw your bow. Creed, hold your weapon forward as if you were to attack. When I say fire, shoot your arrows at the ones closest to the portal. Fire once every few seconds. Creed, you need to swipe in the air. Imagine taking each of their heads from their bodies."

"This won't work. We can't cross, and they won't try to swim to us," Xaris complained.

"Draw your bow, Xaris."

"Ojin."

"Now." Xaris drew back his long bow, and waited for a command in the dark. Pax paced with anxiety. Creed looked at the Ogre, the warrior, and the hobgoblin. He worried that this was no more effective than swatting a hornets' nest. His eyes grew wider however, once he saw the manifestation of Ojin's illusion. There they were plain as day. The four of them blocking the entrance to the underground tunnel, and yet he looked down quickly to see that they remained on the shoreline beside Ojin. This was a ploy.

"FIRE!"

Xaris drew back a bit further, and loosed the arrow. It whistled through the air directly into the neck of a demon prepping unawares. He let out a howl, and broke the arrow's shaft from his thick, scaly hide. The entire island was awoken with eyes fixed on the assault. Ojin waved his arms as if conducting an orchestra, and the mighty faux, four-bodied raid raced about the Mael'deua close to each of Xaris' arrows. The demons struck and swung at the mammoth, but through the dark and constant shadows they seemed to miss. Creed's illusion was not far behind, and when it ran about on the island soil, the candle flames of the altar rose.

Xaris managed to fell three of the Mael'deua through their backs. The island inhabitants were blinded by rage, and trounced one another to annihilate the fomenters. The chaos had been well orchestrated. Creed wished in a way that he could take a few down himself.

"How many more, Ojin? I have twelve arrows left," Xaris called out.

"Shoot three more. I will lead them."

As Xaris drew his next shot, Ojin motioned the raider mirage quickly into the tunnel. The demons poured into the portal, rabid with anticipation. A few stragglers remained on the surface, but as they hurried to follow their brothers, a bolt bounced off a Mael'deua horn. He stopped, grunted something in a dead language, and four others turned around as well.

"PAX! NO!" Xaris exclaimed.

It was too late. Pax had already launched two more bolts, and they fell placidly against their armor. The distance was too great. The Mael'deua bellowed, and the tunnel once more belched forth a handful of willful assailants. The trap was failing. Creed feared what was yet to come.

Ojin dropped his staff, and immediately threw his hands into the dark water, seemingly grasped by something fixed and rigid. With his hands immersed and elbows bent, a wave of frost and froth rose quickly through the cavern air toward the island. It climbed high as a storm's tide, and crashed violently into the mouth of the broken portal gate. It became a waterspout of such high velocity the air became turbulent and pulled them all toward the water's edge. "Ojin! Ojin! Stop." Xaris cried, but Ojin was in a trance, and unable to respond. His eyes were dull and gray.

Xaris levied his bow once more and aimed for those closest to the escape. Two arrows flew into the demons' flanks, and with a misstep they became engulfed by an opaque obelisk of ice, motionless, and doomed. The funnel of frost continued deep within the rock opening, and no others were able to escape. The remaining Mael'deua ran away from the impact of frost and fury, and stopped short of the water's edge facing Creed and the others. Ripples multiplied. The altar surface exploded, engulfed in smoke and flame, and the water surface broke. One by one, bodies wrapped in burial shrouds rose slowly to the top from the depths of the Lacus Atromento, each one shoulder to shoulder with the next until a buoyant bridge connected the island to the main shore. The Mael'deua hesitated at first, but the altar shook, and their hooves advanced. The Mael'deua were coming. Creed looked to Ojin, but he was still detached.

"Pax! Shoot them with your crossbow as they draw closer! Creed, come with me!" Xaris barked as he stepped firmly on one of the lake bodies. It swayed like a plank on a rope bridge, but remained afloat.

Xaris charged the Mael'deua. They met in the middle as his blade struck a demon's axe and parried. The Mael'deua loomed over him reeking of sulfur and ash. Creed was mere feet behind them, and looked for an opening as four more demons battled forward. Xaris and the Mael'deua struggled for space and leverage. The demon turned and with a backhand struck Xaris across the face knocking him onto his side. Creed stepped over him, and lunged with a thrust to the demon. The Mael'deua was quick, and countered. They locked weapons once more, but Creed could feel his weapon vibrate. The burnt bronze glowed. Creed spun away with a half step courting the demon forward, and as if on cue, the spear end of Creed's glaive met its target just below the adversary's left collarbone.

The Mael'deua bellowed, and the altar's flames spilled over onto the island rocks. A violent crash from behind thrust Creed and his opponent on top of Xaris who had risen to a knee. It was yet another demon in line for the kill. The wounded Mael'deua from Creed's spear, fell into the dark lake, and never rose again. Creed lay on his back as the next battle-axe fell with fury, but he managed to brace the impact with the shaft of his glaive. His eyes turned to the water, and barely beneath the surface, he saw the partially unwrapped scalp and face of a decayed Caedere. The image was unsettling. It appeared similar to cadavers he recalled from jars and tanks in medical school.

The attacking Mael'deua bore down fiercely upon him, grunting and snorting for Creed's demise. The demon stepped back to strike again. Creed fumbled to gain his ground, quickly enough to duck and miss an overhead blow as Xaris backed away a few feet to settle. Creed drove his spear end into the demon's thigh as Xaris jumped upon his back, and plunged both blades into the trunk. As blood streamed over their weapons, the lifeless body fell into the lake. Xaris lunged forward to attack the next, but a well-placed bolt pierced the Mael'deua's eye, and he too fell into the waters, drowning frantically. The remaining Mael'deua raced back to the island.

A great rumble shook the caverns, and the ceiling seemed to fall. Rocks crashed about the lake sending water high into the air, and then something gargantuan fell to its feet crushing a Mael'deua beneath its claws. The beast stood on its hind legs and roared.

Before Xaris and Creed, stood a forty-foot bear. She stomped the island repeatedly until the rock altar was crushed along with the remaining Mael'deua, and the fires extinguished. The bear went to all fours, swung, and shattered the ice funnel pouring from the lake and Ojin's magic, leaving only the solid, frozen tomb, laden with dead demons. The tunnel mouth was no more. Ojin fell back, and his eyes returned. He was exhausted, cold, and shivering. Creed turned to run as did Xaris, both barely making it to shore by the time the last body sunk to its unsettled grave. The bear roared again. Creed looked up, and could see the bare, ivory skull with its hollowed socket on one side.

"*URCINIS!*" Ojin exclaimed. He stood shaken, pointing, and attempted to bow. He looked at Bog, Pax, Xaris and Creed. "BOW!"

They obliged, and the bear paced back and forth sniffing the strangers from across the water. She rolled each dead Mael'deua into the lake, and rubbed out the broken portal chains and charred altar rocks until they too sank to the bottom.

"I did not believe she existed. I thought it a myth. Something to keep people from the Ashi."

"What is she?" Creed asked.

"Guardian of the Lacus Atromento. She protects the souls in the lake."

"Did you see any of what happened to the Mael'deua? Could you see their origin deep within the tunnel? Was Acrom there?" Xaris asked.

"No, only shadows and a presence of something very dark. I focused my mind's eye on the demons as they fled into the tunnel. I could see a circle of fire at the end of their long path. I tried to reach the fire with the Haunsa Frost, but as I got close to sealing it, my vision was shattered."

"We fought on risen bodies from the lake. I saw what looked to be a Caedere corpse," Creed mentioned.

"It is possible. Their remains must go somewhere."

"I envisioned them going to the Undüavalle," said, Xaris.

"Most do. I am not sure why they would be buried here." The bear roared again stomping the earth. She seemed agitated. Ojin raised his open hands peacefully.

"Urcinis, forgive us. You saw the demons cross. Some foul force pushed the Mael'deua here. We sought to close them off. The chains had been broken." She sniffed the ice where the chained rocks had lain for millennia. She clawed at the ice.

"Urcinis, no. Please." She growled at him.

"Once it sets, if you disturb the ice in any way, it will grow. It will expand, and spread." She clawed the ice once more despite Ojin's warning, and pieces fell into the lake. Each frosted fragment spawned an expanding sphere of solid ice. The water became encapsulated one sphere at a time until an entire section of the lake had become rigid as stone. Urcinis placed a paw on the ice shelf. It held her weight.

Creed, Xaris, and Ojin backed away slowly, mounting their steeds, wide-eyed and fearful. Pax hid low within the bench upon Bog's back. Ojin steered them toward the road upon which they first entered as Urcinis scratched more ice from the tunnel into the water. Each fragment did as before. The Haunsa Frost over the tunnel grew also, spilling out slowly like bubbling tree sap, and created a glacier along the other end of the island. Now the bear had enough room to stand halfway across. She snorted, and lurched forward. Bog picked up the pace, and soon Nos and Creed's horse did as well. Urcinis walked slowly mere steps from the expanding front as she approached the lake shoreline.

"RUN!" Ojin commanded.

The wayward group dug into the gravel, and lurched into a full sprint. The bear was coming for them. Urcinis clawed once more, and now the ice reached the shore. The glacier became a means of pursuit. The bear leapt and slipped briefly, but she readily gained traction, and it wouldn't be long before she cornered them all. Creed looked back only to have his heart sink. Urcinis was gaining ground immeasurably. Ojin bellowed.

"Bog, keep going! Run! Faster! Faster! We want nothing to do with that!" Urcinis roared, and the caverns shook as she bounded toward them. Bog's stumpy, beastly legs of burden moved as fast as a mammoth possibly could. It was no use. The bear was gaining ground quickly, and appeared to be making a straight line to the mammoth. Creed knew of no other way to stop her. He held onto his glaive tightly with one hand, and pulled quickly on the horse's reins with the other. He jumped into the sandy loam, and charged the bear.

"HERE! HERE! OVER HERE!"

The others were focused on racing for an exit, and did not notice Creed had left them. Urcinis took her focus away from Bog and Ojin, and stared at the blue light and solitary man before her. She slowed her pace, and walked toward Creed, sniffing the air. Creed stood ready to buy what little time he could provide for his friends. He heard a whisper; inquisitive it seemed, curious about him, and the shiny weapon he held.

"Who are you? What do you bring before me?"

He looked about as the bear approached. He couldn't see anyone else. His friends, in their fear, were easily a hundred yards away. The whisper grew in his mind, and he looked back at Urcinis.

She stooped and lowered her burly head, sniffing the ground all around him with her one watchful eye keyed in closely to his every move. Creed could see that half the fur was missing from her skull and face as if someone had taken a razor to her flesh. He looked closer, and saw crystal centipedes crawling beneath her hide, eating her tissue despite its attempts to granulate back onto the exposed bone. It was an ebb and flow of decay and growth continuously on her expression. She seemed agitated, angry. Creed slowly stepped closer. He could smell her breath. It emitted aromas of dewberries and honey. The blue fire within the glaive's blade grew, and the weapon became increasingly warm. Urcinis growled and stood on her hind legs, but Creed stepped onto the ice. She was talking to him, and so he chose to speak with her.

"Breathe. Just breathe. Settle. I won't hurt you. Let me take a look at your face." Urcinis showed her teeth.

"Let me look at it one more time. I won't do anything else." She went to all fours, and this titan of a bear, looming high above him, slowly reached her snout to his outstretched palm. He smelled of trolls, and she huffed as her head jerked away, but with gentle coaxing, she looked back at him once more. The crystalline creatures scurried when the blue fire of Üstor came near them. Creed had an idea.

In the distance, Creed heard someone screaming. He turned to see Xaris charging forward on horseback with swords drawn as if he were planning to attack the bear. Creed waved his arm in an attempt to stop him.

"Creed! Get back! CREED!!" Xaris yelled. He was getting closer, and Urcinis looked up, teeth gleaming in the glow of the glaive.

"STOP!" Creed replied. Xaris kept coming as Creed waved him off. "Give me a second! STOP, XARIS! STOP!"

Urcinis' eye looked quickly at Xaris, which was just enough time for Creed to swipe the blade, broadside, across her exposed bone like a paddle. It hit hard and flat as a hammer on an anvil. Fragments of blinding sparks burst across the facial rot, and settled sizzling into the mange. Urcinis cried out, jumped, and stood upright once more with a paw drawn to swipe at Creed. He did nothing more than lay the weapon down, and put his hands out gently. She roared in his face, and his chest shook in the acoustic percussion and heated breath, but then Urcinis settled. She sat back on her haunches, and rubbed a paw across her face repeatedly as if it itched. Centipede bodies fell onto the ice, curled and lifeless. Her pain was gone, and Creed stood before her with an outstretched hand once more.

A moment passed in a familiar way. She touched his palm with her snout. Her tender flesh crawled across the bone, and began to repair the damage the centipedes had done. Blood vessels, fascia, and muscle layered quickly about, and encircled her eye socket. A white bulb grew in the back of the orbit, and enlarged to fill the space. It shifted twice, and then the eye was fully formed. Her hide set root over the rawness until everything seemed as new. It was as if she had never been infested. Xaris pulled Nos to a stop.

"What did you do? I don't understand." Urcinis growled lowly at Xaris, but Creed patted her face rhythmically.

"It's okay old girl. He doesn't need to understand."

"It appears we've finally found our Hippocrates," Ojin said, arriving atop Bog with a smile.

Urcinis was healed. For a moment, everyone stared at her. Ojin marveled at her size and demeanor. Creed just grinned. He patted her on the neck as he heard the whisper once more.

"*Thank you, Hippocrates. Venture well.*" Urcinis turned to walk away. She meandered back across the ice, and into her den above the lake. She disappeared into the dark, and the cavernous, cold Lacus Atromento was quiet once more.

"What were you thinking?" Xaris asked as he sheathed his blades.

"I knew we wouldn't make it in time, so I decided to take a chance. Once I got a look at her though, I figured it out."

"What do you have there, Hippocrates?" Ojin nodded toward the weapon in the soil. Creed leaned over to pick it up. It had cooled, and the blue light, though present, had dimmed to a gentle calm. "I'm not sure really."

"May I see it?" Creed handed it over to Ojin, and the fire dulled in his hands. "I remember a weapon much like this, but it was ages ago, and the weapon I remember was brilliant silver in the command of a general. Serena will like to look this over. I'm sure she will know its history." He offered it to Xaris. The warrior looked it over as well.

"It's too heavy to be thrown. Well balanced though. Odd to see it in a troll camp, don't you think?" He returned it to Creed, and the weapon's fire grew once more.

"The Ashi holds many secrets, Creed. I'm thankful this one served a purpose." The hobgoblin grinned softly.

Ojin reached for a flask of Mebum on the side of Bog's saddlebags. He took a long drink, and offered it to the others. They all quenched their thirst, and took a moment to gather themselves and their articles. They attached the horses to Bog once more, and Creed climbed atop the bench to sit beside Ojin as Pax fidgeted with his quiver in the back. Xaris, appearing much stronger than before, lead the party forward along the path.

The glacier, now formed within the Lacus Atromento, continued to crack and snap as it spread slowly up the streams displacing boulders and crumbled thoroughfares. The ice appeared to stop short of the falls, and the cavern had become much colder. Pax huddled beneath a large animal fur tucked within one of Ojin's bags. Xaris chewed on jerky while Ojin smoked his pipe. Creed kept touching the blue fire within his weapon, allowing it to climb and roll over his hand. It was as alive as he was. Ojin cleared his throat.

"What happened back there, Creed? In the troll camp?"

"It's weird. I closed my eyes, and allowed the fire to consume everything. It was cathartic."

"We felt the fire grow as the cauldron became unbearable. I suspected as much. You seem different, however. What else?"

"I keep having these flashbacks. Intense. Sad. Violent. Then they're gone. That worries me because that feeling... I can't seem to control it either."

"When the Luxatio were first so named, it was at the request of Serena in order to provide stewards on Earth once the realms were split. The Luxatio were chosen, so that they could represent what man was capable of, a group destined to light the way for others. They would bring the Lux to Earth with each life, and when they returned to Mürindür they would grow in strength, and the Lux, only to return more prepared than their last visit. For every moment in human history where violence was quelled, science advanced, or art was birthed, a Luxatio was at the heart of the moment. Their impact, your impact, has always been monumental, but there have been drawbacks nonetheless." Ojin took a long slow draw off his pipe.

"The problem first came to our attention years before you took your oath. Luxatios who had traveled many times, found their return to be more difficult with each visit. They brought with them the pain and anguish they witnessed, and it would take longer to heal from that before they could remember who they were. The sacrifice was cumulative. We began to question how much tragedy and sorrow, the human mind could truly take, Luxatio or not.

Mortals have only so much space for so much living and so much loss." The pipe smoke rose softly like an aromatic, vanilla cloud about them.

"Do you think that is what's going on with me?" Creed asked.

"Perhaps. You have traveled more than most remaining Luxatio, and those memories you see are trying to fit their way back into your mind even though your heart has never lost them."

"You act like I have an expiration date."

"How do you mean?" Ojin's ears perked with curiosity.

"When does the path of a Luxatio end? When do they move on?" Ojin drew another long puff off his pipe.

"Luxatio give up their right to the Endüerduul, willingly," Ojin explained.

"Right. I can't ever go."

"No, you can't, but should you choose to forego returning to mankind, you can stay here for as long as you like. For some, however, they couldn't get through the images of their past. It ate away at them. They couldn't move beyond the pain. We had to devise a means to give them peace."

"How so?"

"Should a Luxatio choose to never go back, and they wish for peace, they are allowed to pass, and their soul becomes one with Mürindür. Serena felt because they sacrificed everything for mankind they should be rewarded as much."

"So, I could pick a rock or a squirrel?"

"Hah! No! More like a mountain or a forest! It is said that even the Ashi was once a Luxatio," Ojin exclaimed.

"They got a pretty raw deal. They're infested with trolls and everyone keeps picking at them," Creed smirked and Ojin chuckled.

"I don't think the Ashi was truly a Luxatio, but I do believe the creatures within it could be. Legend has it that Urcinis was once a great Luxatio. She was turned into the beast you saw back there. I didn't know if those stories were true until now. She didn't stop to look at you because you have a way with animals. She stopped from attacking you because even though so much of her memory is gone, she still can recognize one of her own. The heart never truly forgets."

"I did feel something when she looked at me. I swear I could hear her in my head. I felt unafraid."

"I'm sure she felt it likewise. Luxatio always form an endless bond."

"What happens to my body should I go someday?"

"We take the remains into the Redemptio Keep into a special chamber where they are preserved and protected." Ojin's face grew solemn.

"Protected from what?" Creed asked.

"The energy you have within you doesn't simply go away when you die, and there are those who would choose to take a Luxatio's bones for untoward ends. There is a great deal of power within Luxatio remains, and that is why they must always be protected."

"Like an honor guard?"

"Somewhat, yes."

"How does one choose when they leave, Ojin?"

"They know when it's time."

"I'm not sure I'm ready for that." Creed looked about, and tried to picture Celeste. He wanted something beautiful, right then, in his mind.

"Well I should hope not, my friend!" Ojin's face was animated once more. "You have a baby on the way, and a wife to wed."

"Yes, I do!"

"You have a great deal of life ahead, and we all want you to have it." Ojin patted Creed as Nos pulled to a stop.

"We are here!" Xaris yelled, pointing to a large arched hall. It was the exit out of Ashi.

They marched further until a broad doorway, overgrown with vines and weeds, lay bare the view. Creed saw the vast amber grain waving gently in the breeze.

"The Fields of Effugere," Ojin said with great satisfaction.

The air was fresh and dry unlike the dankness they emerged from below. As the band considered briefly the task at hand, Creed looked back once more into the Ashi. He wondered if the trolls were able to escape, and would they come searching for the man who set their camp aflame. Perhaps Urcinis would find the trolls beforehand. He wondered what it was like for her, alone, but without the pain of prior lives and losses. He wondered if she was happy, and he wondered if he could enjoy such an existence someday.

Then a memory of his love entered his mind. His anticipation grew. He would finally see her again and their unborn son. She was his family, and the memories of their time together flowed freely. Those mental murals were welcomed and embraced. He turned back toward the fields searching for some sign that she was nearby. He could almost feel her somehow. No movement in the grass below, but the openness was novel and inviting. Hope hastened, and the band moved forward.

Chapter 13: The Fields of Effugere

As they stepped past the broken stone threshold, field larks and sparrows filled the air. Although it was late afternoon, the sky was ablaze in blue. The field sat as a grain bowl between mountains, and golden wheat grew wildly about.

"Ojin, why couldn't this place be further down the mountainside, closer to Durdan? Seems difficult to reach."

"The Fields of Effugere are protected here, and they serve as a challenge for those who found this purpose. To the west, you have the Ashi. To the East you have the Groves and Pools of Cordis Loci backed by the highest mountain peaks of all of Mürindür. All are fraught with trials," Ojin explained.

"Seems cruel," Creed noted.

"Cruelty forges strength for many," Ojin replied.

"And death for many more?"

"Those that seek the grain of Effugere are purposed as such. Should they die while serving the realm with grain, many go onto the Endüerduul."

"A purpose of grain?" Creed asked.

"The grain is everlasting. The flour ground from the tufts makes the bread that feeds the masses of Mürindür. It is the first food survivors of the Transitio dunes taste within the Redemptio Keep. It is a renewal. A promise." Ojin smiled at Creed and motioned to the fields with his large hands. The wind tussled with Ojin's beard, tugging on it like a small child.

"And such a promise is obtained only through sacrifice?" asked, Creed.

"Simply put, the grain would not be what it is without the willingness of others to give of themselves, their hard work in the harvest, but they are not meant to die, Creed. They are challenged. They are exposed here, and isolated, but never truly alone. Bellatorum and the soldiers of Durdan have always helped to protect them. Together hundreds of farmers bring us hope in the bales you see below, and that sustains us all." Ojin placed his hand on his friend's shoulder.

As they walked further, the slender vegetation towered toward them, much higher than it had appeared from the Ashi exit. The tips brushed Bog's belly as Xaris rode ahead. Periodically, treetops broke the sky as the dark soil beneath their feet folded soft and warm. Pax reached out to touch the tufts of wheat. Creed watched him, and wondered what he was thinking at this very moment. If he had so many questions, surely Pax did as well, but looking at the diminutive Ogre, there was no fear or concern. Pax simply cradled a soft grin as the wheat tickled his fingertips.

Xaris stopped the group to look at something ahead, and Creed used this opportunity to dismount Bog to walk about as well. Mindful of where he was, his curiosity took hold. He grabbed a small amount of dirt in his hands, held it to his face, smelling it. Rich like coffee grounds, the odor was organically soothing. Creed slid his boots across the surface, close to a row of bundled grain. No one was around, but there it sat. Nicely gathered and stacked, six feet tall and ten feet deep, seemingly for pickup.

Perhaps that's how it works here, harvesters and gatherers, he wondered.

The trail was worn, having evolved beneath seemingly hundreds of thousands of hooves and feet. He could almost sense the countless souls toiling in the fields hoping to bring something meaningful home to their brethren. It was an honest and simple path indeed. At times though, he wondered if in fact it could be a trap, so open, and so easily approached from above. It was tempting Fate to work throughout the day here, and yet they would, selflessly for purpose, and for the greater good.

He looked into the sky and noticed the birds were gone as his foot snagged on something harsh, and he nearly fell to the ground with a pull to his knee. Creed knelt down, and dusted the site, uncovering a long dark arrow. The shaft appeared to be a deep rust colored bone, but the arrowhead had been carved from black flint. Its fletching composed of Raven feathers. Dried blood tattooed the shaft.

"Ojin, look what I found."

Ojin's eyes widened, and he jumped down from Bog hurriedly.

"Put that down! Now!"

The arrow seemed to vibrate. Creed dropped it into the trench from whence it came. He smelled a brief whiff of sulfur. As he looked about, he realized debris was all around, spears were broken, and hidden behind veils of stalks, shards of metal lay strewn like shrapnel with horse carcasses half buried in the dust. The wind was still, and the air became quiet.

"Those arrows are from Leterum's Keep. Fired from the bows of Caedere archers. All things dark remain dark," Ojin explained. He spit on the ground.

"When did this happen?" Creed wondered.

"Xaris, do you know?" Ojin questioned.

"Likely days ago, when the last harvest was begun." Xaris rode back to them, and dismounted to get a better look.

"Did anyone try to protect them?" asked, Creed.

"Yes." Xaris stepped slowly off the path, and bent the brush down further. Creed could see golden armor embracing bones. Xaris went to touch them, but they dissipated into a fine gray dust. The wind picked up, and the ashes were gone.

"Who were they?"

"That was what remained of a Bellator," explained Ojin.

"I thought they couldn't be killed." Creed walked over to touch the armor. It was cold, even in the sun.

"Apparently, now they can. This may explain the Centurions and the bridge to the Undüavalle. Serena mentioned it was untethered. The Centurions guarding the gates had to fall for the Mael'deua to escape. This must be what has changed. This is why the Caedere roam freely, and the fighting has escalated. I have never seen such a thing until now." Ojin spoke softly as if he did not wish the wind to hear.

"So, what can possibly kill a Bellator?" Creed asked.

"I do not know. Xaris, have you heard of this?"

"A farmer weeks ago mentioned seeing a Bellator fall, but the farmer died in his village shortly after, and we have no other witnesses. Bellatorum are immortal like Serena. They have existed as long as anyone should hope to remember. This must truly be dark magic," Xaris explained.

"This has never been described to my knowledge, and Serena didn't mention it although she surely knows. Leterum has found a way to breach immortality." Ojin looked to Creed with raised brows. His tusks flattened the fur upon his face. Creed could see he was worried.

"Perhaps she wishes to discuss more privately," Xaris suggested.

"Perhaps. What we've always presumed to be our greatest protection has now become vulnerable to the whims of this foul play." Ojin studied the fields intensely. "I had hoped to see Serena at the Grove's edge, but for now, I see nothing. Make haste. We move to the woods. We have little time."

The hobgoblin held up the Penumbra, and encouraged his friends to enter it. Ojin hopped up on to Bog, but Xaris walked beside Nos instead. Creed attached his horse to the armor hook, and trailed behind. They walked in a solemn procession past abandoned wagon carts full of harvest across the fields. Intermittent pieces of golden Bellator armor lay scattered. The road into the Groves wound slightly, obscuring the next few hundred yards. Creed couldn't help but feel they were being lured into something inescapable.

"Why would anyone attack farmers? Why attack the fields?" Creed asked.

"Leterum is wise to attack the Fields of Effugere. No grain, no food. No food, no Hope. No Hope, and the souls in Redemptio will wither. Leterum has gained ground, shut down supply lines, stopped the harvest of the Fields, and now sewn chaos throughout Mürindür. This was a well-executed plan with something unknown to us for so long, and I cannot help but feel something else at play here. There are more hands than we have accounted for." Ojin continued to speak with a lowered voice despite the Penumbra.

Creed saw arrows buried deep within a series of broken wagons. Something akin to a donkey carcass was riddled with them. Death was thinly veiled beneath the tranquil scene he looked upon from the Ashi doorway. As Creed noticed another set of immortal remains sunken beneath a shield, his back began to vibrate from the metal staff. It warmed quickly. He stopped for fear of it catching fire, and fumbled with the shoulder straps to get it off. In his haste, he ignored the group advancing forward, and slowly came out the back end of the Penumbra. Ojin looked back and shouted to Creed to reenter the dome, but the sound was muffled, and Creed was distracted.

At first the hairs bristled upon his neck when the air shifted violently above. The fields swayed in the tumult like a descending tornado prepares its footing. Dark-winged beasts were coming from as far south as the Mountain pass. Many of them landed on the oak trees nearby. The ground shook with a thud. He looked up to see large vultures all around, and then he heard the whispers.

The wheat tops wove to and fro with a frenetic pace of the impending ambush. He tore his weapon from the ropes, stood, and held it tightly. For a moment, the Ravens and vultures silenced. Creed closed his eyes, took a breath, and opened them in time to see the Caedere enter the open road. Nine of the beastly cursed creatures stood before him. Their whispers were deafening though their woven mouths did not move.

There was no ceremonious initiation. The Caedere charged, and as if to surrender to the inevitability, Creed relaxed into a wide stance. He knew he would not be able to run from them. This was his stand, and invariably he would confront what others could not.

His mind raced uncontrollably to a mid-day training session with the Greek hoplites. He had been weary that day from hours of training, but as the instructor struck at him, he found new vigor. In short time, his teacher lay on his back looking up to an emboldened young man.

Creed's memory broke as quickly as the first Caedere sabre thrust toward his face. Down he struck to parry, and with a turn of his hips the glaive tore through its ashen wing. The Caedere wailed and fell to a knee as tarry blood dripped to the ground. The other assailants followed suit, and Creed swept and lunged to engage them all. He severed a hoof from one, and a head from another. The tumultuous campaign ceased briefly as the headless Caedere corpse fell into the wheat, and the ghastly, grimacing face twitched its last moment of existence.

"Ahhhh. So, you aren't strangers to Death after all." Creed smiled.

He felt strong, and emboldened by the ease with which he moved. An air of confidence enveloped him, and the fight ensued. As his weapon spun in a murderous cantation across the Caedere, something else fell beside him. It was Xaris, back to his back, wielding his blades in unison. Ojin joined them, raised the earth like a sheet with his large arms in a spell, and snapped it down to startle, and confuse them all. This unsettled the Caedere, as the Ravens fled, and now seven stood before them, backing off slightly to form a new line. They crouched as their robes seized slowly in the wind, and then, a loud wail split the moment.

"AYEEEE-SSSHHHAAAAAHHH!!"

An ominous flash crushed the ground before them. A Caedere unlike any other, dressed in robes of yellow and blood-orange hues, held chains with sharpened hooks in either hand. She stood taller than the rest, and long white hair undulated about her neck, but unlike her brethren, her wings were severed at the back, and chains of imprisonment laced her chest. She seethed at Creed, and his glaive glowed white hot in his hands. There was something lurid and unholy with this creature. Creed's smile was gone, and the confidence he had minutes earlier was no more. Somehow, he knew this creature was the reason the immortals were dying. "CREED STOP." But Creed didn't listen to Ojin. There was no other way. She wouldn't leave without her prize, and Creed suspected it was inevitable.

He sprinted forward as did she, her orange robes trailing behind. Rusted, twisted chains whipped the air, and imprisoned his glaive like hellish tendrils. Though he pulled angrily against the restraints, she didn't move. The other Caedere charged once more, and Xaris and Ojin took them on while Pax's crossbow hurled bolts into the taught faces of the enemy, disrupting their attack. Bog crushed one of the beasts between an overturned cart and his tusks. Xaris dove to cut the ankles of one Caedere as Ojin thrust his staff into the chest of another.

Creed slid in the dirt as the enigma drew him closer, and despite his strength, she seemed to move him at will. He pulled once more with all his might as he fell to his knees, and the leader tumbled violently over him into a broken wagon. The splintered wood flew into Bog's reaping tusks as he slung Caedere left and right while Pax littered their crippled bodies with the last of his ammunition. Ojin continued to block and strike with his staff, while flinging bursts of wind into their formation, harnessing their wings into sails of retreat. Xaris thrust his blades into a wounded Caedere, and scissored them through its thorax, halving another creature in the Fields of Effugere.

The leader stood quickly from her fall, and pulled her chains into a whirlwind about her head. She turned from Creed, and thrust the hooks toward Pax. One hook struck the little Ogre in the leg, and she pulled viciously ripping flesh from his thigh. He screamed and gurgled in agony falling into the dirt, and Bog turned too late as another one of her hooks buried itself into his flank just shy of his armor. Before the chains had returned to their master, Bog bled uncontrollably over his fur, collapsing to his side. He let out one last forceful cry from his trunk.

"BRRRAAAAMMMPPHHHHH!"

Ojin turned to see his friend fallen, listless, and vulnerable. As he strode frantically to aid Bog, a Caedere struck his back knocking him to his knees. Xaris ran to his side, and blocked another strike. Three Caedere faced off with him as two more flanked Creed, and another twenty Caedere came from the west. The Ashi retreat was no more, and the Eastern route was held hostage by the fiend. Creed looked to the fields for their escape on either side, but the wounded would never make it.

The leader swung her hooks in a high arc, aiming for the neck of Xaris, but Creed was blocked by the oncoming assault, and wouldn't make it in time to help.

"XARIS!" Creed screamed. The hooks glistened in blood and fading sunlight.

CLANG!

A silver arrow spliced them both, and the chains missed their intent. A horn bugled across the fields with such a deep resonance it made it difficult to breathe. A Calvary of two hundred Bellatorum led by Serena and Celeste tore through the harvest ruins, and drove into the Caedere like waves upon the shore. The Bellatorum impaled their spears into the chests of the Caedere, and the creatures burst into sand and ash. Two Caedere were upon

Creed with weapons raised, but arrows felled them with deep strikes to their skulls. One Bellator cut through a Caedere with his blade, and rode ambitiously toward the wingless Matriarch. She slung him from his saddle to the ground by his boot, and thrust her fists into his chest. She ripped his soul in two, and the immortal grayed into oblivion. His ashes rose as smoke from a funeral pyre. Creed stood astonished. He readied himself for the impossible. "TO ME YOU WITCH!!"

She turned, and her face wrinkled into a strained grin. She ran and jumped into the air; her chains striking inches from his feet as Creed lunged backwards. She towered above him, and her reach was nearly twice as long. They clashed once more. Her speed met by his. His glaive incensed the air at times carelessly wafting past the dry wheat chaff. Embers glowed within flickered flames, but Ojin held out his hand to snuff them with frigid bursts of air between each of his breaths. Creed struck at her once more, but as she ducked, her chains wrapped his legs like serpents. She pulled him hard, and his head struck a rock. Creed's eyes watered, and his movements were slowed despite his efforts. He held up his hand to block her claws, but she kicked it away. She struck at his chest, but he managed to drive his glaive across his stomach to tear into her back leg. Shrieking with hatred as her black essence seeped into the soil, the beast raised her clenched fist to end him. Creed held his breath.

Twin arrows buried themselves within the witch's shoulders locking them in place, and knocking her back a few feet. Celeste leapt from her horse, bow in hand, and three arrows drawn. She stood over Creed, and the women stared at one another.

The Ravens flew away, and the vultures had all but vanished. Xaris held pressure on Ojin's wounds, and a motionless Bog lie withered beside the trail. Creed's vision returned, and the presence of Celeste strengthened him into an instinctive rage. He thrust the glaive, and severed the chains across his legs. The Matriarch stumbled from the sudden break in traction. She reached slowly to her shoulders, and broke off the arrows; their shafts dissolving in her palms. The chains about her chest lengthened into her hands once more, and now spikes dangled on either end.

"Be gone, *Anima Capere*! Your Caedere are no more! Leterum is absent. You will die in these fields as the vermin you are!" Celeste's aim and voice were unwavering as the bowstring held taut with vengeance. Serena rode up and dismounted behind her.

"Celeste, step back."

"She is contained."

"The *Anima Capere* is never contained. Where is your master, demon? Call him to me!"

The whispers were high pitched as if in laughter. Serena looked to the ground and saw the disheveled armor of her fallen soldier. Her eyes lit with fire, and Creed felt his hands burn. The Anima reached back with her arms to strike, but no sooner had she done so then she disappeared in a wave of smoke and wind. Celeste let loose her arrows, but they flew into the fields ahead. The Anima was gone.

"Celeste, you are with child! It is a not a promise to take lightly!" Serena admonished.

"Neither is my promise to this man," Celeste countered. The Princess looked to Creed and her face softened.

Creed stood, vigilant, adrenaline pulsating through his vessels, but he wished to hold her. They stared at one another for a moment. It was all too brief as Serena motioned to her Bellatorum.

"Celeste, it isn't safe. Let us move to the Groves. We need to tend to the wounded."

"Understood, Mother."

Creed's warmth faded as he looked around the road. He felt guilt for his brief reprieve while his friends lay bleeding. Pax appeared to be in shock, and Bog wasn't moving. Although Ojin tried to get to his friend, he was too weak, and Xaris had to hold him steady. Creed grabbed the little Ogre instead, and carried him from the ditch to the road as Bellatorum circled the caravan.

Pax struggled to breathe, and the large wound in his thigh had seemingly severed a vessel, but he still had a pulse. As Creed tore fabric from a wagon to place a tourniquet, Serena walked by, and slowly massaged the wound as she closed her eyes and sang enchantments softly. The wound beneath her hands steamed and cauterized itself. Serena breathed into Pax's mouth, and he coughed up clotted blood repeatedly until his eyes opened. Unaware and scared, Pax drew up into a ball, rocking and crying. Creed spoke to him, rubbing his head.

"Pax! Pax, it's me. Just breathe. Breathe. You're safe. They're gone." Celeste worked on Bog as Serena went to a struggling Ojin.

"Serena, get me to Bog," the hobgoblin pleaded.

"My old friend, didn't you know Caedere should best be avoided?"

"Yes, but where would the adventure be in that?" Ojin winced as she pulled back his cloak to unveil the raw, exposed flesh beneath his fur. She did the same for him as she had for Pax, and within moments the wound was covered by tender pink granulation tissue.

"Mother, Bog isn't responding!" Celeste shouted, tearful and dismayed. Creed ran to the mammoth along with Ojin and Serena. Bog wasn't breathing, and his wound had been bled dry.

Ojin kneeled and laid his head to his friend's chest, gripping the mammoth's fur with angst-laden fingers. His ears wished for anything besides the vacuous reality he faced. Serena placed her hands on Ojin for what was now painfully apparent. Bog was gone. "I'm sorry, so sorry, my friend. He was truly beloved, and a wonder to behold."

Ojin wept, and buried his face into the wooly fur, sobbing. Everyone held their heads low, but Xaris fumed and kicked a Caedere corpse as Creed paced, running his hands through his hair. This was his fault. He lost the initiative, and now a friend lay dead. "Is there nothing more that can be done?" Creed asked.

"No. I'm afraid not. Once Leterum senses the end, he takes what is his." Serena stood beside Ojin with her hand upon his back.

"NO! NO! NO WAY! Leterum can go to Hell! He gets nothing! NOTHING!" Creed was beside himself with anger as he reached into the wound, and felt its coolness. He ran back to his glaive, and thrust it into the cavity. The clotted blood bubbled and boiled. The wound edges reached for one another once more, but as the flesh grew slowly across the gaping hole, the color did not change. It was gray and as pale as before.

"He needs blood! We need blood!" Creed shouted.

"How do you plan that we do that? Haven't we spilled enough today?" Xaris questioned angrily.

"Ojin, you said the Luxatio remains are powerful," Creed reminded him.

"Yes," Ojin confirmed.

"Remains are tissue! Blood is tissue! My remains! Use my blood!"

"No, my love!" Celeste protested.

"It's safe. Just a few pints. We need some line. Something like a small tube that's hollow inside." He looked about, and grabbed a wheat stalk, breaking it off to see if the inside was indeed hollow. "We'll use these. Bind the ends together. We only need a few," Creed instructed everyone. They gathered enough unbroken stalks for tubing, and Creed burrowed under the fur to find Bog's femoral vein.

"Xaris, give me your knife." Xaris scowled, and shook his head in refusal.

"Here take this." Celeste handed him her dagger. Creed cut the hide just deep enough, shoved the stalk into the blood vessel, and then shaved off the other end. He looked at his arm briefly, and then stuck himself as well. The pain was sudden, but not too unfamiliar. Slowly, the tubing filled with his Luxatio blood.

"Ojin, I need you to do whatever it is you do when the earth moves and the air becomes heavy. You need to compress his big chest between the air and the ground, repeatedly until I say stop. Your Grace?"

"Yes," replied Serena.

"Do for him as you did Pax. Xaris, stop the infusion when I pass out."

"I'll have no such part of this black magic. Things dead are best left dead." Xaris walked away as Ojin looked at him painfully.

"Look at me, Ojin! He's not dead! Not yet. Celeste, please. When I begin to look pale, pull the tubing from us both, and hold pressure over my arm, and Ojin you can put pressure over his thigh. This will work. We need electricity of some kind. Sparks."

"I can provide the sparks as well," Serena acknowledged.

"Ok. Once the blood is on board, and the compressions and breathing are going, deliver the electricity to his chest. Specifically, here," as Creed pointed behind Bog's right shoulder.

"I can do that," Serena affirmed.

"Ok. Ok then. Let's go."

Ojin stood and forced Bog's chest to compress over and over again. Serena closed her eyes, breathing forcibly into the mammoth's face, so much so that his cheeks bulged from the pressure. It began to rain and a gentle mist settled about them. The wheat stalk fragments were aglow with Creed's blood, and as the sun set, the tubing cast a dim light from Creed's arm to Bog's thigh. They continued for what seemed to be half an hour. Creed's head became light and his breathing shallow as he looked to Celeste, and everything became gray. He couldn't speak, and his pulse was in his ears now, beating rapidly. The last he remembered was Celeste kneeling at his side, and sparks coming from Serena.

Chapter 14: The Groves

He awoke to Pax squatting beside him tucking a blanket beneath his chin and arm pits. The Ogre's eyes grew when he saw Creed move, so he hurried to the boiling pot above the fire, and brought his patient a wooden bowl of steaming broth. Creed glanced about, weakly and marginally nauseous, to find Serena speaking with Ojin while she rubbed his back wound. Creed didn't see Bog, however. He felt panic, and hoped his fears were premature. Although his stomach muscles cramped and twitched, Creed spoke loud enough to draw everyone's attention.

"Where is Bog? Bog? BOG!" Serena looked to him and stood, as did Ojin. Their faces were stern. They walked over slowly. "Where is he?"

He sat up, despite the ground spinning somewhat, and as he listed to his left a little, a gentle, warm hairy trunk embraced him, and sat him upright again.

"Well, you happen to be laying on him my friend." Ojin hunched slightly as he made his way to the makeshift infirmary. Creed looked over his shoulder, and saw Bog's big eyes, heavy with fatigue, staring right back at him. The eyes and the gentle stroke of his trunk assured Creed he would make it. The physician teared up with relief. He grabbed a tuft of fur, and hugged as tightly as he could, exhaling the guilt.

"They came out of nowhere, and for a moment I... I wanted it to happen. I never once thought about any of you. Bog, I'm sorry." Bog licked his face.

"Ha! He hasn't done that in years!" Ojin smiled as he leaned on Creed's shoulder.

"Creed, I saw you fumbling with your weapon. It seemed to create smoke off your clothing. I knew something was amiss, but you couldn't hear me. We know you didn't do this intentionally. You likely felt something very familiar when they charged you. That's good. You will need that." Ojin smiled and his tusks stretched it a little further.

"It worked. I'm glad he's alive. I can't believe it worked!" Creed said excitedly.

"Yes, it did, Creed," Serena noted. "We were all amazed. I have healed many things in Mürindür, but never have I seen Leterum lose his prey. Shortly after you collapsed, Bog's eyes opened. He's very weak, but has been awake since." Serena clasped her hands.

"Just science, and a miracle," Creed added.

"More than that. Your blood was something we've never used before. Luxatio blood is unique, and I doubt anything else truly mattered."

"You both are weak. We suffered back there, and are lucky to be alive. Tonight, we need to rest. Bog may not be able to travel far. It will put us behind schedule, but at least for now we have regrouped." Ojin stretched and winced. Creed looked to him.

"Where is Celeste?"

"She is gathering herbs from the woods," Serena explained.

"Alone?" Creed sat forward, a bit more. Serena smiled, and placed her hand on his face.

"Besides the Bellatorum around our camp? Xaris is with her."

"Oh." Creed didn't know why, but that didn't seem very reassuring despite it all. He looked at his bowl of broth. Had he an appetite, it was all but lost now.

"How long have they been gone?" he asked.

"An hour perhaps. She wished to make a salve for Bog, and another broth for you. We moved here to the Groves once Bog was strong enough to stand, but it won't be long before Leterum launches another attack."

"Exactly, so why is she in the woods?"

"She isn't alone, Creed. Settle." Ojin patted Creed's back.

"She's alone with him," Creed noted.

"Xaris has watched over her for years. He's been an excellent guardian for us both." Serena looked at him gently.

"Not always. Not when I am with her. I need to get up. I need to go."

"No. You need to rest. We trust him, Creed. You should as well." Serena motioned to her Bellatorum nearby to come assist Creed to a bed.

"Well I'm here now. Which way did they go?" He stood and lunged, but as if in a drunken stupor, his body invariably tumbled to one side, yet again, as his hand searched for the nearest tree trunk.

"Easy. Easy. They will be back soon." Ojin steadied his friend.

"Where is my weapon?" Creed asked.

"You mean this?" Serena held his glaive upright as she addressed him. The blue flame grew as it neared.

"Yes. I need that. Please give it to me." He held his head, as it seemed the entire camp was spinning.

"You need to sit down, listen right now, and not speak. I'm not sure you are aware of the significance of this artifact. Do you know what this weapon represents? Do you even know its name? Ojin tells me you found this in the troll camp."

"It simply came alive. It called to me." He took a few steps, and then leaned on one of the tents. He managed to clasp the shaft of the polearm, and steadied himself looking at Serena.

"Yes. I'm sure it did call to you." Her face relaxed, "Of that I am certain, but the question is why? This has not been seen since the Cataclysm, much like its brother Ejiciam, and the original master of this weapon died in the battle."

"Who was it?"

Serena looked at the engravings, scrolled as knurl about the spine. "He was an archangel named Elyptos, my General of the Bellatorum. We fought side by side during the Cataclysm, and this weapon was his alone to command. He named it Üstor, forged from within the Endüerduul. When it was employed in war, Üstor shown brightly and its heat could be felt hundreds of feet away. I still remember when its blue light faded as Elyptos fell. The weapon was lost those many years ago, and now you stumble upon it in the Ashi. Hidden all this time amongst trolls. It seems too readily convenient, honestly."

"Üstor?" Creed asked. Ojin leaned in closer to inspect the relic. "Üstor nearly killed Leterum, scarring his face, and imprisoning him on Mürindür. It is not something Leterum will take lightly should he see it." Creed looked at Üstor, and could feel it reaching out to him. Serena could feel the heat as well. Creed let go for a moment to wipe his brow of sweat, and Serena laid the weapon against a nearby stone.

"Get some sleep. I believe I've told enough tales for one night."
Creed leaned to secure Üstor when he heard leaves rustling behind
them. Serena turned and smiled.

"Celeste, he just woke."

"My love, what are you doing up?" The Princess had just returned
with Xaris, carrying satchels full of herbs. "You need to regain
your strength."

"Why did you leave?" Creed questioned.

"To make you well. Please, sit." She hugged him tightly, and
escorted him back to rest beside Bog.

"Xaris was with me, and we weren't far."

"That's supposed to make me feel better?"

"Why yes. Normally I would go alone, but Mother insisted."

Creed didn't care anymore as he reached for her face. It was soft
and as beautiful as he remembered. Her eyes were intoxicating. She
leaned in to kiss him, and reveled in it for a moment before their
lips touched. The kiss was enticingly warm, and as Creed's heart
sped, his skin raised up as goose bumps, which she could feel with
her nails across his arms. She opened her eyes, and laughed gently.

"After all these years, I still have a way with you, don't I?" Creed
paused to regain his mental footing albeit cumbersome just the
same.

"Yes. I'd say so, but another go may confirm my suspicions."
Creed grinned.

"Another go, eh?" she quipped.

"Okay now," Ojin interrupted. "Save some of that for the wedding
night, you two. Let us eat, and make plans for the next stage. We
still have to travel, and there are many preparations needed before
the ceremony can take place. Now, in your best interest," as he

looked at Creed, "I recommend you drink some more soup, and rest."

The hobgoblin limped to the dinner meal as Xaris walked off to unload the herbs he and Celeste had collected. As Serena conferred with one of her generals, Ojin could be seen turning multiple spits around a large fire of hickory. Various meats cooked slowly as pots simmered in unison. Pax and Bog played a simple game of tic-tac-toe in the dirt. It was surreal for Creed to witness such comfort and peace when only hours before all of them were on Death's doorstep.

"The farmers of the Fields would often rest here beneath the shade as they snacked on the walnuts, pecans, and peach trees," Celeste explained as Creed looked about with his bowl of soup. "Now they scarcely have time to harvest the grain, and each time they do, it is at their peril. I hope to see the day when they all can sit beneath the leaves once more, and laughter fills the air. That would be a wonderful day indeed."

The Groves extended for thousands of acres, dense with communes of old walnut trees, pecans, great oaks, and fruited shrubs. Blackberry bushes carpeted the landscape along with strawberries and honeysuckle, while fig trees speckled the foliage.

"We used to spend days here, camping beneath the two moons and infinite stars. You would always fall asleep in my arms." Celeste smiled, kissed Creed's forehead gently, and stood to walk toward her tent.

"Where are you going?" Creed asked.

"I'll be right back. I need to get something." Creed watched her disappear behind the tanned hides of her doorway. She returned with something in her hand. A cylinder wrapped in silver.

"What's that?" She laughed and kept it out of reach as he leaned for it.

"It's not for you, silly. It's for him. It's a smaller variation of my own." She looked over to Pax, and motioned him to come forward. "Pax, you were very brave back there. Few souls have ever willingly stood up to one Caedere let alone an entire raiding party. Ojin tells me you also helped fight off the trolls, and if it weren't for your precision and persistence, my husband might not be here now. This is a small gift of thanks for you, and your bravery at all costs. It is an Infinitus quiver. It holds an endless supply of bolts for your new crossbow, which my blacksmith just finished. Let's see if it works."

She motioned to her tent as a Minotaur walked forward with a small silver crossbow in his hands. He smiled at Pax, and knelt down to offer it to him. Pax was indeed intimidated, backing away briefly until Bog nudged him forward. The Ogre held out his tremulous hands, and the Minotaur placed the bow within them. Pax held his arms stiff and dare not move. Celeste smiled, and placed the quiver on top of the bow. Pax looked at everyone, and turned to Bog sitting with his back to the crowd.

Pax studied the quiver, and rubbed the shiny, silvery case. Creed looked it over as well, and noticed that the entire apparatus was finely hammered into overlapping scales. The Ogre laid the quiver down, and raised the crossbow. The weapon was a perfect fit to his shoulder and cheek, and it had two flight grooves for shooting simultaneous bolts, Creed noticed. Pax pulled the string quickly into its latch with his foot buried in the stirrup. He reached into the quiver, and placed two bolts into their resting positions one beside the other. With his back to Creed, he aimed at a nearby peach tree.

218

THWACK!

Both bolts decimated their peach targets no more than a few inches apart from one another. He shook his left hand repeatedly, and grunted excitedly toward Bog. The gentle trunk patted him on the back. Pax turned toward Celeste, and awkwardly bowed. She bowed in return as he looked excitedly into the quiver once more. Not a single bolt was missing.

"Where's my gift?" Creed protested.

"Oh? Is that how it's going to be then? What about this gift I carry for you morning and night? Hmmm?" She stood close to Creed, and he laid his cheek softly against her belly.

"Oh, well I thought that was your idea."

"Ohh! You!" The couple laughed as she swatted at Creed's hair. Serena watched from a distance, and sat down next to Ojin in front of the campfire.

"He seems his old self, but I can sense something unsettled," she said.

"He isn't completely where he needs to be, but he will be soon. Remember, you often wouldn't see him for days once he fell before. It didn't take long for him to jump back into combat this go-round. I think we will all recognize our Hippocrates very soon," Ojin explained.

Creed could scarcely overhear them. His smile lessened, and he feigned disinterest while straining his ears.

"Perhaps," the Queen replied.

"He is different, however."

"How so?" asked Serena.

"When he has been confronted, upset on a few occasions since he arrived, his emotions become volatile."

"In what way?"

"His fire is inextricably derived from something otherworldly. More so than anything I could hope or fear to conjure. I haven't seen anything like it. The ferocity at times is frightening."

"That may explain why Üstor calls to him," Serena pondered.

"The fire is sudden and devastating, Serena. He destroyed an entire troll camp by himself. He nearly blew Durdan Keep into oblivion. He is aware of it, and I have warned him not to tap into it until we could talk with you."

"He's never done this before?"

"No," Ojin confirmed.

"Fire is a great weapon."

"Yes, but fearsome and unpredictable. Do you know why he would discover this now, Serena?"

"No, but you mentioned ferocity. The weapon he holds is rare indeed, and it is not happenstance that it found him in the Ashi mines. Elyptos had a great deal of ferocity too. In battle, I would often have to bring him back from the front lines because he refused to seek peace. He often suffered from a righteous bloodlust, and it was all that I could do to keep him restrained. Peace was always tenuous if he were involved in the negotiations."

"Was there ever really peace with Leterum?"

"You forget what Mürindür was like before the Cataclysm. At times, so do I. The only enemy back then was Acrom. Often times, when the battle horns yielded, nothing was left on the field but broken souls, remains of mortals too naïve to understand the path they had chosen. It pained me to see the casualties. The demons would return to the nether, but the souls had no choice but to be imprisoned, tortured indefinitely. Elyptos saw no need of mercy for any of them, despite their torment, because he felt their choices deserved punishment. His compassion was virtually nonexistent, and although he was a brilliant warrior, his heart was too hard for diplomacy. He very much saw a line in the sand for which not to cross. Everything either stood on one side or the other. There was no middle ground to be had." Serena stirred the fire slowly with her hand.

"Diplomacy often blurs such lines," Ojin said pointedly.

"Indeed, but for peace, diplomacy must transpire. Elyptos couldn't see that."

"I had heard of Elyptos, and met him once on Earth. He was disguised as a farmer. An entire race was enslaved, and he sought to topple the empire that confined them. We talked briefly about existence, and his words remain within my mind. 'Truth is the only light, and without it, Justice forfeits victory'. He seemed to be quite honorable."

"Yes, he was. His convictions guided many of his Bellatorum. They believed in him. Even when we disagreed, they believed in him."

"That must have created quite the dilemma."

"Not so. I am not too blind to forego reason. There were times when his counsel was well served. He chose where to place Durdan. I wanted it further away from the Mountains, closer to the Capital, but he argued it was the ideal strategic location. By guarding the River Ebon, it created a border unlike any other. We built the city exactly where he wished it to be."

"I wasn't there when he fell."

"No, I sent you away to find more reinforcements." Her face became solemn.

"And by the time I arrived, the major fighting was over." Ojin recalled.

"Yes. The Cataclysm was all but over. We had driven Acrom beyond the Great Divide, and when Leterum rallied his troops in an attempt to flank us, Elyptos charged alone to challenge Leterum. He offered himself to buy us time, on one condition. They were to forego their ethereal form, and fight as men. Leterum was too bold to refuse. He had long thought himself the most powerful, and as the Angel of Death, he foresaw what he presumed to be his future. His pride was blinding. Leterum and Elyptos fought across the Divide. Acrom was trapped within the chasm, and the Bellatorum were building a wall of his demons' remains. All that was left was the gate."

"Once I had returned with help, the gate was already standing," Ojin added.

"It wasn't without great sacrifice," Serena noted.

"I've heard the stories. Leterum killed Elyptos."

"No, not exactly. I rarely speak of it, so people have constructed what they think to be the truth." She paused for a moment, seemingly lost in thought. Celeste had gone back to her tent, and for the last few minutes, Creed had moved closer, leaning behind a nearby tree to listen.

"The battle between them raged on for days. We recovered our wounded, our ranks swelled once more, and once we invaded the Undüavalle to put an end to Acrom, Leterum made a crucial mistake. He sent his legions to our rear hoping to trap us within the Undüavalle. He had no idea I negotiated a weakened Acrom's surrender. We had already returned in the Fuga, victorious, by the time his last troops had entered. Leterum was surrounded and alone. I told him what I had done, and insisted that he follow suit. He refused. With that, he rose into his ethereal form, and struck Elyptos in the belly with his blade. Elyptos forbid us from intervening, and as he struggled to breathe, he cast upon himself a flame much like the brightest of stars. It was searing, blinding, he emerged as an ethereal, and Üstor erupted. The flash was apocalyptic, and in that moment, Leterum fell. Üstor had buried itself in his chest, striking his face on the descent. There they crumbled, two great angels, weary and wounded. As I rushed to Elyptos, Leterum looked at me for a moment, and dissipated into the wind. He was gone, shamed and defeated. Leterum's beasts made an attempt to traverse the Divide. Elyptos called to me, and asked that I help him to the gate. I refused, but as usual, what he sought was in fact the answer. We were losing the momentum." Serena turned her head slightly in Creed's direction, and continued stirring the flames.

"And Leterum?" Ojin asked.

"Gone. Even as his legions bore down upon the gate in a desperate last attempt to escape, he had abdicated his promise to Acrom. When I brought him to the gates, Elyptos took his hands and coated them in his own blood. He spoke an incantation as he laid them on the wet mortar, and with an ungodly embrace, the gate tore into his soul, and drank him into the stone. It was not enough, for the gate remained open, but inspired by his sacrifice, six more Bellatorum threw themselves upon the arched rock. The gate grew in stature, and sealed itself in an opaque glass consuming my soldiers. Acrom and his demons crashed into it from the other side, but it withstood their onslaught. They were imprisoned. Their fate was sealed with the loss of my greatest champion. Six more of our Bellatorum stepped forward, and promised an existence of guardianship. They would hold the gate until their last breath. I forged the Obsidian Bridge across the Divide, and the Undüavalle Gates were secure. The Gates have held until now. My guardians are gone, and the Gates have been breached. We have been on the run ever since." Serena sighed.

"How did this happen, and how do we not have more demons ravaging our lands?"

"I'm not sure how it transpired, Ojin. Mürindür shook as you know, and I went with my army to investigate. We found the remains of two centurions as piles of ash within their armor. I do not know what happened to the others, but the Obsidian Bridge was broken, and the Great Divide was unbound once more. I could see the gates were cracked and twisted, which makes me wonder about Creed. If Elyptos had escaped his imprisonment, it is possible..."

"What's possible?" Creed interjected.

"Creed! Go sit down," Ojin directed.

"It's okay, Ojin. He's been listening the entire time. It's good you wonder too, Creed. It must be confusing with so much going on inside your mind."

"At times," Creed replied.

"You mustn't let that disturbance within, define who you are. Remember that, my son. You are more than a single moment in time. You are Luxatio. You are one of our finest," Serena reminded him even though Creed struggled with what that even meant.

"We found demons in the Lacus Atromento, Serena." Ojin glanced in the direction of the Ashi as if the mere mention of them would send Mael'deua over the hill, scurrying for an attack.

"I wondered. I heard the Ashi cry out. It felt as if it were in pain."

"Urcinis was there," Ojin replied.

"Yes, my kind-hearted guardian. How does she look? I heard she'd fallen ill."

"Kind? She nearly ate us," Creed said as he made his way to sit beside them both.

"Yes, I'm sure she did. She is a giant bear after all." Serena laughed.

"Creed fixed her infection. Within moments, her face was as good as new."

"You've never ceased to amaze me, Hippocrates." Serena spoke glowingly.

"The Mael'deua were preparing for something. An altar was empty, but responsive. What do you think that means?" Ojin stretched his back once more, and bent sharply from the pain.

"Acrom. He is probing every possibility. He will not rest until he finds the means to escape."

"Can the Gates be repaired? Replaced?" asked Creed.

"I do not know. We did not have enough time to study the damage. Acrom sensed our presence, and the demons were coming for us."

"Did this have something to do with the witch back there?" Ojin wondered.

"That witch I suspect, the Anima Capere, has *everything* to do with it. I fought her outside the Capital of Guillarne as she attacked a caravan from Redemptio. I witnessed her kill a handful of my Bellatorum before we cornered her. As I assumed, she was trapped, I turned but for a second, and she severed the body of my general before disappearing into smoke. Never before have I seen something so easily defeat my immortals. Leterum created her somehow through vile means."

"Have you seen him?"

"Leterum?"

"Yes," Ojin confirmed.

"No. Not in some time." She stood as well, rolling yellow flames across her fingertips like coins.

"He has violated the laws over and over again. Is there nothing he won't waste in his path? It's as if he wants the entire universe to burn." Ojin shook his fist at the two moons.

"He doesn't necessarily want to destroy Mürindür, Ojin, but he does not, cannot have this baby boy born. That destiny will be his undoing, and likely forever imprison him on this plane. Hippocrates, I mean this, truly. Nothing else matters beyond the birth of your child. Celeste knows this, we know this, and you should know this too. Your son will bring an end to Leterum's oppression, and we must see this through," Serena warned him sternly.

"Everything seems to be falling into place for Leterum now," Creed yawned, "He's impossible to stop from the way you two speak of him."

"Perhaps, but there is still much to be done. Much that *can be done*, and that is what we must focus on."

"So why do we travel east, Serena? We should go to Durdan. Shelter there until the baby is born. We are only heading closer to him and his stronghold if we continue." Ojin took a sip of the bubbling stew.

"If we move west, we lose any chance of keeping Redemptio alive. Thousands of souls will perish each day, and his armies will swell. There will be Caedere on every inch of this land. We must make it to the Capital of Guillarne where we can maintain some semblance of balance. We can hold the middle ground of the Highlands, keep the supply lines to Redemptio open, limit the mountain pass traffic, and with the Capital Guard, the Bellatorum, and my family…" she looked toward Celeste as the Princess checked each bolt within her quiver, "… we can hold this realm together. Once my grandson is born, Leterum's time is nigh."

"Then we have no choice, but to travel east," Ojin conceded.

"Yes. We travel east. We will rest tonight, but tomorrow at daybreak we will move onward to the Pools of Cordis Loci." Creed limped toward his bride-to-be as Serena and Ojin spoke with each other a few moments more, over steaming bowls of broth. Creed placed his hands-on Celeste's belly, and kissed her. They embraced, and she helped him to their tent for the night.

Chapter 15: A Promise

They broke camp the following morning, and Bog stood up steadily. He wasn't strong enough to carry passengers or wear his armor, but it did everyone a great deal of good to see the one who escaped Leterum's grasp, so eager to continue on their journey. Creed felt much stronger as well, and once the horses and carriages were loaded, the army of Mürindür began its procession through the Groves. Xaris and three dozen Bellatorum forged ahead as the tip of the spear, while Creed, Celeste, and Serena road behind them in a fortified carriage. Ojin followed closely in an open wagon pulled by four horses as Pax eagerly sat beside him with his new crossbow. Bog and the remaining battalion of Bellatorum made up the rear. Land travel was antiquated, but much safer than the Fuga for now. Leterum knew only the presence of Hippocrates, but not the whereabouts, explained Serena. It became a race for geography; no longer was it question of when but where.

"You know, Creed, I didn't like you at first." Serena teased him slightly with a smirk.

"Well that's reassuring," Creed answered sarcastically. Celeste chuckled.

"It wasn't you per se as it was more the way my daughter looked at you. She seemed to be infatuated with you."

"Mother, please." Celeste rolled her eyes.

"It's true. She had never been so interested in a human before. Even prior to when you took your oath, she looked at you with wonder and curiosity."

"It was his eyes. They were so fiercely sincere." Celeste held his hand.

"I have fiercely sincere eyes?" He mockingly enlarged his eyes for dramatic effect.

"Ha! Well not right now. When I first saw you, you did. My mother and I arrived with the Bellatorum to confront the Caedere in the desert, and there you were, alone with a spear, fighting incessantly with your back to the Vagus. You placed yourself between them and an absolute certainty. You turned to look at us, and I will never forget the intensity in your eyes. You turned back, and struck a Caedere in the chest, and kept moving forward." Celeste squeezed his knuckles with remembrance.

"You were unaware of where you were or why, but your first instinct was to protect, even if it meant your own demise. I knew two things on that day. You would become a Luxatio, and my daughter's heart was forever yours. She is my only child, and for thousands of years before that day and since I have loved her with every fiber of my being. To think someone would potentially be so close to her, especially a mortal, was not something I could so easily condone." Serena patted Creed's knee.

"Mother forbade me from seeing you," Celeste added.

"Only out of love. Why would anyone wish to see their child cry each time their heart passed into another realm only to return as someone else for a time? Over and over again each time more difficult than the last. I asked her to reconsider, but one evening I walked into her room, and you had fallen asleep on her lap. I believe you had just returned a few days prior from a life in the Dark Ages. I looked at her eyes as she stroked your face slowly, and it was then I realized that we cannot choose whom we fall in love with. Her love was yours and yours alone, so I readied myself for a son." Creed looked at Celeste and smiled.

"Creed, we know you here as Hippocrates. That is who you were that day in the Dunes. It was the man she fell in love with, and the son I welcomed with open arms for so many years. If it is ok with you, I would ask that we call you by your ancient name in our ceremony, your true name."

"I am willing, and I hope to make you proud," Creed affirmed.

"As I know you will." He gazed out the window of the carriage, and was quiet for a moment. He felt Celeste staring. She squeezed his hand, and he turned to look at her. It was strange for them all to be so comfortable with the present circumstances while he continued to struggle with reconciling everything he had seen and heard over the past few days.

"Can you tell me more about the day I took the Oath?" he asked.

"Don't you remember?" Celeste questioned.

"Vaguely. Right now, my mind just flashes, visions of things I was a part of, but hearing these moments from you seems to bring it all home for me."

Serena began.

"You fought alongside us for years. I had come to trust you with leading our troops into battle, and the Bellatorum gave you their respect. I still had not come around to accepting you for my daughter, however. One day following a prolonged fight, the enemy was crushed, and the portal to Earth and the Endüerduul opened for you. It was odd. Typically, you would have only one option, but the Universe had given two. You asked me what they represented, and I was conflicted. If you were to go into the Endüerduul, which you very much deserved, I would never have to worry about my daughter again. Her heart would be safe. On the other hand, I would lose a fierce warrior, and my daughter's spirit would be broken. If you returned to Earth, you would live out your short life there and return to Mürindür unlikely to remember us at all, and Celeste would have to watch you, heartbroken once more. I explained to you the choices. You could choose the Endüerduul, or choose to return to Earth." Creed looked to Celeste and saw a tear roll down her cheek.

"Are you ok?"

"I remember this day well. I wondered what it would mean if you stayed, and how it would affect me if you left. I worried for you."

"Yes. She wept, as did you. You asked if there was any other way. We all knew how you cared for her. It was silent for a moment. My General stepped forward and made a request. They asked that I make you a Luxatio."

"Now I see." He closed his eyes for a moment.

"In what way?" Celeste asked.

"In Durdan, I couldn't fathom why I would ever make such a choice. Give up seemingly everything," he looked at Celeste, "now I can't imagine never having that opportunity."

"None of us can. We rode to the Pools of Cordis Loci that day, and arrived at the water's edge. I took the *Patera Argenti* from the altar rock, and dipped it into the Pools. You accepted the honor, and knelt immediately. I offered you the goblet, and you drank. You recited the Oath, and the Endüerduul accepted your promise. At that moment, you became something altogether different. It is that very sacrifice and all the continued sacrifices the Luxatio make that renders them so powerful, and so revered. Although you knew you would have to enter the mortal world once more, you could return for eternity, aware of who you were, and whom you loved. Each time you did, we always had need for you. Each time you returned, you two had one another, once again." Serena clasped her hands with satisfaction.

Creed turned to Celeste. "That must have been hard for you," he said.

"I was happy. I worried you might regret your decision one day, but I also knew you were always meant for Luxatio, and I knew that I loved you."

Celeste touched her forehead to his. He winced for a moment, and she leaned back.

"What's wrong?"

"My head is still a little sore from Durdan. Bog slung me into a wall I think, and I woke up with a big knot on my forehead. You managed to hit the right spot." He smiled, and Celeste kissed the bruise.

"Creed, you mentioned Durdan. Ojin told me what happened there and within the Ashi. I wanted to talk with you about these experiences."

"Durdan was a fog. My mind was so numb and detached from what I'm accustomed to. I had fallen only hours before, and as I kept asking Ojin questions, my heart raced, and my body felt tight. That's when he told me I would never be able to go to the Endüerduul. Everything felt unfair, unjust. I was angry. My skin began to burn. I'm not sure what happened after that. I woke up in the ruins on the way to the Ashi."

"And what happened in the Ashi? How did that make you feel?" Creed paused for a moment. He had a brief memory of sitting in the counselor's office.

"It's funny. You remind me of a lady I've been talking to back home. A counselor."

"Interesting." Serena smiled. He looked at Celeste, and realized he had seen those eyes recently, outside of a dream in fact.

"Celeste?"

"Yes?"

"Did you like the Monets?" Creed asked. She blushed, and laughed slightly.

"The two of you were there all the time? All this time?" he wondered. Serena shook her head.

"Not always, no, and it was mostly Celeste. I watched you walk into the counselor's office, but I chose not to interfere. I feared it would unsettle you in some way. Celeste, however, made it a point to see you once or twice."

"When was the other time?" he asked.

"I watched you run in the middle of the night, and I watched you walk about the parks. I wanted to hold you, and see your smile, but every time I caught a glimpse, you seemed as if you were grieving, troubled. Once I witnessed you walk into the museum, I had to try."

"I wish you would have said something."

"You wouldn't have understood. Mother is right. It would have been too unsettling," Celeste explained.

"It is forbidden for immortals to cross, that is until the Caedere began to trespass after the Gates fell. Mürindür always sets to maintain balance, and once they slipped through, Celeste and I managed to do so as well. We needed to know you were ok, and that they hadn't found you. This jump for you would be the most important, and we thought we had more time. As we leapt to check on you, we came across Caedere in different forms, and removed them from that mortal plain. Some, even made it to your home. We had hoped to stop them all before they found you."

"One of them did," Creed noted.

"Yes. We missed him by mere moments. Leterum coordinated it well. First, he attacked Durdan with Ignis, and then he set his chaos upon the villages. We snuffed out the attacks quickly, always wary of distractions. He then sent his witch to the Capital of Guillarne, and we met her and an army of Caedere. In the middle of the battle, we sensed a breach, and Celeste and I leapt to Earth. Once we made it to the other side, you were gone," Serena recalled.

"We never saw you or anyone that could have been close to you. We returned immediately, and waited. The battle had all but ended, and then once we saw you fall into the Ember Wood, we knew Ojin would find you."

"Were you there when I slept? Back home I mean?" as he looked at Celeste.

"No, but I did visit you in your dreams near the Pools. It was the only way I could rest. One evening, I sat beside the still waters, and your image appeared below the surface. It startled me at first. I reached into the water, and pulled you through, every night, again and again. I waited there. Some nights you weren't there, but as time went on, I looked forward to our brief moments."

"There was always something coming for us. You would send me away."

"Some of that was your own fear manifested in your dreams. I would sense your spirit becoming restless, and I eased you back into the waters." Creed had cascading memories flood his mind again. He looked out the window once more, and started to realize something had changed. He didn't want to go back home. He didn't want to ever leave, and couldn't help but wonder if that would be possible.

"Do I have to go back?"

"Back to Earth?" Serena asked.

"It is your duty," Celeste whispered.

"How can it end?" asked Creed.

"It doesn't…" Celeste stopped short.

"Serena?"

"It can, but it is rare. The Luxatio ceremony is more than a moment, Hippocrates. It is a commitment to the Endüerduul, to Mürindür and to its people. It is a sacrifice, and one that must be upheld. As of late, it appears some people have forgotten this."

"Who?"

"It matters not for now, but there are those who have chosen to turn their backs on the Endüerduul, and it pains me to know they've disappeared."

"But they don't really disappear right? I mean they leave something behind."

"Such as?" Serena asked.

"Ojin mentioned Luxatio remains were guarded in the Redemptio Keep."

"Yes." Serena nodded as Celeste continued looking out the window. Her face was solemn.

"If there are remains, then they left somehow. Where did they go?"

"They became a part of Mürindür. When you drink of the Pools, that is the promise."

"So, my options are to either return to Earth, or to become part of Mürindür."

"Ultimately, yes. Once you choose to turn your back on the portal to Earth, it closes forever, and your existence becomes Mürindür. Should you perish in battle, you become Mürindür."

"I wish there was another way." He looked to Celeste.

"She does too, Hippocrates," Serena said with a smile.

The caravan came to a sudden stop, and they heard angry voices outside. Serena opened the carriage door, and Creed could see the Bellatorum had gathered near an object ahead.

"What is it, General?"

"More sacrifices, my Queen."

He pointed to a pile of charred bodies near the roadside, stacked high beneath a willow tree, draped by its tallest boughs. The grass was black all around them, and the smell of sulfur was suffocating. Serena slapped her hands high above her, and the stifling stench of decay dissipated with the wind's intent. Creed climbed down as he helped Celeste to her feet, and they walked toward Serena and looked about.

"An Ogre sacrifice. These were farmers likely on their way to the Fields of Effugere. May the Endüerduul, comfort them," said the General.

Serena walked to the site, and laid her hand on the chest of one of the bodies. The entire pile of remains fell into a crumbling gray ash, and as Celeste raised her right hand, a slow breeze cradled them all, withering into the sky. Nothing remained but smoldering earth.

"How did this happen? Didn't you just pass this place a day earlier?" Creed asked Serena as she looked toward him with sadness and frustration.

"I do not believe this happened here. It was too close to us, and had we known we could have stopped it. No, this likely took place in the bowels of Leterum's Keep. Captured, whisked away, tortured, and burned. This smells of Ignis and his Ogres. They placed the bodies here as a threat. They knew we would pass through here eventually."

"If they know we're here, why don't they come and fight?" Creed's hands were clenched, and his chest seemed tight.

"We are too close to the Pools, and Ignis knows he would fail if it were left to me. No, they will attack on all fronts indirectly. Leterum is mocking us. Toying with us. He enjoys the fear that falls before him as he proceeds." Serena and Celeste held hands, and closed their eyes. The ground shook, and dirt roiled about as boiling water. Slowly, it unfurled emerald green grass, and dozens of small trees throughout the site. Lilacs and oleander skittered about until the air was once more fragrant and befit for the Groves. The Bellatorum formed a defensive crescent behind them as Ojin walked forward, and Pax peered scarcely over the wagon's edge.

"Serena, should we not wait for nightfall when the moons are highest and each of you command more sway?" Ojin asked.

"As we venture closer to the Pools, Leterum will not attack. It is our best line of defense. The sooner we're there, the safer these two will be."

"Ignis is likely not far," the hobgoblin reminded her.

"No, I suspect he is not. Pray that he missteps before our next stop, and I will bury him with my rage."

Serena strode ahead to the leading component of their procession. She spoke with four scouts, and they took off quickly, disappearing over the nearby hill. Creed looked back to Bog and Pax as Xaris arrived at the Queen's carriage.

"We should get you two seated, and get going." Xaris motioned to them and the open door.

"I think we will ride ahead, Xaris." Celeste went back and readied her bow. She took two horses from the lanyards, and offered a set of reins to Creed. Üstor was cinched across Creed's saddle back.

"Celeste, I do not think it wise for you to be out and unsheltered," Xaris insisted.

"Xaris, you cannot shelter the storm." She mounted her saddle, and kicked her horse, trotting forward. Creed watched her for a bit, and then smiled as he looked at Xaris.

"She's quite spirited, isn't she?" Creed asked.

"Spirited is an understatement. Stay close, Hippocrates. Leterum is hunting her as we speak, and truth be told, she is the only one that matters here today." Xaris looked to her, and back again toward Creed. "We all must be ready to stand and sacrifice as needed for the sake of that child. Do not leave her side. Promise me this on your life, Hippocrates."

"I wouldn't have it any other way." Creed snapped the reins of his horse, and caught up with Celeste quickly. As he stared back at the charred shadows on the ground, he wondered about the cruelty necessary to commence such an act, and hoped he'd have a chance to avenge the victims. Ignis or not, the forces of Leterum would pay for their savagery.

Chapter 16: A Renewal

C reed and Celeste rode in parallel as thick green vines and grass crawled and sprouted before them, dressing the burned soil as a salve. Within a few moments, there would be no record of the sacrifice, and the horror it signified. They rode quietly for a while afterward. Creed sensed that Celeste was deeply troubled by it all, but couldn't find the words to ease her mind. She broke the silence.

"Mother and I greet every Welfalon soul that enters the Redemptio Keep. Men and women from all over the world with different backgrounds and languages, but they all speak human. They mourn what little they remember of their past life, and they worry about the uncertainty ahead, but soon enough we help them to their feet again. We aid them in discovering a new purpose here on Mürindür, but even then, we can never prepare anyone for this." She motioned to the tree behind her. "This barbarism has trespassed all recognized boundaries of this domain, and yet all I can do for now is wait. It is unbearable at times. I feel trapped. Caged."

"I'm sorry."

"I am as well. It still hurts me when I see a Vaga fall in the dunes even though they're supposed to be the forsaken ones. There are few things more disheartening than to hear their screams in the transformation, but we uphold the order of things. We cannot change their fates. We are stewards, protectors, charged as peacekeepers, and yet we cannot lift a finger even for them. In each recess of this realm, where we no longer stand, Leterum rules in tyranny." Celeste looked to the sky sternly, and Creed marveled at her expression. He saw the ferocity of a ruler behind the kind eyes of his love. She turned to him, and smiled softly.

"You stare at me as if you don't know me."

"I barely recognize myself nowadays," Creed said pointedly. Celeste's smile faded.

"I'm sorry. This must all still feel foreign to you. I forget at times. Naturally, I wish we could just pick up where we left off. We used to always spend our reunion time together in isolation, running about the land before we had to relate to others. It gave us the time we needed to reconnect. I wish I could have afforded that for you now."

"We have all these things about to take place, and haven't had a chance to breathe, let alone talk in private. Are you sure you want to do this now? Maybe in a few months we can reconsider? Maybe spend some more time like you say we used to," Creed wondered.

"We don't have months. We don't have time, my love."

"Why?"

"Certain things need to be done now before it's too late," Celeste replied.

"It just seems rushed and artificial to a degree."

She pulled on her reins, and sat up in the saddle. She was quiet for a moment.

"I know. Nothing seems to be as it should. We were to be married, and spend the next few moons preparing for our child. I thought we had enough time, but that is perhaps the worst assumption we could have made. You seem different. I seem different." She sighed. "We need to do the best we can, and make it through the upcoming days. As things settle, we will have what we both desperately want, and get to know one another again, as we once did." She forced a smile, and spurred her horse to travel further.

The army rode quietly for another hour, winding like a wary worm across the plain. Pax fiddled with his crossbow, checking on Bog as the mammoth walked steadily behind them. Xaris shifted on Nos, and kept a constant watch on Serena and her carriage. As they rode eastward, Celeste continued to stare at the horizon to the north. Creed noticed she seemed distracted.

"What is it? What do you see?" he asked.

"Something familiar lies just over those hills," Celeste answered.

"Like what?"

She smiled mischievously.

"Come on!" She kicked her horse into a gallop, racing northward past a series of rolling hills and gray rocky crags. Creed was caught off guard, and looked around confused.

"Wait! The army! What are you doing?" It was too late. She was easily fifty yards ahead of him. He looked back at the caravan, and saw the Bellatorum quickly heading his way lead by Xaris.

"What the Hell?" He too spurred his horse, and off he flew in pursuit. Celeste's steed was very fast, but soon Creed was within earshot of her.

"Wait! Wait!" She turned back at him and laughed. Creed looked to Xaris and the oncoming Bellatorum as well, but saw them slow to a stop. They returned to the caravan as Serena called to them, and Creed smiled. He understood.

Finally, some peace, some time with her! She laughed, and he couldn't help but chuckle. It was a race of no purpose, but for the sheer joy of it. They wove back and forth on horseback like a braided escapade. The ground climbed steeper, gently, until the hill peaked with nothing easily seen in the valley below. As they slowed to a gentle gait, a thick fog had settled onto the northern grasslands. Their horses' heated breath hung in the heavy, cold air, chests heaving, and a smile adorned her face. Tranquility.

"Celeste, why did we…"

"Shhh. Listen," she replied.

Everything was still as before an approaching thunderstorm. The horses were quiet, but a dull, distant vibration took hold. Creed's stallion began to lift its head, bucking the bit and reins. The fog was as a veil, but as the thunder became louder, ivory horns skated above the low-lying precipitation. The rumble grew until the ground began to quake, and the horses paced. Celeste comforted her steed with a pat to the neck. The fog ebbed, and there they were, antlers raised, emboldened and free.

"The elk of the Ashi Pass have roamed the Steppes of Praedorum for as long as I can remember. I would sit here as a little girl on that very rock, watching them for hours," Celeste whispered softly. Hundreds of them milled below until they came to rest within chest high Tengery, an orange luminescent plant with three-pronged tips. The elk settled and grazed. Occasionally a bull would raise his head above the others and announce his presence. The wind was slow.

"Why are we here?" asked, Creed.

"You'll see," she replied.

"We should get back. We're likely miles from the road and your mother by now."

"Shhh. Do you remember this place? Our place? This is where we would go to get away from everyone. Our escape."

"Vaguely. Not well. I mean… wait. What was that?" Something caught his eye.

"Shhh. He's hunting."

Far to their left in the valley below, a large creature low-crawled over a boulder onto an outcropping of snow-covered rock, and his shadow scarcely moved but for a breath. The elk were unsuspecting, and the creature had the wind on them. Step by calculated step, the mass inched closer to the herd. In a blur, it rose high into the air, and crashed into the mass of startled bulls. The herd launched and fled, and the tumult stirred the fog so that a small clearing became visible within the grass. Upon a fallen elder male, stood a massive beast of claws and lumbering wings. From its mouth came a raucous roar, and in the rays of the sun, Creed saw a magnificent manifestation. His eyes widened.

"A lion?"

"No. Not just any lion. This is the alpha male of the Volantum Leonarum. He is hunting for his pride. He hunts the Steppes, and rules the northern lands. The Leonarum have been my most precious beasts in all of Mürindür."

The alpha roared again, and then sank his jaws into the side of the giant elk. The lion's body was muscle and sinew wrapped in a thick hide of pearl white fur, swirled with hues of yellow and tan. The black claws contrasted the lightness of his legs, and his lengthy mane hung heavy across his shoulders. The wind shifted slightly as he looked up at them. His yellow eyes fixed fast on Celeste, and he leapt, disappearing in the mist.

Before Creed could speak, the beast landed squarely before them with a thud, towering above them both. A monster of such dominant fashion and form, the lion was breathtaking. His lips were bloodied, and he snarled briefly showing fangs the length of Creed's forearms. His wings spread high, and then settled onto his flanks. He sat back, and looked down upon them, chest heaving. "Creed. This is Morsu. It has been quite some time."

The winged lion peered at, and then charged Creed as his horse stood on its hind legs and nearly fell to its side. Celeste smiled, but Creed was terrified. The lion's breath smelled of fresh kill, and his throat guttered a deep resonance.

"He is my closest companion. My friend. My confidant. He welcomed you right away the first time you saw each other. I knew he saw something in you as well."

Creed reached to smooth the hair on his neck.

"Careful. We haven't trimmed his quills in some time." Slender black spears for quills hid just beneath the thick furry mane. Between the four-foot feathers of his wings hid many more. One swipe could take a man's head off cleanly, she explained.

Creed stepped off his horse, and placed a hand on Morsu's ribs. The beast's heart pounded through the chest wall, adrenaline still surging from the hunt. His smell brought back a rush of memories for Creed, hundreds of years of hunting excursions on this mighty king. Morsu leaned into him, and then in an instant, pushed him down with one paw on his chest. Creed could barely breathe. Celeste laughed.

"He still has to show you who the alpha is even if he does love you."

"Apparently..." Creed whispered slowly through a gasp.

"Morsu, up."

The lion stepped back, and arched his shoulders into Celeste. They embraced although she did not seem wavered by his weight.

Despite the barbs, she stroked her hands through his mane, and Morsu's body shook. Creed looked in the valley below and saw the Leonarum pride encircle the kill as the lionesses fed first. The males sat back, most of them cloaked in thick black manes, waiting patiently. Creed found this curious.

"They let the females feed first?" he asked.

"The males let the females feed first, so that they may nourish their young. The pride understands that the cubs are their legacy, and Morsu gave up his kill for the pride."

"Why is he so much lighter in color than the others?"

"His coat draws attention, deflecting danger from his pride. The alpha male is always lighter, often white or gray and other creatures know better than to confront the leader. The King."

"The King indeed." Morsu raised his head and let loose an epic roar which thundered through the Steppes.

Creed worried why now of all things, they made no effort to be quiet. He wondered how vulnerable they were at the Steppes. There was no desire to hide. No attempt to disappear. Everything was intentional, exposed, unadulterated primal practicality, and yet not a Raven was in sight.

"Aren't you worried about Leterum? We're at war, standing in the open. Alone."

"We are never alone. We never have been. Though my mother worries about it all, I know our purpose. I know what is destined to be. Leterum doesn't venture to the north. He doesn't venture to the pools. If his vermin flew here, they would be eviscerated, and the Caedere wouldn't stand a chance. This whole land has historically been balanced by the good and evil you've seen today even if for now the balance is skewed. These lions represent more than just beasts. For millennia, man has envisioned them, dreamed of them. Used them as symbols of strength, apostles, kings, and warriors. These lions are all those things and more. If there was any way for the Endüerduul to walk the plains of Mürindür, it is this pride upon these Steppes." More lions joined Morsu as she spoke. They stood before Celeste and Creed, wings stretched, and jaws wide with yawns of full bellies. One of the lionesses leaned heavily on Morsu, and purred.

"Who is that?" Creed asked. Celeste smiled with his curiosity.

"She is La-mala. His queen. When they fly, they fly as one. When they battle, they are synchronized. They have watched over these Steppes for eons, and she has raised all of his lion cubs. They have been together for as long as I can remember, even longer than us. This is Morsu's pride, and although there are many lionesses, he has only one Queen." La-mala looked at Creed, and smelled his air. Her eyes were as intense as Morsu's.

"You talk as if there have been other alphas."

"Few, but yes. In the beginning, when Acrom walked these lands, he sought their strength. The Volantum Leonarum knew his darkness even before he fell from the Endüerduul. They refused him, and fought valiantly. I know of two alphas that died over the centuries. Morsu is the third alpha."

"What happened to the others?"

"I don't know. Leterum was there for the last one to fall. He carried the carcass away to his Keep. Some suspect that his mount Sēpein is what became of it."

"That's horrible."

"Yes. Leterum finds ways to reinvent the undead. Slaves to his will."

She stroked Morsu's mane, and patted La-mala on her neck. They purred with content. The bull elks, once safely away, bleated to their herds to venture west. The sounds were as French horns across the Steppes. It broke the foreboding air.

"Do you want to fly?" Celeste asked, looking to Creed with a flirtatious glimmer.

"I'm not sure that's a great idea."

"It will be fun. Trust me."

"It's not you that I don't trust," Creed replied.

"He won't bite unless you make him angry."

"Right." Celeste laughed at Creed's unwillingness to partake in adventure.

"Morsu, may we?" She bowed gently, and Morsu knelt down. Celeste mounted Morsu, patting the space behind her.

"You're kidding." Creed's hands were on his hips as he shook his head.

"Come on," she insisted.

Creed thought for a moment, and decided it couldn't possibly be worse than anything else at this point. Death by lion wasn't necessarily a bad way to go. Not one for fool-hearted abandonment of caution, however, he took Üstor and strapped it to his back. The horses lingered near a felled aspen tree as he sat behind Celeste, and placed his arms around her waist. She smelled like honeysuckle, and her hair was warm across his face.

Morsu roared, lurched, and launched into the sky as his pride looked on from below. The acceleration was so great that Creed unintentionally pulled Celeste tighter as he slid to the rear. She laughed with her hands gripped deep into Morsu's mane, and they climbed effortlessly to the stars.

The clouds were infinite, and Morsu wove through them like water. As they soared higher, Creed could make out a distant blue horizon. It appeared to be the origins of an ocean. The Steppes were thousands of miles of open land, a realm befit this king. Ohh the exhilarating freedom! He gripped Celeste tighter as she closed her eyes and smiled. A moment. It was a reconciliation of all that had transpired, a sense of loving stability in a world cold from uncertainty.

They soared towards the ocean, and then took a brisk turn west to follow the coastline. The air caught each of his breaths and molded them into tiny crystals, but Creed felt warmth. He felt solace. Peace crept into his mind even if for but a moment as alien as it was. They descended quickly below the clouds, and the beaches shimmered. Small caves littered the rock cliffs, the last extension of the Steppes before the ocean waters. The smell of salt spray filled Creed's lungs, and Morsu landed pointedly onto a dune. He shook his mane, and roared as the couple stepped down. Celeste turned to the caves behind them.

"Come on!"

She took off like a rabbit, bounding over debris. Creed ran after her up the dunes towards a doorway of timber laced in moss like an arbor. She took him inside the dark cavern within the cliff, and walked briskly as if she could do it in her sleep.

"Where are we going?" Creed asked.

"You'll see!" Celeste laughed as she pulled him onward. He could barely keep up. Nary a shadow was separate as they melded into an opaqueness of secrecy. Suddenly, they turned a corner and stood before a towering roughhewn, granite wall.

It curved along the entire vault with a mural of Mürindür landscapes, and a young couple staring at one another, hand in hand. Creatures of all forms seemingly moved about the wall in animation. The woman was wearing the silver and white gown that Celeste wore now, and the man looked very much like Creed. The seasoned leaves of the trees in the backdrop glimmered in the small amount of light trickling down from a crevice above. The floor was worn river stone, and the entire room smelled of fallen rain.

"Who are they?" Creed wondered.

"Us, silly!"

"When did you have time to do that?"

"Time? I started these murals the first moment you went back. I had to believe that our paths were united for a reason. As I thought of you, these images came to mind. I enchanted the rock with our memories, our stories, and our future that I would catch in my dreams. I knew this would come to pass someday, and here we are." She smiled, satisfied with her work, happy with the outcome.

"Those are the exact clothes I'm wearing now."

"Yes."

"Can you see into the future?"

"Not exactly. There are many things, many beings, that alter the final moments, but I know what I wish to see, and how things have come to pass."

"What happens to us then?"

"I don't know. That's what makes this all so exciting!" she exclaimed.

"Not even a little hint of what's to come?" The woman in the mural now had her hands on her belly as Celeste did the same. She smiled.

"I know this. We are here for however long, for whatever purpose. We have one another in this moment, and for us," as she looked down at their unborn son, "that is all we have ever wanted."

Creed placed his arm around her waist still amazed by the work. He felt as if they were in the art museum once more. In the distance, there was a bridge, red and endless. He thought about its significance, and where it might end. No destination seemed to exist. It was unfinished along the expanse of the gray stone. All their battles, their triumphs and their influence upon the realm were lovingly expressed across the cavern, and it all lead to that bridge.

As he looked about, left to right, it followed a timeline of sorts. Moments he had returned to her, and moments when he had no choice but to leave. Cities were built, armies reborn, and yet in all this tumult, they remained side by side. His recollection of Mürindür was rapidly curing in his mind as each picture triggered something meaningful. He belonged on that wall with her, and nothing seemed more real than now.

"This is our story painted on these walls?"

"Yes'" Celeste affirmed. Creed studied the murals for minutes, quietly thinking about it all.

"Remember when we took that old oak sail boat into the Seniorem Sea, and sailed for weeks alone with one another? Do you remember that sea turtle as big as an ox?" Creed asked.

"I do! He kept trying to climb into the boat, so you threw the cargo net over the side, fixed it to the sail mast with wooden joists, and he climbed into the net. That turtle traveled with us for miles, napping in his ocean hammock," Celeste recalled with joyful inflection in her voice as she laid her head on his chest lovingly.

Creed's eyes savored the blues and greens of the undulating currents as he watched the small boat traveling toward the horizon. It rocked to and fro across small waves beyond another scene nearby, where he battled a contingent of Leterum's army as Celeste hovered in the clouds with lightning in her hands. A few feet away, there was a depiction of her launching arrows at a large two-headed dragon while Creed lunged forward with a golden spear. They appeared as a majestic reckoning in each scene, and he marveled at her tenacity. She was so gentle, but could tear the world asunder if she saw fit to do so.

"All of it is so beautiful, Celeste."

"I've improved over the centuries, haven't I?"

"Well yes, but I meant our life. Our *life* is so beautiful. I'm so sorry that it isn't readily there for me, for my mind, when I come back, but when I do remember, I wonder how could I ever forget?" His gaze sunk halfheartedly to the stone floor, but Celeste cupped his face gently, kissing his forehead.

"My love, the *heart never forgets*. The mind will sleep and wake as it always has, but your heart beats true, and nothing can ever alter that. This mural is always here for you, as are all the memories that reside within it. When you need it most, our stories will light the way. Now, let's go. I'm sure Mother is anxious for our return."

She took his hand in hers, and walked him outside to the waves slipping, recessed into the standing lagoons. Celeste knelt down and cupped a handful of seawater. She turned to him, kissing his eyelids softly as they closed in acceptance, and bathed his scalp in the cold brine of the northern coast.

"Hippocrates, unto you I bestow my heart. Within you, I rest. For where eternity is but a blink, our love will remain steadfast. The stars will dress our dreams, and our family will bless these lands. Unto you, I am forever yours. I give you myself willingly. *Cor numquam operae praebitae obliviscitur.*"

He stood there, and thought for a moment as a familiar calm overcame him.

"Celeste, for millenia long since past, and the many lives I have suffered, you have waited. You have loved me. You have healed me. My broken spirit walks because of you. I am willingly yours, forever, and when the sun sets on existence, I will hold you infinitely, and love you without bounds. *Cor numquam operae praebitae obliviscitur.*"

Creed dove his hands into the lagoons as she had done, and placed them over her head as they kissed once more. A thunder, unlike that from above, rolled slowly across the Steppes. It was as if the world exhaled, and for a few moments, Mürindür held fast in a loving embrace.

Chapter 17: The Vagus

As Morsu carried the two back toward the peak over the Tengery grass fields, Creed marveled at how the lion pride and their horses rested beside one another, undisturbed, content. He dismounted first, helping Celeste down, and looked into the king's eyes, touching his muzzle mostly out of awe. Morsu stared back at him, and Creed noticed a golden flicker of light, seeing his reflection for the first time. His hair color was similar to Morsu's, and it gave him pause as Celeste whistled for the horses. Climbing onto their saddles, they strode away as the lions lingered, observing, and nuzzling one another. Morsu stood high on all fours, and roared once more. The fog rolled across the grounds, and the lions disappeared. Majestic indeed.

Celeste took them a different route than the one earlier. They traveled eastward before turning south in hopes of meeting up with the group in time. The terrain was more rock than grass, and Creed found himself shucked from one side to the other in the saddle as his horse's hips shifted. After an hour, he wished they had flown Morsu back to the camp.

"What can I expect at the pools?" he asked.

"Ojin will perform the ceremony, and people will get up to speak. There will be a feast in our honor, and dancing."

"Dancing?"

"You love to dance," she explained.

"Since when?"

"Oh it was the greatest. You would come back, and show me the newest dances from civilization each time. Some were pretty funny while others were amazing."

"Dancing. Didn't dance much in this past life."

"Oh? I'm sorry." Celeste looked at him quizzically.

"It's not your fault. This last one was especially hard. I seemed to have lost everything except for medicine. It was my only constant. My compass I guess. When I felt lost, it kept me moving. I don't remember feeling this way in my prior lives, but as time goes on here, it's just become another book on a long dusty shelf of bound lifetimes," Creed mused.

"Your return this time has been difficult for all of us. Even when we saw each other at first, I could tell you weren't well."

"I have a great number of thoughts and images that flood my mind every so often. It's confusing, really. I don't know if I want to do it anymore. No sense of balance. War is everywhere. It's here. It's there. I go back to a world full of violence and hate when I leave. It just seems endless. Constant struggle. I'm tired."

"What will you do should the portal present itself?" asked Celeste.

"I think I'm ready to walk away, and whatever time I have left to spend, I want to spend it here with you. It would be nice to rest for once."

"I suppose you should get your rest in now," she jested. "Once the little one arrives, I suspect we'll be busy."

"How do we even hope to raise this baby? Is it even safe?" he wondered.

"Mother and I have plans. We will likely need to stay at the Capital of Guillarne. Every day will be a challenge. I'm not sure what to expect, but there is a first time for everything." Celeste rubbed her belly.

"In what way?"

"Well for starters, I've never had a baby." Creed chuckled.

"Well that's good to know."

"Have you?" she asked, teasing him.

"Um, no, and I don't remember having children in any of my lives. Any of my visits I suppose. Not even sure what to call them anymore. It will be new to both of us then."

"It will be new to everyone. A child with mortal blood has never been born in Mürindür. There's no telling what it may do to the balance, but I am hopeful. That's why this ceremony is so crucial. We need the Endüerduul to accept our son into existence, and bless our family, the union of mortal and immortal lives. Once that takes place, we will know which direction to take."

"Well it's not like we can exchange the child if he's not accepted." Celeste frowned at him.

"Well no, but…"

"So, then we're good," Creed smirked.

"Ugh. I see what you're doing, Creed."

"I'm just teasing."

"This ceremony helps us form our family, but most importantly if we are blessed then we know that our hopes will be fulfilled. It will make you a member of my family, and our son will come into a unified house. It's important, and to receive the blessings of the Endüerduul is always significant. I hope you understand that." Celeste's amusement was dimming.

"Okay. Okay. I do understand. It's a big deal. Got it. Let's change the subject. What do you think he will look like?"

"My mother thinks he will look like you, but have my strength."

"Your strength?"

"Yes of course." Creed looked at his chest and flexed his arms humorously.

"Yes they are very nice." She laughed harmoniously as he smiled.

"Will he be immortal too, Celeste?"

"We don't know. I hope so, for what he is intended. He'll need to be."

"That sounds ominous," Creed replied.

"He will be the keeper for our realms. He will have to be kind, strong, well versed in the Laws, and determined enough to keep the balance. It won't be easy for him or for us. We will have much to teach him," she explained.

"Feels like I'm not in any condition to teach anyone."

"You will be." Celeste smiled and spurred her horse faster towards the old gray road before them. They raced once more, and the groves could be seen to their right on the horizon. The road had opened up slightly, and then disappeared again to the left within a dense forrest. No caravan could be seen, but presuming it was because the two had been gone for hours, they continued forward, hoping to catch up.

They slowed through the clumps of waist-high purple fountain grass, and entered the tree line, heading southeast to the Pools. The air had become quiet. Even the rustled leaves were muted. Creed knew they were no longer within the safe confines of the Bellatorum, or the watchful eye of Morsu. He felt Üstor getting warm, and as he moved to uncinch it, Celeste drew her bow.

"I sense it too," she said.

The road funneled beyond their eyes, and the surrounding timber loomed darkly above. There was no sign of their group, but as they stepped down from their horses, there were faint, horrible sounds echoing from a distant ravine. They edged closer, knowing something horrific waited for them. Celeste nocked her arrow, and Creed held his glaive. The horses seemed uneasy as a wail of anguish sped toward them through the air. The two walked quickly, hunched over, along a small game path through thorned thickets. The ground continued to decline toward something quite malignant, and as the brush thinned, they crouched above the ravine's ledge. Below, they could see the work of an eager and deprived mind.

A half dozen Vagus were bound, some sobbing, with their hands behind their backs, and dark hoods pulled over their heads. MultipleOgres lumbered about, doing what they do best. Taunting. Torturing. One Vaga's body lay lifeless behind the group with its severed skull a few feet away. The executioner walked to his tent, and came back with a chain of barbed hooks. He labored the flesh of three more victims, lashing them repeatedly despite the cries. Creed prowled forward while Celeste grabbed his arm, shaking her head in protest. His chest pounded, churning with the witnessed injustice. Celeste pulled on him, but he didn't acknowledge her. It was too late.

Creed thought not about consequence or complexity. Not for a second. Even as he fell through the air, rage merely effervesced, intoxicating him beyond reproach. He may have heard a faint dissent from Celeste, but it was too easily ignored once his knee and foot fell with a resounding thud into the sod. His stance readied. Creed was within their midst, and for a second the Ogres stared in disbelief at this aberrant abomination.

The executioner was the first to act, and he lunged with anticipation of an easy prey.

"Uurrrggggghhhh!! HA, HA, HA!!" The executioner was much bigger than the others, and he outweighed Creed by 400 pounds. Nearly twice as tall, the beast salivated with excitement.

"COME TO ME VERMIN! I SHALL SHAT YOUR BONES!"

The chains of hooks, bloodied from the corpses nearby, whistled past his ears, but Creed remained lurched and unwavered. The atmosphere was heavy, slow, and as the Ogre charged to but three feet away, Creed swept fiercely. His weapon awoke, and he found himself standing tall as the torso fell. The other Ogres laughed with glee, none pausing even a moment for their fallen comrade as they encircled with their weapons in hand. Creed turned slowly watching their movements, anticipating who would strike first. He counted twelve in all.

"Ahh yes. The mighty Hippocrates! How wonderfully delightful to meet you." An obese Ogre bowed mockingly.

"I heard he's been a little off as of late." A skinny bald Ogre proclaimed.

"Off? You mean weak!"

"Yes! He's weak! Not the Hippocrates of old now is he?"

"No. No brother. He's weak as they come!"

"This should be fun then!"

"Yes. Yes. Take it slowly brothers. We want him to bleed!"

"I get the head. You got the last one!"

"This is Hippocrates! I will take his head! It will fetch a great deal on the market!"

"There's more than one who wants this trophy, boys. We'll divvy up the parts and pieces later. NOW MOVE," yelled the obese Ogre.

They attacked at once, fiercely. Creed blocked and parried as he tripped one adversary, and drove Üstor through its target into the boggy soil. He withdrew it in time to stop two blades from clipping his neck. Something stung his calf from an errant sharpened edge, and as he spun he caught images of light from the corner of his eye.

Shwoosh.

Shwoosh.

Shwoosh.

The arrows found their marks briskly, as the fight blurred, and bodies fell lifeless to the sod. Creed engaged three as Celeste made quick work of more. Curved blades bit Üstor, but unfazed, the relic was true. Creed shuffled through the blood-soaked leaves and twigs of the ravine's floor without inhibition. The spear tip eviscerated one beast as the blade severed another through its upper back. An Ogre looked briefly up the embankment to witness Celeste loose another arrow, and he threw his spear toward the unflinching Princess. The lengthy flung weapon was close enough to waft her hair, but she released another volley into an Ogre that had successfully flanked Creed.

Though the Ogre missed with his spear, he suffered the vengeance of a furious man, and Üstor fell heavily into the Ogre's skull, flaying the monster's body, and burying itself into his pelvis. The awkwardness that was an Ogre effigy stumbled, halved, and fell as a broken "Y" into the mud.

CLANG!

THWACK!

Then silence.

Creed turned and found no others to engage. Celeste maintained her perch high above with arrow at the ready as he stuck Üstor into a fallen tree. Mangled bodies were strewn about with Ogre blood pooled at his feet. The smell was repugnant. Three bound Vagus remained, crying, but alive. Creed moved to free them, and tossed their hoods and bindings into the nearby camp fire. All three were disheveled, wild-eyed, and pupils so dilated there was scarcely any color of an iris to be seen. He looked at each of them, two men and a woman, noting the forearm scars, seemingly self-inflicted, on each. They served as emotional tattoos amongst the fresh weeping wounds, products of the Ogres' willful derangement. One man raised his arms in defense while the others looked dazed.

"Do not eat me! Do not eat me! I am covered in worms!"

"Stand. I am not going to eat you," Creed replied.

"Get them off of me! Get them off!" But there were no worms to be found. The man was hallucinating and agitated.

"Sir, relax. There are no worms. You are safe." The man pointed emphatically at his arms and legs. He grabbed a knife from the wet leaves nearby, and cut his bicep's flesh for proof.

"STOP!"

Creed couldn't move fast enough. The man thrust the blade toward his face, and the knife found its way beneath the mangy, bearded chin even as Creed's hands grabbed the weapon and stiff wrist. The damage had been done with the hilt buried at the jaw. The man's eyes rolled back, and the death rattle emanated slowly. Creed stood shocked. Paralyzed for a moment. He let go of the arm, and the body crumpled in defeat. He felt Celeste's hand on his shoulder.

"Vagus. They are deranged. Confused. This one was lost before we ever arrived."

"He was, was sick. I've never…"

"It happens so often. We can do very little for them here. We need to find the army, and my mother."

"What about the other two?"

"If we can convince them to come with us, they can ride our horses, but it will double our travel time. I'm not sure we can afford any more delays."

"We can't abandon them," Creed protested.

"More darkness will be here soon. The blood rises to the nostrils of beasts we don't wish to see. Grab them and move."

Creed grabbed Üstor, and reached for the other man while Celeste restrained the woman. Despite their delirium, the former captives complied, and made their way slowly out of the ravine to the waiting horses. Both were lifted up high, and Celeste tied leather straps around their waists onto the saddles to seat them securely. Creed looked below, and saw smoke rise from the blood through the thicket. Not a bird was seen, and nothing for sound was born. They made their way back to the trail, and eastward to the Pools of Cordis Loci.

Creed and Celeste walked for hours through the wood. The two Vagus survivors were clearly disturbed. They stared into the sky, and swayed to and fro with the horses' gait. The woman mumbled to herself, disconnected from reality, as she would pick at things in the air, and place them in her mouth, though nothing could be found. Creed looked up at them and cleared his throat.

"What happened to these people?"

"They fell into our realm this way. From the moment they entered Mürindür, they have been twisted into what you see. These are the lost ones, the wanderers, the Vagus. They become Caedere one way or another."

"It doesn't seem to be their fault."

"What do you mean?"

"They're sick," Creed replied.

"Yes." Celeste nodded stoically.

"I mean it's an illness, a disease. Why would we punish someone with a disease?"

"The mind is very much a representation of the soul, Creed."

"No. No it isn't. Not here. I disagree." Celeste looked up from the ground and into his eyes. Her brow furrowed.

"They came here, and what you see is a consequence of what they did on Earth. They chose to die. They inflicted harm consciously and willingly even if it were due to vices of their own desire. They forfeit the natural order of things. None of us can change that or them. Not *you*. Not *me*. Not even my *mother*. No one in the Endüerduul can change these people. They are manifested as the creatures they are. They were granted free will, and with it they chose an end."

"So that's why they're here? Like this? Punished with a deranged mind here for having suffered with a sick one back home? That's cruelty. No, maybe you can't change them now, or cure them, but you can help. We can find a way to treat them."

"With what? What could you possibly give them that would make them as Welfalon souls once again? These aren't your patients back home. You cannot undo what has been done."

"No, but it seems as if they had been given the chance to think for themselves, escape as the others do in the Dunes of Transitio, then their entire outcome would have been different. Ogres or Caedere wouldn't have chased this Vaga beside me. He would have had a chance at renewal like everyone else. He would have sat at your tables in Redemptio," he argued.

"What you see is a manifestation of their judgment."

"I know, but I am saying the judgment is unfair. It is unethical."

"Be that as it may in your mind, they have done some horrible things," she replied.

"Would you have let them die back there?" Creed asked.

"No. We had the high ground. I felt we could have helped them from there," Celeste explained.

"Why did you pull me back?"

"There are traps, distractions everywhere. We are being watched, and an ambush is always just a thought away."

"Didn't the screams bother you?" Creed continued, concerned and bewildered. "Doesn't any of this bother you?"

"Always, but I hear them every day. That is the way here. We wouldn't pause for a second to hear the wailing of those imprisoned within Acrom's domain. Those souls were found in trial to deserve damnation, and yet we don't question it. There is a Hell for a reason, Creed, and although we try to help the Vagus, we can't save them. Now, we have to find a way to care for these two. We will get them back to the Redemptio Keep somehow, and try to rehabilitate them, but they will end up at the Keep forever because they will never be safe to release into Mürindür," Celeste replied sternly.

"Were they this way on Earth?" asked Creed.

"I do not know. Were they sick on Earth, and that lead them to perform the acts that they did, or were they not diseased but merely starved of virtue?"

"Can you tell the difference, Celeste?"

"No. Can you?"

"I don't suppose I can," Creed acknowledged.

"Either way, their choices lead to them becoming what you see before you. They may have been sick, but the Endüerduul is not cruel. This male Vaga is different, as is she, and they are cursed. Whether or not they were good or bad, they chose their path, and it has led to this."

"In my many lives, the one constant remained. Mental illness always played a role in the most horrific of things."

"What did you do back then for them?"

"As science advanced, we had medications. Therapy. Things we could do to help them lead normal lives. If not normal, then at least functional." Creed motioned with his hands.

"For all the times you've come back, I don't recall it hurting you this much." Celeste appeared uncomfortable, rubbing her belly over and over again.

"I don't know. It isn't just, or fair. More should be done. The answer can't be that we allow them to waste away in a desert."

"But it *is* the way, the dividing line for moments and choices unseen. When my mother and I walked the Earth, it was different then. We could guide their lives, but once the Cataclysm took place, we were no longer permitted to intervene."

"No wonder they wail. They have been abandoned."

"No, Creed. They have been judged."

"Exactly." Creed looked into her eyes for some semblance of similarity, but he only witnessed her pained expression as she turned away, fumbling with the horse's reins.

They continued on toward a small pasture of lilies and clover. The horses grazed with their burdens, and Celeste walked ahead to study some broken branches on the nearby aspens. Creed stared at the two Vagus victims. Seemingly unaware, they scarcely moved unless something bothered them like an itch or unseen pain. The athetoid, snake-like, movements reminded him of the Caedere. Eerily he wondered if Leterum truly converted them at all when he found them. They were already blind and mute in a way. What effect could the blindfolds and mouth sutures truly have on them? He watched Celeste, and she seemed troubled, but as he walked toward her, she turned in time to address him.

"These branches were freshly broken. I've noticed tracks along the way, and we may have been seen. I should have known! We can either ride together, or the Vagus can be left behind, but our family is in danger!" Celeste's eyes were aglow.

"Who could it be?"

"I'm unsure." She pointed to the ground. "These tracks are not the mark of an Ogre. The scout was likely mounted. We need to move!"

She unfastened the male Vaga, and Creed carried him to the other horse. He could feel the man's ribs beneath his ragged clothing. The Vaga's heart was beating fast, and despite his delusional state, he wrapped his arms around Creed. There was a subtle humanity about the Vagus, and Creed couldn't help but look upon them with pity. He felt responsible for them now, and bound them both carefully to the saddle. He took their horses reins and tied them onto Celeste's saddle hooks. As he looked up to his bride, she moved forward begrudgingly, so he climbed on behind her, resting his chest against her back. Creed looked at the Vagus, and then ahead upon the encroaching wilderness. Time was inescapable, and it had no patience. As they kept an eye out for the evasive scout, the wedding couple made haste to the Pools of Cordis Loci.

Chapter 18: The Pools of Cordis Loci

They ventured along a small bend in the forest, and Creed witnessed Ojin working fervently. The hobgoblin fed a series of encircled fires with shorn timber, building them about a shallow body of water at the forefront of the Pools of Cordis Loci. There was a mortared mound of moss-draped stones, which served as an altar, and Ojin seemed to mumble small enchantments as the pools shimmered. Lilies, lilacs, roses, and orchids adorned the elder trees and rock columns. This was the '*Sepulcher of Covenants*', Celeste explained. It was a monument and reminder of rebirth and renewal. The ancient willow tree, *Matsudana*, hung its boughs as an attendant over the holy grounds. "When anyone seeks approval, they kneel beneath that tree. That is where you took your Oath, and where we will take ours. I can remember that tree when I was a little girl, and I would lie beneath it, staring at the Pools, as its roots would cradle me, and the wind played its limbs like fingers upon a loom. I did not think after all this time, I would stand beneath it once more as a bride." Creed listened as she continued on about the traditions, and the rarity of weddings in Mürindür.

Granite boulders and broken cliffs formed a barricade much like a castle's walls, while hundreds of bodies of water coalesced through falls and streams, making up the Pools of Cordis Loci. A soft glow emanated from their depths, and the Pools had nary a ripple despite the winds slowly picking up as the day grew long.

Serena attended to the banquet tents, lengthy wooden tables of food, and directed security for the perimeter. Roasted game rolled slowly over flames amidst the chefs along the line of maple trees. Creed felt Celeste's body relax as she looked about quietly at all the activity. Her cheeks rose through a subtle smile. Although he had nothing to do with the planning or orchestration, he did hope it was as she wanted it. They rode a little further into camp, and he noticed Ojin shuffle quickly toward Serena in his purple and black ceremonial robes.

"Serena, they've been gone for hours. Should we send someone after them?"

"Xaris left an hour ago. He will find them." Serena reassured him.

"This doesn't bode well," Ojin complained.

"They need time. We've been with them ever since he arrived, one way or another. Let them have it," she explained.

"I think it unwise. The sun will set soon as well."

"Yes, it will."

"Does it concern you?"

"Very little." She finished tying the last of the willow wisps into an arch.

"The timing is everything, Serena," Ojin protested.

"Yes, it is. Perhaps you should look behind you." She smiled as Creed and Celeste arrived on horseback. Ojin grimaced as Serena walked over to welcome them. He appeared displeased with their newfound cargo.

"Welcome home you two! Have a nice jaunt?" Serena asked.

"Mother, we came across Ogres on the way. It was a full pod of them, and one was a Ferris Executioner. They slaughtered some men and women, but we managed to bring back these two survivors."

"Did any get away?" asked the Queen.

"No. We killed the band, but I found tracks running from our encounter, likely a scout. What kind I do not know, but it was headed this way. I feared something more was coming."

"Nothing yet, but Xaris just left looking for the two of you. How all of you didn't run into one another I'll never know. He may intercept the scout you speak of." Serena looked toward a few more Bellatorum. They wore their ceremonial silver armor and crimson half-capes over their left shoulder. One Bellator, a Captain, walked over to her as she whispered something, he nodded, and took a contingent of Bellatorum with him to catch up with Xaris.

Serena then walked over to the Vagus. She looked them over, as they continued their obtuse movements and hallucinations, and touched the knee of the seated woman. As Serena closed her eyes, her grip tightened, and when she opened them, she saw a very disturbed and angry being.

"He comes for you! Leterum calls to you Serena, and you will answer him! The Anima Capere comes for your soul!" The woman's crinkled face twisted with humor and horror as she turned to Celeste. "The unborn will be no more! The path you walk has ended!"

Celeste stood tall and walked to the Vaga.

"Tell your master, his weakness is manifest through your presence. Tell him I welcome him, and he may enter the Pools at any time." Celeste now stood inches away from the malodourous wretch, and her eyes became luminous. Creed stepped forward not knowing what was about to take place.

"Celeste, she's confused. She's trying to get under your skin." Creed placed his hand on her shoulder.

"I can easily account for her skin," as she pulled a slender dagger from her robe's sleeve.

"Ok. Ok. Enough." Creed waved his hands. The Vaga smiled at him as he tried to create some distance between the two.

"Ahhhhh, the mighty Hippocrates! Leterum welcomes you! Come to him. His arms are wide open to those who seek it. All you must do is ask." The Vaga drooled as she cackled with glee. Creed stared at her as he sidestepped her threats. He managed to squeeze in between the Vaga and Celeste, and could smell the weeks of mange on the delirious heckler.

"You, Hippocrates, will burn a thousand deaths in Leterum's mighty hands. He will baptize you in the sands of the Transitio, and glass will fill your…"

THWACK!

She fell off the horse landing face first with a thud. Ojin stepped back with his wooden staff, and wiped some of her blood from the jade orb.

"I don't enjoy them very much." Ojin spat on her backside.

"Ojin!" Creed scowled.

"What?" The hobgoblin rolled his eyes.

"He's taken a liking to them, Ojin." Celeste sheathed her dagger.

"Celeste. They're sick. That wasn't her. Something else had control of her mind."

"My old friend," Ojin reminded him, "they are cursed. These are the larvae that become the very beasts that nearly killed us all in the Fields of Effugere. It begins with them. You cannot cure them.

270

These are not good souls. They did dark things, and this is the consequence."

"Then why are they here? Why didn't they go straight to the Undüavalle once they died? Huh? Celeste tells me the Vagus are souls who chose their end. They didn't harm anyone else, but they deserve damnation? For suffering?" Creed questioned angrily.

"I don't know, but they were meant to become Caedere. We can't change that. We can only delay it," Ojin explained. Serena interrupted.

"Creed, we care for them at the Redemptio Keep, but they will never be normal. They can *never* be trusted. They may even be able to communicate with Leterum, and you brought them here. We need to keep them bound, and put them in confinement. Tonight is very important not just for you, but for us all. We can't afford for them to alter or hinder any of it." The Queen spoke calmly.

"Guards!" Ojin motioned to armored Minotaurs who walked over, grabbed the Vagus, and carried them into a tent far towards the end of the grounds. Creed shook his head.

"Can you imagine what it must feel like to show up here confused and scared and then suddenly you're face down in molten sand? You can see it in their eyes. Their minds are sick." Ojin put his hand on Creed's shoulders.

"They are not *you* my friend, and you are *not* them. Everyone feels confusion when they arrive here, but not everyone deserves the same fate. Now, they will be fine. Let us rejoice in your celebration today, and bring this all to a wonderful *beginning*. Why do you think they were up here far away from the dunes, Serena?"

"That I don't know. The Ogres likely took them as prisoners for their twisted purposes. They've never been this close to the Pools either, which I suspect is quite intentional," she replied.

"I didn't think bringing them here would jeopardize anything. I just felt we couldn't leave them there to die. Celeste?" Creed reached for her arm. "Hey."

"What?" She stepped away, irritated.

"I'm sorry."

"Why are you sorry?" she asked.

"I'm sorry for potentially ruining the day. I won't discuss this anymore. This is our day, and a time to celebrate us and our son."

"That's fine. What is done cannot be undone. I need to freshen up. You should do the same." Celeste walked toward her tent, and disappeared behind the curtains. Ojin chuckled and patted Creed on the back.

"My friend, she is tired. She is pregnant, and Vagus for a wedding day, well, they aren't much in the way of a wedding present."

Creed stood back and looked up at him.

"Damn it! That's right! I don't have anything! Ojin, I'm getting married and I don't have rings, presents, or…"

"You arrived naked. I'm sure she will understand, but until then, take this." Ojin dug in his robe's pockets, and fished out a carved wooden box. He handed it to Creed, and smiled. Creed stared at it for a moment. The engravings alone were beautiful.

"Ojin, I can't. I don't have any way to repay you."

"Ha! After all these years, it's the least I could do. You owe me nothing, but the gift is inside. Open it. Please." Creed removed the lid to reveal an amulet of golden leaves cupping a luminous, pale-green emerald. It was heavy for such a small trinket, but it caught every glimmer of light that came its way no matter how dim, and split it into a thousand beams. It was as captivating as a newfound star.

"This is a piece of jewelry crafted by the very angels of the Endüerduul. Its name is *Oerbuel*. It was designed to project hope, in the rays of all that the Lux could provide, even if the Lux appeared to be lost and forgotten. It has been in my possession since the Cataclysm, and even on my darkest days, I would look upon it, and my sense of loss would fade. We all need to be reminded of hope now and again, Creed. It's so quiet at times, but when we listen, when we look, the world becomes more beautiful when we can envision a better tomorrow. I had hoped one day you would give this to Celeste, and now, here we are! I found in an old script years ago, that its very life comes from the first sun in the universe. It is a brilliant work of art. Now it is yours, my friend."

Creed held it, turning it over in his hands.

"Ojin, I can't."

"You must. When I saw her look at you for the first time, I knew this day would come. This is a fitting gift for your bride. It was meant to be worn by the Princess." Ojin's smiling eyes shone through his bushy brow, and reassured his friend.

"She's pretty mad. Not exactly the kind of mood for a wedding day," Creed said as he stared at the necklace.

"How were the Steppes?" Ojin asked.

"Amazing. She painted a living mural that moves on cave walls. She said she would work on it each time I left."

"She found many ways to pass the time waiting for your return. The Steppes have always been her garden, her safe haven. The two of you would spend days up there away from us all. How is

Morsu?" Ojin turned Creed toward the center of the camp, and walked with him as his heavy arm hung across his shoulders.

"Well enough to tackle and kill a full-grown Ashi bull. As we flew on him toward the sea, I had flashes of him in my mind. Hunting and flying. I remembered then that the Northern Steppes was where I first kissed Celeste. There on the very rocks that we stood today."

"You should tell her this."

"Not sure it would matter much to her right now, Ojin."

"Creed, it would warm her heart. We need you two to be happy, for today we make history. I hope you understand the significance of it all."

"What? Getting married in general or getting married to someone that could make me disappear in a pile of ash with a wave of her hand?"

"Ha! She may have a temper, but I'm sure you'll be fine. She's been just as excited about this day as we all have. She does love you. She always has. You should go to her." Ojin encouraged him as he motioned with a nod toward Celeste's tent.

"I guess I should."

"I need to finish the preparations. Offer her Oerbuel. I'm sure you'll find that she can be quite forgiving. After all, she did put up with you for an eternity," Ojin teased.

"Yes. I guess she did."

Creed smiled, and looked up from the box. He shook Ojin's hand, and the lumbering hobgoblin returned to two cauldrons, mixing the bubbling juices with a large ladle. The smells were quite delicious. Creed stood for a moment, and stared at the sky. He looked down upon the amulet and held it up to the remnants of the sun's day. It emitted a green band of light toward the horizon, reflecting briefly off the snowy tips of the Highland mountains on the western edge. It was quietly powerful. He wrapped the necklace within its small linen cloth, closed the box, and approached Celeste's tent, addressing the guards.

"May I?"

They stepped aside as he drew back the curtains, and found her sitting in a white silken gown upon a gold embroidered stool. Her handmaidens were helping her adjust her crown while another brushed out her long golden hair. Her blue eyes caught a glimpse of Creed in the mirror as he walked in. A series of small torches strung across the tent imbued the room with warmth.

"Hey," he said.

"Hey."

"You look beautiful."

"Thank you. You need to change your clothes." She spoke curtly.

"I don't have a tent, and if I do, I don't know which one it is."

"You do. They can escort you in a moment." She continued to brush her hair.

"Well I wanted to talk if that's ok."

"Of course." Her tone was still cool.

"Never a dull moment around here I suppose. One minute we're flying on a white lion, and the next we're hunting Ogres." He weakly chuckled.

"Just another day in Mürindür."

"Seems I've had better days here, with you, but I can't seem to remember them all."

"Maybe in due time."

"Maybe. The pieces I do recover are pretty special, though." Creed stepped closer.

"Such as?"

"Celeste, my mind has been flooded with memories since we went to the Steppes. Sometimes they come in small bursts, but this time it seemed all the moments we had there with one another returned to me. Almost like someone released a trap door above my head, and I was suddenly buried within it all."

"Buried?" Celeste raised her left eyebrow.

"Well I mean, you know," he cleared his throat, "I know why you took me there."

"Oh?"

"That was our first kiss. Right there on those rocks so many years ago, so many lives before now. That was the place I realized regardless of time, or distance, or adversary I would never leave your side. That was the cave I promised you that no matter how many lives I lead, I would always come home to you. Just for you." Her expression broke, and her face warmed pink. Creed stepped a little closer.

"I know things are different, but I remember you, and I remember us, and I want that. I want us. I want you. I've never felt more at home or more alive since I arrived, and I thank you for that. Thank you for always waiting. Thank you for your forgiveness. Thank you for loving me even when you could have walked away at any moment. Thank you for being the only one willing to find all my broken pieces."

Celeste's eyes filled with tears as did her maidens'. She put down her hairbrush, stood, and dabbed her eyes with a cloth. She walked toward him, meeting half way.

"I'm not crying. It's the baby. My feelings are all over the place."

"Well it's a start." He smiled as she laughed.

"I guess so," Celeste replied.

"I love you, Celeste."

"I do love you too. I wondered if you remembered any of it. How it all began. The experiences, the years of laughter, and the dreams we shared with each other. It warms my heart to hear that you do. We would lie on the sand for hours dreaming about eternity. We didn't worry about when you would leave next, or what battles awaited us in the world that day. We reveled in the moment for what it was, and what we hoped it to become. Today is our day. Let's make this a beautiful memory too." Celeste leaned into him, and exhaled slow and subtle.

"Agreed." Creed stepped back. "I have something for you!"

He opened the box, unwrapped Oerbuel, and a dawn of green bathed the entire tent. Her eyes grew with wonder. He undid the clasp of the hammered links as she pulled her hair up, and he fastened the necklace about her neck, losing himself willingly in her eyes. They kissed, and apparently the time slipped as their lips lingered a little too long. The maidens cleared their throats more than once to bring some levity. His eyes opened to see hers staring back. Creed smiled again as his fingers fixed the clasp, and he stepped back. It was the perfect length. She gathered it in her hands.

"I remember when I first saw Oerbuel. It lay to the side of the artisans' crafting bench. There were so many beautiful pieces in Endüerduul, but this one always drew me into it. I thought it was lost after the Cataclysm, but here it is. How did you... whom did you?"

"Ojin said he found it. He's kept it secretly all this time waiting for us to reach this day. I'm glad you like it."

"I love it!" she exclaimed.

"Good." She hugged his neck tightly, and kissed him once more. The somber air had cleared, and the ceremony was again, front and center.

"Now go on and please clean up. Many people haven't seen you in ages, and if I keep crying my eyes will be puffy. Now shoo." She playfully pushed him toward the entrance. Reluctantly, he obliged. She blew another kiss to him as the curtains returned to one another.

As he looked about the camp, Creed realized how much work everyone had put into this day. There were banquet tables overfilled with roasted meats, baked breads, and harvested fruits, organized by regions and themes of flavors. Wines were poured into large crystal decanters as the citizens prepped more barrels for tapping. Strings of glowing stones, similar to the ones in the Ashi caverns, lit the tree branches above, and as the sun approached its restful place, the canopies were cast in hues of blue and purple. Musicians strummed their bows and strings while melodies, long lost in his mind, brought Creed back to a place he once yearned.

Looking to his right, he noticed log piles stacked two men high while flashes and smoky tendrils escaped the bellows of the nearby blacksmith. Creed was curious as to why the smithy was working so hard on his wedding day, so he decided to take a look. He ventured behind the tanned hides, and his eyes seemingly deceived him. A squad of sweaty Minotaurs hammered upon a row of anvils. The bellows were panting, forcing air into forges that had not been at the Groves or seen in Durdan. Swords, axes, poleaxes, glaives, spears, shields, and arrows were tossed into piles as men gathered them up leaving through a pass in the back of the structure.

The air was heavy with steam and the smell of burning slag. Raw, molten metal stabbed troughs of mountain water, and were then worked over by the hands of each master. It appeared as if the blacksmiths had been here for months, and with the furious pace of warmongering craftsmanship, nothing was more out of place at a wedding. Creed stepped forward to address the grayest of the Minotaurs. The creature was as tall as Ojin, but smelled of sweaty men and cattle.

"Sir, why are all of you making these weapons? Tonight, is a wedding."

"Yes, it is," the Minotaur replied.

"It would appear that each of you are preparing for war."

"Yes. It appears that way."

"Are you?" Creed asked.

"Are what?" The Minotaur seemed annoyed, avoiding eye contact with the inquisitor.

"Are you preparing for war, and if so, why? Where is the battlefield?"

"All of Mürindür is a battlefield, boy." He swung his hammer hard onto the roughened broad sword under his attention, and the metal bent beneath a bevy of bright orange sparks.

"So, when do we expect this war?" Creed persisted.

"We have been at war for as long as I can remember, but I suspect very soon we will draw lines with the most wicked that creation has to offer."

"Why do you say that?"

"What do you think will happen when Hippocrates and Celeste wed? Hmm? Do you think Leterum will pay a visit with gold and gifts? This ceremony is an affront to him and his legions. It is a promise from a place he can no longer visit for a destiny that will no longer be his. He will do all things within his power to ruin this union and the child it brings." He swung his hammer once more, and when the sparks settled, he looked up, and was startled. He hadn't realized with whom he spoke.

"Hippocrates! Forgive me." The Minotaur bowed.

"Please don't bow. I asked you an earnest question."

"Just the same, forgive me. I shouldn't have spoken so loosely." The giant beast kneeled in atonement.

"I appreciate the honesty. Not so many people have been forthcoming."

"It is your wedding day, and this discussion is best made for late night conversations around the fire between warriors. My name is Jak-rael. It is an honor to meet with you." He bowed again.

"Please stop and stand. I appreciate your respect, but it isn't necessary. When do you suspect Leterum will strike?" The Minotaur stood with hammer in hand.

"Serena suspects it will be any moment."

"But she seems so calm."

"Ha! She has already made ready for war. You have yet to see the battlements and catapults in the valley below around the Capital of Guillarne. The wedding is a brief escape, so of course she seems at peace. For the time being, she can focus on something beautiful. This is the way. We celebrate. We fight. We wed, and we die. Mürindür."

"How long have you been here crafting these weapons?"

"Few days."

"Seems longer."

"This is Helgenschphere, our armory. The Queen calls us to wherever we are needed, and we make the tools of war. It was her solution to supply lines, mobility and mortality. About two dozen of us keep the place running, and when it's time, we leap and reap."

Creed picked up an arrow. It was a solid piece of steel, perfectly balanced from the thin shaft to the serrated edges. Each one was the same, and there appeared to be thousands lying on the floor. He rolled it in his fingertips.

"Jak-rael, back home we had artillery, guns, planes, tanks. Why not use those here?"

"Intent, free will, and the lasting presence of insatiable relics imbued with the finality of war."

"How so?"

"Each weapon here is wielded with intent, and the violent residue of the wielder. That arrow is held fast by fingertips emblazoned with desire for demolition. The spear lying there, this sword and that pike over here they all must be held, embraced in fact, and it is the sudden intent, the willful resolute intent, projecting like fire through each weapon's purpose that renders their victims helpless. I have heard of the weapons you speak, but here in Mürindür, the Caedere do not fall without the intent of a willful man, and the lingering film of ferocity. The beasts of Undüavalle will not fade without the direction of hands hell bent on decimating their ranks. A bullet may sit in a chamber, loaded with intent, and a steel pin may strike it on the back, but that pin does not carry the remnants, the flesh of the one who sends it. The bullet is not held as it is launched, it is merely pushed through a cold mechanism of an impersonal consequence."

"But you can intentionally pull the trigger," Creed insisted.

"Yes, but your hatred, your anger isn't as oil on the bullet itself. This spear however, when in your hands, follows your command, and your intent is driven forcefully into your adversary. The ill will that you set into motion rests in their flesh, and no machine can ever grant you that satisfaction."

"That's almost poetic."

"Our killing in Mürindür is quite intimate." His face contorted into a bullish grin. Creed set the arrow down.

"Do you think we even have time for this ceremony?"

"We have all made time for this ceremony. We need this ceremony, Hippocrates. The war will be waiting for us when it's done. Here," the Minotaur reached into a large white oak barrel that had been halved, "this is for you." He handed the items to Creed as he took a deep breath with a chest bursting with pride.

"You and I came from one of the greatest civilizations of all mankind. Before my race was banished here, we fought amongst the Greeks. I never fought with you, but your stories carried across the sea. I made this helm in your honor for your wedding day. I modeled it after the caduceus with two serpents that you are known for. This breastplate and matching pteruges took me years to make just right." The molded serpents came low and forward as jaw pieces while the entire helm was hammered finely with the surface of scales. Jak-rael fit the helm and remaining armor onto Creed to secure some final adjustments. It all felt light and seamless. Creed kneeled and stretched, but felt no restriction. He looked at the breastplate and saw a large winged lion.

"Is this Morsu?"

"Yes, it is. I felt it fitting for you."

He took Creed to a mirror, and let him see himself as the world did. The bronze colored armor was ancient in appearance but contemporary in its design. In the grooves and engravings, the metal turned a reflective black. Creed no longer saw himself, but an embattled Greek hoplite ready for war.

Suddenly Creed's mind stumbled, and he found himself in the depths of an arena. Blood soaked walls filled his nares with the air of copper. Bodies lay strewn about as he looked at his hands soaked in the remnants of the fallen. The doors above him opened yet again, and he was blinded by the sunlight, spear and short sword in hand. Crowds shouted for his death as two men with axes bore down upon him. One swept for his feet while the other punched him square in the mouth with the pummel of an axe. Creed could taste his bloody tongue. For a moment he seemed anchored in the sand, but rage resurfaced and he kicked the first man in the groin, crumpling his legs. As the second swung again, Creed spun to decapitate the crippled, and followed through with his spear into the eye socket of the last opponent. The bodies fell in silence. Then the crowd roared, a standing ovation for an unwelcomed tournament, a majority approval for the basest of human tendencies. Creed looked into the sun as he could taste the sweat and fear on his beard, then another echo.

"Hippocrates. Hippocrates?" Jak-rael shook him out of the cobwebs.

"Look at me."

Creed looked in his eyes.

"Are you well?"

"I'm… I'm fine."

He took the helm off, and beads of sweat trickled down his brow. He looked in the mirror once more and saw only himself and one giant Jak-rael. Creed's heart was pounding.

"Thank you, Jak-rael. These pieces are beautiful, but I cannot take them from you. I have nothing to offer in return, and these are truly works of art."

"They are gifts. You cannot say no. It is Mürindür's tradition. On your wedding day, you must accept all gifts. I would have made you a spear as well, but the Queen tells me you have something much better."

"Yes. It isn't bad at all."

"I wish you many graces and a thousand blessings, Hippocrates. I hope today is a special one for you and the Princess. I will have my helpers take these to your tent just outside."

"Thank you for the enlightenment, Jak-rael." They nodded at one another, and Creed ventured out into the venue once more.

One of Celeste's maids came out of her tent, and escorted him to a smaller shelter made of animal skins and wooden beams. As he stepped inside, he saw a large bed, a table with wine already poured, and a set of wedding clothes lying before him. A steaming bath had been drawn in a smoothed, maple wood tub. He undressed, stepped into the hot water, and sat there bathing, contemplating the arena flashback. He hoped nothing startled his memories again during the ceremony.

Shortly afterward, his armor stood at the ready on a wooden mannequin beside the bed. He looked at it in the light. The armor was a throwback to an era upon which he had once lived before all of this, when he was likely just a man without burden or expectation. Had he been Hippocrates in that memory, or was it something afterward? Something before? He stared at the wine, but didn't trust his mind. He reached for the towel, and stepped out to dry. The wedding robes were a little cumbersome to figure out, and since he didn't have any assistants, he did the best he could. He sat down and stared at the armor.

A wedding and a war, he thought. What more could be asked of him in Mürindür?

Chapter 19: The Wedding of The Pools

Ojin walked into Creed's tent and laughed. The wedding robes were a debacle, and the look on the groom's face was a mix of concern and bewilderment.

"I can't tell if you're ready for a wedding or a funeral, my friend," Ojin teased.

"Little of both."

"I can see that. Be at peace! All these years, and the two of you will finally wed! We've talked about this many times! It has come!"

"It has."

"I was nervous on my wedding day as well. It's normal. Here, you need to take this off, and turn this around. You have it all backwards." Ojin pointed to the lapels on the Creed's back, and gave a twirl with his stout index finger.

"Figures. Felt a little tight." After some guidance, Creed stepped to the side, and fixed his evening attire. Ojin noticed the armor nearby.

"I see you met Jak-rael."

"Yes."

"This is nice," Ojin acknowledged, looking closely at the artisan work, "He's a fine blacksmith. A master of his craft."

"Well he tells me this is all he does. He follows Serena around giving her war at a moment's notice."

"Yes. He is always, and unfortunately, in high demand." Creed shook his head in exhaustion.

"What are we doing here, Ojin? Why is all this happening, and yet nothing changes? People die and come here. Then they die again, but only if they're lucky. Who would make such a place? Who does this? Let these people be judged. I don't care, but give them their judgment, and give them peace or damnation, but don't waste their time. Don't make them suffer. It isn't humane."

"It's more than that."

"Is it?" asked Creed.

"For most, this *is* their second chance, *their* redemption. Most welcome it, openly."

"What about those two over there," he motioned to the captives' tent across camp. "They were suffering on Earth wondering what the Afterlife would hold, and then something or someone happens to them, and they stumble. They fall. Now, as a result, they're prisoners pending execution from a madman. How does the Endüerduul justify this?"

"They suffered their own fates, their chosen fates, on Earth. You have to trust in that. You have to trust that the judgment was fair, and that what they did was of their own volition."

"Fair? That could be me over there in that tent. Scared, confused, disoriented. When I see them, I see me."

"You aren't them. You did not do what they did."

"Ojin, my mind is burning with memories. Hard, horrific things that make me feel like I'm back there in time, on Earth. These images are vivid. Maybe that's what's waiting for me. Maybe the next time I go back, I become a Vaga. Have you ever thought about that? What if they were Luxatio, and now…"

"They never were."

"How do you know?" Creed asked.

"We know the Luxatio. We welcomed each one of them into this existence."

"Some existence."

"Hippocrates, you need to understand." Ojin spoke with animated hand gestures, emphatic and high.

"Look, I'm over it. I understand. I just, just feel like this is a big puzzle, and we're missing a lot of the pieces. There's something else. When I try to think about it, I feel like I get close, and then a memory blows it all up. I think there is more to this than just letting them burn in the desert."

"Sit down. Let us talk." Ojin walked to the table, and poured two glasses of wine.

"I don't drink."

"Just sit. Have a drink. Just one, and listen to what I have to say." Creed thought for a moment, and felt he needed something, anything at this point. He took a seat beside Ojin, looked into the glass, and drank from it. The dark-red wine was perfect.

"Tonight, is a moment we have all waited for, hoped for, prayed for throughout the ages. But in reality, despite what everyone may tell you, tonight isn't about anyone else other than you and Celeste. It is not about the Vagus, the Caedere, Leterum, Serena, the Endüerduul, or myself. It is about you, and your wife and your child. It is about *your* family. This is something more than anyone or anything can ever give you. Even if we weren't at war, and there was no Transitio, you and Celeste would find one another, and this day would still happen. Remember this, and be thankful for the day. Be thankful for the Princess, and for your life here on Mürindür," Ojin took a long swig of wine, twirling it about in his mouth, "You have been given a great gift among men. You are loved and honored. When you walk out there tonight, remember that too. When people look at you, they see something they are incapable of, and in that they witness hope."

"That's unwarranted."

"No, it is not, and that is my point. You think you are nothing, but that is your excuse. It is a fool's errand, and you do more harm than good by practicing this self-deprecation. You cannot see yourself for what you are to these people, to all of us. You inspire people to be more, and you give so much of yourself, that they cannot help but do the same. Do not abdicate this gift, but cherish it. Hold it close, and know the Endüerduul is kind, it is Love, and it is the path upon which you have been set. Stand with your bride tonight, and hold her close. Love her as you already do, and bury these thoughts for now. They will be waiting for us all in the morning, but tonight, let us live. Let us hope. Let us be the Mürindür we once were."

Creed drank the wine slowly. He thought about Ojin's words, and looked at the mirror beside the armor stand. He saw two old friends, and the need for a momentary ceasefire in his mind. He looked into his cup, and saw that much remained.

"To my wedding." Creed held his glass high for a toast.

"To your wedding." They knocked goblets, and finished the toast. The brotherly warmth was cut short, however, as a Bellator with gray eyes walked into Creed's tent with a cloaked figure.

"Ojin, this woman wishes to speak with Hippocrates. I found her outside the entry."

"For what purpose? Where is Serena?" Ojin stood, as did Creed.

"She readies herself for the wedding. I didn't wish to disturb her, and this woman says she has news that is most dire. She said you would understand. She is a Luxata."

"Show yourself." The woman wore a charcoal colored cloak, which furled its edges in the dirt. Only her chin and lips were visible. She pulled back the hood, looked up to Ojin, and then turned to Creed. A sword's hilt revealed itself just shy of the nape of her neck. "Hippocrates, it is good to see you once more. It has been too long."

"I don't know you." Creed stared intently. Ojin waved his hand, and the light became stronger within the shelter. He looked to the Bellator.

"Thank you. Stand guard, and tell no one until I have the time to inform the Queen. I will do so in a moment."

"As you wish." The Bellator left their sight just outside Creed's quarters.

"Do you not remember the Battle of Borainnos?" she queried.

"If I were to recall every battle, that everyone says I should, I would have little room to remember my name. You, somehow, look familiar."

"She stood with us against the cannibalistic priests of Acrom, the Timaenods, and their army of three-legged giant Boräenstrom. We attacked their temple at the base of the mountain that holds Leterum's Keep."

"I'm sorry. I have nothing."

"Maybe this will help." She walked toward him, and outstretched her hand. In it, was a copper rod speckled with flakes of patina. A sliver of tan parchment was exposed. Creed took it from her hand, and unfurled the scroll.

"You told us if we ever needed your help, you would come for us. *Luxatio aeternum.*" The woman said.

Creed read from the scroll, and he found himself again, in another moment in time, before an audience of Luxatio at the Redemptio Keep. He looked around the room in his mind, and saw the very woman before him. That evening, as he recalled, the likelihood of returning to Earth was high. He felt it in his bones, so he gave his inner circle parchments with instructions should he not return from their nighttime mission. She was the last to receive hers. As quickly as the thought began, it was over, and he looked up at Ojin.

"This was from my last visit before I returned." He looked to the woman, and nodded more confidently than he had suspected capable.

"You are Varsalsae," Creed said.

"Yes, commander," she affirmed. Creed read the scroll.

> *Varsalsae, the Vagus seemingly have grown in number. I sense an imbalance of some sort. There have been reports of caravans of Vagus making their way to the swamps, away from Leterum's Keep. The purpose I do not know, but this appears to be a strategy change for our enemy. Not all have been baptized as Caedere. Take a few Luxatio with you, scout the swamps, and help me determine their fate. If you can rescue any of them, smuggle them to Redemptio, but not if it means your demise. Until I return, Luxatio aeternum. - Hippocrates*

"I remember that night. It was the last time I met with all of you. What became of the others?" Creed questioned.

"I'm sorry to say that from our unit, three remain."

"Only three? The others?" Creed looked at her intently.

"I brought twelve with me that night. We followed the caravan into the swamps, and discovered an internment camp of Vagus. They were sold to the highest bidder like animals. Some were burned alive as their ash scattered to the ether, and some," she paused to gain her composure, "some of them were butchered and sacrificed to Acrom as lambs. Their bodies served as a banquet to the camp. We had managed to cross their perimeter without notice, and loaded three wagons with Vagus. We dressed as Leterum sympathizers, and traveled a few miles from the camp when an Ogre tribe ambushed us. We battled fiercely, and made out quite well, but the numbers were too great. Some stayed back to provide us the time we needed, and we returned with only twenty Vagus remaining. The Queen was not pleased. She felt we had risked too much, wasted valuable Luxatio lives, and that we needed to return to the Capital to await her decision. She planned on speaking with you that evening, but following your mission, you did not return. Once we heard that you had crossed to the mortal realm once more, we regrouped, and left for the Groves."

"You didn't go to the Capital of Guillarne?" asked Creed.

"No. We broke our oaths for what we knew to be right. We turned our backs on the Queen, and one by one when the portals opened to send us back to Earth, we walked away."

"And so now, if you should die here in Mürindür, your path is over. You know this?" Ojin questioned Varsalsae.

"Indeed," she replied. Ojin stepped forward to look her over.

"Does the Queen know you are here?"

"It won't be long I suspect."

"No, I suspect not. She will be irate. This is not the day to bring this to us, Varsalsae!" Ojin's voice was enraged with frustration.

"I'm sorry, Ojin."

"That's not enough."

"Why? Why isn't it enough, Ojin? When will it be enough?" Creed asked.

"It isn't that simple, Creed! Three Luxatio abandon their oaths, and fail to return to the very realm where they are most needed. Varsalsae herself has been venturing to Earth for over a thousand years, and just like that, she chooses…"

"To uphold what the Lux has forever held dear." She stared intently at Creed.

"And what would that be?" Ojin asked.

"Justice," she replied.

Ojin was stressed. He paced about the room.

"Serena was angry beyond anything I had ever seen when you disappeared, and she was mourning the loss of her greatest soldiers. You didn't die. You weren't captured. You weren't twisted into one of Leterum's pets, as she feared. All this time, it was because you decided to spit on everything she did for each of you!"

"Ojin, please. She's here for a reason. If the Endüerduul is as moral and just, as you say, then surely it would not allow any of this to take place unless it served some greater purpose."

"Serena will want to know, and she will want to know everything. There will be a price to pay, Varsalsae!" Ojin's hair rose angrily on the back of his neck.

"I do not wish to hide from her, Ojin. I wouldn't have walked into the festivities if that were the case. I asked to speak with Hippocrates first, knowing that I would face her very soon."

"You will be going back to Earth. You know this," the hobgoblin replied.

"Perhaps."

"Serena needs to know, but can we agree to have this wedding, and then let her know, tomorrow, maybe after the noon meal? Ojin, can we do that? Give Celeste and I the ceremony you promised earlier. Let us have this night, and tomorrow we can delve into this mess."

"Hippocrates, they have found a way to tip the scales in their favor, and the more they sacrifice to Acrom, the stronger he becomes. Leterum's witch has marched across these lands at will, and there will come a time when we stand alone against impossibility." Varsalsae's voice seemed taut.

"Then we ready for war in the morning. Tonight, let me hold my bride," Creed replied.

"You need to stay here, Varsalsae, during the ceremony. The newlyweds will go to their bridal enclave, and in the morning, we will discuss this. Do not leave this enclosure by any means." Ojin wagged his palm at her.

"I will remain."

"Varsalsae, I am sorry that we lost the others. I am sorry that I left all of you that night." Creed shook her hand earnestly.

"It is the Way. Welcome back, Hippocrates. We have faith in you."

"That's what I hear. We will speak again."

"*Luxatio aeternum*," she replied.

"*Luxatio aeternum*," Creed answered.

"Creed, let's go. We have a wedding to attend." Ojin looked sternly at Varsalsae, and escorted Creed onto the wedding grounds. He turned to the Bellator.

"Not a word. Let us have this night, and in the morning, we will proceed with Serena."

"Indeed." The Bellator nodded as Creed and Ojin strode to the Pools to make ready for the evening.

The pair watched the last bit of light defervesce beneath the mountains as they stood at the base of a slow rising amphitheater of stone. Behind them were the Pools of Cordis Loci, and before them sat hundreds of well-wishers. Ojin paced slowly, and Creed placed his hand on the back of his arm.

"Aren't you supposed to be reassuring me? You're kind of the best man."

"Best man?"

"Yeah. You know. The guy keeping me calm before I say my vows."

"What's there to keep calm about?" Ojin wringed his hands.

"I don't know. Marriage is kind of scary."

"You've been together for over two thousand years. If you had issues with commitment, they would have come up before now. I'm more concerned about the Luxatio issues coming to our doorstep the night of this ceremony. Serena will tear the joy from your very chest."

Creed smirked.

"Heh. Yeah. Guess you're right. I'm still nervous, so thanks. That helped a lot," Creed admonished.

"If Serena knows of Varsalsae, we all have to answer for it."

"What happened back then?"

Ojin looked at him, and lowered his voice.

"Creed, you were leading a team to rescue Vagus, to save them from what their fates had long concluded. You did not always let

Serena know what you were up to. When she found out that you had been doing this every night behind her back, she questioned your intent. She planned to meet with you, but the pathway to Earth found you first. She has intentionally avoided it for now, but it will come to light, and you will have to answer to her."

"You think she would banish the father of her grandson?"

"She's only had one in her family up to now. She has done many things to protect her. Let's not find out," Ojin replied.

Creed's eyes widened.

"Ok then. This should be fun."

Mother-in-law from Hell. Fantastic, he thought.

The stringed music began. Everyone turned to Creed's left where the members of the ceremony entered. Serena smiled and walked slowly alone toward the altar. She stood next to Ojin, and looked at Creed.

"We decided to honor some earthly traditions for everyone," Serena explained.

"That's great." Creed's stomach burned a bit, and he forced a smile.

The young satyr fawns, walking down the aisle, scattered white hibiscus petals along the way as their parents smiled with adoration. The music slowed and concluded. High atop the amphitheater a long row of Minotaurs stood shoulder to shoulder. They took a deep breath, and began to chant while stomping the rustic travertine stone. In unison, loud and resonant, it seemed very similar to the old Hakas of Creed's earlier lives. His skin was covered in raised hairs, and as he let the sounds bathe over him, Creed closed his eyes. The moment was empowering. Suddenly, they stopped, and a great roar rolled down the amphitheater like a volcano.

There she was, the moon in the midst of a thunderstorm of emotion. Celeste stood beside Morsu. He had been groomed, and stood proud above his escort. The visitors slowly and methodically slid closer to one another to get a little more space between them and the master hunter. Celeste giggled, and with her left hand buried in his mane, she patted him with her right despite the bouquet of calla lilies.

"Morsu, be kind." The lion looked to her and shook his shoulders. The Princess appeared to have found that itchy spot again. His purr was like a base drum. She looked down to see Creed. Her cheeks flushed, and she smiled that beautiful smile he adored. As Celeste walked down the steps, Morsu followed closely as if she were a newborn cub. Her cascading gown draped the stone as morning light, and Creed couldn't help but hold his breath. He felt a hairy arm on his back.

"Breathe my friend. If you pass out again, you will wake up in water."

Exhale. Breathe. Stand. Steady.

His palms were sweaty, so he wiped them off on his clothes. They made it to the altar, and Morsu stood behind Creed making sure he bumped the groom gently with his hips as he turned to face the crowd. Celeste smiled and shook her head.

"He's the alpha."

"Yeah I know. He makes it a point to remind me frequently." Creed laughed.

The ceremony became quiet as Ojin cleared his throat.

"We are gathered here tonight for the promise of love eternal, and there is no more a fitting place than the Pools of Cordis Loci. For as long as it has existed, this ground has been holy, and the site of many promises. Many of you before us kneeled at these very waters to give of yourselves, and take what was gifted unto you. Tonight, we stand to see the blessings of not just my friend and the Princess, but of the unborn. Never before have we witnessed the birth of mortal man in Mürindür, but in time we will, and with that hope begins a new Age for all." Ojin looked to Serena. "The Queen has asked to say a few words."

She stepped forward.

"My fellow country men and women, for millennia we have watched these two court one another, and despite the wars, the years, and the wait, they have held onto one another through it all. It took me quite some time to follow suit, but my daughter knew from the very beginning that this man, Hippocrates, would be hers. Tonight, it has come to pass. I wish them all that Hope and the Light may provide, and with my blessings I welcome this union. May we forever remember this day. The day the Lux became anew. For Mürindür!" she shouted.

The crowd replied earnestly.

"For Mürindür!"

Ojin picked up a leather-bound text, and opened to the ivory pages he had set the marker.

"I will read from the Praedictum Animarum. '*For unto all those who kneel before the Cordis Loci, the Endüerduul extends its grace unto those who partake, and forever more, none shall break the bond of gift and promise.*' We stand before these two, entwined souls, and offer them the blessings of the Endüerduul, and all that it

298

encompasses." He turned toward the altar, and brought forth the goblet. The water was so clear that if he hadn't caused a ripple it would have appeared empty. Ojin looked to Celeste, and offered her the first sip.

"Drink and know that you take within yourself a commitment to this man, your child, and the Endüerduul. May it nourish and protect you. Will you take and drink the cosmos willingly and knowingly? Will you take this man as your husband forevermore?"

"I take this man as my husband, my love, my passion for living. I promise to love him through war, famine, feast, and family. I take this drink willingly, knowingly, and without reservation for the preservation of my kin, and the salvation of Mürindür." She took the goblet into her hands, and drank fully. Once she was done, she handed the goblet back to Ojin, and looked into Creed's eyes.

"I am forever bound to you and to our child. We are one, and we are free, and for all eternity we will roam these lands together with our son. We are Mürindür and Mürindür is ours to shepherd." Ojin turned to Creed, and offered him the goblet.

"Hippocrates, you have sworn an oath before, on these very shores, and it was a bond that has held fast through many centuries, and countless lives on Earth. You have been a true servant of the Lux, and we ask of you again this day, will you take and drink the cosmos willingly and knowingly? Will you take this woman as your wife forevermore?"

Creed took the goblet, and looked at Celeste as he drank. The water was cold and soothing, and the restlessness inside him dissipated. Creed drank until the goblet was emptied, and he handed it back to Ojin. The hobgoblin cleared his throat and raised a brow. Creed gestured confusion.

"Sorry. Guess I missed a step. I drank knowingly and willingly, and I take full comfort in that it is a promise to the Endüerduul, to my lands, but most importantly to my bride. I take you, Celeste, forevermore as my wife and the mother to our unborn child. As we come together as one, I pray we are forever blessed by the Endüerduul."

"And as we wait for the blessing, let it be remembered that the heart never forgets, and as such never forget your heart. *Cor numquam operae praebitae obliviscitur*," Ojin recited.

The audience cheered.

"*Cor numquam operae praebitae obliviscitur!*"

Creed and Celeste smiled at one another and kissed. She then embraced him, and whispered in his ear, "*Cor numquam operae praebitae obliviscitur*".

They stood hand in hand as Ojin walked with them to the shores. Serena stood beside Celeste as Ojin stood beside Creed. The air and waters were still. A moment passed, and Creed wondered if something was missing. He looked behind them, and he saw everyone smiling back. Bog and Pax stood beside one another along the back wall of the amphitheater, but Xaris could not be found. Creed turned from the amphitheater, and looked to the Pools.

The waters warmed, and the wind stirred the giant branches of *Matsudana*. The willow leaves whisked the air like a brush softly upon a drum. There was a ripple followed by another, and yet another until the Pools seemed to breathe. The waters became cloudy while a soft white light eminated from below the surface, and the fog rolled gently around them like a veiled wall. The four were now secluded from everyone, and a series of unified voices spoke.

"We are the Oracle of the Pools of Cordis Loci. We see a mortal before us, and yet an immortal bride. Within, we see their child, a promise, a prophecy. The Endüerduul has long awaited this union, and for the many, hope has been placed within the few. Knowing that never before has a mortal been born on this soil, Serena, do you approve?"

"I do," the Queen replied.

"Hippocrates, we have watched over you, we have cared for you, and you have kept your covenant with us. You have done well for mankind, and the world has benefitted from your benevolence. We hold you yet again to an eternal Oath, to this woman, to this child. You will be asked to sacrifice much, and with the birth of your son, your destiny will forever change. Will you swear yourself to her, your bride, and to he, your son, and like the time before, yourself beyond mankind and to the eternal cosmos?"

"I do," Creed replied.

"Celeste, child, you have always walked your own path. This day you have sworn to be forever bound to this mortal, this Luxata. You carry within your womb a blessing, and it must be known that he shall face great adversity. Dark forces unite against him, and he will forever need your guidance. Are you willing to sacrifice much if not all for the safety and the purpose of your son?"

"I am willing. I am able," Celeste affirmed.

"Then we grant our many blessings unto you, your husband, and your unborn son. May you live with purpose and prosperity. We accept your vows. We sanctify this union, and the future it portends."

The voices disappeared, and the fog lifted. As the light faded from the waters, they turned to the people. Ojin walked behind Creed and Celeste as they held their hands high, and proclaimed with exuberance.

"The Endüerduul has blessed them as man and wife! Let us celebrate their vows and the days of new before us!"

The crowd stood and cheered as Morsu roared emphatically. They were wed, and a prophecy long since promised had come to pass.

Chapter 20: The Wedding Gift

The evening flowered in joyous exaltation. Creed and Celeste sat at the center of the banquet table as Ojin and Serena sat on either side. Intermittently, the couple would whisper something, smile, and laugh. Visitors came up to the table to pay their respects as Celeste introduced them all to Creed. Music wafted about as others danced beneath the vines and wreaths of lights. There hadn't been this much jubilation in many years. Serena leaned past Celeste and motioned to Creed. "I am happy for you both. This night has been thought about for quite some time. Now you are husband and wife, I have a son, and a grandson on the way! To your health!" She brought her glass of wine to his, and they toasted one another. As he sipped his wine slowly, he looked upon the thousands of visitors celebrating their wedding day. So many strangers, and yet they all felt comfort around him. Celeste's face was beautiful and boundless with emotion. Creed knew she was happy.

He stood up to stretch, and as he leaned over to kiss Celeste, the music stopped and the dancing halted. The floor looked to him as if he were prepared to speak. He was caught off guard.

"I'm sorry. Sorry. Just wanted to stretch my legs, and walk about for a bit. Please continue." The conductor motioned, and the music played once more, as did the various couples' rhythmic movements before them. Celeste held his hand.

"Where are you going?" she asked.

"Just wanted to see the Pools again."

"I can come with you."

"No, no. Please stay seated. I was just curious. I will be right back. Speaking of, when do we get to sneak off and consummate the marriage?" He smiled broadly.

"Oh you! We'll see how quickly you return."

"With that in mind, I'll be back in five minutes." She laughed, and they hugged.

"Seriously, I'll be right back." He walked behind the banquet table, and Ojin motioned to stand, but Creed gestured him to stay put. He needed to see the waters once more, alone.

It wasn't but a hundred yards away, and he looked upon the Pools with awe. Twice he had kneeled here, and he couldn't help but have more questions. He placed his hands in the water, pulled away, and watched it trickle through his fingers. Creed brought his wine glass, emptied it into the dirt, and dipped the cup into the waters, drinking from them again. No ripples this time. No light. No fog. Just peace. He sipped again, and a thought crept slowly into the forefront of his mind.

What was it that made these waters? Why were they so calming? What if they could calm others?

The thought grew, and his idea even caught him by surprise. He dipped the cup in the water once more, and went another direction toward the back of the camp. He walked up to the Bellatorum before the captives' tent, and asked to enter.

"May I pass please?"

"Yes, my lord. Congratulations on your wedding, Hippocrates," one of them said.

"Many blessings, Hippocrates!" said the other.

"Thank you both. Thank you." He walked past them as they held the tent flap open, and looked down upon the patients before him.

The two Vaga continued to twitch and flit about in their minds. The rope bindings precluded any movement with their limbs, so they wriggled slowly like worms in the dirt. He kneeled before the woman as she looked beyond him. It was an educated guess, but one that he couldn't let go. Creed turned once more to make sure no one was watching, and then held out his glass, and tilted her chin. He brought the cup to her lips, and poured a small amount of the waters past her teeth, closed her mouth, and waited.

The woman swallowed, and coughed a bit. She continued to twitch, and then began to moan. Her eyes opened intermittently as she fell to her side in a seizure. The male hadn't moved, and as she grunted violently, Creed looked back to make sure no one was coming. Her arms and legs shook as she frothed at the mouth, and he worried she was dying.

Creed searched for anything to free her hands, and found a pair of sheep shears that had been used to trim their hair and the man's beard. He pried the shears through the ropes, pinched and chewed the bindings until they fell away, re-positioned her body, and let her seizure finish. She was still, and barely breathing. Then a big breath followed by another, and then a cough. The Vaga opened her eyes, but did not speak. She stared at Creed, and slowly he felt her fingertips across his cheek. She appeared calm albeit mute, and her touch was soft and profound. The dirt floor rustled, and he stood up to turn. There stood Ojin.

"What are you doing?"

"I wanted to try and see if…"

"What have you done?" Ojin asked. The hobgoblin's gaze was searing.

"Ojin, look! She's changed. I gave her a drink of the water from the Pools. I just gave her a little. She seized, but now she just looked at me. I think it worked! I think it cured her."

"Impossible," Ojin scoffed.

"Why? Why is it impossible to think there is a way to help them? Look at her." She slowly sat up, sat cross-legged, and held her head in her hands as he had done when he first arrived in the Ember Wood.

"Why hasn't anyone ever tried this before?" Creed asked.

"They have never come this far, and no one would consider allowing them to drink of the Pools. It's a sacred place. They are not worthy."

"What does being sick have to do with sacred anything? It's almost as if no one was willing to try."

"That is not what we have known the Pools to be. We don't even know if it is safe for them, or if this will last. What made you do this? Why would you do this?" Ojin wondered.

"I was mixed up inside at the ceremony. A hundred thoughts were flying through my mind. As soon as I drank from the goblet, the thoughts settled down. I felt relaxed. My mind focused clearly on what was before me, and I wasn't distracted anymore. The echoes were gone."

"The waters are not yours to consume and parcel out to the Vagus. The oracle will be displeased with you. Why chance it, my friend? Why jeopardize what they've given you?"

"I sat there at the banquet table, looking around at the festivities, and wondered what it was. What could be in that water? So, I went back to drink some more, and as I drank it again, I couldn't help but think it might do something for them. I am trying to help them, Ojin. Nothing more."

The hobgoblin stared at the female Vaga. He knelt down, looking over her expression as the woman glanced at him, and patted his furry face. She seemed unalarmed that a beastly hobgoblin was before her, ironic especially for someone who appeared to have just woken from a terrible nightmare.

"Fascinating. She seems unafraid. She does appear different," Ojin observed.

"This was just a small amount. What if we treated her for days? Imagine the impact we could make!" Creed's voice rose with excitement.

"Shhhh." Ojin looked about. "Wait. Don't get ahead of yourself. I've seen similar things with other potions and herbs that we've used to treat my kin, but what initially appears to be a miracle can often be a ruse. Serena needs to know. Surely, she could think of a way to help them all. We could start with those at the Redemptio, and see where that takes us."

"Let me find Celeste first. I want her to know what we discovered. This could change everything!"

Ojin and Creed hurried back to the banquet only to find people standing, and arguing. A riot seemed to be forming lines between immortals and mankind. Creed couldn't see past the crowd, but heard Celeste's voice. Everyone readied themselves to fight for some reason, and from the sound of it, Celeste was willing to do so as well.

"You will wait for my husband to return, Xaris!" Celeste commanded.

"Then where is he my Princess?" Xaris insisted. "Where is Hippocrates? We know what he did, and why he left so quickly last time! Odd, don't you think that he abandons his bride on his wedding night while we have traitors in our midst?" Creed raised his goblet, and shouted.

"Here! I'm here! On my way! Let me pass. Let me get through."

The crowd parted, as some guests patted him on the back. Once he made it past the congestion, he stood before the banquet table, and looked upon Celeste. She seemed visibly upset.

"What's wrong?" he asked.

She looked over his shoulder. Xaris stood there with three Bellatorum. Two strangers were bent to their knees as Xaris held his swords at the ready.

"Hippocrates! I bring before you, *your* brethren! These two disappeared the night you left, and I found them a half-mile from here beneath some felled timber. They wouldn't talk with me, but they did ask for you. They are Luxatio, at least before they abandoned their oaths. Much like you I suppose. I know what you were doing despite the warnings, and when the Queen and I conferred on the repercussions of your decisions, the Queen deemed them traitors. I believe they planned to attack us tonight as retribution. They will be punished accordingly."

Creed put his goblet down, and walked over to the two men. Though they kneeled, it was apparent that they were big and broad shouldered. They too were warriors, and Creed couldn't help but wonder why they didn't resist more. It wasn't folly to assume they could have given the Bellatorum and Xaris a difficult time if they had chosen to. They looked up at him through their dust-covered masks. He pulled the masks below their chins and bristly beards, and saw warming, familiar faces. Creed smiled and placed his hands on their shoulders. These were his friends.

"Yersinitus and Kinklefitz!" Xaris scowled at Creed's exuberance. Creed looked at him, and understood the friction now. Xaris had harbored these thoughts for some time, all this time.

"Commander," the men said in unison.

"Hippocrates, it is good to at long last lay eyes upon you. Welcome home. We've failed you. I am sorry." Kinklefitz bowed his head in a somber fashion.

"How so? Please, please stand. Here," Creed cut their restraints with his boot knife, "You should eat. Have some wine. Welcome home!" Creed helped them to their feet, making sure to stare down Xaris in the process. He did not wish to escalate in front of everyone, but Xaris needed to stop his pursuit now.

"They have forsaken their oaths! This is no longer their home!" Xaris looked about the crowd as they ridiculed his insinuation. "They have failed us all! They will be taken into confinement by order of the Queen!" Xaris looked to Serena and nodded. She acknowledged him in return.

"They fought with me. They bled with me. They saved my life as much as I have saved theirs. I will not step away from this." Creed turned to Celeste as Serena sat there sternly. "Serena, these men, they were with me last, the night I was called back. They were following my orders. Not their own. This is a consequence of my command."

"I suspected as much, but now is not the time to discuss these things. Xaris, take them to the Vagus tent. We will settle this in the morning." Serena raised her hand to dismiss the prisoners.

"Why? Serena, they did nothing wrong. Let them come with me under my watch," requested Creed.

"They forfeit their promises on the very soil you just wed. They have been in exile ever since your departure. We have much to ask of them, so it can wait until the morning."

"It shouldn't wait. Let us all go to the Vagus tent now! I've discovered something!" He looked to his wife, "Celeste, I gave the water to the woman. She changed! The waters did something to her. She is gentle, and she is at peace. I think I found a cure!"

"How?" Celeste asked.

"I don't know. Come with me. Come look!" Celeste made her way around the banquet table when Serena grabbed her arm.

"No! Sit down!" the Queen demanded.

Celeste looked confused, and then angrily at her mother. Creed noticed the crowd had become silent as they firmly supported him and the other Luxatio. Serena spoke up as if to quell a subtle rebellion.

"Everyone, please. Enjoy the night. I ask for calm at this moment. We will be back to have more wine and food. As we know, the issues of our realm won't even cease for a wedding, but I assure you all is well. Servers, please let there neither be a single empty platter nor glass anywhere. We will be back in a moment." She let go of Celeste's arm, and they walked to stand before the Luxatio. Serena spoke with Xaris.

"Bring them with me. Let us see this Vagus experiment." Xaris nodded, and took their captives toward the perimeter. Creed had his hand on Celeste's shoulder.

"Celeste?"

"Not now."

"Celeste, this could change everything." She turned abruptly.

"For whom? For you? For me? For the Luxatio? Why couldn't you just let us have this one night? Just once?" Her eyes welled with tears.

"This is bigger than us, Celeste. What if this is why I'm here?" She rolled her eyes.

"Enough, Creed! This child is why we are here, not those nameless Vagus you've taken pity on! Let us pray you have not doomed them all with your ambition!" Celeste left him there in the midst of Mürindür's citizenry.

Once Creed arrived at the tent, he walked in to see Serena looming over the woman. The Vaga looked up at her and smiled gently. She reached out to hold Serena's hand, but the Queen stepped away.

"Bind her once more. We cannot trust her. She may return to what she was. What of this one?" She pointed to the Vaga male. Ojin reappeared with a full goblet of Cordis water, and handed it to Creed. The Queen looked up at him.

"Ojin? You as well?"

"Serena, please. Watch. Watch him. He wouldn't lie to us. Hippocrates has never lied to us. Trust in him as the Pools have."

Creed kneeled beside the man, and did the same as he had done before. The man drank, and then lurched into the goblet, consuming the entire amount. Some of it dribbled down his beard. The male stiffened for a moment, and fell face first into the dirt. His convulsions were more violent than the woman's. Xaris drew his sword, and raised it high to strike full force into the Vaga's chest.

"He's possessed! Make ready!" he cried, as he drove the sword downward, but the weapon did not move.

Creed caught the warrior's wrist. Xaris looked into his eyes, and bore down with his weight, challenging him. Creed stood, and slid his grasp slowly to the meat of the forearm. He choked Xaris' limb slowly at first, and then more aggressively all the while looking through him. The hand became pale, weakened with a tremor, and the sword fell onto the ground. Celeste stared at Creed, astonished. Xaris didn't move. He couldn't. Small tufts of smoke drifted about the fallen sword.

"You will give him the time he needs. Is that understood?" Creed said slowly as he let go, but Xaris raised his other hand in defiance. Creed leaned forward, exposing his chin as bait.

"Please do."

Ojin stepped between them, and placed a hand on Creed to push him back. His chest was scalding.

"Settle! Settle you two! Look!"

Ojin pointed to the man who sat upright. Creed kneeled to cut his bindings as well, and the man looked over to the woman. He crawled closer to her, and they embraced, weeping. They seemed not to care about the audience before them. Yersinitus spoke up.

"Queen Serena, this man and woman were ours to protect. We rescued them along with many more, but we were ambushed, and fought until we no longer could. We failed them, but Hippocrates has found the means to redeem us." He hung his head in shame, but Serena stood indifferent, quiet.

The couple cried and rocked one another, now fully aware of all that had transpired. They stroked each other's hair, and called each other by their Earthly names as they had done as husband and wife.

Celeste wept. Never before had they seen Vagus touch and act as normal. Creed was right. There was something more to this. The bodies in the Ogre ravine suffered a much worse fate, and had they not intervened when they did, these two would not have survived. Celeste reached for Creed's hand. He stood up and held her as he looked to Serena.

"Serena, I knew something was happening, but couldn't remember until now. My last time here in Mürindür, we discovered that the Vagus were not all converted to Caedere. Many of them were being sacrificed for Acrom, fueling him, and hastening his return. With each soul on his altar, he grew in strength. We sought to end the trafficking of Vagus with hopes, initially, of preventing more sacrifices. We didn't think anything more of it, and had no idea where we could house them once they were secure. We just knew we couldn't allow Acrom to continue feeding. It was never my intent to go behind your back, but I couldn't come to you empty-handed. I needed proof. I had hoped to ride back with them," he motioned to Varsalsae and the others. "Vagus secured, and you would have known everything at that point. These people, and they *are* people, are pawns in a greater game. Their deaths are nurturing a darkness we cannot contain. Leterum is helping this process, and it must be stopped. Little did I know, something as simple as the Cordis waters could serve us so well, but now that I do, I think we've found a way to help them all."

"How do we know this to be true, and not a figment of your imagination or a broken memory?" Serena chastised him bluntly.

"Mother!"

"Celeste, we cannot know unless we ask."

"It's true, my Queen, every word of it. Hippocrates wanted to tell you everything that night. He wanted to show you how it could be done." Varsalsae said as she walked in. "Hippocrates, sent us on our mission that night as he went to an Ogre stronghold. We had hoped to hit four camps, and emerge with hundreds of Vagus. My unit was the only one to survive."

"A third one is it? Where have you been?" Serena asked.

"I met with Hippocrates and Ojin before the ceremony." Celeste looked at Creed, as did Serena to Ojin. The Queen was not pleased. "This day of all days you choose to return, the most significant day of our time? All three of you disappeared that night as criminals. Heretics! *You* chose to abandon *your* purpose. The roads to Durdan became a hunter's ground as Leterum's forces sought you out, so much so that I had to send Bellatorum to guard the city. Caedere and Ogre alike were searching for the Luxatio 'bandits', and yet Xaris looked everywhere for you with no trace. We were trying to recover all of you. Save you." Serena was livid.

"You mean imprison," Creed insinuated.

"Son, it would do you well to reconsider your words."

"Deny it. Deny the fact that you declared them traitors, when their greatest crime was following my command."

"I do not deny that," Serena admitted.

"Mother?" Celeste protested.

"I couldn't discuss it with you. He left that night before I had a chance to confront him. You hadn't even said goodbye to one another. You didn't need anything more at the moment, and I had enough information to know what needed to happen next. These three abandoned their posts, their purpose for something that has existed since the beginning." She looked upon the Vagus and the Luxatio.

"Arrest these three, and secure those two. Take them to Redemptio. We will discuss more then," Serena commanded.

"I won't allow it." Creed stepped before the Vagus, and the three Luxatio stood behind him. Varsalsae drew her sword.

"Easy now. Easy." Ojin reached out with his large hands held high between the warring parties.

"Hippocrates, step aside." Serena motioned to her Bellatorum. As they approached him, Creed's face grew warm, and he took off his robe. He stood with hands at the ready. The room became sweltering as the torches grew.

"Careful, Hippocrates. Today is not the day to cross paths with me."

Serena began to change as well. Her eyes slowly glowed like embers. Celeste walked over to Creed, and grabbed his hand. She looked at her mother, and sought an end to the palpable tension. "This is my wedding day, and I will not turn away a gift, and a gift may not be taken from me. It is tradition. I gladly accept these Luxatio and Vagus as gifts, and I am grateful. Many thanks, Xaris." She nodded to the warrior. Serena was beside herself.

"Child, you do not understand! After all this time, do not let a simple moment tarnish what we fight for. Let us take these people to Redemptio, and discus this in private." Serena's eyes settled into their Norse-blue tone. Creed slowed his breathing, and the temperature ebbed within the confines of their confrontation.

"No, Mother. I understand fully. We have always been stewards of the lives fallen on this plane. Before us sit two lost ones, who somehow by the grace of my husband, have taken a step away from the darkness. We need to know why this is possible, and how we plan to save all the others. This is our purpose, and you know this."

"You know not what you do. You do not know what has transpired. The thousands of Vagus that fall cannot be brought here. Not every time. Then we're left with whom we choose, and whom we discard to Leterum. That is not our purpose. We are not here to serve as judge and executioner." Serena flipped her hand to the air in protest.

"No, but we can find a way, Mother. Somehow, there is a path for them to these Pools."

Serena regained her composure, and clasped her hands tensely. Xaris sheathed his swords, as did Varsalsae. Ojin lowered his hands, and took a deep breath. Serena spoke once more.

"When we wake, I will explain our history, and the reasons why we likely cannot do much for these people. It is how things have come to be on Mürindür." Creed crossed his arms.

"Our guests can stay in my quarters. My wife and I will sleep in the suite. We can let the Vagus sleep here tonight. In the morning, I look forward to the discussion." Serena turned out the tent with Xaris and her Bellatorum following behind. Creed turned to his team.

"Come with me, and we will get you fresh clothes and a place to sleep." Varsalsae looked at Kinklefitz and Yersinitus, and shook her head.

"With all due respect, Hippocrates, we will stay here with the Vagus. They are our flock. We lost them once, but we will not lose them a second time." The men nodded in agreement with her. Creed scanned the tight quarters, and sighed.

"Then we will get some beds in here for all of you." He turned to Ojin and Celeste, but the Princess spoke before he could say another word.

"We need rest. I suspect tomorrow will be arduous. Tonight, has been more than any of us expected. Good night all." Celeste and Creed left for their suite, and Ojin spoke with the Luxatio as they walked away.

"Did any of you know this was possible?" Ojin asked.

"No. We knew we needed to stop the killings. Acrom could not continue feeding," Varsalsae explained.

"However, we did not think it possible for Hippocrates to find a cure let alone catch himself on fire." Kinklefitz was quick to add.

"Many things have changed my friends. Many things," Ojin sighed.

Celeste pulled on Creed's hand to motivate his slowed gait. He reluctantly acquiesced, and the conversation between Ojin and the Luxatio grew to a soft rumble.

Chapter 21: A Revelation

Creed woke to Celeste lying beside him, and watched her for nearly half an hour, smiling at the rise and fall of her chest. It had been quite some time since they had fallen asleep together. Her face seemed relaxed and content.

He marveled at her complexity, and wondered how it could be possible for her to love him. She being a woman of alluring grace and perpetude, and he a simple man, fallible and finite.

What must it be like to know tomorrow will always wait for you, he thought.

Not a muscle moved, and then she spoke.

"It's a little disturbing knowing you've been staring at me all morning."

"Ha! You've been awake?"

"Yes. Resting. This little one doesn't do much for sleep." Celeste rubbed her flank slowly in a massage.

"Is he moving?"

"Yes." Creed placed his hand on her belly. The kicks were forceful and persistent. He was impressed, and smiled with soft laughter.

"Was it like that all night?" Creed asked.

"For the most part. He gets like this when you're around." Creed leaned in for a long kiss. Celeste smiled, and put her hand up, paralyzing his advance.

"What? What's wrong?" he asked.

"I think last night was enough for now don't you?" she quipped.

"Oh, I don't know. How about we give it a go?" Creed nuzzled once more for her lips.

"Give it a go, eh?"

She giggled, and he kissed her anyway despite her feigned protest. As Celeste draped her leg over his hip, pulling him closer, there was a rustling outside. The kiss ended, and they both sat up abruptly as Ojin entered the tent. When he saw a shirtless Creed, he mumbled and looked away.

"Creed, you need to see this. It's important."

Creed stood up and dressed as Celeste lay there. He followed his friend outside, wondering what possibly could be wrong. The camp was dark beneath the thick trees even as dawn broke in the distance. Ojin walked briskly to the Vagus tent, and Creed found it difficult to keep up. His hobgoblin friend seemed disturbed and distraught, but Ojin wouldn't say what had happened. When he opened the tent flap, the shock was evident as Creed looked at his team. They stood over the Vagus bodies, clearly upset.

"When?" he asked.

"We all stood guard. They went to sleep hours ago, and both of them were breathing," Varsalsae explained. "It wasn't until the light came through the front that I realized they were gray." Creed looked upon their ghastly expressions. Eyes open, and the rigor had already set. They were holding hands in death's repose.

"Damn it!" He kicked the pile of blankets beside them, and paced in circles, thinking through the process.

"No seizures?"

"No," Varsalsae replied.

"Any grunting? Sounds like they were choking?" Creed continued pushing for some rationale.

"None. Hippocrates, none of us slept. I don't know what happened. They were constantly under our care."

He kneeled down beside the woman's body. No bleeding. No bruising. The Bellatorum arrived with more lanterns, and Serena wasn't far behind. She hurried in, and paused, paradoxically saddened.

"Any idea what took place?" the Queen asked. Creed stood to look at her.

"No. You?"

"I've never seen this."

"Never?" Creed challenged.

"No. Why do you ask?"

"I just think it's funny that you're angry with what we discovered last night, and then this morning they're dead."

"Careful, Hippocrates."

"What do you know, Serena? What has happened here?" Creed was upset. He felt so close to a solution for the lost ones, and now they lie dead at his feet. The physician in him was inconsolable.

"I don't know. No one has seen Vagus this far north before, let alone had them drink from the Pools. This has never occurred. I have nothing to go by. What you did last night likely lead them to their deaths, but that is not all bad. They are at peace now. No longer suffering. It is much better this way."

"For whom?"

"For them. Now we know. Something doesn't allow them to survive the waters."

"When you said we had to be blessed and accepted by the Pools of Cordis Loci, Ojin, has there ever been someone who died after drinking the water?"

"Not that I remember. Serena?" The hobgoblin turned to the Queen.

"No. Never in the history has there been a death from the goblet even for those refused the blessing," Serena replied.

"What happens if someone isn't accepted? What if the Pools refuse to acknowledge the recipient?" Creed asked.

"Most people who aren't accepted have nothing to lose or gain at that point. They carry on where they left off," she explained.

"Has there ever been someone chosen for Luxatio, but then refused the honor by the Pools?"

"Why do you ask?" Ojin wondered.

"There is something that changed within me when I drank that water, but it did not hurt me. You choose people to be Luxatio because they have certain qualities, certain strengths. Maybe these Vagus didn't have that certain something to survive."

"Some people have been suggested for the Luxatio, but the Pools have declined. Their silence precluded any further thought," Serena attested.

"Who?" Creed stared at her for some semblance of an answer.

"It doesn't matter," Serena stated sternly.

"It might matter to me," he insisted. Serena glanced to the doorway, and spoke. A figure loomed in the morning light.

"Some have not been accepted by the Pools, and they continue to live their lives as such until their purpose is complete. They cannot choose if or when the Endüerduul accepts them despite what they may do for us and for others. A sacrifice is always a sacrifice regardless of recognition or knowledge."

"Give me some examples," Creed demanded. The discomfort in the room was palpable. Xaris stepped forward, looking down upon the bodies, and then stared at Creed. No emotion, but a slight twinge in his jaw.

"Me."

There was uncertainty as to whether something more would come of it. The silence settled the conversation. Varsalsae turned, and gathered the blankets Creed had kicked moments beforehand. She placed them over the Vagus, covering their faces. Xaris looked away, and cleared his throat. Serena left the tent and he followed.

Creed waited with everyone quietly, pacing the room, as his mind raced over the potential causes for their demise. He studied the dirt around them, and looked above for any clues. He walked out and in again. Finally, he kneeled beside them, and pulled the blankets back once more.

"It just doesn't make any sense. I watched them for some time after the seizures finished. What could have taken them? I did this. I... I poisoned them." Creed hung his head in defeat.

"They couldn't tolerate the Cordis waters. There's no explanation besides the obvious," Ojin assured him.

"I don't know. We all drank from the water, and nothing happened to anyone. They drink, and then they're gone." Creed put his hands on his head as he paced about. Varsalsae and Kinklefitz began to roll the man and woman's bodies in the blankets to prepare them for burial. Ojin looked to his friend.

"It was a noble attempt. It seemed that something did matter at the time, something that could have changed everything. I'm sorry, but you tried. You thought of something and tried. It is what you do."

"I haven't done anything, but muddy the waters." He thought for a moment.

Muddy waters.

"Ojin, normally I would order an autopsy when we lose someone without cause."

"You've done those?" Ojin asked.

"I have, not this past life, I mean not all the time. At different times, I've helped. I need answers. I need some way to understand this." Creed's speech was pressured and quickened with a plan.

"There are just some things that cannot be explained with science. Magic abounds, and sometimes that's all we can know. Let this go. We no longer need to speak of it." Ojin motioned to the Luxatio to continue binding the bodies.

"I understand that. Even so, think about it. We're the same in so many ways. Why did we have different reactions? I drink it, and my thoughts slow down, and I feel peace. They drink, and they collapse and die the next day. There is a reason."

"Perhaps, but you are a Luxata. Luxatio have a power all onto their own. The same rules likely don't apply."

"I have an idea." Creed's face was animated.

"Are you sure that's wise?"

"I don't know, but your words don't invoke confidence."

"Well the last few days haven't been easy. How about we just stay within the lines this time? Give them a proper burial," Ojin insisted.

Creed looked to his Luxatio.

"Wrap their bodies and come with me. We're going to the Pools." They stared wide -eyed at him. Ojin protested.

"No. That's sacrilegious! Not even you should do this!" Ojin put his hands up to stop them all, and he stepped back to block the doorway.

"It isn't sacrilegious, Ojin. We need answers. I need to understand. There is more at stake than just the Welfalon. These Vagus can help us understand their brethren."

"You can't put dead bodies in the Pools, Creed! You cannot desecrate those grounds!"

"Ojin, don't come if you don't want to, but I need some guidance here. I need the Oracle's understanding. Pick them up and let's go." The three Luxatio helped with the bodies, and followed Creed out of the tent to the Pools. Celeste was walking briskly to their tent when she saw the corpses. She stopped them, and stood in front of Creed.

"Please tell me I'm not seeing this. Please!" Her eyes begged of him.

"Celeste, give me some time. They died unexpectedly in the night. I need some answers."

"Let this go. Let them go. Give them a proper burial!" she demanded.

"We will. I want to see what happens in the Pools, first."

"You will not do this! You may not understand what the Pools of Cordis Loci are for, but they are not for the dead!"

"You don't understand. I need answers!" Creed's voice rose over hers.

"What don't I understand? That you haven't been normal since you came back? That you keep making these unorthodox decisions with catastrophic consequences? We fought those Ogres, and for what? They could have been taken to Redemptio, but now they are nothing. They are dead! We could have walked past them yesterday, and the outcome would have been the same. You've done nothing for them, and now you wish to poison the Pools with their remains?"

Creed looked at Celeste, broken, and his posture withered. He stared at the ground as he thought about it all. His throat was tight, but he spoke anyways.

"I am doing what I feel is right. I am trying to make a difference, and as the days pass, I remember why. It's because of *you*. I could have died as the others have died, and moved on to a better place, but I'm here because of you and a decision I made that I can barely remember at those same damn Pools you guys keep commiserating over. Dozens of lives later, and I'm left with this swamp of a mind. I have all this suffering, and all the loss, of all the human experiences that *you* will never understand!" Creed's eyes welled with tears. "*You*, fair Princess, will *never* be mortal! You will never understand that fleeting, faint blink of life. What it feels like each day knowing it could be your last, and as the sun sets, you get one step closer to the end regardless. But you want to know something? I wouldn't change that for the world. If I didn't feel that constant presence of death in my mind, I wouldn't have tried as hard as I did to do all the things I have done for mankind. The risks I took to make that fleeting life more sustainable and worthwhile all the while you and your mother sit here judging everyone, and choosing to only save the ones who can think clearly." He spit into the dirt as the tears' salty taste fouled his mouth.

"You judge me too harshly, Creed!" Celeste was crying now as well. Creed wiped his eyes.

"I can't imagine what it must be like to always have tomorrow! *I* don't get that guarantee! I never know when my last moment will be whether it's there or here. I can't know, and that's the only thing that keeps me moving forward. In some ways, it's a blessing. It forces me to live. You'll never understand that feeling, but" as he looked at the other Luxatio, "*they* do. We fight for the Vagus because no one else will, and no one else cares. I am trying to find a way to make them better. I know what my purpose is now, and why I'm here even if you don't."

Creed turned toward Varsalsae, and took the woman's corpse into his arms. He cradled her body gently, respectfully, and walked to the Pools. He looked back toward his team.

"You can take the man to the tent, but I need answers. This could affect everyone, and something inside keeps pushing me that this needs to happen. I can't explain it. I'm not crazy, and I'm not being disrespectful, but I need to see why they died. I want to see if the Pools respond. You can go back. It won't take me long." His colleagues stood there, hesitant, refusing to leave. If there was anything to lessen their guilt for losing the Vagus, they had hoped their leader would find the way. Kinklefitz carried the man's body as Varsalsae and Yersinitus followed behind. Ojin and Celeste stood still. She had tears rolling down her cheeks, tears of anguish, anger, and remorse. Once she regained her composure, she spoke with Ojin.

"This is wrong, and you know it. Ojin, please do not let him do this."

"Celeste, I have protested, but I also know he doesn't get like this unless there is something to it. He is in pain, and he is angry, but his heart is in the right place. Let him be."

"This is reprehensible. It is unkind. It is inhumane."

"He feels responsible for this, and he needs some way to reconcile it in his mind."

"Those people died because of his impulsiveness, and now he seeks to defile the Pools. Ojin, you have to get control of this!"

"With all due respect, he is my friend, but he is *your* husband." Celeste wiped her face clean, and stood in defiance with her arms crossed.

"Then I'm going."

"No sense in that. Your mother will be angry enough. He's pushed her a little too far, and this will likely bring things to a head. Someone needs to remain clean of it all. Wait here, and I will bring word of what took place." She shook her head.

"We go together, and not another word." She stormed off after Creed and his crew while Ojin followed. The hobgoblin looked at the Bellatorum who could be seen mumbling with one another, and held up his hands as if to motion for more time. He wouldn't be surprised if Serena was already there.

Moments later, Creed stood before the Pools of Cordis Loci with the dead woman in his arms. He stared at her face framed by the blanket, and his expression was strained. She seemed to be at peace, tranquil, and lifeless. He had made what he believed the right decision only to accelerate her end. He sought something, even if for a sliver of consolation.

"To the Spirits, the Oracle of the Cordis Loci, I am here requesting an audience, a moment of your time." He waited. There were no songbirds. No movement. The waters were still and translucent.

"I hold this woman, a dead Vaga in my arms, and I gave her the essence of these very Pools. I woke this morning to find her and her husband dead. Gone. I ask for answers and for forgiveness. I can't help but feel the answer lies here somehow. Please show me the way." With that, he walked waist deep into the waters, and held her afloat for a few minutes. Nothing occurred, it seemed, until the ground began to warm, and the waters clouded. Wind stirred the willows, and the air became thin as if something inhaled. Voices in unison spoke angrily, explosively.

"WHO DARES TO BRING THE DEAD INTO THESE DEPTHS?"

"It is I, Hippocrates."

"Hippocrates, the son of Heracleides and Praxithea from the long line of Hercules, you know not what you do this day! You have done much for the living, but there is nothing here for the dead. Be gone, and bury her bones."

"Forgive me, but I have questions. My wife tells me she would pull me from these very pools when I slept on Earth. This is something more than water, something more than the Endüerduul. What are you? What is this place?"

"These are the Pools of Cordis Loci! We were borne of light and life! Poured from the cosmos onto the very soil with which you stand!"

"How did I come here through my dreams?"

"We willed it so."

"Why?"

"The balance was broken. The bridge was no more. No longer were you concealed, but evident you became. A means to an end."

"To Celeste?"

"To the goddess as she wished it to be. You came to her as we had foreseen it. This is not a doorway for the dead!" Celeste stood a few feet away as did Ojin. Creed looked back to them as Varsalsae took the man's body, and entered the waters beside him as well. Celeste motioned to step forward, but Ojin held her back.

"Just a moment, and we will see," he suggested.

"What of this man and woman? Did you will it for them to be ill? I gave them your essence. Did you take them out of spite?" Creed questioned the Oracle. There was silence. Wind moved slowly about the treetops.

"**ANSWER ME**!" Creed's defiance brought his anger to light, and his skin warmed the water quickly with frustration. Steam rose slowly about the bodies.

"We do not decide! We choose not which souls become Vagus or Welfalon. It is made of their own free will! To each of them, their journey begins at their hands!"

"That is not redemption! That is not what I should think the Endüerduul to be."

"We will not be judged by you Luxata! We grant you an existence! **IT CAN BE CUT OFF!**"

"Then do it." There was nothing but ripples and wind. "**DO IT!**" Creed punched his fist in the turbid waters.

A large wave sucked inward, rose, and then crashed at his feet, pulling him violently under water along with the body. Varsalsae abandoned her Vaga, and struggled to regain composure above the surface, nearly drowning in the process. Celeste screamed, and ran toward the water, but Ojin held fast onto her arm.

"Creed! Hippocrates!!" she cried.

Creed's shadow was suddenly dozens of feet below the surface many yards further away from the shore. He held onto the woman tightly. The sounds echoed to him beneath the ripples. He hovered mid depth far below the sunlight. His fire was gone, and the coldness sank heavily into his chest.

"Death becomes you Luxata, and nothing more! You will fall into a darkness that you cannot contain. Your existence will be wiped from the long line of legacies!" Creed's thoughts became loud despite his inability to speak.

"Revive her. Bring her back. I did this to them. Take me instead, a life for a life. I give it willingly."

The water swirled about him as a whirlpool of discontent. There was no answer, but he was pulled viciously back and forth in a rage as though he were clasped in the jaws of an angered leviathan. He was spun violently, but refused to let go of her body. Everything was a blur, and he could feel Celeste reaching out to him, but as the last bit of air gurgled from his lips, the Pools cast him high into the air, and hurled him onto the shoreline. His ribs crumpled into the soft muddy soil. Creed gasped for air, and struggled to his hands and knees, angry and disoriented. The bodies could be seen floating side by side within still waters once more, as they had earlier in the tent. Celeste ran to him as did Ojin, and they pulled him from the mud. The Oracle spoke.

"Hippocrates, you will do well to remember this day, and the oaths you have made. Never again shall you enter this domain with the dead. These souls die not at your hands, however, but those of another, a dark being not of our making. The dark rider Falciparum, has violated the chamber, and the world cries out in agony. What you wish to be undone cannot be undone through the Pools."

Creed coughed, forcefully vomiting the Cordis waters, and stood with assistance and frustration.

"Then what is their purpose? What of this pain? Why do any of this? How can it be stopped?"

"The waters repulse the darkness, but the Vagus need the ash to survive. Look to the Silva Luctus. The bark of the Lamentum trees should be fired, burned, and steeped in our waters. Feed them this for eternity and alter the course of their existence."

"Let me have them back. I will bury them on that hill." Creed pointed to a secluded area nearby.

"This man and woman have suffered enough. Their remains belong to us," the Oracle replied.

"Let me bury them, please."

"Their shrouds will be our waves; their burial will be our depths. They shall know peace."

The bodies floated calmly before him, and then, as if a tide were receding, they regressed into a fog, and broke below the water's surface. The Pools had reclaimed them. The waters cleared once more, and all became quiet.

Chapter 22: The Price for Peace

A commotion arose from camp, and Creed turned to see Serena in an angry stride, heading their way with a dozen Bellatorum. Everything from the night before until now had likely festered, and it was time for Creed to confront it all. This would not be easy, but it would be necessary.

"What have you done? What happened here?" Serena yelled. Creed looked at her and then at the Luxatio. He nodded for them to leave. The four of them walked toward Serena, and as they sought to pass her, she stopped them with her hand. She stared angrily at Creed.

"What did you do?"

"I sought answers," Creed replied.

"What answers do you seek?"

"I asked the Oracle what I could do to save the Vagus. They gave me a directive, and now I plan to ride to the Silva Luctus."

"That's impossible!" Serena exclaimed.

"What's impossible?"

"The Pools do not give 'directives'. Where are the bodies of the Vagus?"

"They rest at the bottom. The Oracle took them." Creed motioned with his head to the Pools behind them.

"This is blasphemy!" the Queen decried, grabbing his arm.

"I'm one step closer to doing more for them than any of you have done for all of their existence. Now, excuse me." She held him there firmly, and for a brief moment he felt breathless. Celeste stepped forward.

"Mother, stop. Let him go."

"Hear me, and hear me well, Hippocrates. I have granted you more latitude than you deserve, but the irreverence you so easily place at my feet has become insufferable. It would do you a great service to suffer the humility you are due. Maybe then your escapades would be put to rest."

"You can humble me however you choose, Serena, but the Endüerduul has spoken. The Oracle of the Pools has spoken. I will do what is asked of me, and if it means I must suffer for the greater good, then make ready. Until then, I need to prepare. I remember very little about the Silva Luctus, but what I do recall, I should bring a weapon, and a handful of hubris."

"Hubris will get you killed, my son," the Queen noted.

"Believing in more than what is laid at my feet is necessary for survival. Ojin, how far to the Silva Luctus?"

"A day's ride," the hobgoblin replied.

"I will take the Luxatio with me, and we will be back in two days."

"I think not, Hippocrates." The Queen lowered her hands and clasped them.

"I don't think you have a choice, Serena," retorted Creed.

"Enough with your insolence child!" She raised her hand as if to strike him, but Celeste caught it and held it gently.

"Mother, the Pools will it so. He took the bodies into their depths, and nearly died. The waters could have taken him, but they didn't. They spoke with him, directed him, and him alone. There is very little left to discuss. I will go with him, and I will be back soon."

Ojin spoke up.

"We could enact the Fuga. It would be but for a moment. He was instructed to bring back the bark of the Lamentum. With it, and the waters here, we can make the Vagus well again."

"The remains of the Lamentum for the souls of the Vagus. It does not seem plausible, nor does it seem moral. The Silva Luctus is not to be disturbed. Its voices can be heard by all, and it is unwise to meddle in their resting place, Celeste," Serena chided.

"Serena, the Endüerduul would not have revealed this unless it were for the purpose upon which he has been set. Let's keep this small and quick. The less we disturb the Silva Luctus forest the better. What say you, Hippocrates?" Ojin asked.

"Ojin, you may come with us. I would ask that Celeste and Serena stay here. The five of us will return quickly. Let's meet at the Pools, and follow the orders as they were given. How we will find more Vagus, I don't know." Varsalsae spoke up.

"We have a base camp in a cavern northeast of the Capital of Guillarne."

"How many?" Creed asked.

"Hundreds," Varsalsae replied.

"Hundreds?"

"Yes."

"How has it been all this time, and we knew nothing of this? Ojin, did you?" Serena stared at him clearly annoyed.

"I did not, Serena. I'm shocked, honestly. I don't know how they could have pulled it off."

"I was waiting to disclose this as well, but since we're all throwing things into the open, then I offer this. We have run out of time. We have to act." Varsalsae reached within her cloak, and withdrew a cracked horn of onyx bathed in the stench of Acrom's army.

"Mael'deua!" Celeste took it, and turned the horn within her hands. Serena looked away at a figure standing watch in the shadows. "There were Mael'deua in the Ashi. We know they have been trying to cross. Where did you find this?" Serena asked.

"Outside of Durdan," Varsalsae reached into her satchel, and threw another horn into the dirt. "this one in the villages outside the Capital", and another, "And this one, mere feet outside the confines of Leterum's Keep. They are everywhere and nowhere. They strike at night, and then retreat. Quickly. Easily. No bodies. No remains, and when the fighting commences, no Bellatorum arrive. The Endüerduul did not answer our cries for help, so we..."

"*You* turned your back on the Endüerduul!" Serena interrupted her. Creed spoke up.

"So, they're driven away and forgotten?" he asked.

"There is much more to this than you know, Hippocrates!"

"Then tell me, or let us be!" he replied.

Ojin looked up from his staff. Creed's patience was waning, and if she wouldn't give him answers, he would find his own. He turned as if to leave, but Serena walked toward a series of boulders nearby, sat upon the largest, and spoke.

"Acrom was bleeding, he was broken and driven from Earth and Mürindür. My men were dying, and Leterum continued to battle despite his losses. It needed to end. A deal was made."

"What deal? What did you barter?" Creed questioned.

"If Acrom died, we would be victorious, but if he lived, unrestrained, all would be lost. I sought to place his head upon a pike, so we entered Acrom's domain, and I confronted him myself. I eventually had the demon on his back, impaled upon my spear, and I felt the end was at hand, but it was not to be. Leterum must

335

have sensed his brother's waning breath, and channeled life into him despite my efforts. While we battled, Acrom bargained. I could not kill him though I tried. Despite knowing this, I could not dare leave him, so that I may confront Leterum, and I could not stop Leterum from reviving Acrom. It was a stalemate. Outside the walls of Acrom's domain, my soldiers were dying by the hundreds. Our best chance was to confine the darkness, and recover our own. I settled for a truce."

"What did you do?"

"I saved our existence. I preserved our realms," Serena argued.

"What did he want?" Creed asked again.

"Souls! He wanted souls, Hippocrates! I had to abdicate the Chamber! I had to step aside. No longer was I permitted to intervene with those that fell lost into Mürindür." Celeste closed her eyes and looked away. The Princess held her stomach, and Serena's eyes watered at the sight of her daughter's disappointment.

"What does that mean?" Creed looked to Ojin. Even the old hobgoblin was shocked.

Ojin looked over his small round glasses and spoke directly to Creed.

"It meant that she could no longer shepherd the souls as they entered the Ostiarius Chamber, the intermediary domain between Earth and Mürindür. It's manned by a titan Cyclops named Amad'al. Most new arrivals she could calm, and ferry toward a peaceful existence before they landed, regardless of what they went through before their deaths. Mürindür was a chance for their redemption, and Serena made it so that millions of souls could eventually make it to the Endüerduul. Each soul Serena salvaged

was a soul Acrom found forfeit. When she left the Chamber…"
Ojin looked at Serena, "… all of that must have changed. Acrom
was ultimately given an endless supply of lost ones, and we find
ourselves here today with an encroaching darkness as he grows
stronger. These Mael'deua horns merely prove that he has found a
way to move his troops about at will." Creed looked up at Celeste,
and wondered. *Did she know all along what her mother did to
Mürindür?*

He knew this much; the Queen was responsible for everything.
Creed studied her with dismay. Serena looked up to meet
everyone's eyes.

"The Transitio had once been a flourishing valley of foothills and
forest, and my dominion was Redemptio. Once we returned from
the Cataclysm, following the truce, the lush vegetation had decayed
into thousands of miles of sand and desolation. I stood there with
Celeste when the first Vaga fell without my guidance. He was lost
and scared. Leterum had taken a point high up within the desert-
mountains, and in moments he sequestered his prey, baptizing him
in molten glass and dragon's fire. We could only stand there and
watch. I listened to the man's screams." Her eyes blinked, and she
paused,."I had chosen to step aside in an attempt to craft peace.
What I had in return was pain and little more. The Welfalon
tumbled around us as well, and we scurried about securing them,
whisking them away to Redemptio while we left the Vagus to their
fates. Leterum built his army of Caedere, and we had lines in the
sand. Mürindür was split in two." Serena cleared her throat, and
wrung her hands in remembrance.

"So, you gave up the souls in order to preserve your realm?" Creed
motioned all around. "Was it worth it?" he asked.

"I have pondered and suffered from it ever since, and if the Cataclysm were to happen today, I would make the same choices. Lose everything, or lose some. What would you have done?" The Queen questioned him with an open hand. Creed sighed, and turned to Celeste.

"I wish you would have told me all of this in the beginning." Celeste opened her mouth to speak, but her mother intervened.

"Would it have made a difference, Hippocrates?" Serena asked. "She did not know why I left the Chamber. She only knew it was the consequence of the Cataclysm."

"I'm not sure. Perhaps. It doesn't matter anymore. For now, we will go to the Silva Luctus, and I will return with an answer for these Vagus. We've run out of time." Creed attempted to walk away when an irritated voice called him out.

"You'll abandon your wife and unborn child to run a fool's errand? Doesn't it get tiresome constantly leaving her behind?" Xaris walked down the slope to stand beside Serena.

"Fool's errand? Only a fool would abdicate their role of protector," Creed snapped.

"Careful, Hippocrates. Collecting twigs for the insane hardly qualifies as heroic," Xaris replied.

"Leave me. We have work to do." Creed attempted again to walk away.

"Always off to something. Always up to something. How do we know if you have other secrets hidden within that broken mind? Mürindür's hopes are misplaced if you be its hero."

"What would you know of heroism? Do you suppose the Pools detected weakness when you sought their blessing?" Creed's eyes narrowed as he stared at Xaris. Xaris felt the insult, and bristled in response, placing his hand on his belt dagger.

"Hippocrates enough!" Ojin cried, seeking to end the saber rattling. Creed looked to Ojin, and shook his head. He backed away slightly only to have Xaris close the gap, and put his hands-on Creed's chest.

"I can't imagine what it must be like to always feel lost, broken, constantly looking for a way home. Your bride deserves better." Xaris' breath soured across Creed's face. Creed tensed, and felt a twinge of hatred in his stomach. It felt fulfilling. He looked down at Xaris' forearm, noted the large purple bruise, and peeling skin. "Does it hurt?" Creed taunted.

"I will show you pain, Hippocrates, if you seek it!"

"I seek restitution!" He looked around and saw dozens of people that had slowly coalesced about them. "I seek restitution for those each of you have chosen to abandon in the dunes. I seek a means to salvage our brethren that burn in the sands of Leterum! They deserve justice, and we will deliver it for them!" Creed turned to Xaris, and lowered his voice. "In more direct terms for you to understand, Xaris, if we remove the Vagus from Leterum's grasp, the very currency of their empire is gone. We cut off their supply line, and strangle them into submission."

"You know very little in the ways of Mürindür," Xaris replied.

"If we find a way to turn these Vagus into Welfalon, you mark my words. The balance will shift."

"We have something to settle before I march off to the Silva Luctus." Xaris' grip tightened on Creed's tunic.

"You're not going," Creed countered.

"You don't command me or the will of these people."

"I do now."

"Since when?" Xaris scoffed, looking to Serena.

"Since I decided to come back and do what you would not. Cowardice isn't a virtue. It's a disease."

"COWARDICE?" The warrior angrily pushed forward into Creed's face. It was a mistake.

There wasn't a hairbreadth of hesitation. Creed reared back, and crushed Xaris barbarically with his forehead, breaking the man's nose, and knocking him into the mud. Blood streamed down Xaris' face and thick black beard. The crowd was silent. Creed spoke to Serena as he stared at Xaris.

"If you send him after me, he won't come back alive." He turned to his team. "Let's go."

Creed's eyes met Celeste's, resolute with resentment and pain. She reached for him, and he sparingly took her hand. He turned toward her, and cleared his throat.

"I'm going to find a way to right what your mother could not, and when we return, make ready. War will be at our doorstep." Creed let go of her, and walked away briskly. Varsalsae and the others followed close behind as Ojin sighed, and strode to catch up. The time for jubilation was gone.

Chapter 23: The Silva Luctus

Creed shook off his wet clothes, and eyed the armor. It wasn't subdued by any means. It would be nice for protection, but this mission needed something less. He rummaged through his things, and found some simple clothing, and chain mail. He discarded the chain mail. It would be woolen clothes, Üstor, and nothing more. He did find a pair of new, dry, brown leather boots, which fit perfectly. He filled a flask with the water near his bed, and stepped into the sunlight. Varsalsae, Kinklefitz, and Yersinitus stood waiting. The four of them were together again in search of redemption for their flock. Ojin arrived with his satchel of food and water. He was dressed in his old kilt of drab greens and browns with an open leather vest. He patted the flasks.

"Brought enough Mebum for us all. If anyone is interested, I also brought some Highland Hoffpepper Mead." Kinklefitz was most intrigued.

"I wouldn't mind givin' it a go before we lift off!" He smiled his big toothy grin. Creed thought for a moment. *Fitz and Yersi?*

"Fitz and Yersi!"

They laughed.

"It's been some time since we heard you mutter those nicknames!" Yersi proclaimed, as Fitz was too preoccupied, swigging away at the mead.

"Ahh. It's got a bite to it," he said once he finished his drink.

"The bees make their honey from the Hoffpepper. Will keep you warm in the mountains. Here, here." Ojin had to take it from him. "I didn't say we needed to stumble blind and drunk into the woods. No more for you. Varsalsae?" Ojin offered it to her.

"No. I'd rather keep my wits about. The Silva Luctus is a morbid affair."

"Yes, it is. That's why I'll take some of that too!" Yersi grabbed the flask, and a few good swallows before wiping his red beard clean. His face burned from the mead.

"Ha! Hope it's nicer to me on the way out, Fitz!" Fitz laughed heartily. They bumped their meaty forearms together.

Creed watched them in their short sleeve tunics and hoods. Their legs were bound in leather wraps to the knees, and he remembered them well. Yersi and Fitz had been Vikings before they were discovered in the dunes of Mürindür. In a series of unwitting ironies, both men had lived with opposing clans. Though they recalled very little of the battles once waged against one another, they did find a certain semblance. For all they knew, they were brothers. Each braided, bearded warrior stood barrel chested at the same height as Creed. Yersi had red hair all over including the thick patches on his forearms and exposed shoulders. Fitz was blonde and twenty pounds lighter than Yersi. Yersi had a tendency to indulge in one too many roasted pigs. His belly still hung close to his torso albeit with some assistance from the wide leather belt.

Creed looked to Varsalsae, raven-haired, thin, and as beautiful as she was deadly. She seemed as a small child when standing alongside the grown men, but Creed recalled she could easily take twice as many brutes to Hell given her speed and slender blade. The last life she had before becoming Luxatio was one of a Spanish farmer's daughter. She mobilized raids at night to steal food for the poor, and during the day, she tended to the livestock, leaving none to suspect her as the night raider. Creed admired her strength and tenacity, and was content to have his team together. Flying through the Fuga once again, however, was another matter entirely. He whispered to Ojin for guidance.

"It's been some time since I've done this. Walk me through it again."

"The Fuga is a fast flight through space and time. Hold on to everything, and keep one hand on me. I can usually handle up to six or seven people. If I tire excessively, I can manage two or three. The less we have to enact the Fuga, the better. I am hoping we jump in, harvest what we need, and jump out. The less time we're there, the safer we will be." Ojin motioned to everyone, "All of you form a circle on me. Hold one another with one arm, and hold on to my cloak with the other. You may feel a little heat. Creed, I suspect that won't bother you much." Ojin grinned as his tusks glistened. He tired of walking, and with Bog safely resting under the watchful eye of Pax, this would be much less of a strain on his spirit.

"*Nobis Fugere!*"

Wind shot from the ground as an immense white light blinded them all. Creed could feel his clothing swirling about him as Fitz held his waist and he held Yersi's. Roars and echoes engulfed their minds until Ojin yelled at the top of his lungs.

"Brace!" They hit the boggy ground as if they had fallen from a mountaintop. Creed rolled away from the others, and sat up from the indentation in the sod.

"Honestly, I thought we would have had a smoother landing, Ojin."

"Well we would have had I known this one was coming!" Ojin picked the creature off his back, and set him down.

Pax had somehow snuck up on them, and leapt just as Ojin had begun. He was lucky he held on at all. The hobgoblin angrily confronted him.

"Pax! What were you thinking? You could have gotten us all killed." Fitz stepped back and gripped the handle on his battle-axe. Pax cowered, and stepped behind Creed.

"Oi! What's this bloody Ogre doin' 'ere?" Fitz asked. Creed was none too amused either, but what could be done now?

"Men, calm down. At least when we go back, we will have a proper count. Pax, you were to stay with Bog. Who's watching Bog?" Pax stirred the dirt with his fingers. He had drawn a woman with long hair. Ojin looked at it.

"Celeste is it? Fine, fine. Get up then. Don't imagine you've brought your bow, have you?" the hobgoblin wondered. Pax stood up, and beneath his gray cloak, he swiveled out his crossbow and quiver, grinning.

"Well, at least he's prepared," Creed acknowledged. "Pax, you could get hurt here. We were coming back. I asked you to wait." Pax stared at Creed and just smiled.

"Right. We've already stumbled afoot with the plan. The forest is ahead. It's best if we stay hidden for as long as we can. Stay close, and remain quiet." Ojin raised the Penumbra, and they made way toward the nearest tree line hidden from wandering eyes.

Surrounding the trees for hundreds of yards, there was an absence of growth. No shrubs or grass, just fine gray silt with faintly exposed roots padding their boots as they ventured north. It was difficult to navigate. Each step was awkward as if one tried to walk

344

unevenly through an eroded cemetery. As they drew near, what appeared to be a large forest, leaf-less through winter, became a solemn landscape of disfigured, knot-ridden giant alder trees. The wind tiptoed through their eves as birds flew high above in hopes of avoiding calamity. The forest was alive, though it appeared not to be so, as the troupe sought a path through low-lying limbs into the meadows.

Ojin took a long slow breath, and exhaled as if to whisper. His breath mingled with the hapless breeze, and the roots and limbs withdrew, revealing a sunken rock trail lined with pale green lichens. He turned to each member, including their stowaway, and whispered his precautions.

"Do not veer from velvet green. Nigh are those dark souls unseen. Venture wayward, undue rest, an untoward reward behest. Travel true and penitent, oft align with time well spent." Creed looked at him, and raised his brow. Ojin frowned, and began the verse once more, but Creed raised his hand.

"What do you mean?"

"Shhh. Exactly what I said. Stay on the path. Do not leave it under any circumstances."

"I don't remember ever being here. I remember the name, Ojin, but not much else." Creed motioned about.

"The Silva Luctus is where tortured spirits come to reside." Fitz mumbled carefully. They ventured forward a few paces, and when Varsalsae looked behind them, the limbs lowered once more leaving them with no option but to proceed forward. She peered up to their left, and a slight glimpse of the mountain pass was visible, but fell away as the clouds crept across the elevation.

"None of us have ever 'been here', Hippocrates. We avoid it. Most people use it as a waypoint to the Capital. I don't know of anyone who has willingly gone into the woods. The trees whisper and cry out when they seek retribution," Varsalsae explained.

"Do they favor Leterum or Serena?" Creed wondered aloud.

"Neither," Ojin affirmed.

"How do you mean?"

"They no longer care of the deeds of beings on Mürindür. They are souls rooted in the soil, but yearn to reach the sky."

"Who were they, Ojin?"

"Caedere," the hobgoblin replied.

"Ojin, you said Caedere go to the Undüavalle when they die."

"Most do. Some are salvaged from their fates if permitted to speak, however."

"How do you get a Caedere to speak?"

"You cut the stitch, Hippocrates. You stab them in the chest, and as they die, you cut their lips free. As the last bit of air escapes their lungs, they tell their story," Varsalsae replied, twisting her dagger in her hand. Fitz and Yersi looked at her quietly.

"They can speak?" Creed asked.

"Only some, the ones that whisper the loudest. They are restless until they do. Most warriors do not take the time to listen, or care to free them. They kill them and move on," Fitz added.

"Yes, but some victors grant them grace." Yersi looked to Varsalsae. She gazed into the woods. Creed stopped, and noticed the odd air about them as they spoke of the forest.

"Varsalsae, have you seen this take place?" he asked. Yersi spoke up before she could.

"She has freed many, but the one she looked for most…"

"Enough! That's enough you two!" Varsalsae snapped at Fitz and Yersi. Fitz protested.

"I didn't say a word, Varsalsae. We've talked about this, and I agreed never to speak of it again." She rolled her eyes, and shook her head slowly. The words seemed difficult for her to share.

"I had a brother. In the beginning, before I came here, I had a brother. He was gifted in many ways. He played the harp, he could sing, he could paint, he could dance, and he memorized every star in the sky. He was my baby brother, and I was his protector. When I was in the fields one day, he came running to me with blood on his hands. Crying. He wasn't more than 14 years at the time. Our father had beaten our mother once more, and as he attempted the finishing blow, my brother stabbed him in the chest with a kitchen knife. He wept as he buried the knife into the man who raised him. Held him. At that time, if he were found, my brother would be executed for murder. I dropped my bushels, and we stole a horse from a nearby farmer. I gave him my daily bread, and sent him to the coast to set sail in exile. Before he left, I held him as I did when he would cry at night. I told him to talk to no one, and I told him goodbye. I promised him I wouldn't be far behind." Varsalsae continued after a long look down the narrow path ahead. They walked slowly as she spoke. Her face grimaced.

"When I returned home, I found my mother crying over our dead father's body, and she wailed for the damnation of her son. I remember looking at her in disbelief. She would forfeit her child to the memory of an evil man?" Varsalsae wiped her eyes. "The village elders arrived, and they sent word to the surrounding communities. My brother was a fugitive. When I was pressed, I sent them inland, away from him, hoping to buy him time. Later

347

that night, I packed my own satchel for the road. I raced my horse toward the harbor, hoping to make it there by daybreak, but outside of town, in the boughs of an old chestnut tree," she swallowed her tears, "I saw his feet swaying in the thick air. He had taken his own life out of fear or out of shame, but he was gone. I wasn't there for him at the end as I had promised to be, and I couldn't protect him anymore." She rubbed her face hard on her sleeve. Creed found himself mentally adrift, back in the trauma bay the night Jessie drove her vehicle off the cliff.

"Varsalsae, I'm sorry." He put his hand on her shoulder. She looked briefly, nodded, and stepped aside to collect herself as Ojin spoke to the group.

"Creed, all of you have moments that connect you clearly to the lives on Earth. Those bonds hold you Luxatio together, and they lend you empathy for those you are sworn to protect. Here, the past lies in wait, and although it would do us some peace to find those each of you lost, it would do us no good to waste another second. We need to keep pressing forward."

"Wait. Varsalsae, what came of your brother?" Creed asked.

"He became a Caedere," she replied.

"Did you ever…"

"Once. It was during a raid on an outpost at the mouth of the River Ebon. I noticed a beast that held the sickle as he once held the harp, but this time he did not sing. His movements were that of my brother, my Efron. The wrought bindings on his face couldn't hide him, and as I charged to end his misery, they sounded a retreat, and he disappeared once more. I hope to find him, and even though this forest will become his resting place, it will be a far better judgment than the sentencing he received once he fell here in the sand."

"Ojin, how does that make any sense? Who could blame him for protecting his mother? Can you imagine the heartache he felt?"

"The mind poisons the heart, and there is nothing anyone can do. His punishment was not for the father, but for the rope. He fell as a Vaga a long time ago, and his path was set. He chose that tree, and that conclusion."

"I don't accept that. Varsalsae, you have my word. If I find your brother, I will give him peace, but not before you get to speak with him one last time." He reached for her forearm to shake in solidarity. She ignored the promise, and turned to Ojin.

"Let's go. I don't want to be here any longer than we have to. The woods bring a chill to my bones."

"Agreed. Let's continue down the path until we reach a clearing. We do not wish to disturb the trees. If we do, we are isolated here, and Leterum will descend upon us," Ojin affirmed. Creed lowered his arm.

"How do we get the wood that's needed then?" he asked.

"We should be able to find downed trees. Lightning of the Endüerduul will sometimes strike the trees within the middle of the forest nearest the Rock of Soliloquy. The trees burn slightly, and then the spirits are released. That wood, the remnants, will not cry out for they hold no voice. We can use that to infuse the waters from the Pools."

"What happens to the spirits freed from the trees?"

"The Endüerduul claims them. For those that seek it, redemption is merely a promise away, Creed."

"And the other trees? What of them?" Creed wondered.

"The forest moves. It lives and breathes. When one tree falls, as a spiral, the others entwine themselves closer to the Rock, pulling towards it as some beacon of hope. The newest arrivals grow from the silt on the perimeter, which we have passed. They tussle to be closer, but the others, much bigger, wedge themselves in front. It is a slow, constant struggle for escape. If you truly felt there was a purgatory, Creed, it is the Silva Luctus. The trees, even anew, are struggling for moisture and light. Their bark is plagued with mites, and you can see the ones that bleed are most afflicted."

Creed and the others looked about. Many of those long ashen white trunks were lashed with wounds, and the blood trickled slowly like tree sap. Other trees had large burled holes in their flesh. Creed stared at those the longest. They did not weep like the mite bites, but instead were black in color. Something much larger fed on them too. It seemed to Creed the trees were restless and in pain, and there was no doubt that their current fate was hardly an improvement from their former.

"An entire landscape of dead Caedere. This realm never ceases to confuse me. How do you know so much about this place, Ojin?"

"It is a place of study for many hobgoblins ,my friend. We spend years at various sites throughout Mürindür studying the ways of the imposing elements, trying to understand the purpose of things. I spent some time out here within the mountain pass, and I have ventured to the Rock many times. It speaks whether or not you ask anything of it. It truly is a marvel of knowledge. It even speaks of you at times, Creed."

"Where does the voice come from?"

"From them." Ojin pointed all around as the group focused beyond the penumbra. Nothing but trees.

"The trees?" Creed asked with a tinge of doubt.

"The Caedere spirits within them, and all their past lives, experiences, observations of the world. They speak about on goings they can see, and actions of the past. Their wisdom is a collection of centuries of life and death. Once we get close enough, if you listen, you can decipher many things. There is great wisdom in these woods." Something snapped nearby, and Yersi looked to his left quickly.

"Steady." Ojin held up his hand, and although a soft fog obscured the path before them, the treetops were readily visible all around. Seemingly looking at them, searching for them.

Creed could feel the warmth of Üstor on his back. He unharnessed it, and held it firmly with both hands. Ojin readied his staff as Varsalsae and the two Vikings spread out within the Penumbra. Pax inched closer to Creed. The group paused with their backs to one another searching for the sound bearer. The wind wept, and slowly Creed's brow became wet with the hovering dew. Nothing but breath from one another could be heard, then another snap, and a rustle of broken roots. A swirl of mist roiled over something moving.

Yersi leaned forward trying to get a better look. He took a small step and then another, but his boot hung up on a rise in the path, and his soles slipped on the moist rocks. He stumbled, but as he leaned back once more to slow his momentum, the moss, forfeit his recovery. Ojin broke his whisper.

"WATCH IT", but it was too late. Yersi fell out of the Penumbra into the under thicket mere feet from the path. It was like watching a wild boar caught within a snare.

"AHHH!!! For the gods, this burns!!"

He became entangled in the thorny roots and vines, and was slowly pulled away from the path. His fingers dug desperately into the soil. Despite the thorns tearing into him, he managed to stay somewhat composed. The ground stopped moving, and he re-gripped his axe. Creed could see his hair and arms moving about. "Do not veer from velvet green!" Yersi recalled out loud. It appeared the harder he pulled, the tighter the roots became. Yersi took his axe, and began chopping violently at his captors. The roots were tough, but as each one became splintered and severed, two more took its place. The trees swayed toward Yersi, and faint cries could be heard all around the forest. The Viking screamed.

"Varsalsae!! Fitz!! Hippocrates!! HELP ME!!" Ojin threw his arm across Creed's chest, holding him back. The fog enveloped poor Yersi, and they could no longer see him, but the pleading for help was deafening. For now, they were still protected from wandering eyes within the Penumbra.

"If you go out there, we will die," Ojin warned everyone.

"Then do something! Do the Fuga!" Creed admonished.

"That's not how it works. I set foot out there, I will not make it back which means no one will make it back to the Pools. Look around. There is no escape. No exit. There is only forward." The Luxatio winced as they heard Yersi cry. Creed had enough.

"I'm done. I'm getting him", but before Ojin could protest, Creed stepped out from the Penumbra, and yelled to Yersi.

"I'm coming brother! HANG ON! Stop swinging that damn axe! You're just pissing them all off!"

Varsalsae and Fitz followed quickly behind him, and Ojin let the Penumbra down. Pax hovered right behind his hairy legs. The trees made notice, and the forest came alive with trembling voices, and shrieks heard hundreds of yards ahead. Their presence was now known across the forest. Creed took a rock the size of a small melon, and threw it into the nest of crawling roots. In an instant, the rock was embroiled with vegetation. Üstor was glowing. Creed looked at the others.

"Stand back!"

He raised his weapon high into the air, and struck the earth with fervor. The explosion shook Fitz and Varsalsae, and Pax fell to his knees covering his ears. Ojin flinched, shielding his eyes from the blinding flash. The rift of heat and light burned through the roots and fog clearing a path around Yersi. He stumbled, thirty feet away, and fell into a brief clearing of singed ash. On his hands and knees, he tried to stand, but then screamed again. This time clawing at his back, swatting it as if it were on fire. Fitz ran and screamed at his friend.

"HOLD ON! HOLD ON!" The crew sprinted even as the path closed slowly making way for vegetative reinforcements.

"Fitz! My back! My back is on fire!!" Yersi howled.

"I'm almost there, Yersi! Stand! Stand up!!" Yersi couldn't. The pain made his large legs buckle. Then Creed saw them.

Thousands of bright red mites swarmed out of Yersi's clothing, and burrowed beneath his big red beard. His face was obscured by the parasites. Ojin swung his staff into a nearby tree sending a wave of excruciating sound straight at Yersi. The mites fell suddenly onto the ground, and lay stunned in the bog.

"Now! Get him now!" Ojin commanded. They were mere feet away when a large shadow slithered in the background. Fitz hesitated for but a moment. A loud crunch, and Yersi bellowed in pain.

"AHHHH!" Varsalsae dove for his hands, but she missed by inches as Yersi was forcefully snatched up into the darkness. Fitz screamed.

"YERSI!" He went into a rage, and began chopping into trees left and right, angrily seeking his friend. Ojin yelled.

"Stop! Stop it! You will kill us all! Exit the woods! Now!"

"No! No! We follow his trail for whatever beast took him!" Fitz argued.

Fitz lumbered forward until a root lashed onto his leg and then another. It cut into his right thigh, but as another root worked its way up his back to his neck, Creed landed a devastating blow into the nearby tree from whence the roots came. The tree crumpled in one strike, standing sixty feet above them all. As wide as a doorway, the trunk fell directly toward them. All narrowly escaped by falling to either side, as the trunk crashed into the earth, sending Fitz to the ground, and Varsalsae momentarily lost her sword.

The forest floor was tumbling like a disturbed ant mound, and mites dug into Creed's skin. The burning was unbearable and disorienting. He attempted to stand, but the pain was too severe. He fell to his knees with hands outstretched toward the sky, and then curled into a ball of agony. The inner sanctum of his mind became molten, and containment was impossible. He screamed.

"AAAAHHHHH!"

The air was torn asunder.

Creed's rage exploded, as did everything around him, and when he opened his eyes in a daze, dozens of trees were engulfed in flame. Black smoke choked the air, and beyond his companions' voices he had no concept of which way to run. He looked at Üstor and his arms, and realized a blue, intense flame covered him as oil.

Ojin grabbed Fitz and Varsalsae. Pax had already retreated to the path as he ran across the felled trunk. The fire spread quickly and haphazardly as the trees cried out in agony. Creed heard Ojin land with a thud on the fallen tree, so he hurried in the same direction until he came to the severed end of the trunk. He climbed it and ran, staring at his feet hoping not to fall again. As the trunk narrowed, he paused, and could see his friends and the green path once more. Creed looked back onto the burning woods, and witnessed what appeared to be small pearls of light floating into the upper ether.

They gathered, resting nervously for a moment, when suddenly Fitz broke out into a war cry. He shook his fists at the sky, and then heaved a boulder back into the embers and black smoke. The rock rolled through the ash coming to rest at another tree engulfed in flame. Creed looked to Varsalsae, and she shook her head in defeat. Ojin took a long drink from the Mebum flask, and then offered it to everyone else. He looked upward and saw the huge funnel of black smoke towering to the clouds above as he cleaned his small glasses with a silk cloth from his vest pocket. Creed watched the spreading blaze, and knew they needed to leave immediately. He drank from Ojin's flaks, and handed it to Pax. After a few good gulps, the Ogre gingerly offered it to Kinklefitz. The beastly man swatted the Ogre and his flask away.

"I won't drink after Ogres." Fitz proclaimed as he spat at Pax's feet.

"Fitz, drink. Pax has no ill will to you despite what you may feel for him." Creed took up the flask, cleaned off the spigot, and offered it again.

"Hippocrates, I will not put my lips onto the spittle of that beast. His kind has wrought enough carnage on our people. I'll take the Mead."

"No. Water. We still have a fight ahead," Varsalsae stated. "Ojin, we need to…"

"Get out of here. Creed, we have signaled every beast within a thousand miles. We need to manage what we can, and head home."

"We need the felled wood!" pleaded Creed. Fitz angrily replied.

"Look about! What the hell do you call all of that?" Fitz readied his axe, and walked to the large tree trunk. He took a swing, and buried it deep into the weeping, red bark. He continued for a few minutes, and crafted quite the pile of timber.

"Now you all can go! I will find my brother!" Fitz yelled as he reached into his satchel, and pulled out some twine, forearms sticky from the bloody tree resin. He kneeled, and began bundling the wood when they heard a loud scream. Fitz took to his feet as everyone crouched to fight. Ojin admonished him.

"You'll do no such thing. Get back here! He's gone, Fitz! We need to leave now!" Ojin instructed. "Hold onto my cloak, so we can leave." But it was too late.

"I'm not going!" Fitz replied as more screams echoed through the Silva Luctus, and he sprinted down the path with axe in hand. Ojin grabbed Pax.

"We need to go now! We can't stop him!" Creed shook his head in defiance.

"We're not losing anyone else!"

Creed raised a brow at Varsalsae, and ran after Fitz. She followed as Ojin stared in sadness. The hobgoblin stood beside the Ogre as Pax's eyes were watering, and his lower lip was taut. The Ogre hopped on Ojin's back once more, and they chased after Creed as small roots slowly climbed over the fallen tree, attempting to take ground upon the path. As a wayward rootlet touched the path's stone and lichens, it seared in smoke and ash. The fallen tree however, was quickly engulfed in thorns.

Creed could hear screaming, and an admonishment. A shrill, beastly cry echoed down the trail along with the sound of a thousand boots marching, making the ground quiver.

"Come on you blood sucking sack of shite!"

It was Yersi. He was fighting something monstrous. Fitz was the first to make it to the clearing followed by Creed. Before them, stood a giant rock, white with islands of quartz veins running through it. It towered above them as large as a two-story tavern. Yersi was perched on top, wounded, lying on his side. Fitz called out.

"Yersi! Yersi! I'm here! Coming to get you! Hold tight!"

"No! Fitz, run away! This thing is ghastly. Go home! Fitz! Go home!"

The thousand boots rattled Fitz's stance, and the creature was ghastly indeed. Varsalsae, and Ojin with Pax, arrived shoulder to shoulder in shock. What loomed before them was something straight out of their nightmares.

"*Olopendra*!" exclaimed a dismayed Ojin as he pointed to the beast.

A giant, articulated centipede encircled the rock like a boa. Hundreds of yellow eyes covered its black, glossy head, and a carapace of gray speckled bone interlocked as hundreds of shields of a slithering phalanx. Long fangs percolated thick, brown venom, and where the venom fell, the ground became as brittle as moth wings. Its thousand legs were barbed, red, and its tail forked as ten-foot segmented pikes. Skulls were impaled upon the tail segments, and they rattled when the beast became agitated. The creature smelled the smoke and bloodied trees, and then noticed Creed. It spiraled down the rock, and stopped before him as the sound splintered from skull rattles. They stared at one another, measuring, calculating an attack. Creed looked back briefly to see his friends were too far to help, and the creature too close to evade. Yersi screamed once more from pain. The trees launched an attack, and Olopendra struck.

Chapter 24: Leterum

Creed rolled quickly to his left as he saw his friends entangled in the nearby tree roots. Their mouths were covered in thorny vines, and all that remained visible of Pax was his small Ogre feet. Creed needed to get to them, but the beast struck again, narrowly missing his thigh. He needed help.

Fitz had disappeared, but out of Creed's eye, he caught a glimpse of the blonde warrior high upon the Rock. He was trying to salvage Yersi. Creed would serve as the distraction. He rolled once more, but this time struck Üstor into Olopendra's belly, and the centipede screeched in pain. Creed shouted to Fitz.

"Fitz, you gotta move! I can't hold this thing off by myself!" Fitz looked over the edge at him, and nodded in affirmation.

"Yersi, take my hand. Give me your axe! We are going home!"

"I wish I could join you my friend. My life is leaving me. It spills upon this wretched rock."

Fitz rolled Yersi onto his back. Creed could see maroon blood pumping down the side of Soliloquy. The quartz veins absorbed each drop.

"Fitz! FITZ! YOU HAVE TO HOLD PRESSURE ON HIS WOUNDS! HOLD PRESSURE!" Creed shouted.

Fitz took off his cloak, and rolled it into a tight compression. He pushed the clothing firmly into Yersi's side hoping to stem the hemorrhage. Yersi's face was pale even more so than usual. Creed leapt to the back of the monster, stabbing it again, but this time struck the hard carapace of the beast with nothing to show for it.

"FITZ! HURRY!" Creed screamed.

"Yersi! Listen to me! You will make it home. I will bring you home! Give me your hand!" Fitz pleaded.

"I know you will Fitz. You always do. You always have."

Yersi's bloodied palm, tried to pat his brother's face, but it fell short, smearing his mortality on Fitz's beard. Yersi's death rattle echoed through the rock, and all anyone could do was listen. Fitz stared in disbelief, and Creed hesitated with shock. All this time, all this way, all these years, and for it to end here upon this rock seemed so insignificant. Fitz wiped his eyes. Creed was struck on his back by the monster's legs, and fell to the ground on his side. Fighting for his life, he called out to Fitz.

"FITZ! NOW!" Creed turned and could see Varsalsae turning purple with Pax and Ojin being dragged nearly beyond sight into the woods. This would be an unenviable death. Everything seemed for naught.

Fitz jumped from high above with vengeance in the air, and his feet crashed into the soft soil behind the creature.

"ARRGHHHHHH!!!" Fitz jumped onto the back of the centipede, and struck his axe onto its carapace. The vibrations through the handle were so severe his hands went numb. Not a blemish on the shell, and Olopendra was unfazed Creed shouted to Fitz.

"Get to its tail!! Its tail has no armor!" Fitz turned, and as if on a steep slope, slid on his feet down the creature's back. Olopendra tossed and bucked hoping to rid itself of the bearded man while lunging for Creed.

Fitz jumped from the last segment, and crashed his weapon upon the tail. His mighty axe chopped through the sinew as the juices splattered upon his chest and neck. Although not injected, the venom sacs' excrement burned and smelled of carrion. One of the forked ends was severed beyond reproach, and it sent the monstrosity into a blind rage. It turned on Fitz, and head butted him into the Rock. Fitz lay unconscious.

The monster rose to strike, but as it did, Creed lunged in front of Fitz, and drove Üstor's spear tip deep into the ground with both hands. Olopendra launched forward for the kill, but the glaive split the monster's mouth in two, and the shock of the strike and fire, avulsed both fangs. They fell at Creed's feet spilling their toxic contents before the Rock, and the centipede curled up in a defensive posture. Its eyes roving for an escape. Creed held his ground, and looked back to Fitz. He was slowly moving, but wouldn't be able to run. Creed and the centipede stared at one another. The air stirred above them, and Olopendra arched its eyes upward. With great haste, it fled, scurrying down a trench along the backside of the Rock, and was gone in an instant.

The trees whimpered, and their roots fell into retreat. Creed's friends were freed. They slowly rose up, dusted themselves off, and Varsalsae assessed her wounds as Ojin wrapped Pax's. Creed looked at Pax, and saw him stare at something above. The sky was dark. Lightning splashed the air, and the wind threw the dust into waves of grit against their skin.

"Ojin! Did you do this?" Creed asked pointing to the sky. Ojin shook his head, and his expression of fear was well evident. Üstor glowed white hot, and Creed felt something he hadn't felt in quite some time. It was a sense of reckoning.

A large chimera of crimson, indigo, and ivory hovered above them as his wings flung the air like felled hope. Creed could taste bitterness in his throat, and knew the creature upon which he stared, for he had a long, tortuous history with this nightmare and its master.

"*Sēpein*," Creed whispered.

The chimera, Sēpein, was an abomination unlike any other, three heads, to control an ungodly beast. Upon the left shoulder, a hide-less goat skull with spiraled horns and ivory bone, its bronze eyes meant to see all those who despair. Before the right shoulder, a red-skinned dragon with silver eyes to sense one's darkness, and a gullet that births fire. But in the middle, rose the alpha, a fierce beastly lion of black and auburn mane with tempest eyes of gold. He finds the fear in men's hearts, and hungers for it as the heathen gods of Acrom's kingdom. Sēpein's shoulders and chest were of lion in origin, but the flanks and hindquarters, were those of the dragon. Its tail, a long albino serpent with eyes of diamond, eager to strike its prey with paralysis, kept a watchful gaze on the lustful desires of mankind. The creature was indeed an amalgam of vile depravity, but as fearsome as Sēpein truly was, it was the rider that fetched the woes of men.

Upon Sēpein's back rode the Reaper, Lord Leterum himself. He sat tall within the saddle as they remained mere feet above Yersi's body, high upon the Rock of Soliloquy. Leterum was draped in dark robes, which undulated about him slowly as waves on a cold, distant shore. His arms and legs were armored in gauntlets and greaves of silver scales, while his face remained hidden, behind a menacing helm of roiling black smoke within his hood. Ice glistened on his clenched metallic knuckles as the reins remained steadfast within his grasp.

Creed gripped his weapon, and readied himself for an attack as Fitz came to, and stood with his. They backed up slightly to take the ominous view in all, while Varsalsae, Pax, and Ojin ventured forward a few feet to join their friends. There was silence now besides the lamentations of the woods, similar to the deep tones of iron bells strung together upon a cliff of destitution. Nothing stirred but the wind and dirt. It was eerily serene. Leterum leaned forward slightly in his saddle. Creed could feel his eyes.

"Do you know me, child?" His voice was deep and resonant.

"Does any man?"

"Aye, men know me. They fear me. They sense when I am within the room. They pray to avoid my calling, and yet, you're not just any man, now are you?"

"I am, just a man," Creed replied.

"No. No, your falsehoods are easily transparent. You've prayed for me, Hippocrates, as if we were kin. Perhaps we are, though now, I can't place you so easily upon the family tree. If so, where would you belong?"

"None of us belong here, but these trees seem to know you well."

"Aye. They know their father."

"I know of you, but I do not fear you, Leterum. You're nothing more than a ferryman." Creed gripped Üstor tighter, and the heat from the ethereal weapon reached the rock. Small fissures developed within the quartz, and the others stepped back from the stifling air.

"No. *You* are not afraid. I've found this most endearing. You wish for it so desperately, and yet you remain despondent in denial. I've pondered what merit there lies with delaying the inevitable, when it is so willingly hoped for. You have fought me with one hand, while with the other, invited me into your home, as a beggar for an end to what you consider to be insufferable. Yet here we are. A man who eagerly awaits me, an army who yearns for my demise, and a universe so blind to its indiscretions, that I have become the very evil it hopes to obliterate, despite the truths that lie buried within this very rock."

Sēpein landed forcefully on the Rock of Soliloquy with a crash, and buried his talons into Yersi's body. Dark blood oozed from his broken ribs with the tension while the last of the corpse's breath exhaled. The desecration infuriated Fitz.

"Here you! You foul-mouthed demon! Come down so I can skin your bone-borne body!" He spat upon the Rock.

"Ahhh. You mourn, as you should. Fear not. His soul and bones will serve yet again, a higher purpose."

"Don't touch him you piece of shite! Come to me you corpse sucker!"

"Ha! Such vigor, Kinklefitz! I've watched you with scarce intrigue. You follow this man, this idealistic failure like some kind of mute lap dog." Leterum nodded toward Creed. "Would you like to sit beside me tonight at my banquet table, Kinklefitz? I'm sure you and your friend will find the conversation quite inspirational." Leterum leaned back and sat high within the saddle once more.

"I'll roast your bones!" Fitz proclaimed.

"Careful, child. You humor me, but mildly. Your time is nigh, and none shall hinder my direction."

Sēpein sniffed the corpse within its grasp, but then turned to take a look at the mighty morsel bellowing below. The dragon's head drew in a deep breath, and before Fitz could contemplate a move, a fire spewed forth, incensing the very air they tried to breathe. Unbeknownst to everyone, Pax had brandished his crossbow, and unleashed two bolts right below the dragon's left eye as the fire spilled from the tongue. It was enough to alter its aim, and time for Creed to jump toward Fitz, embracing him with his back turned to the Rock. The dragon grimaced in pain, and belched a boulder, a burst of magma toward Pax and the others. They all fell to their sides scarcely dodging the boiling ember as it ultimately exploded in a grove behind them. Fire spread quickly throughout the desiccated alder trees.

The chimera turned downward once more, and unleashed flame onto Creed and Fitz as the lion's head roared. The flames fell feckless, however, for Creed shielded Fitz, and the fire scattered, scalding the earth about them. Leterum laughed softly, and sat forward again, with a motion of his right hand to the forest below. Fitz stepped back with his axe, hoping to have a chance to strike, but the forest roots struck first, and within a moment, all of Creed's companions were restrained once more in an organic entanglement. It was Creed and Leterum, alone.

"Hippocrates…"

"It's Creed."

"Ahh. Creed is it? As you wish. Have a bit of longing for the last life?" Leterum asked.

"It's who I am. It's who you would declare should my time arrive."

"Ha! You remember. How exquisite. The ancient declaration of my prize to the Book of Ages."

"I will not end up in that book today, Leterum."

"No. Not today, but Hippocrates would be the proper name, I'm sorry to say. It is who you are. I remember the day you arrived. I watched you from above. Puzzling as it was to see you run toward me, toward the chaos. Ever since that day you've been a hero of the people, yet now, here you have returned, and the realm has had little time to enjoy you."

"I am here, now. If you wish to fight, then release his body. Come down, and we can end all of this." Creed's chest was burning, and a light blue flame trickled across his shoulders. "Let us bury him, as is the tradition, and place his remains at Redemptio. Let them all go, and we can settle this here upon the Rock." Creed stepped back in preparation with Üstor at the ready.

"I would enjoy that very much though you've changed, Hippocrates. I can smell it. Acrom wafts about you. Fire has become your novelty, and your weapon brings back fond memories. You know, its master was once a close brother of mine. I do not favor you wielding it as such since it is a bit insulting to his memory."

"You're welcome to come retrieve it, my Lord." Creed mockingly bowed. He kept hoping Serena would arrive at any minute. He remembered Ojin's tales of the Bellatorum striking from the skies, but no one answered the call.

"Hubris. Ahh yes, my brother Elyptos mastered that as well. In due time, my child, but unfortunately, as elements in motion so often do, we too must wait for the series to conclude. I have pondered you, Hippocrates, for as much as you hold such withering disdain for me, you do marvel at my necessity."

"Perhaps."

"There are things darker than my hands. I bring peace. I end suffering."

"And what of Acrom?"

"Acrom is something you could not possibly comprehend. We were all brothers and sisters once. Serena would like to simplify the complex. We heralded the Dawn of Creation. We were the shepherds of the new world, but when man arrived our purpose changed. We questioned the reasoning behind their very existence, and yet we did as we were commanded to do. All things have a price, however. With Light, there is judgment. There is a revelation of all that transpires, but with Darkness the mistakes, the errors, and the ugly scars of human experience disappear. In the shadows, there is reconciliation. Darkness is more than an absence of light, Hippocrates. It is a promise unlike any other, and yet, Acrom lies in prison while I command the realm. His captor has little room for judgement as I'm sure she has explained to you."

"Serena has said nothing to me." Creed looked back to his friends as they lay helpless in the dirt, bound, gagged, and bleeding once again.

"Your lies are poorly crafted, child. For you have found yourself here at the direction of the Oracle, and I suspect the knowledge attained therein did little to win the Queen's favor. No matter. Serena would do well to speak with you. It is customary when one so readily deploys their pawn."

"Release Yersi and the others. Now, before I strike you down. We can end this all here, amongst your slaves."

"Slaves? These trees, these Caedere graves, were my children. Forsaken and forgotten. I gave them purpose. I gave them sight. I gave them life in the sands. Soon, my Caedere will cover this world, and all will bow to what they know to be peace. A resurrection of an existence we once knew." Sēpein seemed restless as Leterum tightened the reins.

"A world of death and decay will never find balance. Your Caedere will yield, Leterum."

"Perhaps you should discuss that with them now. Fight fervently, Hippocrates, or you may be dining with me tonight as well!" Leterum laughed heartily.

With that, Sēpein thrust his wings downward, taking flight with Yersi in tow. They flew through the funnel of smoke now billowing about the charred forest, and once they disappeared, the Ravens and vultures poured forth, blotting the sun with their numbers.

Creed turned to see hundreds of Caedere striding, unscathed, through the Silva Luctus. They tore through the trees and underbrush, and the thorny vines did little to slow them. The black-feathered sages began to roost about the forest much to the chagrin of the surviving timber. Creed ran to his friends, and severed the roots that held them captive. They readied themselves as Fitz seethed for retribution. Pax was trembling, as he loaded two more bolts into his bow, and Varsalsae breathed slowly through her nostrils as blood trickled from her lips. Ojin gathered his wits along with his staff, and prepared himself, though weary, for one last leap in the Fuga.

"On me! Now!"

The hobgoblin settled his glasses upon his snout. They all grasped his robe, and Pax held tightly to his leg, aiming for the closest impending villain. The Caedere were fast approaching, at a gallop, lustful for the kill.

"Wait!" yelled, Creed. He ran to the outskirts of the Rock of Soliloquy, and gathered as much felled Silva wood as his arms could carry. Fitz and Varsalsae were getting anxious.

"Creed! Now! There's no time!" Ojin beckoned.

"We're not coming back! If we fail, then this was all for nothing!" He bound the timber stack with sinew from the tissue of the centipede's tail, threw it over his back, and ran once more to Ojin and the others. They all looked at one another. The Caedere raised their blades and dove into their midst. Ojin whispered once more with his head held recumbent.

"*Nobis Fugere.*" There was a flash, and they were gone.

Chapter 25: A Remedy

T he wayward expedition party fell from the Fuga a few trees before Celeste and Serena, as they sat waiting on a marble bench. They were facing the horizon of the distant Silva Luctus, and had seen the smoke. Celeste raced to Creed as he lay on his back beside the others as Ojin struggled to stand, leaning heavily on his wooden staff. The weary hobgoblin reached for a nearby tree for stability. Fitz and Varsalsae crumpled into the grass, bloodied and beaten, while Pax was the only one to seem stoic. Serena sought them aid.

"Get them water! Bring them fresh bandages! Let's get them inside. Take them to my quarters!" A flurry of activity, and a team was tending to their wounds. Celeste kneeled over Creed.

"You've been crying," he said. She smiled.

"Yes. I saw the Ravens fly to you. I knew Leterum would not be far."

"I met him."

Her face grew grim.

"What did he say?"

"He said he was doing this for a higher purpose. He took him, and then left us to his Caedere."

"Did he say anything about you, or about an attack?" Celeste's eyes were wide.

"Something about a family tree, the truth was in the Rock, and that I was a pawn for your mother. He didn't mention a battle, but when I challenged him, he said it wasn't time, something about 'things set in motion'. I don't know. A great deal happened. The woods were alive. Our plans were thrown away the second he fell into the briar. We tried to get to him, but those woods are haunted, vile." Creed hung his head.

"Who?"

"Yersi! We lost Yersi!" He looked to Fitz whose head lay solemnly against an oak tree.

"Fitz is taking it pretty hard." Creed started to tear up, but quickly choked back the emotion as he looked about.

The entire group struggled with their grief. Yersi was a force to be reckoned with on the battlefield and the beer halls. His humor and gusto for living in Mürindür shed light even on the most opaque of days. His loss left a palpable void in the small band of Luxatio. Pax walked over to Creed, and offered him the water that had been given to him. Creed took a long draw from the glass, and when it lowered, he looked at Pax, always faithful, and never deterred.

"Pax surprised us all, Celeste, when he jumped on Ojin's back, but when Sēpein wished to end us, it was his quick thinking and sharp aim that gave us the reprieve we needed." Creed reached for Pax's shoulder. "I'm sorry, my friend. I thought we could pull it off. I thought we could stem the tide. If it hadn't been for your bow, the dragon would have taken Fitz as well. We're alive because of you, Pax. Thank you." As Creed slowly lowered his head, Pax knelt down and patted his scalp gently. Ojin came over, offering his hand.

"Pax, you were very brave back there. I too am sorry. If you can forgive me for how I've treated you as of…" but before he could finish, Pax leaned in and hugged the hobgoblin's leg, releasing a sigh and a brief snort. Ojin's hand cradled his back. Celeste wept as she looked at her husband and his friends. Their pain and heartache were apparent. She walked over to assess Varsalsae and Fitz.

"I'm so sorry for your friend." she said. Varsalsae looked up at her as she finished her drink.

"He died honorably. After all these years, he finally had his hero's death." Celeste paused for a moment, and then responded.

"Yes. He died with honor and bravery. He will be well remembered."

Fitz was less inclined to celebrate.

"He died! That's what happened! That monster fookin' took him! I failed him! We failed him, and there's not a damn thing any of us can do about it!" He threw the goblet into the tree, and then looked at Celeste.

"You immortals don't know a damn thing about bravery, about honor. You think living forever in Mürindür makes you brave? Try living and struggling on that dust heap back home, and then come to this godforsaken place knowing that any misstep, and you could be some dragon fodder." His voice trailed off in misery. "We end up dying all over again. There, here, no matter. Suffering, all over again. Until you feel the fear of the End, and know that you will not live to see another moon or sunrise, don't talk to me about honor! Don't ever mention the word bravery in front of me again." Fitz stood, and stumbled with assistance from some nearby Bellatorum. He grabbed a flask of mead, and drained it quickly in his sorrow as they escorted him to Serena's quarters. Creed called over to Celeste as he recovered.

"He is hurt, Celeste. He knows you didn't do this. Don't take his words to heart." She came back, and sat onto her legs beside him.

"My heart can't help but take his words. They have been with you, with us, for many, many years. In a second, your brother is gone. He didn't even have the chance to choose a path. His path was taken from him. Now he lies within Leterum's Keep, a soul under confines."

"It all happened so fast, Celeste. The woods, this beastly worm, and then Leterum. It was like he was waiting for us as if he knew we'd be there. One minute, we're racing to the rock, and the next he's hovering in mid-air, taunting us. He could have taken us all out with the wave of his hand, but he kept us in the middle of that hell."

"Leterum plays his games as he so often has throughout time. He revels in the control. The souls are like puppets to him."

"I'll kill him someday. I'll plunge Üstor into his empty chest."

"You cannot kill Death my love." Celeste placed her hand on his scalp.

"I can try."

"No. We need to get away. We need to find a new home, and raise this child. Leterum can have his desert of Caedere. He can keep all of this suffering to himself."

"I've been here so many times, and after seeing him again, I remember, I realize how incessant he is with his pursuits. His smugness, his ego, will be his undoing. There is something I recall each time I've faced him. There is something that has been left undone, and when I discover what that is, I will finish it." Celeste simply placed her hand on his neck, and kissed his forehead.

Pax went to lie next to Bog, and the mammoth curled his trunk around his best friend. Within moments, the two were asleep beneath a red maple tree as the campfire crackled nearby. Serena stood with Ojin, and as they walked toward the campfire, she listened to his observations. Creed looked up as well.

"Leterum was stronger. I could feel it, Serena. The entire forest could feel it. I believe that as his Caedere grow in number, he and Acrom will likely feed off that energy. I can't help but acknowledge at some level, this world is about to be split in two. If that happens, there is no longer an intermediary. There truly will be a Hell on Earth."

"This calamity has always been on the horizon, but this child was also foretold. It cannot end before it begins," Serena replied.

"Leterum could sense the change in Creed. He knows something. I wish *I* knew what has changed," Ojin looked at Creed and locked eyes with him.

"He withstood Sēpein's flame, Serena. I have seen that beast turn sand into glass, decimate entire villages, and yet this man turns his back, and nothing comes of it. Not even a singed hair."

Creed looked down. He sensed angst in Ojin's voice.

"I don't know, Ojin. I have no understanding what this means." Serena lowered her voice slightly. "I've asked Xaris to keep an eye on him. I feel his behavior has become too unpredictable."

"That won't likely end well. Those two have been at each other's throats from the beginning," Ojin protested. Creed stared at the dirt.

"Perhaps, but I need someone to report to me their findings. I would ask you, but your friendship likely clouds your ability to remain objective."

"You are correct. I would prefer not to spy on my friend," the hobgoblin replied.

"Ojin, we are on the verge of losing everything. Nothing can withstand a full Nether Army with Acrom at the helm. He and

Leterum, Damnation and Death, will destroy every living thing in this existence. I think 'spying' on your dear friend would be a small consequence if it meant avoiding that conclusion."

Creed interrupted.

"Let him watch me. I have nothing to hide." Creed stood and placed his arm around Celeste. She laid her head on his shoulder.

"Creed, Hippocrates, you have changed. That much is true, and I need you to find a way to settle your mind."

"Well I am trying."

"You need to try harder," Serena instructed.

"Mother, please. He's been through too much these past few days."

"We all have my child. The time for passivity is gone. We need to begin our preparations, and ready ourselves for what's to come."

"Serena, forgive me when I say this..." Ojin interjected.

"Then say nothing."

"What you may perceive to be coming our way, will always be tainted by your perspective. We both know something has prevented *you* from seeing the recent events. Whatever that may be, could also be forcing you to see things yet to occur, twisted in a contortion. Maybe what you think should happen is only what you've been convinced may happen."

"Do you question my capacity, Ojin?"

"No, but I do feel I am the only one who will say it. We can no longer rely on what you may see now, either. We will have to reason through our planning. The strategies will have to be built off of real observations in the field. Send out more scouts. Move your camps. Decide on where we wish to hold a stand."

"The Pools are all that keep him from sheer domination," Serena replied.

"Then build a fortress here," Ojin countered.

"And what of Redemptio?"

"We can find a way to keep it safe, but the Capital is no longer our best option, Serena. Please. You know this. I saw the refugees in Durdan." Ojin gestured emphatically with his large hands.

"I evacuated the weak and aged."

"Evacuate them all then, if you choose to remain here."

"What of the Capital Guard? Let them fall?" Serena asked.

"Call their retreat. Let the Capital fall, but have the populace join us here, or Durdan. I don't care which, but we cannot be divided across the Highlands. Our resources are too diluted."

"What of the Welfalon? We abandon them in the desert?"

"No. If we can shore up Redemptio by consolidating our forces, we'll be stronger in the long run. Establish new supply lines through the mountain passes. Hold the North, and keep Durdan alive. Durdan, the Pools, and Redemptio would suffice for now. A new border of control."

"We will be relinquishing half of our territory should we let the Capital of Guillarne fall, and the Vagus will overflow the lands. The numbers of Caedere will be insurmountable."

"No. We can stop this. All of it." Creed dropped the Silva timber at her feet.

"We don't have any more time for your experiments, Hippocrates. The losses up until now are quite evident," Serena opined.

"The Pools sent me on that mission. The least we can do is try."

"On whom? The other Vagus that were so haplessly thrown into our camp are dead." Serena looked at Creed coldly.

"The Caverns. Varsalsae said they are holding hundreds of Vagus in Caverns beyond the forest. Help me make this medicine. Come with me, and let's try to save the souls we can."

"It won't work," Serena admonished.

"It might," Creed insisted. Serena was exhausted, and let out a long sigh.

"If it fails?"

"Then I'm done. We fight your way to the last man. We get Celeste and the baby somewhere safe. Wherever that may be, and we fight until the end."

"I would prefer Creed's odds, personally." Ojin nodded toward the timber. Varsalsae came to stand beside them.

"The Caverns are hidden well. The rock doors are enchanted, and Leterum does not know where they are." Varsalsae looked to Ojin.

"How is that possible?" Serena asked.

"His brothers helped us."

"Ojin?" The Queen was visibly frustrated.

"I had no knowledge of this." Ojin waved his hands, and looked puzzled at Varsalsae.

"We were visited in the night by three brothers. They had watched us for weeks, apparently. They promised to help us keep the Caverns hidden by enchanting the doors and walls. We were provided with grain and fruit trees that would grow in the dim light. They also gave us lanterns and torches from the Tree of Amaranth. With those gifts, and the waters of the Caverns, we had a reprieve from the Caedere. This is why we have been able to hide for so long, and keep so many lost ones."

"Have the Hobgoblins turned on me as well, Ojin?"

"No, Serena. I've received no word of this. Up until now, most of my people have shored up the defenses of our homeland. The apprenticeships have stopped altogether. We haven't taken on any new pupils in quite some time. Naturally, I assumed I was one of the few stubborn enough to remain."

"Why would they… why couldn't I sense…" Serena paused.

"We care as much about these lands as you, Serena. These brothers I suspect did so without notice. Had the elders known about their whereabouts, I'm certain they would have called for an end to it. They also would have, by courtesy, notified you. Regardless, I have more faith now in this Vagus refuge you speak of."

"Then it's settled. Help us make this medicine, Serena, and I will take it to them." Creed untied the bundle of wood.

"If I do this, then *we* will take it to them. Ojin, what were we to do with this Silva wood?"

"We are to char it. Take the burnt pieces, and steep them in the waters of the Pools. Then we feed it to the Vagus."

"There likely won't be enough for the hundreds you speak of."

"Likely not." Creed looked to Ojin and Varsalsae.

"If I must go back, then I go back alone. I will bring more Lamentum wood."

"No! Absolutely not! You barely made it back home to me. I won't allow it." Celeste stood with her arms crossed.

"No. No, she's right, Creed. That's not an option. We will dilute what we can. We will give them drink since it is difficult to make them eat. Give me the timber. I will char it, and then I need four cauldrons filled with the Pools medium. Serena, we will need a means to carry the medicine." Ojin noted.

"We will use the barrels of wine from the wedding. Men, drain the wine! Empty the barrels! Bring them to me."

People uncorked the wine barrels, and within minutes, pools of dark maroon saturated the dwarf grass. It eerily resembled something more morbid than simple wine. Ojin shook his head in disappointment as Fitz came out of the tent to the smell of wasted fermented grapes.

"Oi! What goes here?"

Creed walked towards him.

"We are making the medicine, my friend. I need your help as well as Varsalsae's. We will go to the Caverns, and try it on the Vagus there."

"Fine, but just Luxatio. The men will be happy to see you again."

"We bring everyone we need," Creed assured.

"Your mother-in-law can stay right where she is. I don't trust her with the whereabouts of *our* Keep." Fitz motioned to Serena, and she raised her chin sternly.

"At some point, we all will need to get past what transpired, but until that time, I need you to trust me. Can you trust *me*, Fitz?" Creed asked. Fitz kicked the dirt a bit with his boots. He looked to his axe lying beside a nearby black walnut tree, cleared his throat, and spit on the wine-soaked soil.

"Aye. I trust you."

"Then let us make right what we could not so many years ago, my friend." Creed patted him on the shoulder.

They did as Ojin requested, and brought four cauldrons with fires stoked beneath, and poured buckets of the Pools' precious water into the iron pots. Ojin tended to the fires, and sifted the embers to manage the heat. He divided the Silva Luctus wood evenly between the four fires, knowing the timber needed to be charred, not made ashen. As the heat accelerated, the blood of the felled timber blackened and popped, leaving splatters about the dirt. Creed noticed where the cooked blood fell, mushrooms arose. Soon, there was an entire harvest of orange-capped fungi ringing the base. Pax walked over out of curiosity, and attempted to eat one. Ojin slapped his hand.

"Put that down! We don't know where that's been. For all you know, that could turn you into a swamp monster."

The mushroom tumbled into the fire, sparkled, and then exploded, sending embers sporadically within a ten-foot radius. Ojin raced and stomped them out before they had another bonfire on their hands. The Silva wood remained intact and charred. Serena ran over as Creed investigated the mushrooms further.

"What in the Ether was that?" Serena asked.

"I don't know. The tree sap fell and formed mushrooms everywhere. One mushroom fell into the fire, and blew up," Ojin explained.

"Interesting. May be helpful," she muttered.

"I have no concept of what they are, and how dangerous they may be, Serena."

"Even so, gather them up in a sack. We'll take those with us."

"For what end?"

"If anything, they can serve as a diversion," Serena exclaimed.

"You can carry them then. They'd be much safer in your hands, Serena." Ojin motioned to the Queen with his fire stirring stick. Serena looked at Pax.

"Pax would you mind taking these with you when we venture to the caverns?" The Ogre shook his head emphatically.

"Good. Then it's settled," the Queen concluded. Creed smirked. Serena clearly misunderstood Pax's unwillingness to carry the explosive mushrooms. She walked off to gather her items for the trip as Pax looked to Ojin and Creed, whimpering.

"Don't look at me. If you hadn't tried to sample that garbage, Pax, neither one of us would be in this predicament. I need to tend to the timber. They almost look done. You gather the mushrooms, and careful not to drop them in the fire. The whole place could blow up from those things." Pax begrudgingly gathered the explosive mushrooms, and placed them carefully into a green sack. As he did so, Ojin turned the timber with metal tongs until they were all blackened and sealed.

Four cauldrons bubbled and steamed from the clear waters of the Cordis Loci. The heated mist created a ring of fog about his workstation. Ojin took two charred logs for each cauldron, and placed them in the bottom of the boiling water. Once the timber had been added, the water became viscous with a pink hue like that of hibiscus tea. The cauldrons percolated the air with smells of tarragon and white truffles. Creed and Celeste walked over to examine.

"Ojin, it smells like soup."

"Well it is Caedere, so anything is possible I presume."

"How much do you think we get from all of this? Will it be enough to treat those in the Caverns?" Creed wondered.

"We likely have enough for two thousand Vagus let alone two hundred. I have no idea how much to give, or how concentrated this elixir may be, but the good news is the logs do not appear to change in size or conformation. Theoretically, this water could be ready, and then we simply add more water over time. If the smells and color dilute, then we will know the strength has lessened. I've already asked the workers to brand an 'X' on each of the barrels for the first batch. The next batch will be 'XX' and so on and so on. I've never worked the sap or bark of these trees before, so I wouldn't suggest giving them all the strongest barrels. Maybe we wait for the second go round?"

"It's all uncharted territory. We need to try it. I wasn't given any more guidance from the Pools. Maybe if we…"

"I will be there. We will try it on a few, and then try the other barrels on a few more. Their options beyond this gamble are few to none." Serena stood there sternly with her hands clasped.

"Ok. Fine. How many of us are going?" Creed looked about.

"I'm exhausted. It was all I could do to get us back here. I cannot help in the Fuga. We need Serena." Ojin looked behind Creed and saw Varsalsae and Fitz approach.

"By my count, it would be the six of us, and we might as well include Pax again, so seven. Seven altogether."

"I'm not comfortable bringing the royals. All these years, and only Luxatio have managed the caverns. We've been in hiding for some time. If I brought you all there, I would be looked upon as a traitor," Varsalsae petitioned Creed in protest.

"We have little choice, Varsalsae. Maybe it's time we brought this all out into the open. If we continue to fight amongst ourselves, we have already lost. How many Luxatio are there?"

"One hundred."

"One hundred?" Creed's mind raced. Had he met them all? Who were they? How had they remained hidden for so long?

"How many Luxatio are left serving then?"

"My last count would be another two hundred left between the worlds." Varsalsae looked at the forlorn Serena while Celeste spoke up.

"This would explain so many things. Perhaps this is why the mortal realm has spun so quickly out of control?" she wondered.

"Unlikely. We noticed for some time the number returning had lessened. Leterum has stolen many of them as he did with your friend, Yersi. It's unknown how many Luxatio remains he has acquired. We have no idea what he has in store for any of us, but the Luxatio have likely done little to hurt our fortifications. Varsalsae, I understand your hesitation. Many of them likely assume they will be punished somehow for disbanding." Serena tried to reassure them.

"You did have us arrested when we came to talk with Hippocrates." Varsalsae replied.

"A reflex. It was an attempt to regain control over something quite unorthodox. You have my word. No harm, judgement, or punishment will come to the Luxatio."

"She stays outside." Fitz was not willing to be so accommodating.

"Outside? I am your Queen…"

"She will stay outside." Celeste walked to her mother, and took her hand.

"Mother, we will go, and we will wait outside together. If we wish to regain their trust, we must meet them halfway." She turned to the group, "We've lost precious time in assigning blame and responsibility. If we are to survive, and protect the souls that continue to come here, we must find a way to get through this together. Luxatio and Immortals have always been of one purpose, and regardless of what stories we may hear, nothing has changed."

Xaris stood nearby. His eyes blackened by Creed's blunted response earlier. Xaris looked at them all, and spoke firmly.

"Aye. We all go. We do this together." Creed listened, and paused.

"Ok. Eight then," he replied.

"And I will bring one hundred of my Bellatorum," Serena instructed, but Ojin merely coughed.

"Serena, we cannot do that. Those Bellatorum will draw too much attention. It has to be just us."

"My daughter is coming with us, Ojin. I want my guard around her."

"Mother, we have Luxatio. They will protect us as they always have. Trust in them. No Bellatorum." Celeste and Serena exchanged stern looks.

"Celeste, that is unwise," Xaris interjected.

"Xaris, trust requires risk. This is worth the risk."

"If Leterum knows you are unguarded, we have little to no means to stop him."

"Then we best be quiet and on our way," she affirmed. The allies went about the camp quickly to prepare for the journey.

Ojin directed the workers to siphon the fluid into the barrels, and cork them for transport. He then had others refill the cauldrons with more of the Pools' water, and acquired the second batch of medicine as well. When they refilled the cauldrons for a third time, Ojin saw no change in the liquid's composition, or the bulk of the charred timber.

"Curiously," he mentioned to Creed, "there is no dilution in our mixture. We may have many more opportunities just from the wood you acquired. I hope this works."

"Me too. Are we ready?" Creed asked.

"I believe so. Let me gather the others."

Everyone arrived, and Serena kept her word. Only the eight of them would go with the hopes that the remaining Luxatio would be willing to take them in. They gathered around the barrels, and Serena gave a few final orders to her guard. They would continue to prepare the medicine in their absence, and hold the camp grounds unobtainable to the hordes. Serena then handed a sealed parchment to one of her Generals at Ojin's request, and directed seven Bellatorum scouts to escort him, bringing word of retreat to the Capital Guard of Guillarne. They would be at war soon, and despite her wish to be there to deliver the orders herself, she hoped the Capital Guard would abandon their post, and come to the Pools. The citizens would continue to be escorted to Durdan in the meantime.

Everyone gathered about the Queen. Creed cinched Üstor to his back, Pax slung his crossbow beneath his cloak, and Xaris brought a spear, buckling it to his harness. Ojin readied his staff as the jade orb swirled, and Varsalsae and Fitz appeared eager to go home to their Luxatio family. Celeste took a deep breath, and exhaled slowly as she rubbed her belly. Creed looked to her with a raised brow, but she simply offered a reassuring smile. Serena then entered the circle, and enacted the Fuga. Bright light, and they were gone.

Chapter 26: The Caverns of Lorem

They arrived at the base of the caverns careful to remain hidden in the timber far below. Ojin raised the Penumbra, and one by one, the Luxatio carried the barrels of medicine up the narrow path to an outcropping of limestone. When everything was in place, Creed, Varsalsae, and Fitz stood at the gray rock-face while the others watched from a distance. Fitz turned and grabbed a barrel of medicine, and placed it on his shoulder as Varsalsae spoke with Creed.

"I warn you. These are the Caverns of Lorem, and what you are about to see will likely be disturbing, but this truly is the only means by which we've been able to protect them. Nurture them. Some are sicker than others. The Luxatio here have all forsaken their oaths to care for these Vagus. There is bitterness here for most. They feel abandoned by the very source they once served. Word has spread that you have come home, but no one knows that you have wed. I think it would be best to not mention your bride or the Queen for now until you gain their trust. I will introduce you only as Hippocrates. Now step back. Rocks often fall from above when I do this."

Varsalsae stepped forward and placed her hands on the smooth surface, and then on her lips. Her incantations were as song while her fingers strummed the rock like a harp. It was rhythmic and repetitive. The rock shuddered, and an archway of light emerged from within the stone. Glyphs were illuminated with a soft red light. Debris fell all around them as the arch became a doorway, and slowly recessed into the soil. Once it was done, Creed could smell the musk of men.

Varsalsae took a torch from the entryway of the mountain, and walked down a slow winding path. The rumbling of the door muted the sounds of dripping limestone as it rose and sealed itself once more. They followed the flitting shadows and flickering light for quite some time until the ceiling rose high above, beyond their sight. As the ground and stairway leveled, below them, in the open caverns, a multitude of lanterns were seen staked throughout the darkness. Faint wails echoed. A group of hooded men with torches took notice, and formed a line at the end of the cavern path. When Creed, Fitz, and Varsalsae approached, the tallest man held his hand up.

"Hold. Varsalsae, it has been some time. How fair you?"

"Cold and tired. We have continued to scout the northern plains for Vagus. We lost a small group following an ambush. Then we received word."

"Word of what?" Varsalsae stepped aside and motioned for Creed to come into the torchlight. There was a moment of vetting with the eyes, and then suddenly the cavern patrol bowed respectively.

"Hippocrates, welcome home." The man was about to kneel, but Creed grabbed his shoulders with one hand while pulling his hood over tighter.

"Please do not kneel. I am home as are you. Family doesn't bow to one another." Creed smiled at the patrol. They were familiar, but their names escaped him. Fitz let out a groan and rolled his eyes. Creed chastised him with a look.

"What? This barrel's heavy." Fitz set the medicine down.

"What did you bring us, Fitz?" the patrol leader asked.

"Medicine from Hippocrates. We worked hard for this. Yersi died because of it."

"Dead?"

"Yes."

"No portal? No journey back?" the man asked.

"No. He had barely..." Fitz's voice broke, and the sentence lingered.

"Leterum claimed him before we could," Varsalsae finished it succinctly.

"May the Endüerduul accept him someday."

"Yes. One day we hope."

Creed thought about Varsalsae's comment, and pondered what did await them all should they forego their oaths to the Endüerduul. It seemed cruel to sacrifice so much only to be thrown away. Creed explained the purpose of the serum.

"The medicine we bring is an elixir made from the Pools of Cordis Loci and the tree sap of the Silva Luctus timber. I questioned the Pools' Oracle, and this was their answer. We have not tried to treat any of the Vagus yet. I found two Vagus survivors in the wood, and had them drink the waters alone. At first, they seemed much better, but by the next day, both were dead."

"Poisoned?" the man asked.

"No. Yersi, Fitz, and myself stood guard all night. Nothing ventured into the tent. We think it was because of the waters," Varsalsae replied.

"Ha! Makes sense doesn't it, Varsalsae? We have all seemingly been forsaken by the Endüerduul."

"No. We have not been forsaken. The waters needed to be combined with whatever it is in the tree sap," she replied.

"The bones of the Caedere and the waters of Cordis Loci. Sounds like a disaster." An older, white bearded man walked toward them from below. He held a torch high into the air to look upon Creed. He stared for an uncomfortable moment and spoke.

"And yet, you keep coming back, don't you, Hippocrates?"

"This time was sooner than most." Creed kept his hood up for discretion. A number of Luxatio gathered behind the older gentleman.

"Hippocrates, you left last time at a crucial moment. We all struggled to survive."

"I did not have a choice." Creed stared at the elder.

"We always have a choice."

"Some. Others have a path they must follow regardless of the price."

"Hmm. Still the pragmatic philosopher."

"Still the salty old man." They stared at one another for a moment. This man, he remembered.

"Ha. Yes. Yes. I guess I am." He reached for Creed's upper arm in a warrior embrace. They stared at each other, respectfully, as they shook.

"Pescus. It's been ages."

"Intentionally," Pescus replied.

"Of course." Creed smiled.

"You still roaming about with that overgrown ape?" Pescus asked.

"Ojin"

"Yeah. The hobgoblin."

"I'd be dead if it wasn't for him, Pescus."

"Maybe."

"Pescus, I don't recall you having an issue with…"

"Things have changed. Many things. He is the lap dog of the Queen." Pescus looked about as if Ojin would be present.

"And?" Creed waited.

"Varsalsae? Does he know?" Pescus asked.

"Know what?" Creed looked to her confused.

"He knows," she affirmed.

"We have all been disavowed! All of her mighty children have become castaways. Unmentionables. We are betrayers in the Queen's eyes! No one is even allowed to speak our names! Rumor has spread that she has indeed placed bounties on all of us!"

"I know she feels she has lost many Luxatio, and she does not know why. She still seems to worry about all of you, however. I understand you have gone into hiding out of fear, but she has not mentioned anything of a bounty for any of you," Creed assured him.

"So, you've spoken with the Queen?" Pescus asked while Varsalsae threw Creed a warning glance.

"I have not heard of her placing a bounty I should say," Creed clarified.

"We wouldn't be in this mess if it weren't for you. We did it because of you. You lead us to a cliff edge, and flew away." Pescus spit on the cavern floor.

"I was called back, Pescus. I did not wish to leave."

"We have all been called back, but that night we chose to turn away. We found our purpose here with our own mortal brethren, and now you've come back, hoping for forgiveness. Take a look around."

The lanterns flickered throughout the darkness, and Creed could see bodies huddled together near baskets of food and urns of water. Some paced in circles while others whimpered in corners as Luxatio tended to their needs. A handful of Vagus lashed out in their rage and confusion, and when they did, they were held down forcibly, tied to wooden racks, and left until they fell into exhaustion. It was far from humane, but everything here was a shade of something better than the prior foregone conclusion. Creed was disappointed to see it all, saddening and maddening within the confines of this earthly catacomb.

"This is… umm…. not what I expected, Pescus."

"What *did* you expect?"

"I don't know. A second chance, perhaps. A means to…"

"We moved from encampment to encampment. We killed Ogres, we killed trolls, we fought and lost to many Caedere, but we saved these souls. This may not be the Endüerduul, Hippocrates, but it is a place of rest."

"Maybe, but we can do better. This might possibly be their remedy." Creed motioned to Fitz.

"Such as this medicine you made in that barrel?" the old man questioned.

"Yes, Pescus," Creed replied.

"Have you seen it work?" Pescus asked belligerently.

"No."

"So, from whom is the cruelty best derived now? Hmmm?"

"There has to be the first patient, Pescus. There is always a first." Creed cleared his throat.

"I know this better than anyone, Hippocrates. Take your pick, healer. Look about. You can take any one of these you want."

Creed looked around the areas closest to the exit path. If this went awry, he wanted something to his back for an escape. They were potentially safe here, but the animosity was evident. To his right, Vagus held one another, rocking continuously. Beyond them, clusters of Vagus paced and scratched at the cavern walls, clearly more agitated. The six before him would do.

"Let's take those patients over there. If you have any seats, benches of any kind, please bring them here. They will likely seize once we have them drink this."

"This should be entertaining." Pescus spoke with mockery in his tone.

"Pescus, we have no other way. Now, seemingly all that fall from the skies are lost. Leterum has found an endless supply of servants. We cannot defeat his numbers. We can only prevent his troops from surging. If this works, everything changes."

Fitz placed the barrel on a footstool, grabbed a ladle, and uncorked the belly. He had borrowed a spigot from the camp, shoved it into the hole, and filled the ladle with medicine.

"Who's first?" Fitz asked.

"How do you choose which life to forfeit, Hippocrates?" Pescus nodded to the ladle full of rose-colored serum.

"I don't."

A Vaga, out of curiosity came toward Fitz, and grabbed the ladle from his hand. He drank the dose quickly, and licked the metal. The Vaga started to bang the barrel with the kitchen utensil, forcing Fitz to take it from him. Creed watched the man. His movements were the same, and walked in circles as he had been seen doing moments before. It was as if nothing happened.

"Seems your theory has failed," Pescus smirked.

"Maybe. This one isn't seizing though, and that is progress."

Suddenly the patient fell to his knees, and his face contorted into a distortion of human semblance. His eyes blackened, and as if he were to scream, he took in a breath, but when his chest contracted nothing but black smoke fell like cold ink from his lips. There was no sound. Not even a gurgle or a gasp. Just a pale Vaga reaching for Creed's cloak ends.

Creed stepped back, and watched the man fall to his face. There was a small twitch of his leg, and then nothing. Creed kneeled, and turned the Vaga to his side, slapping the man's back repeatedly until the man curled into the fetal position and belched. He proceeded to vomit weakly, and Creed made sure to hold his head steady to the side, wiping his mouth. The Vaga took a breath, and then another, and another until he was sleeping. The black liquid he had managed to expel sat as a puddle for a moment, and then dissipated into a vapor, never to be seen again. Creed checked for the man's pulse along his neck. His artery bounded strong and steady as he looked to Varsalsae.

"Let's get him to a bed. Bring the others, and let us see what we may see."

Varsalsae brought the next few patients, and all reacted the same, weakness, collapse, silent agony, and loss of consciousness. Within an hour, there was a small infirmary of dozens of Vagus within the caverns. Creed watched over them for some time taking note of their pulses and respiratory pattern. He checked their pupils with the torchlight, and some would purposefully shield their eyes from the heat. None would talk, but Creed could see something different this time than before.

He was lost in thought as Varsalsae and Fitz went about the camp talking with the other Luxatio. They spread the word that Hippocrates had returned, and there was new hope for all Vagus. It wasn't long before Luxatio crowded shoulder to shoulder to catch a glimpse. Creed was unawares until he stood up to check on another patient, and suddenly realized he was within a large circle of curious Luxatio. He hesitated, but then collected himself. Now was as good a time as ever. He stood tall, removing his hooded cloak, and motioned for Varsalsae and Fitz to join him.

"My fellow Luxatio. It is good to see all of you. Although it may take some time for me to recognize everyone, I do feel a calm sense of belonging. I've been reminded constantly of how much I had hoped to achieve here before I was called back once again, and how many of you, all of you, were left holding the line until my return. For that, I am truly sorry."

"You left us! We've been alone all this time!" shouted a voice from the back.

"I understand. There was still more to do, but I am not leaving now."

"Why should we believe you?" voiced another.

"Well, trust requires risk, I suppose. I have much to gain from each of you, and I don't expect anyone to feel comfortable just yet, but we bring hope this day. I bring a promise."

"We don't need empty promises!" a woman yelled.

"We need peace!" shouted another.

"Friends, please. Listen. I have fleeting memories of my last visit here, and the knowledge that we discovered something we could no longer ignore. We discovered a purpose. It has become our path to steward those that have been left behind. Our brothers and sisters, the Lost Ones, are ours to save, and ours alone!" Scattered clapping could be heard in the back as others nodded in agreement. He continued.

"I am not alone today. Varsalsae and Fitz stand with me. We fought hard to acquire the means to save these souls. We lost a brother in the process. Yersi fought bravely and relentlessly." A few gasps were mingled with mumbling, but he fought until the end. I've honestly never seen anything like it." He paused to look at Fitz and Varsalsae before addressing the crowd once more.

"We stood at the inner circle of the Silva Luctus, but before we could get to him, Leterum took him from us! Leterum has taken everything from us! We don't have to travel the realm, to know that something, everything, has changed forever. The balance has been broken. Our oaths to the Endüerduul have been dissolved by our own volition. This world stands to rip itself in two, but I believe we've found a way to end the suffering. I have brought some mild hope with us, and I have given this opportunity to those you see lying behind me, resting, and I hope, recovering."

"Does this mean you have forsaken your Oath as well, Hippocrates?" Pescus probed.

The grumbling throughout the caverns softened to dull murmurs. Creed glanced at the souls resting on the benches. He looked to Varsalsae and Fitz, and settled his eyes on Pescus, who, for some reason, felt it necessary to challenge him incessantly. He cleared his voice.

"Today we have bigger things to wrestle beyond your opinion of me, Pescus." He turned to the crowd, and raised his hands. His voice resonated with those that had sought him out. "Today, I promise all of you, that I will not leave, and I will not rest until I see this through!"

Varsalsae and Fitz acknowledged one another. Fitz smiled. The Luxatio cheered in unison, some shook their fists in triumph, and others hugged in celebration. Pescus spit on the ground, and wrung his hands as old men do. He slipped away into the crowd, and ventured down the path toward the inner orchard, plucking peaches along the way. Creed watched him disappear into a tent of Vagus.

When the crowd had dispersed and shared their appreciation with him, Creed spoke with Varsalsae.

"Look after these Vagus. I need to talk with Pescus, and then head outside. It's been over an hour. We're probably sorely missed at this point."

"Yes, but you were missed here."

"*We* were missed. Let me speak with Pescus. Something doesn't feel right."

"He's likely just his usual self, needs more wine. We should check on your wife before anything else."

"You're right. Ok. Fitz, come on. Let's go check on Celeste. Maybe now we can bring them down here for a reunion."

He marveled once more at the patients, but with little change, he, Fitz, and Varsalsae walked up the steps toward the cavern door. Creed was contemplating how best to introduce everyone. He felt he barely was accepted, and imagined the Luxatio would be far less hospitable to Serena and his bride. Suddenly, there was a commotion near the medicine barrels and bedded patients. He turned abruptly, and his colleagues followed. One of the younger Luxatio women was jumping for joy. Her smile was contagious.

Creed looked at her in the lantern light, and recognized that face immediately.

"Evalynn! What is it? What have you found?"

"Look, Hippocrates! Look!" He did indeed, and witnessed something miraculous. After thousands of years of cursed Lost Ones falling from the sky, the Vagus were awake, and talking.

"Where am I?" asked one.

"Why is it so dark in here?" asked another.

"I don't understand. What do you mean I 'died'? Where's my family?"

"Who are you?"

Creed was puzzled. How is it now, after so many years, the Vagus distinctly remembered their last moments as he was slowly forgetting his last shift, and even the people he had worked with weeks before. The patients stood, and struggled to regain their balance. Others stumbled and fell into the arms of their caregivers. Evalynn was overjoyed.

"Hippocrates! It worked! The Vagus are awake! They speak!"

"Yes. Yes." He couldn't help but smile in amazement. "I can't believe it. They really are awake. I can't wait to tell Ojin." Creed looked to Evalynn.

"Eva, I need you to do something for me. We need to get back to camp."

"What would you have me do?"

"I need you to take these patients down below, and recover them quietly in private. They are awake and aware, and likely scared. I don't want them feeling intimidated by the other Vagus. We brought a barrel of medicine. We have many more outside. Bring the other Vagus up here in groups of twenty, and give them each, one ladle full of medicine. When they wake, take them to join their brothers and sisters."

"Consider it done. What do we do when we run out of serum?" Eva asked.

"We'll bring the other barrels in shortly. For now, let's set up a system of treatment, and start bringing these souls back to reality."

"It's good to see you again, Hippocrates," she exclaimed.

"It's good to be back."

Creed nodded to Varsalsae and Fitz. They walked upward along the stone stairs, and continued toward the entry of the Caverns. Creed noticed the Luxatio below. They were patting backs, and laughing with joy as they escorted their patients to areas of rest. Many of them looked once more to Creed, and cheered. He waved to them in reply. Hippocrates had indeed returned with hope in a barrel.

Chapter 27: Ojin's Decision

Ojin watched the cavern door long after the trio disappeared behind the stone. Pax sat cross-legged on the ground near a cedar shrub while Xaris leaned on a man-sized boulder. Serena and Celeste sat with one another on a felled oak tree, its bark bleached by the Mürindür sun. All was quiet, and beneath the protection of the Penumbra, the waiting party hid from the wildlife milling about. A fawn walked nearby, and paused as if startled by something. Ojin held his breath, hoping the fawn hadn't sensed them, as he watched it sniff the dirt and grass cautiously. Without much fright, the baby meandered slowly down the mountain slope, tail flagging in the breeze, to its patient mother waiting on the ridge. Celeste teased him.

"Scared of little deer now are we, Ojin?" She smiled gently.

"No. No, but I am tired. More so than usual, and I fear my magic may be waning for the time being."

"Well, mother and I are here, so rest easy friend. You don't need to do much more for the day."

"Let's hope not, *Princess*." Ojin teased. He knew she hated the royal title.

"Ohh. Keep it up old man. We'll see who has the last laugh today!" Ojin chuckled. It was odd this far from any reinforcements to feel so carefree, but looking upon Serena and Celeste, he couldn't imagine a safer place to be. Xaris was less inclined to jest.

"It'd be best if we remained quiet. We've caused a great deal of activity out here in the foothills, and I wouldn't be surprised if scouts didn't head our way. We can't expect to delve into this much magic without provoking something in the sky."

"Xaris, there is nothing in the sky. It won't be long, and we will be inside with the others," Celeste explained optimistically.

"How so? I doubt the Luxatio will so willingly take Hippocrates back into the fold. They've been missing for years, and he's been absent for many more. We should be thinking about a plan to get them out should he fail."

"You've never been willing to give him a chance, Xaris. His heart is good. He means well, and others who choose to see it often feel the same. He inspires men to reach for something more. They will follow him again. He will be out here soon, and we will finally have time to sit and break bread with our lost soldiers."

"Lest you forget, Hippocrates lead the rebellion behind your mother's back. He sowed discontent throughout the Luxatio. He has changed, Princess, and until I can understand why, I will keep him at arm's length," Xaris replied.

"You should. Last time you got a little too close." Ojin smirked behind his thick beard. Celeste snorted and looked away to her mother as Xaris' face grew red with indignation. Serena interrupted.

"Stop it you two. Xaris is right to a degree. Hippocrates has changed, and we just need to make sure until he settles in once more, that we leave nothing to chance. Once he comes back outside, we will have an opportunity to rebuild lost trust with the Luxatio. I am eager to see what they have to say."

"Mother, I... UGHHHHH!"

Celeste leaned over heavily, holding her belly. She went to a knee, and grimaced.

"Celeste! What's wrong?"

"I don't know, but it hurts into my back and legs. It's the baby, but he isn't ready!" Celeste started to hold her breath.

"Breathe, my love. Breathe. My child, infants arrive when they wish to. Have you been feeling these for some time?" Serena asked.

"Not much. Not like this. This one, this one hurts." Her breathing slowed for a moment, and Serena helped her to her feet.

"Let's walk."

They paced in slow concentric circles as Pax watched them continuously. He stood and followed them careful not to get too close. Ojin warned Serena and Xaris.

"If this happens again, we will need to leave immediately."

"Agreed," stated, Xaris.

"We can wait until my husband comes back. The baby has many more weeks to go."

"We may not have that luxury, Celeste, and Serena is right. Weeks, days, or hours may all seem the same to that little one. We need to get you to the camp at Cordis Loci," Ojin suggested.

"I'm not leaving," she replied. The pain seemed to ebb somewhat. She motioned to sit down.

"Child, you and that baby are first and foremost in our minds. Your protection is our highest priority," Serena said patiently.

"Mother, I need to be here to help you find the middle ground with the Luxatio. Standing with my husband will serve as a reminder that we are one."

"It does us no good if you go into labor in those caves," Ojin warned.

Celeste reached for his arm. She had another contraction, and it buckled her for a moment. Beads of sweat broke out onto her forehead. Ojin steadied her as Serena grabbed her hand.

"We need to get you back! I can take you, and Ojin can stay for Hippocrates," Serena assured her daughter.

The Princess was gasping for air, trying to speak.

"No! Mother, Creed is in there without us. We have no idea how many, or how loyal these Luxatio may truly be. For all we know he could be walking into a trap... Ahhhh!!" The pain was intensifying. Ojin shook his head.

"Celeste, you must go. Now! You cannot have this child here. You and your mother must leave, and I will bring Creed home. You, have my word." Ojin hesitated.

The hobgoblin looked about to make sure the Penumbra still held. He was exhausted beyond reproach, and suspected all eyes were searching for the Princess. If his focus faltered in any way, no matter how slight, his magic would fail. She needed to be gone soon. Pax and Xaris kept vigilant. While Serena and Ojin counseled Celeste, Xaris caught movement on the dirt trail stretched below them, disappearing behind a mound of tan boulders.

"*Shhhhh. Everyone. Quiet,*" he whispered.

Ojin followed his outstretched arm toward the boulders, but saw nothing. They held their breath watching for telltale signs of the enemy. After a few minutes, Ojin relaxed enough to momentarily let slip his staff, and the butt end struck a flat rock soundly. He winced, as the group cringed, and there was an awful sound. Ravens settled briskly upon the boulders. Their claws scratched the rock like nails on glass. Their beady eyes stared into the woods, and the secret gathered beneath the boughs had been violated.

Ojin kneeled as he picked up his staff, noticing Xaris had already drawn his swords. Serena sat with a pained Celeste, and Pax made aim with his crossbow. Ojin felt weak, and knew they were trapped, but if the Luxatio emerged from the caverns, he would not be able to get his friends home. He could leave with Serena, but no one would be aware of the impending ambush, or he could try and hold the ground until the Luxatio arrived. Ojin looked at Celeste, and noticed tears in her eyes. He couldn't jeopardize their hope anymore. He made a decision.

"Serena, take her home. I will stay behind, and rally the Luxatio. I may yet have enough strength to open the cavern doors, but you must go now." Ojin's voice was worrisome and strained.

"Indeed," the Queen replied.

"No, Mother, please! Get me to Creed. Get me inside that mountain!"

"It will be a trap, my love."

"I don't care!" Celeste replied.

Slowly, over the rise, Ojin could see an army of Ogres. All strode steadily up the path as a scouting party, covered in dust and grime from many days of marching, settled about the entrance. They appeared as they always did to him, hungry for bloodshed and viciously vile. They scoured the area, a few walking along the rock face, as others ran their hands across the marbled grain at the very place the door had been opened. They could not find the doorway.

"He said it was the first bald rock off the path," One Ogre exclaimed, pointing to a large orange and tan boulder void of moss or lichens.

"There is nuthin' 'ere," another replied.

"Look for tracks." They milled about, staring at the ground, but fortunately the winds did a reasonable job of stirring the dust and dirt in disarray. All they could see was muddled walkways, and old broken timber strewn across the landscape.

"When were they 'ere?"

"Two moons ago. An old man with a grey beard stumbled outside, and took a piss into the briar over there."

The Ogres took their hounds, large speckled, yellow and orange creatures, in a grid up and down the slope. It wouldn't be long before they reached Ojin and the group.

"*Jaiuleynas*," Ojin whispered.

He looked at his friends, and worried. These hounds would easily detect their scent through the weakened Penumbra. For now, Ojin hoped they had the wind in their favor. Serena whispered in return.

"Ojin, stay for Creed. Evade the patrols down the mountain slope for as long as you can. I will get the others to Camp. When they are safe, I will come back for you and the Luxatio."

"No, Mother. No!" Celeste shook her head in defiance. Xaris tried to reassure her.

"I will stay with him as well. We will get Creed home alive. I promise." The warrior placed his hand on Celeste's shoulder. Pax reached for Celeste, but pulled away. The Princess took hold the Ogre's hand, and held his fingers gently. She buried her face in her mother's shoulder and sobbed.

"You don't understand! We need them. We need them to know that we're here. We need them to know that we've come back for them, for peace. They need to… AHHHHHH."

She doubled over again.

"We don't have time. We go now!" Serena raised her hands when suddenly a hound turned toward them, and stared directly at Celeste. It growled in a low grumble, alerting his pack to the new find. Ojin knew it was time.

"GO!" he shouted to Serena, and the Queen touched his cloak once more as a farewell. In a flash, mother and daughter were gone. Ojin, Xaris, and Pax made ready. Ojin let down the Penumbra. "HERE! Here to me you godforsaken pitiful shites! Bring those flea bags to me!" Ojin struck the ground with his staff, and a quake sent rocks and boulders rolling towards the enemy troops below. The Ogres on the high ground laughed with anticipation.

"It's been some time since we butchered ourselves a hobgoblin boys! Let's do it slowly!"

The Ogre band charged from above as the ones below clambered through the rocky avalanche. The hounds were the first to attack, and Xaris wasted no time in removing the nearest hound's head from his shoulders. Pax shot two bolts into a fat Ogre on his right, and as the green beastly carcass rolled downhill, the others took note.

"Look there! Is that Traelore's runt from the Ferris Clan?"

"I think it is, brother!"

"Good! His head will fit nicely on my wall!" the Ogre grumbled in a thick-throated voice. His eyes seemed to grow at the prospect of having a rival clan's remains.

"Traelore? Pax, is this true? The Chieftain is your father?" Ojin questioned, knowing he wouldn't get an answer. Flashes of his dead wife and sons blinded his forethought, as a spear glanced his face, severing beard hair from his chin.

"OJIN! With me! Focus! To my back!" Xaris yelled at the hobgoblin.

Ojin's eyes welled with tears, and he raised a fist of rage. Lightning churned above him, and struck decisively about the charging horde. Their bodies burned as charred grease beneath a roasting pit. Ojin's hair rose upon his back, and he pulled his hands apart from one another, tearing a crevasse into the earth. Ogres fell one by one into the depths below, their screams echoing to their ends. The hobgoblin roped the very essence of the wind, and blistered the Ogre's green hides with sheering torrents and shards of flint and debris from the mountainside. Then it stopped.

Ojin's head pounded with exhaustion, and he fell to his knees, holding weakly onto his staff. He looked at Pax, and wept. Pax stumbled before him, placing his body between Ojin and the forces inbound while he loaded his crossbow once more. There was a momentary reprieve with the chasm before them. Dozens of Ogres were dead, but now his worst fears were realized. Ojin looked below, and saw a legion of Ogres form rank as the remaining patrol and Jaiuleyna hounds circled around for another pass at the three.

As was Ogre tradition, each column in the army announced their presence with a unique bugle of their unit. The sounds resonated from broken mammoth tusks carved to instill fear in their enemies. Bellowing of the legion was slow and methodical. Each sound echoed off the mountains before the next unit began. Once they were done, Ojin counted nine tones all together, and estimated nearly two thousand Ogres within earshot. This was an impossible task.

"Ojin, can you use the Fuga to get to Creed?" Xaris yelled.

"No. No. I have nothing left."

Ojin pulled himself to his feet to stand once more. He stared at Pax, and placed his hand upon the little one's shoulders, patting him gently. Ojin knew that if Traelore was his father, Pax likely suffered immensely at the hands of the Ferris Clan leader, an Ogre who exceeded all ambitions of cruelty to hold his position of power. Ojin's heart broke for Pax, both for his tortuous past, and the knowledge that nothing more could change their fates. They were trapped within a maelstrom of the mountainside.

Chapter 28: The Queen Returns

C reed, Fitz, and Varsalsae failed to look through the walls' fault lines for intruders as was customary before lowering the defenses. The three were in good spirits with the knowledge that a simple thought of redemption had now turned into a possibility for renewal. Assuming the team they left outside would thwart any wayward warring parties, Varsalsae lowered the stone door unawares. As the rock settled, Üstor warmed rapidly, and the Ogre horns were the preeminent sounds cascading through the valley. Creed looked to Varsalsae for an answer, but the door lay bare the caverns' inner sanctum loudly in conclusion. For a moment, everyone froze, breathless, and paralyzed. Creed's eyes met with a scowling Ogre's.

The Jaiuleyna alpha, nearest the entrance, growled gravelly. It salivated as its jaws snapped over and over to an aggressive cadence. Six other hounds did the same, and their trackers drew maces prepping for the easy kills. The remaining Ogres from Ojin's counter-assault gawked in unison at the doorway, as the Ravens' off-key song rose in pitch and anticipation. Fitz drew his axe as Varsalsae's sword settled forward at mid-height. The hounds' leashes fell onto the sandy loam, freed to hunt their prey. The alpha gave a command. Creed gave his.

"LUXATIO AETERNUM!!"

His battle cry echoed down into the Caverns of Lorem. The remaining Luxatio stopped in their tracks. There was a flurry of activity as they took up arms, and sprinted by the dozens up toward their commander. The young warrior Eva led the group, and as she saw the light fall over the shoulders of the silhouettes before her, blood and fur struck her face.

Creed's strike was brutal, but clean, and as the beta hound's head rolled toward Fitz's feet, the Viking's axe struck another hound in the back, crippling it to the ground. Varsalsae had just pushed a carcass from her blade as Eva came to her side. Luxatio were climbing the stairs shoulder-to-shoulder behind him, and Creed looked back to take in their numbers. The odds were easily ten to one against them, but he knew if they failed, the Vagus in the Caverns would be dead within minutes. The Ogres could not be allowed to pass the entrance.

"HOLD THE LINE!! HOLD THIS GROUND!!" he ordered. The voices behind him yelled in return.

"*HOOORAHHH!*"

Creed faced the slope, and the fervor of battle warmed him as did Üstor. He smiled slightly, and leapt into the air. The earth shook as his feet hit the rock, and the impact thrust Ogres haphazardly across the slope. Fitz charged to cover Creed's left flank as Varsalsae covered his right. Eva ran at the forefront of the charging Luxatio army. Swords, spears, and glaives whipped the air, severing green flesh with each intent strike. The Ogres had unwittingly woken a den of wolves, and the Luxatio were hungry. The Ravens took flight, and disappeared into the cloudy sky, leaving the Ogres to fight alone.

Creed scanned the battlefield as he struck his opponents, hoping to see his wife. He found his friends, following their hasty retreat, encircled within the trees, but did not see Celeste. He feared the worst, and sprinted toward them, driving Üstor through two Ogres like a skewer. An Ogre pikesman tried to run his spear through Ojin's back, but Creed managed to get to him first, and the now, one-legged Ogre fell into the briar as his severed leg twitched in the sun. Creed yelled to his friend over the tumult of clanging steel and battle cries.

"WHERE IS CELESTE?"

"GONE!" Ojin replied. He seemed to be breathing heavy.

"GONE? WHERE?" Creed lunged to dodge another sword strike, and split the Ogre's back in half.

"Serena took her back to camp!"

"What? Why?" as Creed stabbed another Ogre, he blocked a thrown spear nearly striking Pax in the back.

"Pax! Get behind me!"

Pax shook his head, and took aim. He let loose one bolt into a large hound, and the other into its handler's eye socket. Both targets tumbled down the incline. The Ogres were running en masse. Xaris drove his swords into an adversary only to stumble as an axe pommel caught his ribs. He coughed harshly, and spit blood, but without hesitation spun to chop the axe wielder's arm off at the shoulder. The bewildered Ogre cried out in anger and pain, but he was quickly disposed of when the swords of Xaris fell once more.

Pax fumbled around with the sack of explosive mushrooms on his back. He threw the sack to the ground, unraveled the bindings, and began lobbing the mushrooms one after another into the field. Ojin saw this, broke a tree branch over his knee, and set it on fire with his fingers. The hobgoblin then launched the limb near the mushrooms. Creed watched astonished. One by one, the mushrooms exploded into brilliant orange clouds of ballistic might.

Dozens of Ogres fell dead near the craters of the organic grenades, and some fell back into the split earth of Ojin. It slowed their advance, and gave the Luxatio reinforcements time to emerge, spilling forth in waves from the cave mouth, while the Ogre ranks wilted from the barrage. Vengeance was brutal and swift.

The lead hound leapt onto a Luxatio's back, and ripped his shoulder from the neck. The man screamed as the alpha finished him off. The hound turned to Varsalsae, and as it tried to leap towards her flank, Pax shot two bolts into its chest. The impact threw the hound's trajectory off by mere inches, and its fangs tore through Varsalsae's cloak as she decapitated another invader. The alpha tumbled, and fell beyond view. Fitz made quick work of three spearmen, and managed to throw their bodies off an unseen cliffside to his left. Eva spun and kicked an Ogre in the throat, and as he collapsed, she split his ribs with her sword. Xaris shouted over the noise.

"We need to get back to camp, now! Ojin get us to the Cordis Loci!"

"We aren't leaving my men!" Creed responded.

"Hippocrates, Celeste is not well! We have done what you have asked. Let us go back and regroup. We cannot finish this!" Xaris argued.

"We lose this, we lose them all!" Creed shouted in return.

"The Ravens have gone, Hippocrates! Leterum knows we are here! It is only a matter of time! We should go, now!"

Creed paused long enough to kick an attacker in the belly while Ojin broke their neck with his heavy staff. The Luxatio, though outnumbered, drove the Ogres further down the slope past the boulders, and into a small ravine. For now, the Luxatio held the high ground, and for a moment the battle tempo slowed. It seemed eerily premature.

Creed and the others finished off what stragglers remained near the trees, and made their way to the ravine where the Ogre leader stood defiantly at the forefront. He was taller than the rest, broad shouldered, and covered in pearly scars and fresh, weeping wounds. A red tribal tattoo marked the left half of his face as a symbol of his rank. He held a pike in one hand, a horn in the other, and had instructed his troops to fight until the last Ogre. They would not fail him.

"You there! Tell your men to stand down!" Creed commanded.

"I will spit on your bloodied bones!" The Ogre replied.

"I think it unwise to threaten me when we have so easily handed you a defeat."

"Defeat? Ha! Child, we aren't the force you had hoped to destroy. We were merely the diversion!"

He laughed obnoxiously loud, thrusting his fist in the air as an affront, and the humor was infectious as the Ogres followed suit, inspired by their leader's taunts. The Luxatio paced for a moment. Creed continued.

"We will grant you mercy, and offer you imprisonment over death! Drop your weapons, and kneel!"

"Death you say? Aye, I know Death, Hippocrates. I walked with him the other day. We spoke of you. He has foreseen it all. Leterum rides toward us now, and all will come to an end! Enjoy this last breath, Luxatio! We won't grant *you* mercy!"

The wind unfurled as the rustling of feathers overtook the discourse. Creed and Ojin gazed across the horizon, and saw the Ravens fast approaching. In the distance from the cover of the rock and ravines, a thousand Ogres marched toward them as well. Dirt danced from their battle cadence. Ojin looked to Creed and Xaris. "This was a trap! We're stranded, and I cannot get us home! I do not have the strength. If we face Leterum alone, we will perish. I am sorry my friends, but the best I can offer is a hurried retreat, a distraction. I will do what I can. You must go, and I will slow them with what I have left."

"Ojin, we can make it back to the Caverns in time! Gather up the wounded! Quickly! Now! All of you! Gather our fallen, and get them inside the walls! Leterum is coming! We must go!" Creed ordered everyone to fall back.

The Ogre commander laughed.

"Hippocrates! Run! Run! Run! Hide from Le-ter-um!"

THWACK!

The commander's body slumped, crumpling to the side. Pax's bolts found themselves deep within the Ogre's skull, and as he fell, the Ogres were enraged. They drew swords, and charged. Spears and arrows flew toward Pax and the others, as they lunged and rolled to avoid them.

"**ARGGGHHH!!**" The Ogres cried out.

As the beasts climbed out of the ravine, the Luxatio stood their ground, and impaled the ambitious horde. The Ravens returned high above, and the trees began to bend from dark figures stampeding to the battlefield. Vultures circled them all, and knowing what was coming, Creed beckoned his troops once more. "To the caves!! To the caves!! Now!! RETREAT!!"

He heard the whispers, and their angst was deafening. The Caedere crashed through the timberline, as the Luxatio turned and ran up the hill toward their home. The Ogre diversion had been well planned, and now the Luxatio, drawn from their defenses, would be the ones to wither. With the front lines broken, the Ogres ascended the slope once more, and Luxatio fell to their deaths as they turned to escape. The Caedere had outflanked them in a race to the top, and Creed looked to see the Cavern entrance wide open. "Ojin! We must close that entrance! NOW!" Creed bellowed. "We won't make it in time, Creed! Look! The Caedere are there!"

They indeed were too far. The Caedere would soon pour into the Caverns of Lorem, knowing what waited for them deep within the mountain, and their master wished for them to take it all. Xaris and Pax covered Creed's escape as he sprinted until his lungs burned, and Ojin scarcely managed to blind the Ravens with bursts of light.

The sky blackened, and heavily charged clouds collided with one another. Creed glanced up, fearful Leterum was descending on Sēpein. Lightning grew and crawled across space like fuel to a flame when suddenly a large white bolt struck at the forefront of the Caedere. Their bodies fell to one side and the other as the energy traveled amongst them in splatters of light. Multiple lightning bolts followed suit, forming a column of brilliant, bright chaos before the entry. It was a formidable barricade.

The Ogres screamed in fear, as their Caedere cavalry fell, one by one. The Ravens and vultures were struck as they flew, and their burnt bodies were cast to the ground. The lightning column spread aggressively in its circumference, and into the molten limestone and carcasses, an incensed Serena made her meteoric mark. Her body flickered with erratic and angry light as she crashed into the battle, eyes aglow with unwavering tenacity. Her hands directed the means of desolation for those who fought against the Luxatio. Where emboldened Caedere had stood, ash wafted in her wake.

Nothing of Leterum's will was to remain. This mountain was the Queen's.

The energy pulsated about her feet as she strode from one victim to the next, destroying all things dark until she came upon a weakened Caedere. She looked into its face, and ripped the stitches from its mouth. The Caedere exhaled, and a faint shriek of a voice escaped. It was a young woman, and she pleaded for forgiveness. Serena paused for but a moment with her hand in the air. As she stared at the blind demon, she calmed herself, and the lightning disappeared. The clouds dissipated, and she placed her hand onto the Caedere's leathered scalp.

"Be at peace."

The Caedere arched as if in pain, and a small light rose as a paper lantern gently from its body. The light climbed higher, and blew passively with the wind as pollen toward the Silva Luctus. Serena looked down upon Creed, and summoned him to follow her into the caverns. As the Luxatio made their way uphill to the Queen, Creed noticed that the Ogres, Caedere, and Raven carcasses littered the ground so heavily not a blade of grass remained visible. She had killed them all.

Varsalsae and Fitz approached the doorway. Angry yet afraid of Serena, Varsalsae spoke with frustrated hesitation as she looked about the dead Luxatio.

"Had you come sooner..."

Serena stared at her intensely.

"I am here *now*." Varsalsae attempted to hold her gaze, but she looked down quickly. Serena turned her temper to Creed.

"This fool's errand you have set us upon has endangered everyone. These Luxatio souls, extinguished before you, will be heavily sought after by Leterum. Had I not returned, all of you would be at his table."

"But you did, and I thank you. As do all of them." He pointed to the crowd before the caverns. Serena looked with indignation.

The Luxatio all bowed their heads in respect. They had spent years sequestered behind this rock, hiding from her and the others, but today they owed her a great debt. Today, they were unafraid to look upon her with gratitude. First Varsalsae and then Fitz kneeled, and the eighty remaining Luxatio did as well. Creed lowered to his right knee while he held Üstor, and spoke.

"Thank you, Serena for saving us once more. We ask for your mercy as we welcome you to the Caverns of Lorem."

Serena softened her gaze, thawed with reminiscence. It was an emotional reunion for them all as she motioned for them to rise. Hands stretched towards her as they sought acceptance, and she embraced those with open arms. She wiped the tears away for those that wept. These were not her subjects. They were her children, and though they broke her heart to a degree, as any mother would, she sought reconciliation.

"Let's bind their wounds. Gather the dead," she sighed, "all of you, inside. Get inside." She paused for a moment before she entered the archway. Creed's hand rested gently on her shoulder. She exhaled. She had finally found her flock.

"Come with me," he said, "I have some people I'd like for you to meet." He offered his hand out of habit, and she chuckled. The absurdity of it was apparent. As they entered the foyer, the walls closed slowly and soundly. Every Luxata was accounted for. The camp was safe. Creed's mind shifted to Celeste as they walked down toward the cavern camps.

"Where is she?"

"Back at Cordis Loci. We put her to bed, and it is time for her to rest. I promised her I would bring her husband home *alive*." She patted him on the back.

"Thank you for that." Creed smiled.

"You're welcome. You appear to have walked right into an ambush."

"I had assumed our second half would have given us fair warning." Creed winked as Serena smirked.

"I'll admit none of it went as planned, and Celeste was in no state to help. She wanted to be here, but her labor pains crippled her."

"Labor? Is she ok? We need to go!" Creed's eyes were wide.

"Of course. You're a doctor. You know these things take time, but when the moment arrives, time becomes inconsequential."

"Is she in pain?"

"No, and we will make it back soon. You won't miss it. That much I'm certain."

Creed took a breath, and stopped with her at the end of the steps. The caverns opened up before them, and she marveled at the enormity of the space. It was a large commune; an underground village complete with all the trappings one would hope for in a township. Creed walked her over to the dozen tables and cots now occupied at the apex of the village.

"In the short time we were down here, we've treated two groups of patients with the first barrel. As you can see, they've woken." Serena approached a woman lying on her side in a bovine-hide cot. "Do you know where you are?" The lady looked at her with tearful eyes.

"No. No, I don't. One minute, I'm putting the kids to bed, and the next," she covered her face and sobbed.

"What happened?"

"I had a few drinks, and then... I took the pills, all of them. I don't remember anything else. Now I'm here. Where am I?"

"You're in Mürindür, sweet child."

"I don't understand. What does that even mean?" She sat up, and one of the Luxatio came to her side, offering her tea and fresh fruit. Another Vaga whispered quietly.

"I know I cut them. I held the razor in my hand; I was in the bathtub. Now I'm sitting on this dry blanket. I'm so confused." The woman continued to rub her bare wrists. Serena walked over to another. This one was a man with a short white beard and receding hairline.

"Sir, how are you feeling?"

"I feel really good. I'm not tired anymore, and I don't know what happened, but that tightness in my chest is gone. I knew the drugs would get me someday, but I kept hoping I'd figure out a way to stay on the wagon. You know what I mean?" He smiled back at her. They seemed to be Welfalon, but she saw the wounds on their bodies, and knew they had come under hard times. She stepped back and clasped her hands.

"All these were Vagus?" she asked.

"Yes, all of them. The first group is in a tent down near the orchards. Let's see how they're doing."

Xaris and Ojin observed from a distance while Pax hung close to the hobgoblin, eyes flitting about nervously. He occasionally noticed Luxatio staring at him, and it made him quite uncomfortable. Ojin turned to him.

"Come now, Pax. It does not matter what they think of you. They will know you soon enough. No one will harm you. That I can promise. Stay by me, and we'll take a look around."

Pax rubbed his own cloak for a bit, and held onto Ojin. The hobgoblin walked over to some of the patients. Listened to them, and observed. It truly was remarkable, and beyond anything they could have hoped for. This signaled the end of the Vagus, and the Caedere altogether. Xaris appeared wary, however. He chose to linger in the shadows near the steps. Occasionally, he would look up the path monitoring for intruders. Creed beckoned them to follow.

As Creed and Serena ventured further, Ojin and Pax caught up. Creed showed everyone the first patients to try the medicine, and most were clothed, eating their first meal as Welfalon. Serena smiled, and cleared her throat.

"Ojin, I believe we will need a bigger Redemptio."

"Yes, Serena. I believe you're right."

"Have you ever seen such a thing? A Vaga become Welfalon once again?" she asked.

"No. It's astonishing." Ojin marveled.

"I wonder how all this came to be?" Her face became solemn and tight. "We should have tried something sooner for all these souls, all those Caedere," she said. Creed stepped in and interrupted. "Nothing can be done about the past. I suspect all of us accepted things for what they were. Like you for a while, I assumed this was already part of the plan. I realize now what we had been working on for so long. We had hoped to create a place such as this. A haven for them, but I didn't dare ask you until we had everything in place. In all honesty, it was Pescus that asked me to think about it."

Creed glanced about, but couldn't find the old man. He asked one of the Luxata nearby.

"Have you seen Pescus?"

"Yes. He's in his tent as usual down by the streams. Follow the cobblestones and torchlights. You can't miss him." The Luxata replied.

"Indeed. Thank you. Serena, feel free to stay here for a moment. Let me find him, and bring him to you. He likely doesn't even know you're here." The Queen nodded, and carried on admiring the patients sitting about the banquet table. Creed smiled. Serena seemed to finally be at peace.

Chapter 29: Humility and Hubris

Creed ducked as he entered the large brown tent by the stream, and his warmth of optimism was soon swept away as he looked inside. Everything appeared decrepit, a wanton ward of comatose patients. Pescus slumped at his desk, rolling a small glass vile back and forth while the Vagus lay on the floor in filth. They were all asleep, drooling and smelling of urine. The rhythmic snoring became a symphony of soft, surreal metronomes. Pescus refrained from making eye contact.

"Here to see what you've been missing have you?" Pescus mumbled.

"Came to check on you, old man. I expected you to come flying into the fray outside."

"Aye. I heard about it. I don't really fight anymore." He licked his dry lips. "Don't see the need for it, and who you calling old?"

"A younger man who used to look up to you."

"Ha! That was your mistake, not mine. You know, you've been cocky ever since I first met you. Bold and brazen, but dumb as a rock."

"I've managed."

Pescus stood up, and shuffled through some of his papers. He found his old maple wood pipe. Stuffed it full of twisted orange tobacco, and lit it with a small twig candle from a basket nearby. He drew two long puffs, and let them out slowly. The smoke rings hovered for a bit, and went their separate ways.

"What do you think of our humble abode?"

"You have endured much," Creed replied.

"Ehhh. We live as refugees. Beggars. No longer are we the honored children of Mürindür. These Luxatio gave up everything for you, Hippocrates. We committed ourselves to a life of imprisonment."

"I know that."

"Do you?"

"Over the last few days, yes. You seem angry. Let's have it."

"Oh, do I? What possibly could have made me loathe to even speak your name?"

"Well, speak then. Make your peace."

"Now?"

"It's as good a time as any. Say what you wish to say." Pescus walked around the desk, and stood over one of the sleeping Vagus. "This realm is dying. We are crumpled as trash in Leterum's hand. We're losing, all of us. Every day, we lose ground, we lose Welfalon, we lose Luxatio, and we lose hope."

"Why? Why do you think that is?" Creed asked.

"Something has broken. You can stand in the desert right now, and there are no Welfalon. Not anymore. Every soul that crashes into that sand is lost, confused, and psychotic. Vagus as far as the eye can see; stumbling about crying for help, but no one comes. No one cares. This entire world has become an asylum of suffering. The numbers at Redemptio have stagnated." Pescus spit on the cavern floor. "The Immortals have done nothing! Serena has done nothing! We scouted villages, roads, camps, and all you see is strife. Hundreds and hundreds of lost souls, and the Immortals do nothing! We finally had enough. We all had our roles, but they abdicated theirs. We combined our forces, and now we save whom we can. We rescue the groups, bring them here, and we wait, seemingly for some miracle that has yet to happen." Creed looked all around.

"Have you not seen the Vagus up the path? They're talking, Pescus. They're waking. We've discovered the miracle you wish for."

"We'll see how they fair. I'm not so certain it's as impactful as you suspect it to be."

"Why not?" Creed asked.

"Nothing changes for the better here. Mark my words. Something worse is coming," Pescus motioned to the slumbering patients at his feet. "This is the most we can truly hope for."

"How is it every one of these people are sleeping?" Creed wondered.

"This."

Pescus opened a drawer, and within it was a number of glass vials with yellow powder in each. He took a pinch of it, and placed it on the back of his hand, snorting the whole dose through his nostrils. His pupils enlarged, and then constricted, as pinpoints, slowly over a few seconds. He staggered for a bit, and sat down forcefully, puffing his pipe. He jarred the desk, and vials of powder fell across the floor. Creed stood there stooped in disappointment.

"Is this why you didn't join us in battle? You're too busy getting high on powder? Is this what you've been doing, hallucinating while the world falls apart at your feet?" Creed clenched his fists angrily. This was his friend. His mentor, but now he was a shell of something once great.

"What would you have me do? What did you do? Huh? You flew away like a frightened sparrow! *We* stayed behind. *We* followed your direction! *We* were here! *You* were not! These Vagus are not dead! They are survivors only by our hands! They are not butchered upon the hall tables of Acrom's Keep! They live and breathe, but they are still sick. Uneasy. Restless. This, this is medicine," Pescus held the vial high, "this keeps them calm. They sleep like newborns on a cloud of righteousness."

"What is this? Is this what I think it is?" Creed grabbed the powder and gently smelled of the vial. Its sweet perfume was familiar. He touched a bit to the tip of his tongue, and the burning sensation confirmed it for him.

"Yes. I have the honey over there in jars. Gallons of it." Creed looked to his right and saw the bookshelves of red colored honey, crusting at the brim. "The fields of our mountain basins are full of purple *Ponticum* flowers, and the bees have been busy." Creed shook his head. His heart was broken. This was the delicacy of madmen. History was never kind to those that imbibed it.

"I remember when the Persian King Mithridates employed the honeycomb against the Roman army. They never had a chance. It was a massacre," Creed recalled.

"Yes. It was glorious," Pescus chuckled.

"I somehow remember things differently than you. The Romans were so intoxicated they began slaughtering their own. They appeared to be as disoriented as the Vagus."

"Fancy that," Pescus replied with a smirk. Creed stared at him. Small beads of sweat gathered at the gray man's hairline.

"As I recall, mad honey tends to make you confused, sick, dizzy. It generally induces delirium, but it doesn't make you comatose, Pescus."

"You would be correct, Hippocrates. This is not just *Ponticum*. I found a way to cross-pollinate with the Poppy." Pescus reached under his desk, and brought out a potted brilliant purple flower with yellow stripes and red stamens. "I call this *Nefarium Somnus*. My sleeping flower." The old man chuckled.

"Why would you make such a plant?" Creed admonished.

"Look at them. Look! They do not cry. They do not scream. They do not pluck at the air or their skin. They rest. I have brought them mercy."

"There is someone else who claims to bring the Vagus mercy, and we do not honor him here, Pescus. This is wrong. You've drugged them into oblivion!"

"I've taken them to paradise."

"What happened to you? I left you in charge. *You* were the leader. You were the one the Luxatio trusted, and would follow into the abyss in my absence. Have you no idea what you've become? Why? What lead you to this?"

"Loss and disregard," Pescus replied.

"You've lost nothing. Nothing that could possibly justify this meaningless existence."

"We've lost everything, and none cared to right the sinking ship!"

"The Immortals are stewards. Nothing more. They did not know our plans. They did not know what we hoped to accomplish," Creed muttered with frustration at Pescus.

"They walk the plains as royalty, and turn their noses to the suffering. 'The Universe's will' or 'it's their judgement'. Bullshit! No one deserves this." He motioned to the room. "Find me a compassionate Immortal to the human plight, and I will call you liar!" Pescus attempted to stand, but stumbled back into his seat drunken from the pollen dust.

"Stay in your chair. Your body can't make up for the mistakes of your mind. You're a shadow. You're an addict, and a weak excuse of a once honorable man, hiding behind this!" Creed spun the vial of pollen on the desk. Pescus snatched it up, and held it carefully. He stared angrily at Creed.

"You left us! You weren't here! You have nothing on me, Hippocrates, keeper of the realm! Ha! This bloated carcass of a realm. You can have it, my lord." Pescus mockingly bowed.

"The people of Mürindür needed you! The Luxatio needed you! These souls at your feet, they needed you! You're an illusion, a fraud. You will never lead the Luxatio again! You need to come with me. This charade ends now!" Creed insisted.

"I'm going nowhere you pup!" Pescus stood staggering once more, and dropped his pipe. He walked over to Creed, and came within inches of his face. Creed could smell the sickening sweet syrup on his beard.

"Sit down!" Creed ordered. Pescus grabbed his wrist.

"Make me child!" the old man replied.

Creed's skin became exceedingly hot to the touch, and suddenly his eyes glowed white. His pupils were lost to anger. He grabbed Pescus' wrist in return, staring into his eyes, and seeing the fear. The sweat dripped from the elder Luxata's brow. He muttered and mumbled.

"D-d-d-demon... Let go of me!"

Creed's voice deepened.

"Your time here is done. I will happily take what remains of you to Leterum myself!"

"Let me, let me go… go…. go... let me," as Pescus quivered, "You are not Hippocrates…you're something else, something different!" Creed squeezed the man's arm as a vice, and seared his flesh with fire.

"AHHHHH! AHHHHHH! STOP! THE BURNING! MAKE IT STOP!"

Pescus wept loudly, shrieking in agony. Creed staggered, and the room was spinning. His head felt heavy. The vials of yellow pollen, fallen from the desk in the tumult were cracked, and a yellow haze hung about the tent.

"NOW SIT DOWN!" Creed shoved him over the desk, and Pescus fell backwards into his books and piles of papers, left to wallow on his hands and knees, shaking his head in disbelief.

Creed's temper ebbed as his eyes returned to normal. He quelled the intensity of rage toward Pescus, turned to breathe, and prepared himself for what he needed to say to the others. The air was thick as a dense fog, so he hurriedly unlashed the tent sides, and peeled back the cloth walls. Nausea and vertigo overwhelmed him as he tumbled outside. Varsalsae and Fitz stood beside the entrance. By the look of Fitz, they had seen everything.

"Don't go in there." Creed warned them. "Pollen dust everywhere. Pescus is sick. We need to get him out."

"You're angry," Varsalsae noted.

"I'm angry because he's sick."

"You looked like you were going to kill him," Fitz noted.

"No. You missed what happened. He grabbed me, and I reminded him…"

"You had wings," Varsalsae held her hands wide, "spread as if you were to take flight."

"What?"

"She's right. Big ones. They curled out above your head. We walked in and you looked as if you were ethereal. When we saw you, we stepped out to get Serena."

"That's ridiculous. You guys must have inhaled that stuff too." Creed responded with doubt in his voice. Serena walked down the path toward the three.

"What happened? Why was there screaming?" She looked at Creed with concern.

"Pescus... he," Creed looked toward the open tent flaps.

Serena quickly strode into the tent, and slammed her open palms together. The burst of air split the yellow fog, and the room became clear again. Pescus could be seen moaning behind his desk, clasping his burnt arm in pain. Serena looked to Creed.

"What did you do?" Before he could answer, Varsalsae interrupted. "My Queen, Pescus has fallen ill, and Hippocrates discovered a substance that has likely been the cause of it. He was trying to save him, but was overwhelmed by the dust." Varsalsae nodded to the collection of glass vials and honey jars. Serena looked at the flower on the wooden desk.

"Hmm. Pescus, stand." The old man mumbled to himself. "Pescus, I say stand before me!" He looked to Serena, and shook. Pescus rose slowly, but glared at Creed as if he were studying something grotesque. When Pescus realized who was before him, he was visibly displeased.

"Who...who...who let her in? Why is she here?" He looked to Creed. "You dare bring her to our camp? Was it not enough for her to place bounties on our heads? Did you need to escort her into the caverns?"

428

"Enough, Pescus! She saved us from the battle you refrained from."

"She merely delayed the inevitable." Pescus spat on the ground near a drooling Vaga.

"Pescus, you look like you have aged, my old friend. You don't look well."

"Living as a refugee does that I suppose, Serena," Pescus replied.

"What do you have here?" She asked, motioning all around.

"Nothing. Nothing at all." Pescus turned quickly to gather his flower.

"These Vagus lie here unawares, and you seem beside yourself. What is in those glass vials, Pescus?"

"Medicine."

"Oh. Medicine is it?" she chided.

"He created a strong sedative. That's why they lie here undisturbed and unawares. Pescus, unfortunately, has been self-medicating as well. I think it has taken over his ability to lead." Creed handed Serena a vial. She smelled of it, and her eyes narrowed with scrutiny. The Queen walked to Pescus, and placed her hand on his shoulder.

"Why?" Serena asked.

"What do you mean 'why'?"

"You were the first, one of our strongest. Why did you stumble?"

"I didn't stumble. I leapt."

"Why?" Serena persisted.

"I am nothing here in Mürindür. I have nothing. I cannot return to the place of my birth, and despite my best efforts, I cannot leave this world." He motioned to a broken knife on the bookshelf and bruised wrists, "You used to speak of our destiny as if we had a choice, as if we have any say in the matter."

"Destiny *is* the path towards understanding our purpose, Pescus. It is a journey of our own choosing."

"Destiny is merely a sword bent crooked 'crost an anvil of fear, hammered by the cold resolve of charlatans, and wielded as a lustful masquerade to the ruin of a people too blind to see the truth." Spittle trickled down his chin as his speech slurred.

"No one seeks to wield a masquerade, Pescus. Destiny *is* truth. Truth *is* Destiny. The Universe has purpose, provides purpose, and yields peace through purpose for those who seek it. You must earn the fruits of your labor."

"Earn? I fell time and time again in that godforsaken desert. Got up. Dusted myself off, and went to serve the Lux. I served you. I served whatever purpose you sent me to. I never asked questions. I never challenged you. When asked to go back, I did without hesitation. Over and over like some sick recurrent nightmare, and yet I never would have peace. Not from my past or the knowledge of what lie ahead for my future. I would forever be enslaved with no reward. No peace. This peace you speak of, do Luxatio ever truly know peace?"

"That is not for me to decide."

"Not bloody likely. There is no decision to be made. It is in fact a sentence passed upon unsuspecting souls. It's sold as an honor, a gift. It is no such thing. It is a noose. I do all that you ask of me, and then this man comes along," as he pointed at Creed, "I come back from yet another nightmare of human suffering, and suddenly he's in charge. I hated him for it. I've traveled more than anyone. I've seen Luxatio come and go, but I have never faltered. I've seen them wilt under their recollections and flashbacks. Their frailty was exposed, and they gave up. I watched them choose Mürindür and fade away. I never faded, and you never gave me peace! One night I realized, there is no future for any of us. We were duped into choosing an existence with no end. No hope. No joy."

"That is not why we choose Luxatio. There is no shame in that destiny. You were revered. Honored above all other men."

"That does us all a great deal of good, doesn't it? We live in fancy castles, and all the wine and gold… oh wait. That's right! We live in the same quagmire as everyone else! We die and come back, over and over. No better off than the first comers. We might as well have been farmers and gatherers in the Fields of Effugere!"

"You do not realize your significance."

"No. *You*, don't realize our significance," Pescus replied.

"It is a shame you feel this way. Your disillusion is self-imposed," acknowledged Serena.

"Maybe. I could not forget the things my mind had seared into its flesh. The nightmares had become unbearable, and nothing anyone said made them any more benevolent. I told Hippocrates one day that we were no different than the Vagus, and in fact maybe worse. I told him I wished we had a means to make it disappear. We needed an end to the labyrinth of our memories. That's when he started with his ideas of finding some treatment, a cure for all the mental anguish. I felt if he did discover a way to numb the mind, I was all in."

"So, you sought not a solution for them, but an escape for yourself?"

"I sought the means to wipe clean the atrocities that visit me in the wee hours of the night. I sought a bridge to anywhere but here."

"And yet, all you've done is take them into oblivion without a line to return." Serena motioned to the Vagus lying about in their gray, torn tunics. "You are sick, my old friend, very sick. Hippocrates, instruct everyone to gather the Vagus, and meet us at the entrance. We will bring everyone back to Cordis Loci."

"That is a great number of people, Serena," Creed replied.

"You doubt my vigor, Hippocrates?" she asked.

"No, not at all. I'll let them know."

"And the dead?" Varsalsae asked.

"This will become their resting place. This will forever be hallowed ground. Bring their bodies here to the stream, and I will seal this as their tomb."

"All my work! The flowers, and the medicine what of those?" Pescus pleaded.

"They stay as well," Serena turned to Fitz, "Get Pescus to the top of the stairs, keep him from the others, and wait for us there."

"Gladly."

Fitz walked toward Pescus as the old man flinched, anticipating a strike of some sort. The looming Viking gathered him by his shirtsleeve, and pulled him from the tent. Serena looked to Creed.

"I want everything to stay here in the depths of these caverns. Is that understood?" she directed Varsalsae and Creed.

"Understood," Creed affirmed.

"Hippocrates, what happened here when I heard the screams?" Serena asked.

"Nothing. He refused to leave, and I told him there was no other way."

"Is that all?" She looked intently in his eyes.

"Yes." Creed stared back. He wasn't sure what happened, but he remembered feeling angry. He had no means to explain that to Serena now.

"Varsalsae, is that all?"

"Yes, my Queen. Nothing else happened." Varsalsae replied.

"Fair enough. Let us go."

Serena motioned them up the stairs as others came to collect the sedate Vagus. The command had been given to evacuate, and the caverns were alive with hope and preparations. As Varsalsae and Creed ascended the stairs, she looked to him, and grabbed his arm.

"I saw what I saw back there. You had wings like an Immortal, and your eyes were ablaze with fury. Promise me you have not turned to Leterum on my brother's soul."

"Never. Not in a thousand lifetimes."

"Swear to it."

"I swear." Creed watched Serena walk off toward the woken patients, and when she was far enough away, he continued.

"Nothing has changed, but I was angry. I will do a better job of controlling that next time."

"Mürindür is not what it once was, and all things have turned sour in their own way. We need you to be healthy and whole."

"I'm working on it."

"Work harder. If that happens on the battlefield, the Luxatio will lose faith."

"It appears Pescus has lost faith," Creed noted.

"He did years ago, but it wasn't until he started playing with plants that his mind warped. We've kept him here where it's safe while we roam the woods. He needn't leave the caverns otherwise we'd have another mess to deal with."

"It appears we all are leaving the caverns."

"It's been my wish for some time. I don't know what a life at the Cordis Loci will mean, but I'm willing to try." Varsalsae grabbed her satchel, and helped a woken Vaga to their feet.

"Go upstairs. I'll be there shortly. We are finally going home." Creed smiled.

Varsalsae nodded, and walked off with a few patients to gather them shoes. Hundreds of people made their way out of the only home they'd known for years. They left the tents and plants they had tended to, and for the Luxatio it was bittersweet. There was a sense of freedom and liberation to live on the fringe, hidden from Mürindür in an effort for something deemed impossible. Now they were going back to what they scarcely recalled.

Creed ventured to the top. He looked down below, and saw the fires in the distance. The sounds of trickling water were soothing, and he marveled at how profound it was for everyone to have survived here for so long with little support or guidance. They lived in isolation for a just cause, and he hoped they felt welcome in Serena's presence. The Vagus broke his thought as they occasionally moaned and screamed from their delusionary state. Everyone awaited Creed at the rock wall of the doorway. Serena nodded to Varsalsae, and she whispered the incantations once more. The rock doors lowered, and the sun cast an orange light into the depths one last time.

The crowd made way into the fresh air as each Luxatio tended to their assigned Vagus patients. They milled around outside waiting for all to exit. Leterum's dead, lay undisturbed before them, and even now, the wind was still. Creed watched for signs of Ravens or vultures, but nothing flew as he wished for a speedy exit. Once everyone had left the Caverns of Lorem, and the final head count was made, Serena had them gather in as close as three hundred souls possibly could. The dead would remain safe and enclosed within the hallowed halls of the now decommissioned refuge. Serena looked about. Her eyes lit up like the incandescent lightning she cast earlier. The rock door closed slowly, forever, and then a brilliant flash. They disappeared into the ether, and a sonic boom echoed through the mountains. All was quiet once more.

Chapter 30: Three Brothers

The flash was gone, and the gathered crowd, found themselves within the shaded grounds of the Pools of Cordis Loci. Creed ran to their wedding tent to check on his beloved. Celeste lay in bed with her back turned to the entrance, and when he came to her side, he saw she had been weeping. She was startled at first, but sat up quickly to throw her arms around his neck, nearly squeezing the life out of him.

"Well," he choked out, "there's no good in your mother's efforts if you're just going to kill me anyways." He chuckled, and she loosened her grip with a soft laugh.

"No. No, I suppose not." She pulled his filthy face close to hers, and kissed the sweat from his lips. Creed felt at ease, once again. "How are you?"

"Tired and worried. He acts as if he is coming soon, but I know he isn't ready." Celeste rubbed her belly gently.

"Babies have a timing all their own."

"Yes, but he won't survive if he comes now."

"He won't come now," Creed assured her.

"How do you know?"

"He's meant for great things. Great things don't simply disappear."

"Great things can disappear. It's the need for great things that never does," Celeste replied.

"The baby will be fine. You're here now. Just rest. No more wandering about the deep dark woods with me."

"No more wandering the deep dark woods without me," she countered.

"Fair enough. Let's stay here by the Pools until the birth. We can make a home here. Safely."

"It isn't that simple. Souls are falling as we speak, and no one is there to rescue them."

"We found the cure." He smiled.

"Really? Did it work?" Her expression widened.

"Something in the Silva timber made the waters safer. We've treated three dozen so far, and they all seem to be normal. We may have found a way to cure them all."

"I so hope that you have, but what good is it if they all become Caedere?"

"But they don't. You've seen it now. They are shuffled and sold as cattle. They have become a source of sacrificial power for Acrom. If we take them, we heal them, and teach them to fight. It would be detrimental to Leterum's forces while we build an army of our own. Acrom will weaken. The balance will be restored," Creed explained with confidence.

"We have an army, but he still has dominion."

"And that I don't understand. I saw your mother decimate an entire field of Ogres and Caedere. It was a single strike, and everything fell. Everything died. Why hasn't she done more?"

"It has everything to do with her agreement with Acrom. She stepped aside, and made way for the realm to be split in two. She said it was to keep the realm intact, but we can see that failed somehow. I think whatever was agreed upon has passed, and she is making up for lost time."

"I don't know what happened, but she could easily wipe out half his army in minutes. I understand now why he hasn't confronted her directly. Leterum would lose."

"Leterum has calculated each move with precision. He isn't as willing to dive head first into combat unlike some people I know."

"I'll be fine."

"What happens if you die, and our son never meets you? It will be as if you never existed. I know what that's like. I do not wish that for our son," Celeste said sternly.

"Neither do I, but on that mountainside, I couldn't risk allowing them entry to what was below."

"I don't enjoy seeing the slight amusement with war you seem to have acquired. I saw it in the Fields of Effugere, the Ogre ravine, and I suspect the same on that hillside. Each time, you revel in it. I am asking you to stow it away. Stay with me, and let us welcome this child. I'm certain, whatever my mother did, it has given Leterum pause."

"She was pretty impressive."

"And?" Celeste asked.

"And… I won't seek war so readily," he replied as he kissed her forehead.

"I've seen my mother strike the way you describe a few times." Celeste looked out the tent, and stared at the moving grass. "I wish after all this time she would have done more sooner. I feel her lack of engagement likely drove the Luxatio away."

"The Luxatio missed her. You should have seen the reunion. Even with all this talk of rebelling and oath breaking, I could see how much they missed her. She missed them too."

"She has always thought so highly of them, as her own children, that when they disappeared one after another, she was bent on finding out why. She heard rumors they had abandoned her and Mürindür, and I honestly think it broke her heart. She kept much closer tabs on all of them, especially you."

"Me?" Creed wondered.

"Yes. She felt if you were gone, no one else would stay. She would seemingly have nothing of the Luxatio in the world of Earth. Inspiration and the moral compasses of world leaders would be gone, and the human experience would be null and void."

"I've lived quite a few human experiences, and I can tell you that none of it was easy, and most of it was painful. I'm not sure how much morality or inspiration I truly bring to anyone."

"I have seen it within you. I thought about your words outside the tent with the deceased woman in your arms."

"I'm sorry, Celeste. I was upset and frustrated."

"No. Your words resonated with me. You think I don't wonder what it's like to live and feel as you do? I have. What would it be like to be mortal even if for a day? I see your passion in every moment, and I envy you. Would the sun seem different? If I said goodbye to you not knowing if I'd ever see you again, would it make the farewell more poignant? Would we embrace longer? Life must be sweeter when you know it will have an end. I've never known existence the way that you have."

"I hope you never will." Creed held her hand firmly.

"Morbid curiosity, I suppose, as you said in the museum."

"You know, we talk about choice around here so much, but in reality, I don't feel any of us had a choice until now. Seeing my old friends, and hearing their stories, it reminds me how fleeting even this time on Mürindür can be. In a way, I feel trapped."

"Are you trapped when there is a knowledge that things will change yet again, or would you feel trapped knowing nothing would ever change?"

"I guess it depends on your perspective." Creed looked at Celeste and could see she was tired.

"Perhaps. There are many similarities between your experience and mine. I can still remember the early days as a child. Long before mankind ever rose from the clay. The stars were still so fresh and new, that I felt them to be too delicate to play with. My mother raised me to understand many things, nearly all things, but what I never understood is why they made man mortal. They felt immortality was good enough for them, but somehow, man, their greatest child needed to be confined. Limited. Over the years I've wondered many things, but none were more impactful than the realization that it perhaps had more to do with fear and jealousy than compassion. Imagine a race that lived forever. There would be little fear instilled in them. Living things fear the end of things. The unknown. If there were no fear, how could my people maintain their station in the universe? Who would respect whom, and who would rule? Mortality was created to instill order, and yet many of you have turned living so succinctly into something beautiful. You were given chains, and crafted them into wings. I don't wish to have mortal bearings, but I do wonder what it's like to live like you live, and to love like you love."

"Wait? You don't love me like I love you?" Creed jested. She laughed.

"No silly. Ugh. A meaningful conversation, and you splatter humor and wit all over it."

"Just a dribble," Creed replied.

"I love you more than the stars and their feral playground. I love you for being human, and with all your faults, I love you for existing. You are the father of our unborn son, and to have given me this life, by far, has been the greatest gift known to my kind."

"Well, you're welcome." He smiled smugly.

"Oh! You! Could you give me at least a moment of sincerity?" He stared at her, sincerely, albeit comedic.

"How's this?"

"It'll do I suppose." He leaned over and kissed her forehead, and then her lips. His hand gently laced her belly. Their son was very active at the moment.

"Celeste?"

"Yes?"

"If this child is immortal, what good am I as his father? I'm just a man, and an imperfect one at that."

"You are *his* father. You will be present, and he will feel love. Immortal or not, his understanding of you and our place in this world will be all that he could ever need."

"What about your father? You never speak of him."

She paused. He could see a change in her mood.

"An angel much like my mother. He was very powerful, or so I am told. I don't remember anything about him. He and my mother were birthed from the first star. He helped bind the universe into constructs, and created the means to intersect the realms, much of which we have today. The bridges he built were unlike any other, and the Immortals used them to travel and transport the intent and will of creation. He died when Acrom rose to power. Acrom stole him from us which led to my mother imprisoning the demon the first time."

"First time?"

"Acrom has escaped and threatened the order of things twice before. Each time he was imprisoned. It has been foretold that the third will be his liberation, and all things long since known will be abolished, and chaos will be absolute." Celeste's voice trailed off.

"I don't understand. I thought the Cataclysm was his imprisonment."

"No. The Cataclysm was something far greater in its consequence, worse than before. The Cataclysm split the Immortal forces in two. Many chose to abandon the Lux, and followed Acrom with his promise of new life and boundless possibilities. The Luxatio aren't the only ones that have become weary of the order. In prior battles, Acrom and his army would fall at the might of the Bellatorum. Each time he would get closer to victory, and each time the fall was that much greater. The Cataclysm, however, revealed his true intent, and this sent our worlds into a difficult fall. He managed to convince some of the elder beings to fight alongside him, and none were more feared than Death himself."

"Leterum?"

"Yes. The possibility of Acrom and Leterum joining forces in war was something no one had foreseen. Death and Destruction together as brothers. Creation had little chance of survival."

"Why did he join Acrom?"

"I do not know. During the Cataclysm, we had little time to discover his intent. We had hoped to imprison him along with Acrom, but the plan faltered. Leterum attempted to strike at my mother, and in an instant, I saw more power and anger from her than anything I've seen before or since. The Abyss widened as if being torn, and she decimated Leterum's forces casting him to the ground at Elyptos' feet. We could have conquered Leterum at that moment, but she turned her focus on Acrom. Once the constructs were crafted, and the walls erected, mother lead a charge into Acrom's Keep. Leterum sent his Raven Guard behind her, and the rest is history. Leterum was wounded, Elyptos died, Acrom was imprisoned, and Mürindür was forever changed."

"Where were you?"

"I held the line before the Abyss. Ojin was sent off to find more help. I watched my mother go into the darkness not knowing if she would return. When Leterum sent troops after her, I sought to join her, but knew Leterum would use that as an opportunity to drive his forces into the world. I waited. It was excruciating. I wondered what I would do if she were to fall, and I was left to defend it all. She returned, and our ways of magic and worldly intervention were over. An existence hurdling toward a vision held fast by Acrom and his legions." Celeste ran her fingertips gently over Creed's forearm. They were quiet for a moment.

"What did Acrom have on your mother? Why did she seem to give up so much?"

"I truly believe at the time she was trying to protect the balance, and knew that despite how sick it may sound, evil is necessary. There is no balance with one side attached to the scales. She saw an opportunity to end this, and it was time. I know she weighed what was asked, and she did not give up completely. Acrom had not realized he would be imprisoned, and completely separate from the world. She won her peace."

"And yet they want to eliminate ours."

"Balance is not even a fleeting afterthought for them."

"So then what hope do we honestly have?" Creed worried.

"This peace has always been tenuous. My mother realized that fairly quickly. How can you honestly split a world in two, and hope to live across a desert from those who wish to see your end? There are times I feel it may have been best to let the lot fall where it may. We might have won without compromise. Without a treatise of darkness."

"Perhaps, but it won the day, and it saved you and all the others. Had I to choose again, I would have done so. Lifetime after lifetime." Serena had been at the cusp of the entrance, and walked toward them both, sitting down on the nearby stool.

"Mother."

"Celeste."

"What now?" Celeste asked.

"Well, we heal those that have suffered long enough. We solidify our forces, and we wait. Leterum's troops vastly outnumber our own, but we have Bellatorum and have gained a great number of Luxatio. We cannot attack him, so we wait for his move. I've called the Capital Guard to us. We will make the Pools our stand for now."

"And Leterum?"

"He no doubt knows what happened at the Caverns. The promise I made is broken, and the seals once secured have faltered. He knows this too, and will seek his claim. We won't likely wait long." Serena smiled gently as a mother does in a thunderstorm.

"You've been holding back for a reason," Creed acknowledged.

"Do you think I wish to see the disease, the pestilence overwhelming our beautiful home? Leterum ruled unchecked, and I have remained fettered. No more. The walls were breached long before I chose to strike."

"That's why you've been playing defense all this time," he said.

"Seals between deities are sacred regardless of the parties involved. My blood served as the wax upon which Acrom stamped his own incarceration. The walls will crumble now, and Acrom's armies will rise. He remains trapped by his own volition, but we will see Leterum surge to war."

"Then how do we sustain his barrage?" Creed asked.

"Me," Serena confirmed.

"You alone?"

"Leterum knows this. He has always known this. This war will not conclude until we've met on the field. I have offered him this, today on that wicked soil, but he likely won't choose to fight face to face. He will use what he has, and leverage that across the plains. We will need to rally all men to us. All magical beasts sworn to the Endüerduul need take heed, and either run or stand with us. We will garner our support here, then advance to the plains before the Capital. Leterum will be too tempted not to engage. On the Maundae Plain we will face one another, and put an end to this once and for all."

"And Acrom?"

"Your son will bring him to his knees. This child must be born, and grow into the man he is destined to be. This is why the blessings of the Pools were so important, and why he needs both parents to raise him, one of mortal and immortal blood. This child will become a man beloved by both, and sworn to unify them all. This child *is* the promise. Regardless of whether I or Leterum fall, this child must stand."

"And when Acrom is gone? This world is predicated on balance. No evil, no balance." Creed stood to pour himself a glass of water.

"There will always be evil. There will always be Death. There will always be hope. There will always be Life. The forces at play never end, but the role players do."

"So, you think Acrom can die?" Creed asked.

"My son, regardless of what you've heard, even Death can die," Serena replied. Ojin came into the tent, and Creed turned to look at him. His orange eyes were big behind his low-lying glasses.

"Ojin, what is it? You look concerned."

"I'm sorry, but we have more Vagus arriving. Hundreds."

"From where?"

"I don't know, but they are here outside our camp." Ojin looked to Serena for her thoughts. She stood as well, and walked to the opening.

"Well, let's welcome them home." She left with Ojin behind her. Creed spoke with Celeste once more.

"Stay here. I'll be back. Just rest."

"I'm fine. Let me come and..."

"No. Doctor's orders." He smiled. She grinned enough to acknowledge the humor.

Creed walked outside to join the others. Pax was busy smoothing Bog's snout with a wire brush. Bog looked good, and his color had returned to normal. He was standing and eating the pile of fruit before him. Pax seemed pleased to see his friend recover so well. Ojin walked over to him, and leaned his heavy head onto Bog's.

They stood that way for but a second, and the sentiment was well understood.

Serena stood at the peak of a moderate sized hill, and below her were hundreds of Vagus. Torn clothing, bloodied flesh, and yet here they stood, stuporous and silent, seemingly waiting for absolution. It was odd. They were not corralled by force, but when she stepped forward, she felt a presence. Serena stiffened her stance, and within seconds, they were surrounded by Bellatorum as Ojin and Creed made their way to her side. Üstor was not warm, but Creed felt uneasy as if they were being watched. Xaris stood behind a nearby tree with his bow drawn. Creed looked over to him, but Xaris shook his head. Serena smiled.

"Show yourselves younglings. I can feel you're here."

Ojin snorted. He wondered what that smell was. It was the smell of home. He cast his hands in the air, and sure enough he found their Penumbra. With a snap of his fingers, the light transgressed, and suddenly before them stood three young hobgoblins, adolescents by hobgoblin standards. Startled, they bowed. Varsalsae ran over, and smiled broadly.

"You are alive! I feared after the last time, we'd never see one another!" She hugged the tallest in the middle. His underbite peaked.

"Hello, Varsalsae. It's good to see you too." The hobgoblin looked up at Ojin, and held his hand open and high.

"Master Ojin. How fair you?"

"Well enough. Well enough."

He tried hard to hide his smile with a façade of displeasure, for the young ones were not allowed to venture off the island, especially into the depths of Mürindür. They would likely be punished by the Tribunal of Elders when they returned home. To be here like this, required a bit of courage and a twist of disregard.

"How long have you been gone from home?" Ojin asked.

"A few lifetimes it seems."

"Oh?"

"Yes. We barely finished our schooling when we each had dreams within the same night about the lost ones. We came here to discover the dream's meaning. That's when we found caverns hidden from the sky's eye. They seemed big enough to house a hundred thousand, so we began to rescue what we could."

"According to Pescus, he found and rescued them." Creed interjected.

"Hah! We found him lost one night in the woods, scarcely an hour's walk from an Ogre camp. He would have made a nice stew for them that evening. Pescus told us of what you and the Luxatio were planning, and we felt we could help each other. We showed him the caverns, and we brought many of them home."

"How are they so subdued for you three?" The hobgoblins looked at one another. The shortest reached into his satchel, and produced a large flask of red honey. Ojin smirked.

"Mad honey?"

"It works."

"Not efficiently."

"It was readily available in the mountain plains nearest the caverns. It allowed us to gather them, quietly, without them being harmed." The hobgoblin explained. Creed spoke up.

"I found Pescus eating that like candy, and snorting the pollen as well."

"Pescus has a problem," the young one affirmed.

"Naturally," Creed replied.

"Yes, naturally. Welcome home, Hippocrates." The hobgoblin bowed.

"And you are?" asked, Creed.

"I am Sylvestrae, these are my brothers, Maeylincus, and Coliquis."

He motioned from largest to smallest. Even the baby brother was bigger than Creed. Their beards were mangled, and their brown kilts unkempt. Burs hung in their fur. They clearly had lived within the wild for some time, with little to no concern over appearance. "It is an honor to meet you Master Ojin. At times, when the little ones went to bed, the elders spoke of you, planting wild ideas of adventure in the ones old enough to be bold and young enough to be daring." Sylvestrae stared at the large harmonious jade stone in Ojin's staff. Their staves were devoid of stones since they had yet to complete their crucible.

"The stories say you took that from the back of an *Heremeticklops.*"

"Indeed. He wasn't too pleased with me to say the least."

"How did you get him out of the volcano?"

"Hah. Now that's a tale for mead and Festorbius!"

"Ojin," Serena said, "Perhaps we need to take these Vagus into our new home, and treat them as the others."

"Yes. Yes of course. We'll discuss that story later my friends. We've found a serum of sorts that will likely fix these lost ones for good."

"A serum?" Sylvestrae asked.

"Hippocrates" Ojin replied.

"Ahhh. Well done then!" They nodded toward Creed, and he acknowledged their gesture of respect.

The young hobgoblins rounded their Vagus up gently like cattle. They may have been novices with magic, but their kindness and compassion to these souls demonstrated wisdom beyond their years. Ojin observed for a moment, and then joined them, rallying up the stragglers in the back of the group. Serena requested more lodging for the newcomers, so she stood with her blacksmiths and engineers, scripting a model for more permanent structures to be made. This would be their stronghold.

A new Keep needed to be built nearest the Pools, she explained, and the surrounding buildings would prove necessary for livestock, weaponry, and housing. Well within the woods, the perimeter was already established, and now with solid footing on their plans, Creed watched Serena craft walls of stones and petrified wood from deep within the soil. Granite and quartz were hewn, and stacked in tight compressed columns. He helped where he could, and within hours, the Vagus were resting on pallets of soft grass, and the walls had been completed. The Keep of Cordis Loci was becoming a reality.

Celeste had slept in the meantime, and when she awoke, she ventured out into the now enclosed inhabitance. She shook her head in disbelief as she watched her mother drink a glass of wine. "How long have I been asleep, Mother?"

"Ages it seems, my love."

"Ages indeed. You've been busy." Creed smiled at her as he scooped ladles of medicine, and filled bowls with the serum. "We found the three brothers responsible for hiding the Luxatio and Vagus. They know of Ojin, and they seem relieved that their little adventure has come to a close." Serena pointed over to the large central camp fire of the Keep.

Ojin regaled the brothers with tales of their homeland, and the murderous ploys of Acrom during the Cataclysm. The hobgoblins had scarcely finished their mead from the first serving, having perched permanently on the edges of their seats. Bog opened his eyes briefly, and shook his ears as Pax slept soundly, snortling a few times. Bog rolled him over in his trunk, and closed his eyes to rest once more. Creed had taken to administering the Silva water to as many Vagus as he could. A few hundred patients in all now slept soundly in their cots. Varsalsae and Fitz sat with Pescus as he rested.

The Luxatio helped build structures for the village, and served as lookouts alongside their Bellatorum brethren. Once again, the warriors of the Lux stood side by side. Serena placed calls out to the realm, and slowly, legions of men and Bellatorum returned, surprised to see the newfound vigor of their command. Within days, they would easily reach ten thousand troops, Serena explained to Creed as they walked about the camp. A fraction of Leterum's forces indeed, but they would overshadow what bite he could provide. They needed the Capital Guard of Guillarne. The city would likely fall within hours of their departure, but the souls she had evacuated to Durdan would be safe. Serena had yet to hear from the Capital, but hoped they would proceed as she commanded. As of late, men had a way of leading with their hearts in lieu of their minds.

Chapter 31: A Battle Cry

Creed noticed glimmers of armor breach the horizon on the Maundae Plain. He reached for Serena's shoulder, as the commotion garnered everyone's attention, and they stood beside one another to witness the large caravan of warriors approaching. Men cloaked in black, and armored in silver with gold trim, swayed upon Arabian steeds. Swordsmen in the front, and toward the back of the convoy, the pikesmen, all galloped in a similar rhythm and pace. They formed a crescent in front of Serena as she met them in the narrow meadow. Celeste stood beside her mother as a Captain dismounted, and approached the Queen.

"Queen Serena, we have come at your request." He bowed respectfully. She looked at the men before her, and was not amused.

"This is not *all* the Capital Guard. Where are the others?"

"The Commander sends his respects, and apologizes he could not send more. We are a hundred men ready to serve you."

"Where are the others?" Serena asked again, slow and insistent.

"The Capital Guard stands at the ready to defend the city and its people."

"I ordered evacuations days ago. I sent for a retreat as well."

"Yes," he replied.

"I saw evacuees on the Road of Borainnos to Durdan," she said.

"Yes, your highness, however, we have suffered many casualties since Leterum last attacked. The Ogre raids have been relentless. We've lost hundreds of men, but worse yet, many times over as many citizens were wounded. They still lie within the infirmaries of the Capital. They are too weak to leave."

"How many remain ill?"

"Last count was nearly a thousand Guardsmen, and two thousand citizens in beds. The Commander asked to transport them, but their caregivers say they are too unstable to move."

"Why was I not informed of this?" Serena asked.

"We tried, my Queen, but we suffered another attack two days ago, which is when we suffered the most losses, and although we sent scouts, they did not apparently make it to you. We haven't seen them since. We sent signals for help, but none answered." Serena winced.

"Leterum has timed the strikes across the land perfectly, each major battle in succession as we try to salvage our army. We seem to always be a moment behind the pandemonium." She requested to speak with her generals. They arrived shortly, and she met with them and the other officers of the Guard. The impromptu summit was in front of everyone as members of the Keep of Cordis Loci gathered around. Serena raised her voice slightly, and then lowered her head.

"General Reqwarnst, can we get them all to Durdan in time?" she asked.

"Unlikely. If what the Captain says is true, they will not make the Fuga, and we can no longer go by ground. Time has escaped us once more," General Reqwarnst advised.

"So, thousands of our Guard stand alone against Leterum's forces to protect thousands of wounded, many of whom may not survive next week let alone a few more hours."

"Yes. It appears so, my Queen."

"I called for a retreat! For whomever remains in Leterum's path, will perish. There is nothing we can do to stop it?"

"We can counter," another General suggested.

"For what purpose? If we leave this new settlement, exposing our flank from the mountains, we'll be cut off from returning. We go to Durdan, and everyone in the Capital dies. We descend on the Capital, and Leterum will cut us off from everything surrounding us with no escape."

Ojin interrupted Serena.

"You mentioned you dare not lose the Capital for there would be no help for Redemptio at that point, and all the Welfalon would be sacrificed along with the Vagus. Why evacuate and give it away now?"

"General Reqwarnst, would you like to share with Ojin what you shared with me moments ago?"

"Master Ojin, no Welfalon have landed in many days, in fact almost two weeks. We have scout reports of the Dunes of Transitio, and all that fall are Vagus. There are no more souls to rescue."

"How is that possible?" Ojin asked.

"Leterum has infiltrated the Chamber. It's the only explanation, but before we can address that very issue, we must make a stand at some point. We must choose and hold ground. Redemptio will withstand a barrage for many months, but the lands to the west will be burnt to the ground. I chose to move everything, taking your earlier advice under consideration, Ojin, and consolidated our forces here at the Keep of Cordis Loci. I want our Capital Guard here. They are the very men that have held that line for eons, and to lose them would be to lose many honorable souls, and with regard to morale, forfeit a symbol of strength. It would be a significant victory for Leterum. If they had withdrawn as I asked, and the city fell, he would have gained nothing but stone and rubble."

"What of Lord Haergen and his army to the east? Any word? It's as if they hide behind their great wall ignorant to it all," Ojin wondered.

"Haergen has not responded, and with his silence I accept it as refusal. Even if they were to advance, they would be slaughtered westward on the way to the Capital," Serena replied.

"Not necessarily. If Haergen would assume his mantle once more, he could challenge Leterum himself," the General surmised.

"Haergen lost his wife, and fears for his daughter. I have not seen him wield his weapon since the Cataclysm. He prefers a defensive posture."

"Then his refusal should be deemed traitorous," said the General.

"Haergen is not the enemy, and although he ignores our requests, his wall has created an insurmountable boundary. I am thankful it prevents Leterum from heading further east into the remainder of our lands. Remember why we constructed that wall. At the very least, he still holds it for us all," Serena explained.

"We are paralyzed then. We cannot move the citizens of the Capital. We certainly cannot sacrifice them. What little choice do we have?" Ojin asked.

"Leterum has given us none," she replied. Creed listened to it all.

"Then we should descend on the Capital, rescue that city, and the lives within it. Order your army to assemble, Serena. We will protect all that is west of the city." Creed looked around at the gathered crowd. The Luxatio were nodding in agreement.

"Hippocrates, this would undoubtedly be Leterum's intention. He has set this trap, and you would merely trip its spring," Serena replied.

"My Queen, we should bolster our forces here. Build up our defenses," the General interjected. "The Ember Wood crawls with darkness, and it is likely now that Acrom's army will attack from the west as Leterum's attacks from the east. If we hold here, the lower lands will be gone, but with the mountains to our backs, we can fight them from the high ground." Serena looked at the General, frustrated at his suggestion.

"So, we simply let Mürindür fall, so that we may survive?"

"We need time, my Queen."

"We are out of time, General! If Acrom will fight from the Ember Wood while Leterum attacks the Capital, we will have to divide our forces. With the citizens evacuated and walled up within Durdan, they are *our* people. They *are* Mürindür. We must not let Durdan fall! Our goal for the Capital of Guillarne should be to evacuate whomever we can, while holding the line. My intent, and expectation is the Capital will be no more once we engage. All survivors are to be taken to Durdan. We will carve out the mountain passes as our supply chains. Ashi will be the midway of our lines. We will need Bellatorum to establish safe passage through the Ashi."

"We give up the Maundae Plain for the Ashi?" Ojin asked.

"We give up one city so that we don't lose two," she replied. The strategists were at an impasse.

The sky became cadaveric as the air moved slowly, in a suffocating darkness. Celeste and Serena readied themselves as the hobgoblin brothers gathered to launch a Penumbra, but Ojin stopped them, and urged them forward. The four readied their staves. The ground rumbled, and as Creed looked at his feet, the pebbles danced haphazardly over his boots. It was evident that something wicked was at play, and all eyes were fixed on the valley below.

An apparition appeared in a flood of ebon mist. The eyes of Sēpein shown through with hunger and hate. The giant chimera's claws crashed into the rock, and there upon him sat the Enigma. Leterum was silent behind the smoke within his hood. He gripped his reins, and it sounded as bones breaking slowly. Serena had been too distracted and too distressed to feel his presence as he landed between her and the hundred, mounted Capital Guard. The ground continued to shake, and soon it was apparent to them all. Countless Caedere, hundreds upon hundreds, were now behind the Guard mere yards down the slope of the terrain. The Keep of Cordis Loci had been flanked, and cut off from the Capital of Guillarne altogether.

"Ahhh. Here we are, yet again," the dark angel proclaimed. "Leterum you will not survive here. I would very much enjoy your visit if you so choose to stay a little longer." Serena was resolute. The Cordis Loci Pools glowed in the distance, and their fervor made Leterum's cloak smolder. Wafts of white smoke emanated from his body.

"The Endüerduul does not wish me to stay fair Queen, otherwise I would oblige. I do not come to fight. I come to bargain. If I recall, you rather excel at compromise."

"There is no middle ground here, demon."

"Demon is it? How cruel. You've become distant and cold, Serena. I remember once you being altogether different."

"Betrayal does many things, Leterum," Serena replied.

"Look around, Queen Serena. This is your betrayal. These lands are dying as Vagus fall like lice upon the sands. The bargain you struck with Acrom has now come to harvest."

"And who better to reap what I sowed than you?"

"Aye, but I come with an offer," Leterum countered.

"I suspect it won't be to my terms."

"One term only. A proposition. Give me what's mine."

His gauntlet knuckles unfurled slowly with an open hand toward Celeste, and he turned his palm upwards as if to invite her upon Sēpein's saddle. The ebony lion's head roared. Serena and Celeste's disgust was only superseded by Creed's anger.

"Go to Hell!" Creed walked forward to the gamekeeper, and spit at the feet of his mount. Sēpein's chest rumbled with intent to char all before him, but Leterum yanked the chains, and discouraged him from doing so.

"Ahh, Hippocrates. I see you've been busy scampering about the land scavenging half-living remains. Does it fulfill you somehow to 'rescue' a damned soul only to see it disemboweled on the field of battle?"

"If it means less souls for you and your *master* then, yes. Worth every second." Leterum leaned forward, and his eyes lit up fiery red behind the helm's fog.

"*My* master, child? How petty and poor. I expected much more from you, Hippocrates. Do I seem so vain as to think much of it? Acrom is a means to an end. He is a harbinger of the revolution, and nothing more. There is one end to existence, and it must always go through me."

"Leterum, no such 'end' exists. Acrom will devour you as he has the others. None shall exist through or beside him." Serena was aglow with electric energy.

"We have lived a long time, Serena. You and I both know the strengths we possess. Acrom will have his desire, but I will have dominion. Now, give me the child. I will allow you to live in your Keep. You may gather as many souls as you wish, and can live out your eternity safely. Plant your fields. Have your flock as you see fit. That is my offer. If you so choose to refuse me, I will burn this world to the ground. You will watch with your own eyes the travesty of your lack of foresight." Leterum rescinded his hand, and sat high upon the beast.

"That is not your offer to make," Serena countered.

"I need no such condition."

"What of Acrom?" she asked.

"He has his plans. I have mine. Even now, our forces approach the Highland cities. Once they fall, there are only a few steps left. The remaining regions with their townships will fall one by one. Give me Celeste and the unborn child. I will give you peace."

"If those are your terms, I choose war, Leterum." The clouds rumbled with anticipation above.

"Then you choose death. *You choose me*. How satisfying, Serena. I look forward to dining with you all." The white smoke thickened above his shoulders, and though few could see it, he shifted in discomfort. Creed sensed his presence did not please the Endüerduul.

Leterum focused intently on Serena, as her hatred permeated the air. Her hands began to roil aflame, and the skies were laced with encroaching webs of lightning. She would do this here and now. Creed tensed, waiting for the moment to charge. Leterum sighed. "Ah, Serena. Foolish and forewarned!"

Leterum yanked hard on Sēpein's reins, and the spikes dug into the chimera's flesh. The dragon's head roared, fire brimming the nostrils, as Sēpein spun around quickly on his hindquarters, and decimated the armored men before him. The flames were too quick for Serena to react, and their blistered bodies crumpled in agony. Serena felled her power loose upon the field, and struck forcefully at Leterum, but as soon as the lightning avulsed the ground, he and his Caedere army had disappeared in a black mist of Fuga. Leterum had once again gained the upper hand, as Serena was left with a field of angst and atrocity.

Screams echoed as if afar for Creed's ears still rang from the thunder. Movement tussled around him, as recovery efforts launched in disarray. The sudden light from Serena's attack was so blinding, that as Creed stumbled down the hill to the wounded, he fell numerous times, relying solely on the smell of seared flesh. The Luxatio and Bellatorum ran toward the ill fallen as well, and the others made way for stretchers and bandages.

Serena lowered her head, half the men that had come before her were dead, and the other half burned beyond function. The ground was infested with green flames, and the heat made it difficult for the rescuers to respond to those most in need. Celeste raised her hands, and the sky became opaque with grief. Cold rain pummeled the fields until no fire remained. Serena ordered her Bellatorum to move the wounded into the Keep of Cordis Loci, and within minutes, the infirmary was at capacity. The hobgoblin brothers hurriedly constructed more temporary wooden structures with their magic and the nearby trees to house the wounded and resting Vagus. Serena looked to the Guard's Captain.

"I will avenge your brothers," she said. The Captain looked about as Creed met his eyes. The young officer appeared sickened.

"I think you have likely condemned us, my Queen. Soon, there will be nothing left to avenge at all." He put on his helmet, and strode toward his fallen. He too carried as many men as he could with the others. Serena stared down the slope, trembling with rage. Leterum had accomplished what he had set out to do. Sowing discord within the factions was merely the beginning.

Creed closed the eyes of another casualty, looked across the carnage, and noticed Xaris, weeping. A man seemingly made of stone mourned the men he had commanded for centuries. Creed wondered had Xaris been in the Capital, would these men still have survived? This was too much apparently for the solemn warrior to bear. He turned away, knelt, and wiped his eyes, repeatedly. After a few minutes, Xaris spat on the ground, and stood to address Serena.

"My Queen, let me lead the men. Send me to command the wounded's escape to Durdan. I will hold that wall until the last soul is delivered safely to you."

"Xaris, I will need you to go to Durdan."

"Your highness, these men..." Xaris pleaded.

"Your men at Durdan need you now more than ever."

"Then who will go to the Capital?" he asked.

"I will." Creed stepped forward. Celeste was within earshot, and immediately condemned his decision.

"Absolutely not!" she said.

"It makes sense. Let me go. I can lead whomever you send, and I can tend to the wounded as we get the others out quickly. I cannot triage the populace unless I am there. As soon as we get everyone out, I will leave. I promise."

"You will not save everyone this time, Hippocrates. People are dying, and they will still die. You could die as well. It does us no good if you simply cast your life away haphazardly. I've witnessed you become careless in battle, and that hubris will only serve you for so long. We need a quick exodus, and nothing more. Engaging the enemy full force is not an option. I will assign those to facilitate the Capital retreat," Serena assured Celeste.

"What I ask of each of you in this dire time is to consider what is at stake, and the role each of you will play. We will have to surrender the city, and likely many souls within it, but in the meantime, we need to acquire the remaining Guardsmen and any wounded that can travel. The objective is to get in there, and be gone within hours. Not days as some had suggested earlier. Leterum will obliterate every soul and stone to prove his point. The city is nothing more than a symbol now. If we strengthen Durdan, it will hold, and we will control the northwest region. That cannot be altered. It is our best bet. This is a time for man to salvage immortality's remains. Mürindür is set upon a path of decay, and we need man to garner a foothold. This is why I ask the remaining Luxatio to honor my request in rescuing your brothers at the Capital." The Luxatio had gathered slowly, and the mumbling ensued. They had just escaped a near-death, and were now ordered to virtually secure another.

"Hear me. The Luxatio have always been the bridge between man and Eternity. The Luxatio are the ambassadors of good will and strength, and for thousands of years, this has inspired a multitude of souls. The Guard and the people of the Capital need this now more than ever. I will send with you my Bellatorum. They will take on Leterum's hordes while you gather those that can stand and fly. I am sending my daughter along with Ojin and his kin to Durdan."

"Mother! I can fight! I can help the…" Celeste was angry.

"No child. Your son's birth is nigh, and we cannot risk losing either one of you. I ask you, Ojin, to gather up your team, and get Bog and Pax to the Durdan Keep. Xaris, I task you with the high command of Durdan. Tell Perrindor I plan on making Durdan the new Capital, and we will expand its girth and resources once we empty the halls of the wounded."

"I wish to go to the Capital instead, Serena. Send me with your Bellatorum and Luxatio. I will secure your success," Xaris pleaded.

"No. I've decided. Luxatio and Bellatorum will facilitate the escape while all of you embolden Durdan."

"Mother, where are you in all of this?" Celeste asked.

"It is time." Celeste's eyes grew big.

"No," the Princess pleaded.

"I will confront him on the field of battle. I am going with my warriors to the Capital. This will buy us the time we need."

"You could perish," Ojin protested. Serena looked about.

"Part of me already has. I will lead the forces. Each of you will travel to Durdan. Generals…" the officers formed a line before her, "Is the plan understood?"

"Yes, my Queen." They bowed in acceptance.

"Then gather the resources. Equip the Luxatio with weapons. We leave in one hour. Ojin, make ready." The protests were kept at a whisper, but the command had been given.

They would divide to mitigate the conquered. Celeste spoke with her mother in private, and Creed could see the disbelief in his wife's face. Serena placed her hands on her daughter's shoulders and simply kissed her forehead. The Queen walked away to prepare, and Celeste stood there quietly.

"She will make it back," Creed assured her.

"I'm not so sure," she replied softly.

"We have to hope."

"Today we need something more. I asked that she join us in Durdan, and let Leterum have his momentary joy, but she feels this is unavoidable. She is tired of running. She only did it this long because of our son, and he will be here any day. We've moved from one region to another barely a step ahead of a wolf obsessed with our trail. She is done. She is ready." Tears streamed down her face.

"Are you?" he asked.

"I will be." she replied.

"Good."

"Gather your belongings. I will gather mine. By nightfall, we should be ready within the walls of Durdan." Celeste kissed his cheek, and she turned toward her tent.

Creed nodded, and as she disappeared behind the trees, he walked toward the collection of bodies, gingerly gathered up by the grieving Luxatio and Bellatorum. The dead Guardsmen lie shoulder to shoulder in a formation of fatality, their armor charred and disfigured. He stepped slowly down the line, as his mind clawed for understanding, staring at the human hands, laxed and lifeless, their burnt faces tightened in a posture of torment. Creed sought retribution, and it would not be found in Durdan. He glanced toward the Keep, and noticed Fitz grinding his battle-axe. A thought crept into his mind, and Creed made way, speaking with the Viking in confidence. Not all battle plans were finalized, and today would be the day the Luxatio reclaimed their honor in the eyes of Mürindür.

Chapter 32: Change of Plans

The flurry of activity about the camp was hectic, but purposeful. The Luxatio were clad in armor and equipped with the weapons of their choosing. The Minotaur blacksmiths of the Helgenschphere had been hard at work finalizing the details. A contingent of Bellatorum and men would stay behind at the Keep of Cordis Loci knowing the dark legions would likely crumble to ash should they ever attempt to come close to the Pools. They continued to treat and recover the Vagus, as hundreds of people were newly woken, and asked what lie in store for them. For now, they would be fed and clothed within the confines of the Keep; a new Redemptio as it were. Creed prepared his things, and went to visit with Celeste. She was ready, sword across her back, and bow with quiver in hand. She looked to him and spoke.

"Where are your things? We're leaving now."

"I will meet you there."

"No. You're coming with me. We have a great deal of work to do," Celeste insisted.

"I've already spoken with your mother. She agreed to it. I will treat and tend to the wounded a bit more here, and then Ojin will come back to get me. A half-day at most."

"What are you up to?" Her eyebrow rose with doubt.

"Nothing. Serena is leaving shortly, and you guys are headed to Durdan. I will meet you at Durdan. I promise." Serena walked over to speak with her daughter one last time before they went their separate ways.

"Mother, Creed stays behind?"

"Just for a moment, my love. He will be with you soon. There is some benefit in having him treat and manage more of the Vagus and wounded Guardsmen. Once he has them stabilized, he will join you and the rest at Durdan. He will be safe here." Celeste looked at her husband.

"I don't like this. Not one bit. What if the child comes, and you aren't there? Either one of you?"

"I will be there. Ojin promised me that," Creed assured her.

"Where is Ojin?" Celeste asked.

"He's suiting up now. Bog is in his armor once more, and Pax is beside him. Everyone, including Xaris, is ready to leave. My child, go to Durdan. Your husband will join you soon, and I will be there as quickly as I can."

Celeste stared at the two most important people in her life, and shook her head. Serena kissed her on her cheek, and left the couple to each other for a moment. Creed reached in for a hug, but Celeste put up her hand.

"Don't. This is unacceptable. I don't care what my mother says. You're coming with me."

"Once we make it to Durdan, we won't be coming back anytime soon. Some of these people I can help, and it wouldn't set right with me to do otherwise. Let me do this, and I will be right there with you. Besides, most of today will be spent on supplies, bedding. Nothing more." Her blue eyes scanned him closely.

"I promise," Creed assured her. Ojin walked towards them.

"Celeste, it's time to go. I am better now, but with the brothers' help we will likely only need to leap once."

"I will fly us, Ojin," she replied.

"No. Too risky. You need to reserve your strength. If we do it now, we can ready the Keep for you and your child before things get tedious."

"Did you know about this?" She pointed to Creed.

"Yes, but Serena does as well, and I promise you, I will get him before sunset. He will be sleeping beside you tonight." She looked at Creed once more, and leaned in slightly, a mediocre invite for an embrace. Creed took it, and pulled her in tightly. He felt her body relax.

"Celeste, I will make it back to you. It's only a few hours. I will be there."

"Yes, *you will*, and not a minute later. Sunset, Ojin?"

"Yes" the hobgoblin affirmed.

"Sunset it is." She kissed Creed, and walked out into the light as Ojin followed. He looked back with tail twitching stressfully.

"Creed, be here in this tent before sunset. The moment the light lies low over the mountain crest, I will be here. Don't be late. Tonight,will be long. We need our tribe together."

"I won't be late my friend."

"Indeed. Creed?"

"Yes?"

"It's been good to have you back, my friend. You had me worried."

Ojin's tusks spread his smile wide.

"Travel well, Ojin, and please watch her closely."

"I will," Ojin replied.

"Good luck."

"No, Hippocrates. Luck is for the ill-prepared. We are ready. Don't you worry."

Ojin turned and walked to the large gathering of allies before them. Creed followed, and saw his friends all join hands. Celeste faced him with worry. He smiled in an attempt to cure it, noticing the green glimmer of Oerbuel through the ties of her robe. It settled his spirit. Pax, Bog, Celeste, Xaris, Ojin, the three brothers, and all the others disappeared instantly into the white light. They were gone, and Creed stood there alone. After a moment of collecting his thoughts, he ventured into a nearby recovery tent, and checked the wounds on one of the younger Guardsmen.

"Sir, are you Hippocrates?" the soldier asked.

"Yes. I am."

"The men in the Capital mentioned you had come back."

"How are they?"

"Morale is dying. We have watched the dark masses gain strength from afar. They wait for the word. They've toyed with us for days now. They could have consumed us anytime, but they wait. Our best estimates, Leterum has over thirty thousand soldiers at his command before the Capital. We have no concept of Acrom or his forces. It has been difficult. It seems darkness lives everywhere."

"It seems near impossible doesn't it?"

"At times. I remind myself that this too is merely a transition, a waypoint on some long journey. Regardless of how its ends here, perhaps something better lies ahead."

"What if there is nothing beyond Mürindür?" Creed asked.

"Well, sir, what would be the point in that?" the Guardsman replied.

"I don't know. What is the point of any of it?"

"The universe is benevolent, sir. I believe that it is kind. Why should any of us be brought here merely to suffer the end of something beautiful if there isn't something more beautiful ahead? The Endüerduul is where we all wish to be. It's a place of peace. Imagine being surrounded by grace and love for all of your days. It's something I have prayed for, many times. I feel it is close."

Creed analyzed his eyes, and hung his head. The patient had become delirious, and appeared to be embarking upon another journey of his own.

"It is close. It is, my friend. Rest your eyes and breathe."

Creed watched solemnly as the soldier's breathing became more erratic. He stared at his charred face, and kept patting it softly with wet gauze. As the body stiffened, it soon relaxed, and the last breath was had. Creed sat there quietly. No matter where he lived or what he experienced, the human need for something 'better and beyond' was constant. How could it ever be otherwise? He glanced up, and all around. His senses were inundated with suffering, pain, and fear. All of Leterum's fodder lay before him as a banquet on Death's table.

Creed hadn't realized how long he had sat beside the soldier's body. He hoped he'd see something miraculous, but instead it was just silence. The workers came over, and covered the man's face with a white shroud. They bound his body with rope, and carried him away to another building, which housed the deceased. Creed heard someone clear his throat. It was Pescus.

"It never gets easier does it? Watching them die. Each one with hopes and dreams falling victim to random human happenstance."

"No. It never gets easier," Creed replied.

"When I first took command, it was only twenty of us. A small group tasked with miniscule objectives. Observe an outpost here. Gather up Welfalon over there. Nothing big. We thought ourselves to be very important. That all changed one night when we were caught in the dark, showing our stupidity in the process. Caedere picked us apart like fruit from a tree. Eight of us survived. Serena was angry and frustrated that so many were lost. We hadn't seen any Luxatio die in Mürindür before, and when we went back, we gathered their remains. Placed them in catacombs in the base of Redemptio. I sat with them for days afterward. I wouldn't eat or sleep. It was Serena who finally came down and sat with me. She told me I needed to go to Earth for a while. Live a little if it were, and when I returned, I would be ready to assume more responsibilities. I felt it to be a punishment, but she sent me anyway right then and there. When I came back, not much had changed. I still thought of the souls lost. I became more conservative. More protective. More indecisive."

"That's understandable. You were afraid to lose more."

"Aye, but you were different. When you took command, you lead four times as many Luxatio on any given day with them coming and going. You would lose a few, but head right into battle as if it were nothing."

"It wasn't 'nothing'. It was necessary," Creed explained.

"Aye, but so is grieving. If you never allow yourself to fall apart, you can't rebuild and grow. You can't get any stronger. You can't evolve."

"I grieve, but I grieve differently from you. My anger serves as a warm winter coat. I do not pause to give what's lost more time than it is due. I burn it up, and move forward. Each step. Each loss, another step." Creed looked down at his boots for a moment as he cleared his throat.

"That is a painfully finite way to measure one's purpose," Pescus said pointedly.

"I've survived this long with rage. It sustains me."

"A belly full of fire is it?" Pescus asked.

"A soul full of fire," Creed replied.

"Yes. That much is true. You've changed quite a bit for the better I might add. I did not like you when we first met."

"I hear that a lot," Creed smirked.

"I finally came around. Over time, I even looked up to you. Whatever it is you have planned for us, don't leave us again. It will break us." Pescus seemed more vigilant and aware than before in the Caverns of Lorem. He appeared to be sober.

"I will not leave. That much I know even if it means I must break my Oath. I will not leave again."

"Well, I hope not," Pescus replied. Fitz walked over.

"It's time," Fitz said.

"Agreed."

"What's time?" Pescus asked.

"We are leaving. You two need to get dressed," Fitz explained.

"Alright. It's been a while since I've made it into battle, but…" as Pescus turned, Fitz caught him across the back of the neck with his axe handle, and he slumped into a nearby gurney.

"We haven't much time," Fitz reminded Creed. "They will head into battle soon."

"I know." Creed looked down at the old Luxata on the ground.

"I'm sorry, Pescus. When you wake, you'll hopefully understand."

Creed took the satchel Fitz brought him, and walked behind a wall to change. Fitz disrobed Pescus, and threw his clothes to Creed as Creed threw his back. Soon, Creed emerged, appearing to be the elder Luxatio. He wrapped Üstor in leather and slung it over his back careful that not a glimmer was visible. Fitz helped him dress Pescus, and pulled his hood low to delay detection. Creed pulled on a dark woolen mask, and slung the satchel of armor over his back. The clanging noise inside made Fitz take a quick look around.

"You keep that up, and you'll sound like a sheep with a brass bell. Might as well tell everyone," Fitz admonished.

"It's secure now. We're good. Let's go," Creed replied.

"Serena is gathering everyone out front as we speak. The Luxatio are excited in a way I've never seen."

"Nothing is more invigorating than leaping with a sense of purpose even if the chasm seems dark and wide."

"You're starting to sound like that old man," Fitz teased.

"I am an old man. Let's go."

They walked out of the infirmary down toward the open meadow. Serena, her Bellatorum, and the remaining Luxatio were encircled now, ready for war. Serena spoke some last words of encouragement.

"We ready ourselves for something far greater than anything we've ever known. We head into impossibility with hope. I cannot promise that any of you will return with us to Durdan. It is highly likely that we will fail in doing so. I *can* promise you this! What we hope to accomplish will instill vigor and legend into the minds of those who do survive! WE WILL DECIMATE LETERUM'S

PROMISE OF RETRIBUTION, AND SPIT IN THE FACE OF ANNIHILATION!"

Her voice echoed across the Keep of Cordis Loci.

"**AAAAAAHHHHHHH**!!" Her legion replied.

The crowd was emboldened and grateful. Nothing seemed more honorable than to stare down Death himself. The Queen raised her hands just as Fitz and Creed joined within the outer circle. Varsalsae squinted angrily at the two. Fitz informed Creed earlier they had argued because the Viking insisted on bringing Pescus much to her chagrin. After all, what good would it do to bring a derelict to war? Fitz beamed a toothy grin at Varsalsae, and she turned away with disgust. They all looked to Serena as she spoke softly. There was a flash, and they were gone.

Chapter 33: Capital of Guillarne

They arrived at the forefront of the Castle's courtyard nestled deep within the heart of the Capital of Guillarne. Screams were heard all around. Serena motioned to her troops to spread out and take the walls. Creed and Fitz separated from the others, so they could watch the Queen. She flew quickly to the wall's walkway, and looked eastward to the foe. Creed sprinted up some nearby stairs and stood behind a rock column. On the horizon, he could see dark figures milled about, and above them the sky was infested with black wings. Serena's generals joined her side as Bellatorum filled the battlements. Luxatio searched the inner buildings and found hundreds of wounded lying about the halls below. Outside the Castle, within the Capital streets, Creed could hear shouting. The voice was familiar to him.

Serena peered into the market, and found the man. It was the Capital's leader, Commander Sines. Creed could hear him ordering traps and spike columns throughout the main thoroughfares of the city. Serena motioned her hands quickly, and the Commander appeared before her. He seemed shocked, but quickly bowed.

"Queen Serena. Thank the gods you have arrived! We've been requesting aid for days!"

"My apologies. We have been overrun elsewhere. My daughter and I have been on the run for months, and the infant is likely due any day now. I sent for your retreat."

"I am sorry, but I had to disregard your orders. We would have…"

"Left many to die," Serena admitted.

"Thousands," the Commander confirmed.

The city was broken and in disarray. Creed overheard the Capital had been under siege for weeks, and the only peace they experienced was for the last twenty-four hours. The commander explained to Serena that the men were tired, and hadn't slept or eaten in as long of time.

"We just arrived within the Castle grounds, Commander Sines. We have supplies and some food. I will summon more. I see the troops we face," the Queen noted.

"That's just from the east, my Queen. If you look to the south, you will witness many, many more. They materialize out of thin air, and take up camp beyond our archers and catapults. They are waiting patiently for our end as well." Commander Sines motioned to the south wall.

"Then let us offer it to them willingly," Serena advised.

"Pardon?"

"Let us choose the time and place. We leave these walls and bring them to us. Let us step out into the field."

"We will surely perish. They outnumber us…"

"Vastly, but while we do so, you and your men will retreat to the west, and make it to Durdan. Set up refuge there."

"What of the wounded?" the Commander asked.

"Take who you can. My Bellatorum will bring the rest."

"It will take days."

"It will be done within hours. Bring your generals to the courtyard, and we will outline our attack."

He nodded, and motioned to his aide below. The officer toned a signal to regroup through an old pearly-white ram's horn. The sound echoed through the wide cobblestone streets, and after three volleys of the horn, hundreds and then thousands of boots returned from the perimeter. Creed made way to the ground floor as Fitz followed.

Within the castle, the other Luxatio tended to the wounded. As Creed continued throughout the halls, he realized most of them could make it to Durdan. He assessed dozens of soldiers and civilians. Their wounds were moderate in scale, but would not prove to be life threatening in the meantime. He shared as much with Fitz.

"We can get most of these people out of here, I think, if not all. The Fuga should not harm them in any way."

"That is good then." the Viking nodded.

"Very. When Serena formulates her plans, I will infiltrate with the other Luxatio. I'm certain she will assign a few to Durdan, and the others to battle. You should try to make it back to Ojin and my wife. It won't be long before Durdan is attacked."

"Understood."

Creed ventured into the courtyard once more, gazing up at the walls. He could see the Bellatorum when another horn sounded off. The gates opened slowly with the iron chains, and from beneath the bottom of the thick wood and brackets, hundreds of horse legs became visible. As the gates rose higher, the Commander came into view along with his officers. They galloped into the yard, and dismounted. Serena appeared from above, and together, the strategists marked their moves on a map laid out before everyone over an old battered banquet table.

After a few minutes, Serena summoned her forces to the courtyard where she addressed them on the Castle steps. The military planners stood behind her in unison.

"We have urgent need to evacuate the remainder of this city. Though it pains us to see these walls fall, it should lighten our burden to know that we can successfully get most of the survivors to Durdan safely. Soon, the sun will lower, and we will fight in its glory. I ask that the main Luxatio force stay alongside my Bellatorum, while a handful of either party, that I will designate, join the Commander's army, and evacuate to Durdan. Our goal is to impose a barricade south of their main front, and take both assaulting forces as we see fit, on our own terms. If Leterum should wish to show himself, I will take him, but I suspect he will remain hidden within his Keep. At this very moment, our remaining troops from the Cordis Loci have reunited with Durdan's, and are preparing fortifications. Our only job today is to hold Leterum's forces long enough for the others to leap and vacate. When the ram's horn sounds three times, we are to regroup in the center, and I will carry us to Durdan safely. Is this understood?"

"**AYE**!!" the crowd answered.

"Commander, prepare your gates, and make ready your citizens. All of you are going home!"

Thunderous applause followed her as she descended the stairs, choosing the Luxatio meant to escort the wounded away. Creed made sure to stay hidden within the stables for the few minutes she made her orders known. He changed into his armor, and placed the clothing over it. Thankfully, the weight was negligible as he left his helm in the satchel. The assigned parties prepared, and those destined for battle made way to the City's gates. Fitz had been

chosen to escort the retreat while Varsalsae and Eva had been
assigned to platoons of Bellatorum. Creed walked toward a platoon
of his own when Varsalsae grabbed his arm.

"Pescus?"

"Yes?" Creed muttered.

"Wouldn't you do better to stay with Fitz and make way to
Durdan?" she asked.

"How so?"

"I don't believe you've recovered quickly enough to handle a
sword."

"I will do as I have been commanded to do, Varsalsae. Now if
you'll excuse me, I'd prefer to fill my flask before we head to
Hell."

Creed pulled his arm away, and walked toward a nearby well. A
few pumps, and water flowed freely into the leather container.
Varsalsae continued to stare at him as he traversed the city streets
eventually disappearing within the crowds. As he walked, he
noticed eyes and faces of fear through the windows and doorways
of the homes and shops. Eventually the populace was shepherded
out into the light, and funneled toward the castle for their departure.
Animals roamed about the cobblestones as cows mooed and goats
bleated. Creed squeezed and twisted through the crowd of warriors,
managing to get close to the city gates. He looked back at the
castle, and saw that the streets had become a river of refugees. The
mood was solemn, but sincere. He found himself standing shoulder
to shoulder with Guardsmen, Bellatorum, and Luxatio alike.
Outside arm's reach, he heard Luxatio talking.

"Where is Hippocrates?" a man asked.

"They say he stayed at Cordis Loci to tend to the wounded," the woman replied.

"He's needed here."

"Yes, but he won't be."

"This doesn't feel right. What does he know that we don't?"

"I don't know, my friend. I had hoped to see him once more, and fight with us. We need him. We need our lion," the woman replied.

The man turned toward him, but Creed knelt down quickly to adjust his boots.

Suddenly, a foreboding command.

"OPEN THE GATES!"

The ratcheting began and the chains tumbled over one another as the wheels turned. Within moments, Creed found himself staring at an open field of waving grass and stoic rock. Remnants of prior engagements littered the view as far as he could see. Serena's army walked out in lines of thirty, which ultimately merged to lines of fifty and then a hundred. They marched forward until all the men had cleared the gates.

"CLOSE THE GATES!!"

When they concluded, the gates' spikes thudded against their sockets. High above them stood a wary wall of archers estimating ranges. To their front, approached an imposing infantry of Caedere and Ogres, and to their right, a muddled mass of horned Mael'deua with trolls the size of buildings. The numbers were immeasurable, but it mattered not. They would give the survivors all the time that they could. The sky eerily appeared peaceful, with glimmers of an orange sun in the west, as the Ravens surged forth with their brethren of vultures. They circled high above, quietly scouting for Leterum's troops below. The dark army formed columns, and their auburn banners flickered rhythmically, snapping the otherwise utter silence. The horses' heavy breathing seeped into the background.

BOOM!

BOOM!

BOOM!

The sound was to the right of Creed, from the south. The Mael'deua advanced to the beat of war drums, ominous and unified. Bellatorum formed their middle ranks while Luxatio covered the outer lines. Over two-thirds of the Guardsmen made up the rear. Creed could see Serena high atop the wall over the gates. Banners of white linen trimmed in gold danced beside her. Üstor began to warm. Creed focused forward, and readied himself.

"HOOORRRAHHHHH!"

The Bellatorum clanged their shields with their swords. All of them armored, golden and polished. Their helms sat low across their brow, and their crimson capes undulated in the northern breeze. The Bellatorum stepped forward and spread out, overtaking the entire front line. Creed found himself, anonymous and hidden, within the center of the Luxatio column.

In the distance, hundreds of yards away, the black beast, Sēpein, flew over the army, hovering at first, and then slowly listing toward the city. He grew larger as he approached, finally settling decisively in the middle of the battlefield. Sēpein paced the hard, futile ground with his gruesome rider. The white serpent tail whipped about as the chimera viewed all fronts. The lion head roared in a protracted command. Everything became quiet. The drums ceased.

Leterum dismounted and walked to the void between the forces' frontlines as Sēpein rose onto his hindquarters, disappearing into the sky. Seven of Serena's Generals strode forward on their horses, and the archers' bowstrings, along the Capital wall, were taut and eager. Leterum stood as a solitary grim moor. At his greatest height, he stood twice as tall as the largest Bellatorum. From his back, he unsheathed his weapon, a sword twisted and folded into a Damascus pattern. The hilt was translucent with swirls of opaque hues as it had been shorn of diamond-impregnated bone, and polished to a high finish in flame. A knurled skull beset the pommel. He gripped his weapon tightly in his right hand as the sword tip rose to address General Reqwarnst. They were a mere twenty yards from one another.

"This is your last stand, General Reqwarnst, and it shall end quickly. Where is my prize? Where is the Child of Mürindür?"

"The Queen spits upon your proposal. Her daughter is not your prize!"

In symbolic gesture, General Reqwarnst spit at Leterum. Death's posture tightened in frustration as he looked upon the walls. There, Serena stood as defiant as the sun. Leterum's chest swelled with fury, and he turned to the lines before him.

"I will offer no rest for any soul who stands before me! You will bellow with pain in the depths of Acrom's belly! I will revive you only long enough to experience each shearing tortuous grind upon your undead flesh! Lay down your weapons, and I promise you safe passage to Redemptio!"

The wind spun up swirls of dust as high as the city walls. Neither a face broke expression, nor a head turned aside. Their focus was due. A flash, and there stood Serena, staring into Leterum's mask, strong and resolute.

"Leterum, you will rue this day." The Queen's eyes were white flame.

"Have you chosen to finally stand against me, or will you wither off like some poor petulant child?"

"The time has come, and Acrom's prison walls may fall with my intervention, but no matter. On this day, we settle what you shied from so many years ago."

"If I remember, you weren't there to face me. You sent your lap dog," Leterum taunted.

"He was your brother, Leterum!" Serena chided.

"Elyptos was a brave soul. He deserved better."

"You should have offered him better. He was unsettled when he learned of your treason."

"Discovery is not treason, Serena. Knowledge can be empowering."

"Leterum, you failed the Universe as prescribed. Your path, your role, was cast aside the moment you aligned with Acrom. Instead of being the shepherd of souls, you became the executioner of mankind. What you seek now, can never be undone, and your salvation has long since passed. All that you will reap today, is your own demise!" Serena took a half-step back to prepare.

"Did you weep for me?" Leterum asked.

"Weep?"

"Yes," he replied.

"When?"

"When I was cast out from the Endüerduul? Did you even pain one moment for my exile?"

"You chose that path of your own selfish means," Serena replied coldly.

"I was there when they cast out Acrom as were you. All his brothers and sisters stood as stone when his judgment fell like an axe. Down he went, and a new world had begun."

"He too failed to see his role."

"He saw a different purpose for man, a predilection of servitude. I, however, swore to protect them," Leterum rationalized.

"You were to be their guide, and nothing more," she replied.

"I was their guardian, but then my purpose was warped by them!" Leterum thrust his sword to the light-colored moon. "I was tasked with horrible things. Things you couldn't fathom!"

"I was there!" Serena shouted.

"I took those lives. Time and time again. I was sent to do what no one else would. I held the gates between life and the after, and I cared for them as no one else ever could. They worshipped me, and built pyramids for their kings, anticipating an existence solely through my means. Then with the interference of the Endüerduul, man began to fear me. They abhorred me."

"You cared about your prestige. Your dominion."

"My purpose!" Leterum shouted.

"A mockery. It was nothing more than an arena of fallacies in your mind," Serena replied.

"When the universe cast judgment, I walked those souls to Acrom. I ferried them to an eternal damnation, and for what justly cause beyond a decree? A lack of grace? An absence of absolution?"

"It was as it was intended to be." said Serena.

"Heresy!"

"No, you became the heretic!"

"I became the light!" Leterum argued.

"You are not their savior!" she replied.

"No, but I did become their courier, and in that I saw an end. I would make the Endüerduul tear itself apart. They would see the wisdom in my teachings, and mankind would gain freedom not from a trial of tribulation but through me."

"You are blind!"

"I *serve* the blind! I nurture them! They fall, and you abandon them in the dunes, but I rescue them. They are feared throughout the land, and yet they are not the ones lost, Serena!"

"Enough! I am here to right this arc!"

"And, you will lose. There is no Life without Death, Serena." Leterum paced slowly to and fro.

"I will achieve what I sought to accomplish," the Queen replied.

"Then I seek nothing more from you. When you fall, Serena, the Child of Mürindür will be mine. Your kingdom will be dust beneath my feet. This world will burn under Acrom, and I will obtain passage to the Endüerduul. The Immortals will face me once more!"

"WE FACE YOU NOW!"

Serena wasted no more time. Her right hand rose as his, and she flung the sky's wrath like a spear of searing revenge. The bolt struck his sword as Leterum parried, and sent the charge deep into the earth. He roared behind his helm of black fumes, and made a fist with his left hand. The ground shook, and a quake split the rocky ground in two, traveling as a fault line through the Queen's ranks, and into the gates. The Capital walls trembled, and the gates were as leaves strewn too hastily in autumn. The metal crashed in the distance. Serena struck with her bolts again and again. She raised the ground, and sent it as a wave into Leterum, but he flew mere feet above its crest as it decimated a good sum of Caedere fast approaching. Leterum countered with vines of rancid undergrowth, which lashed and bound her limbs. She shouted in defiance, and her skin boiled, turning the vines to ash in her wake. Locusts spun out of the crevasse, and swarmed her, picking at her flesh. She bore down upon herself a thousand bolts of lightning, and nothing more remained of the insects.

"**AAAHHHHHHHHHHHHH**!" The voices carried across the field.

Leterum's ranks broke forward, and the Bellatorum bellowed. At first it was a slow jog, but within seconds the sprint was full, and from above, the Ravens could see the masses bent on one another's destruction. Serena's archers let loose their first volley, and the hail of Jak-rael's arrows pierced the opposed sinew. Catapult ropes were hewn, and burning birch wood, strapped upon granite boulders, could be seen contrasting the cold sky. As the projectiles fell, dozens of Caedere and Ogres fed the parched soil. Creed slung his satchel to the ground while retrieving his helm. His woolen mask and clothing were torn away revealing his burnt-bronze armor, and Üstor was unleashed. He pulled his helm over tightly, and ran full force with the others. As he passed Luxatio, he could hear them call his name.

"HIPPOCRATES! HIPPOCRATES!"

Emboldened, they unleashed their battle cry. Their leader had not cowered in the rear as some suggested, but flew forward into the fray. His armor was bright within the field when the sunrays struck it, drawing malevolent, adversarial eyes to him. He was the alpha. This was his pride. The Lion of the Luxatio had returned.

With Serena occupying Leterum, the allied forces crashed upon the Caedere like bulls. Blood splattered onto the grasslands. The

Bellatorum ripped into the middle of the Caedere, and within minutes the mass of blows and alloy melded. Creed was caught outside the scrum, and found himself battling a fervent Caedere and three eager Ogres. Üstor was buried into one Ogre's entrails as Creed caught the Caedere's hilt in hand. As he pushed back against the hooved beast, his body emitted a flared temper, and the Ogres stumbled back from the searing heat. Creed redirected the Caedere's blade into the nearby Ogre spearman, and with that, withdrew Üstor, driving it into the last Ogre.

With none left before him, he chopped the Caedere's legs from beneath the knees with an upward arc of his glaive. The ungainly creature fell to his bloody stumps, and Creed leaned within inches from its sutured face. He paused, but then severed its head, unwilling to grant it a moment of peace. He drew Üstor quickly above his shoulder, and halted a strike from the side. Another contemptuous Caedere was met with Üstor's flame, and the dark soldier fell in his place. Creed caught a glimpse of Serena from the corner of his eye, and suddenly felt Üstor resonate.

Serena drove her fist into Leterum's chest forcing him to back step, but undeterred, Leterum drove his leg into her hip, buckling her stance into the dust. He raised his sword to strike Serena down, but through a beckoned grasp a molten trident materialized into her hand quickly enough to catch the blade. Leterum leaned heavily into her, but as if merely standing from a kneeling position in her garden, she regained her posture, thrust him back, spun, and her weapon found itself within a hairbreadth of his throat. Leterum unfurled his wings, and flew back with mocking laughter. She leapt to counter, and he to her, but as Serena spun to unleash a flurry of flame, Leterum thrust debris into her eyes with the force of his wings. She was blind. He hurled into her, crashing upon her chest, and as she fell, her back broke the rocks underneath. The vibrations shook the mountains.

Leterum clenched his raised fist, and the dark Ravens engulfed Serena, the Queen lying with her face to the sky. Creed could see Leterum step back quickly, and ready his sword as if to strike the killing blow. The Queen was lost in a tornado of tumultuous feathered fiends as they pecked and clawed her face. She rolled to her side, clasped her hands, and summoned a fiery whirlwind, engulfing the birds with its incendiary arid breath. Hundreds of Ravens were taken high into the sky as they tumbled and squawked only to be decimated with indifference. She rose to her feet, and as she stood before Leterum, smoldering Raven carcasses fell all around.

Serena wiped her eyes clean, and held her trident low. Leterum opened his left hand for a moment, and laughed once more before lowering his sword to her eye level. Serena hesitated for but a blink, but that was all it took, for the fateful indecision was concluded painfully at the hands of the Anima Capere. The strike from behind was so severe it buckled Serena to her knees before Leterum. The Bellatorum generals cried out.

"SAVE THE QUEEN!"

Creed saw the witch with her hand buried in Serena's back. The unmitigated rage took over, as he fought in a battle briar of hurdling bodies and weapons to reach her. The heat mounted, and before the Anima Capere could move, Creed lowered his shoulder, knocking her forcefully, face first, into the dirt with her robes engulfed in flames. Serena gasped as if the air had been stolen from her, but she slowly regained her composure. The Anima stood, seething at the man who was Luxatio. The fire about her robes ebbed, and she brushed the remaining embers to the ground. Leterum laughed. The battleground swirled about them, but did so, as the wind and rain of a hurricane about its eye.

"SERENA! ARE YOU OK?" Creed pulled the Queen to her feet.

"For the love of the gods, Hippocrates, why are you here, child?" Serena spat blood to the ground as she coughed.

"*Luxatio aeternum*," Creed replied.

He smiled briefly then glanced in time to see the Anima's hooks hurled toward his face. He dodged the attempted assail, and captured one of her chains. Pulling hard, the Anima lost footing. Creed's anger felt welcomed, and he used it to threaten her. He jerked the chains just to see her weaken. She pulled, and he countered with a brisk strike of Üstor, severing the chains and sending her stumbling backwards. The Anima gathered her posture, struck again, and this time she leapt toward the side of him, bending backward enough to dodge his strike, and instead clasp his thigh with her claws. She ripped into his muscle sending a mist of blood into the air. Despite the lacerations, Creed felt no pain, and from a fire within he cauterized his wounds. They paused to measure one another. Leterum spoke.

"Poetic wouldn't you say? Antitheses of one another. Life. Death. A man of healing nature, and a creature bent on his destruction. What do you think of *my* creation, Hippocrates?"

"She's an abomination. A farce that only something like you could create." Creed kept his eye on the Anima as they paced slowly in a circle, making sure to keep his back to Serena, granting her time to recover.

"Mmmmm. She angers you doesn't she, Hippocrates? There is something about her you loathe, but you don't know what it is. You can't wait to see her fall into a shallow grave."

"I don't care how she falls."

"Do you see a semblance of what once was?" Creed stared at her, and felt nothing but hate. He knew Leterum was playing with his mind, and likely sowing discord in order to buy time for something far worse.

"She is the same as all the others," Creed replied angrily.

"Ahhh, my friend, but she is *not* as the others. She is powerful, and you have seen this. When she fell, I knew I had something special. Something unique. The Anima Capere is a rare creature indeed only found on occasion when the moons are aligned in sequence. Something of a paradox, a construct of one fallen, but two souls. A creature so bent on their own destruction they willfully conclude the demise of another. This was a gift. For only *those* that can *create* souls, have the ability to *steal* them. When I found her in the Desert of Transitio, she mentioned a name. Over and over and over, like some sick, broken songbird." Creed looked at the Anima who appeared to be seething for a moment to strike. "In fact, I believe the name she shouted with her last breath was…. 'Creed'."

Leterum walked slowly to his left as Creed looked down for a second.

Why would she say my name?

SWOOSH!

Creed caught her hook inches from his chest. Images of his past life came flooding through him like waters of a broken dam. His childhood, his adolescence, college, medical school, and then… then the image of Jessie hung heavy in his mind's eye.

"*Jessie?*" he whispered, staring at the snarled, taut face of the Caedere matron before him.

"In Mürindür, her name is something more, a fitting title indeed. It is 'Anguish' in the old tongue. Finish him, *Asys*! Crush the soul that led you to me, my child. TAKE WHAT IS YOURS AND REVEL IN IT!"

Leterum thrust his sword at Creed as Asys launched her attack. A strengthened Serena countered Leterum with her trident, locking his sword in place, and the explosion sent the four scattered within the clearing of the onslaught about them. Creed coughed and sputtered from his side in the dirt, but jumped to his feet anticipating another strike. Serena was the next to rise, and as Leterum stood, reaching for his sword to charge, she flung her trident into his thigh, and the Angel of Death cried out in pain. The Caedere and Ogres paused as the battle reached an interlude. They stared at their master.

"ARRRGHHHH! YOU HEATHEN!" he screamed.

"Heathens are *your* children, Leterum." She motioned all around, "I *am* the Queen!"

Wounded, Leterum staggered, and slowly pulled the dripping weapon from his leg. He motioned to the darkness above, and his chimera swooped in for an escape. Creed lunged, but was too late. Leterum mounted Sēpein, and they flung themselves into the sky, retreating toward his Keep. Serena held her side still gasping from the strike of the Anima, and drew a deep breath.

"Creed, you must hold this line! The Mael'deua are coming! Do not let them through! When all seems lost at the gates, retreat to Durdan. I will meet you there!"

Asys hissed at the Queen, but it mattered not. Serena melded into the dark clouds above as lightning, and followed Leterum to his sanctuary in an effort to finish the fight. Creed stared at Asys as he shouted to the Bellatorum.

"MARK THE RIGHT FLANK!"

The warriors acknowledged him, war horns blew, and the Queen's army slowly formed a "V". The drums of the Mael'deua encroached as a deafening roar of doom. Creed motioned to his right to shore up the holes in their defense. He knew it was unlikely they would manage to hold either front in isolation let alone two. The ground trembled, and Bellatorum lined shoulder to shoulder. Shields and spears at the ready, they crouched to take on the Berserkers.

Then, as if a cruel ploy, a thunderclap, and a black haze left nothing else to be seen. The Mael'deua were gone. The Bellatorum looked at one another, and turned for guidance at the archers behind them. The high-ground troops had no idea what happened to the Mael'deua flanking maneuver, but now reassured that their gaze would not be split in two, the arrows were once more slung eastward, and flew to fulfill their purpose.

As the line collapsed into a more consolidated defense, the Queen's army gave up modest ground to close off any entry through the gaping hole where the gates once stood. Creed wondered how many could have possibly escaped by now to Durdan. Hopefully, the handful of Bellatorum within the Capital was enough to fly them all. Creed and Asys circled one another. Pacing as feral beasts often do. One of them would suffer this day. That much was certain.

Chapter 34: Ojin's Stand

Ojin hurriedly rearranged the tables in the Hall and Commons of Durdan's Keep. The three brothers organized their items about the forge, and the youngest made way with his set of potions and salves. Xaris was directing his men to the armory, and positioned as many guards as he could along the outer walls. They needed immediate reconnaissance of any wayward movement.

Ojin ran up the stairwell to the rotunda of the mighty Hall, stepped out onto its crescent balcony, and looked all around. He stared longest into the Ember Wood, hoping to detect nothing. The trees were still, not a leaf ruffled, and the River Ebon flowed undisturbed. To his back, he felt a cold air approaching, enough to make his neck bristle. He turned and gazed toward the Capital, witnessing the clouds swirling high above on the distant horizon. Celeste joined him as she took in the view of Durdan below.

"They've begun," she said.

"Yes. Yes, they have." Ojin's tufts of hair swayed at the whim of the tower breeze.

"The diversion likely won't last long, I'm afraid. The wounded will be arriving soon," the Princess whispered.

"Yes. They will." There was a soft pause. "Your mother will too, Celeste."

"I hope so."

Xaris walked up behind them both.

"I think this is greater than her or anyone else for that matter. I can feel the world splitting in two. Though we wish to save what we can, Mürindür is no longer what it was, even days ago."

"Growth requires change, Xaris. Mürindür will be reborn. For now, we must prepare," Ojin reminded him.

"I commanded those men over there, fighting beneath that lightning storm. For centuries, I fought beside them. We bled for the Queen. I buried the ones that could not continue, and yet here I am. The most important battle of my time, and I stand here like a scout, watching from afar. That should be my battle. I should be there with her." Xaris clenched the railing angrily.

"She isn't sustaining a fight. She's feigning one. They will be here, and we will be overrun with people in pain, soon. You will have your battle in due time, Xaris." Celeste rubbed her belly. Ojin placed a hand on her shoulder for reassurance, but Xaris was in no mood to reconcile his displacement.

"Don't you wonder how he can so easily stay behind, Celeste? 'Tending' to the sick? Hippocrates is by the Pools where it is safest. He allowed *you* to come here, but *he* isn't. Why? Why don't you ever wonder?"

"I trust in him. So, should you." She looked into his eyes, weary with concern, and ventured down into the Hall and Commons where she sought to arrange the infirmary. Ojin stared at Xaris as she left.

"We are here to protect *her*. Not to challenge the Queen's plan, *your* Queen. Celeste has enough to fret about without you attacking her husband."

"Your friend. Not mine, Ojin. Not anymore. Not after all he has done. He rests in the cover of the Cordis Loci while we prepare to

salvage what remains of our people. He should be here or there."
Xaris pointed to the Capital of Guillarne. "I don't care, but he
should be doing something more than hiding."

"He doesn't hide from anything, Xaris, for he is waging his own
battle. Soon, I will go to him, and we will tend to our own."

Ojin left Xaris on the balcony to join Celeste below, and as he
walked down the steps, he saw rows upon rows of cots organized
as a grid. Celeste was directing everyone in preparation for the
refugees.

"This will be the resting area for the most ill while those with less
need can be housed throughout the Keep. The able-bodied can stay
within the homes of the Durdan villagers." The workers nodded in
agreement as they brought baskets of bandages and tubs of water to
wash the wounds. The Keep was transforming into a series of
rudimentary hospital wards.

Ojin glanced toward the entrance of the Hall and Commons,
where the giant doors were open, and small brown leaves trickled
past the threshold. There sat Bog and Pax, seemingly mesmerized
by the sky as it morphed through a spectrum of violets and blues.
The two looked synchronized as children, watching with wonder.
Ojin smiled, as they nodded in amazement. Neither one could
speak, but their conversations seemed pithy. Pax rubbed on Bog's
fur, beneath the armor while the mammoth patted his head gently.
Bog seemed different, somehow more at peace, and less afraid than
before. Ojin wished it had never come to that. The images in the
Fields of Effugere were too much to recount, so the old hobgoblin
blinked it away, rubbed his eyes, and watched the lightning show.
He hoped Serena was giving them Hell. Behind him, Celeste paced,
rubbing her belly. Ojin walked over to assess her.

"Pains?" He asked.

"Yes. They're intense, and now they are constant and frequent," she replied.

"You should rest."

"I cannot." The Princess sighed deeply.

"Well, you should try."

Ojin watched her face, tighten with discomfort. He led her to a nearby cot, and offered some cold Mebum, and a yellow apple. As they sat, Ojin tried to distract her while reminiscing about the days when he was a husband and father.

"When Noänja and I first wed, we talked about having a large family. We wanted many children to run throughout our home and fields. I had taken a new job at the University, and we saved enough money to buy a small home just outside of town. Years went by, and we had no children. My heart ached for her, knowing she would be an excellent mother. We thought it to be a blessing we were never meant to have. One day, I came home late, and she was very ill. I went to make her some tea, and that's when she told me." Ojin chuckled. "I had never been happier to see her so sick."

"Oh! That's awful!" Celeste replied.

He smiled as he looked, and lightly touched Celeste's belly. His large furry hand easily covered the little one balled up beneath his mother's robes. He grew silent. Celeste's eyes welled with tears. Everyone knew Ojin's story.

"The boys were beautiful, one with my dark brown hair, and the other with her light blonde. Luckily, they had their mother's tail instead of this gangly mess of a thing," he laughed, "Oh, Celeste. They were so beautiful. My family was everything to me. They were my Universe."

"I know, Ojin. They were beautiful indeed." A tear rolled down her lips as she grimaced, and held her flank tightly.

"I'm sorry, Celeste. Here, take this. Drink. The Mebum will soothe the cramps. Let's lie you down, and raise your legs upon this pillow. You should be resting, and not listening to old man drivel," Ojin instructed. She lay back after a few sips, and rested her hand across his forearm.

"How did you go on, Ojin? How did you find the strength?" she asked through another contraction.

"I didn't. I wanted nothing to do with it. I had wished to die that night there on the cold road beside my family. Strength found me, however. The Ferris tribesman that took them, chased me down in the night as I stumbled confused and bloodied on the mountain pass. He stood there with his spear, and shouted his name, so that I may remember it for eternity. He shoved the spear into my chest, and for a moment, I let it pass. I *leaned* into it. I cared not. Not anymore. As my vision faded, I heard the voices of my sons, knowing they were gone. I grabbed the spear, broke it off, and I pierced the jagged end through his eye. Traelore, the chieftain who murdered my family, fell onto the road, and I fell from the mountain. I should have died that day, Celeste, but I did not. Strength found me, and I found my way home again."

The Hall and Commons shook, swaying the lamps that hung precariously from the high arches. Men's voices heralded the chaos unfolding. Celeste looked to Ojin, and the brother hobgoblins formed around them, staves at the ready. Ojin thought he heard a name.

"It couldn't be. Surely," he whispered. There was silence for a moment. Then the voice of Xaris tumbled like thunder down the steps.

"IGNIS!! IGNIS APPROACHES!! READY THE WALLS!!"

Ojin could hear Xaris shouting to the others to prepare the catapults and tower harpoons. The scouting reports, moments ago, mentioned nothing about movement in the woods. In what Ojin could gather now from the conversations milling about, an army moved on Durdan without much in the way of a rebuttal. Celeste grasped Ojin's hand as she tried to pull herself up.

"Ojin, we can't receive the wounded if we are under attack! We need to send word to divert them elsewhere!" she exclaimed.

"Then where will they go?" Ojin asked.

"To the Keep of Cordis Loci. That's the only way," she said.

"They are overrun as it is, Celeste. They can't assume any more. Besides, it isn't just who remains at the Capital. We would need to evacuate Durdan as well."

"There isn't enough time."

"Exactly. We need to take the fight to them, and then take the fight somewhere else. We need to draw them away from Durdan!" the hobgoblin explained.

"How?" she asked.

"We give them what they want," Ojin suggested.

Xaris had come down the stairs to hear the plan. He shook his head fervently.

"No! Absolutely not! We didn't come all this way, and fight through mounds of hellhounds and heathens only to throw the Princess and her child to the wolves!"

"We need *misdirection*. We need them to *think* they have the Princess, Xaris. That is all," Ojin explained.

"What do you propose, Ojin?" Celeste asked.

"I will confront him."

"You wouldn't last five seconds," Xaris scowled.

"I will hold their troops. When it is time, I will cast an illusion of Celeste running in the Ember Wood. That will buy us a reprieve, and we can get her to safety," Ojin replied.

"Just fly her now. Take her to the Keep of Cordis Loci with the Fuga."

"Xaris, she cannot fly. She is in labor. The child is coming. If we fly in the Fuga, there's a chance we could lose the child." Ojin stared through his spectacles clasping to the end of his snout. Xaris looked at Celeste, and shook his head.

"So, tricks is it? This isn't the Ashi. What if it fails? What if you fail?" the warrior asked.

"I will take him with me into the River Ebon," Ojin replied.

"Idiotic. We need to send troops out to stop them. No tricks. We get Celeste to the Cordis Loci, and we hold the titan here. He is not to gain entry to Durdan. We will meet him might for might!" Perrindor walked briskly up to him.

"Xaris, we never forced Ignis into a retreat. He bombarded our city with fire, and took what he wished. He left on his own accord. As I said before, they toyed with us. Probed our defenses. They never truly attacked us. I am certain that if he knows the Princess is here, he will leave no stone unturned until she is taken. Leterum wants that child. He has made no bones about it."

"We cannot match his might. We have to use strategy!" the master hobgoblin argued.

No one could agree on the next step, meanwhile, the Keep's walls shook once more, and Pax hurried onto Bog's back. The mammoth hugged his friend tightly. They had run out of time, and something needed to happen. Celeste leaned forward.

"Ignis will tear this city apart. We have tens of thousands of refugees from the war-torn Capital who arrived here mere days ago. They have little food. Little strength. If Ignis wants to fight, we have little choice, but to fight. We cannot run any further. *I* will not run any further. Send word to my husband. Bring him here with the remaining Bellatorum. I will meet Ignis! I will send him back to the Undüavalle myself!"

Celeste stood, and her eyes had a soft glow of willful intent. She walked toward the steps of the tower, but collapsed to the floor as another quake moved through the Hall and Commons.

"AHHHHH!"

"Celeste!" Ojin and Xaris picked her up quickly beneath her arms, and Perrindor signaled to the men to bring wooden walls to place around her for privacy. She leaned back onto the bed, and lay to her side.

"Celeste, you cannot do this. I will." Ojin looked to Xaris. "I will get us the time that we need. Find Hippocrates. Now!"

There was a flash and then another in a multitude of brilliant waves blinking about the Hall and Commons. Bellatorum were flying feverishly with wounded through the Fuga. As quickly as they arrived, the Bellatorum disappeared into the Ether once more. Ojin spoke with a nervous appearing scout. The walls trembled again, this time, the dust and mortar shook from the Hall and Commons' ceiling as fragments of concrete fell onto the patients. Ojin touched Celeste gently on the shoulder.

"Ignis is nearly to the tree line. Mael'deua and Ogres are with him. A scout estimates ten thousand. He also reports bugling of war mammoths."

"How did so many Mael'deua come through?" she wondered.

"I think we know by now. Acrom's forces are no longer contained, merely inconvenienced. We can expect them all."

"How is it possible they made it past our scouts?" Xaris asked with disgust.

"They were brought here through the Fuga. Acrom must have somehow been able to see into our lands. With this new insight and freedom, he can direct them at will." Ojin helped another Bellator lay a half-conscious man onto the bed he had slept upon only days before.

"My mother's army must return here now! They need to abandon the Capital! Someone get my husband!" Celeste yelled to the Bellatorum as they moved about. A Bellator came to her side and knelt down with his head hung heavy.

"Princess, he cannot be found. Your husband is nowhere within the Cordis Loci."

"What do you mean nowhere? I left him there tending to the Vagus. He must be there!" Celeste looked at the other Bellatorum, frustrated and worried.

"No, Princess. No, he is not. He fights at the Capital Gates as we speak." Fitz was behind the wall to her left as he helped an older woman with one leg into a nearby chair. Once she had settled, he walked around the trembling stone, and spoke with Celeste. She was livid, while laboring recumbent. Fitz raised his hands apprehensively.

"Your highness, it was his plan. His idea. He hated that his people were going to be slaughtered, and he could not allow the Luxatio to fight leaderless."

"They have a leader! My mother is with them!"

"They needed *their* leader. He fights for man. He does not fight for the Endüerduul," Fitz explained.

Ojin glanced at Xaris with a raised brow, and the warrior nodded.

"Yes, Ojin. *That* is the Hippocrates I recall."

"He is fighting a losing battle! We need him here! GET HIM HERE!" Celeste grabbed the nearby Bellator by his breastplate.

"Yes, your highness. Right away."

Havoc rained as a boulder crashed through the upper most portion of the Hall's tower. The sky peered down upon them as debris fell all around. Celeste looked to Xaris, Ojin and the hobgoblin brothers. Ojin grabbed his staff, and the jade orb churned impatiently.

"It's time. Let's go!"

He snapped his fingers, and they were gone.

When the light of the Fuga dissipated, the five of them stood atop the wall at the city gates of the bridge. They peered through the smoke and fire, and saw the giant's silhouette. His body blocked the view of the mountainside. The trees looked as shrubs barely high enough to brush his waist.

Ignis was ready. At his feet were thousands of Acrom's warriors. The smell of sulfur perforated the senses. Ojin snorted to clear his nares. The Durdan gates opened below them, and Perrindor marched forward with the army of Durdan. Bellatorum landed from the sky, throughout their ranks onto the bridge to join the effort.

"Ojin, you can't defeat that monster," Xaris commented as he pointed to Ignis.

"Perhaps, but I'm not here to defeat him. I'm here to make him lose."

The air rumbled with defiance.

"I seek the Daughter of the Dawn! The one the old Immortals call the Child of Mürindür!" Ignis exclaimed.

"She is gone, Ignis! She fights alongside her mother. I'm afraid you've chosen to occupy the wrong castle," Ojin explained.

"Lies! She is here. Bring her to me!"

"It is only man, and the Bellatorum you will face today. Make ready!" Ojin declared.

"Where is Hippocrates?" Ignis asked.

"I do not know."

"More lies from a mischievous hobgoblin! No matter! There is someone who wished to meet the man responsible for the fall of Leonicus, but he will have to settle for you."

Horns blew across the chasm of the River Ebon, and Ignis stepped aside to allow the passage of dozens of war mammoths and their captains. The lead mammoth was covered in red and white paint, and the Chieftain of the Ferris Ogre tribe held the reins. Ojin grimaced, and his palms tightened about his staff. His breath quickened, and his heart raced. The mammoths stopped short of entering the bridge, and the red and white beast trumpeted its war cry. The other mammoths answered in unison while the river loudly lapped the granite riverbanks in cadence.

Slowly at first, there was another sound. Muffled and distant until it grew in strength and proximity. A defiant trumpet of challenge, and a willful adversary looking to settle something unkind and unjust. Ojin looked below the ramparts to see Bog walking forward with Pax on his back. Bog appeared to be focused solely on the large Chieftain mammoth. Ojin shouted to him with angst.

"Bog! Get back inside! NOW!"

Bog did not look up or respond to Ojin. The Durdan warriors stepped aside, and allowed him to pass. Within moments, Bog was at the tip of the assault, and now, before the enemy, it was quite evident that the baby mammoth they had tortured for so long, had become the alpha in exile. Ojin snapped his fingers once more.

He appeared before Bog on the bridge, and turned for a moment to speak with his old friend. The thought of losing him again was unbearable, and as he caught the wayward glance from Pax, Ojin became profoundly paternalistic.

"Do not do this! Go back inside! You owe them nothing! Go inside, and be with our wounded. What they did to you, is their burden to bear, and not yours to collect."

"BRRRMMMPPPHHHHHHH!" the mammoth replied.

"BOG! Go inside!"

Bog stomped the bridge repeatedly with his leg. He wasn't backing down. A war gong was struck three times, and the Chieftain was lowered to the ground. The large, gray-bearded Ogre stepped forward, covered in scars, and pulled his half helm tightly over his brow. The right side of the helm obscured his face, and bent toward his thick neck. Only his left eye and jawline could be seen. The Chieftain spoke.

"I have hunted for you far and wide old hobgoblin of the mountain pass!"

"It appears we have found our moment, Traelore." Ojin's voice was steady and deep, but his stomach was sick with anger.

"Pity. I don't remember *your* name."

"You lie. You know me well, Chieftain. I slaughtered your people. I speared your war beasts as they charged my kin. I even managed to give you that scar. It's a *pity* you don't show it off to all your friends." Ojin walked forward, and spat on the bridge stones. The jade orb was churning faster and faster.

"Mock me, Ojin? Truly? Coward! Answer this! What hurt more? My spear, or the cries of your family?" Traelore laughed, as did the other Ogres. Ojin ground his teeth as his tusks moved side to side.

"You killed children!" Ojin slammed his staff into the bridge rock as a gavel.

CLANG!

"You killed women!"

CLANG!

"You tortured those too afraid to stand!"

CLANG!

The third strike to the bridge sent a smoky white tendril toward the Ogre troops. A cool fog settled at their feet, and they looked about not knowing what the hobgoblin had done.

"You, Traelore, are the coward! You attack the lesser, the weaker, and the timid. Look before you now. You will die this day at the feet of those you chose to torture and maim!"

The Chieftain looked at Bog.

"You stole my mammoth, hobgoblin. He should be my alpha. I will claim him when I raise your head onto a pike. That beast will learn who his true master is!"

Bog released a bellowing retort, and the sound echoed through the mountains. He inched further, swaying his trunk and broad shoulders in a menacing act of dominance. Pax stood within the bench, and leveled the crossbow at the Chieftain. He trembled in the lantern light. Ojin looked at him, and motioned him to sit down. Pax remained standing, and did not lax his aim. The Chieftain stared at him.

"Who do you have there, Ojin? A Halfling? An imp?"

"Look again. Know who will stand over your body when you fall." Ojin raised his right hand, and the war-bench lanterns grew in size and radiance. Pax was illuminated. Traelore grinned most vile.

"Yümpir? Is that you? Ha! Ojin, I pity you. You have no sons of your own, so you've stolen two of mine. I will take them back in chains, and lay this city to ruin!"

Traelore stepped back, and lowered his spear. Ojin clasped his staff, and the orb was aglow. Ojin's eyes ebbed from orange to a fervent red, stained with hatred and remorse. His tail lowered, and was still.

Traelore lunged with his spear, aiming for Ojin's heart as the Ogre army charged. Ojin struck his staff to the ground one last time, and the fog about the Ogres froze into a solid block of ice. The Ferris Ogres were trapped to their waists. This would be Ojin's fight, and his fight alone. He parried the spear, and spun to thrust his staff into the Ogre's lower back. Traelore stumbled, and looked up to face Pax. Pax placed his finger on the trigger.

"You don't have the strength boy! I should have taught you how to wield a spear instead of that coward's bow in your hands!" Pax let loose his bolts, but Traelore caught them inches from his face. He snapped them like twigs, throwing them to the ground, and laughed.

"When I'm through with this hobgoblin, I will thank you for that with my hooks!" Pax cowered below the bench rest. Bog stepped forward as Traelore turned to Ojin, but the hobgoblin motioned for Bog to stay.

"You do no good spreading false hope like a weed, Ojin, convincing my boy he is strong when he is dim-witted and weak. I will undo whatever you planted in him."

"I did nothing more than believe." Ojin looked to the small Ogre. "Worry not, Pax! This monster will never touch you again!"

"Monster? Monster? I watched my tribe driven nearly into extinction because your brother, Hippocrates, saw fit to destroy generations of rule and Ogre sovereignty! We owned the Ashi pass! We were the strongest of the tribes, and yet I did not see you stop him when he butchered my people, burned my villages, and cast us into exile! Monster? No! The monster lives with you!"

Traelore dove for Ojin once again this time twirling his spear as a saw blade, pushing Ojin towards the trapped Ogre troops. They grunted and yelled as they picked at the ice. Ojin was getting closer to an eager enemy.

"ENOUGH!" Ojin slammed his staff into the bridge, and a blast of frigid air spread outward faster than sound. Traelore slid back to a knee.

"Magic tricks? Fight me with your hands! Fight me like a warrior!"

THWACK!

"PAX! NO!" Ojin cried out.

Pax had released two bolts into the Chieftain's back, and the mighty Ogre grunted. He reached over his shoulder, and pulled them out slowly, staring at Ojin with a dark grin. Traelore spun and threw his spear to Pax's chest.

Ojin froze.

Pax looked down at the spear, and panted. His breath steamed the cold, polished metal. Bog's trunk caught the weapon, in time, with its tip pressed into Pax's tunic. The mammoth turned it to Traelore, and as the giant wooly warrior strode forward, he bashed the bridge with the weapon until nothing but splinters and a spearhead remained. Traelore angrily motioned to Bog as if to take him on as well. Bog simply stood, and stared the Chieftain down. The thick-muscled Ogre laughed as he bent down to get the spearhead. "I forged this piece from the helms of the Durdan warriors when they trespassed onto our lands. I folded it a thousand times to ensure it would remain steadfast. I have carried it into battle for centuries, and it has bathed in man's blood. Today I hold it one last time to bury it into your soul. Come to me, Ojin! Let us finish what began ages ago!"

Ojin walked slowly at first, and then progressed into a slow jog. Traelore did the same until both were sprinting toward one another. Ojin bellowed as his tusks shone in the bronze dusk of the sky. He lowered his head, and dove.

His shoulder caught Traelore on the sternum by surprise, and Ojin took him to the ground, crashing him breathless beneath the watchful eyes of the Centurion statues. Traelore scarcely raised his hands in a weakened attempt to stab Ojin, as the hobgoblin pummeled the Ogre's face with bloodied elbows and forearms. As Ojin tired, he could only hammer-fist the brute while gasping in his bloodlust stupor.

The images of his boys and his wife lying on the muddy ground pulsated through his mind. He struck once more with both fists, and Traelore went limp. A gurgling moan was all that exhaled from the Chieftain. Ojin fell over to his back, wincing from something sharp in his flank. As he reached for it, the spearhead was palpable and deep. He coughed blood onto the ground, and looked up to the sky.

With Ojin's focus broken, the ice shackles of the Ogre army shattered, and they shuffled through the fragments. They blew the war horns, and the mammoths charged. Bog started into a sprint, but Ojin knew the numbers were too great. He would have to watch his beloved friend die at the thrust of the very tusks that abandoned him as a young calf, and that imagery was excruciating.

The hobgoblin stood, weary, and cast his hands to the Ebon below. He turned toward Bog, thrust his arms forward, and tidal waves of frigid water fell over the brim of the bridge, slowing in an ice flow until every one of his allies were trapped behind him. Bog ran into the ice wall, but it was too thick, and too strong to break.

Ojin was isolated, alone to face the onslaught. Durdan's men along with Perrindor and Xaris drove their spears and axes into the barrier, but little could be done. Their voices cried out to their friend.

"Ojin! Ojin! Get out of there!" Xaris beckoned.

Ojin looked upon the faint shadows of his friends scurrying frantically behind the veil. Ignis spoke.

"Enough games, old hobgoblin. Someone grab your Chieftain! He's had a little too much war today I suspect." Ignis laughed heartily as Ojin turned to face him. Three Ogres ran toward him, gathered their Chieftain, and drug the stuporous leader toward the far side of the bridge. Ignis continued.

"I will let my army crush you, and cut your head from your body. I will melt your wall with my breath, and your men will charge through to see you, a failure, before they die. Hope will not survive the bridge tonight, but first, before the Ogres have their revenge,

510

tell me where the Child of Mürindür hides, so that I may take her to Leterum. If you do so, I will take your head cleanly myself as a gift of mercy."

Ojin grasped the spearhead, and pulled it painfully from his side. He gasped from the severity. The clang of the metal to the bridge's stone fell against a backdrop of silence. Ojin looked up, and saw hundreds of Ogres mere yards from him, waiting for the signal to take his life. It did not matter to him anymore.

"Ignis, you will never find the one you seek because she is far from here. You've lost the only thing you were sent to keep. Leterum will not be pleased with you, titan." Blood trickled down his beard.

"TELL ME WHERE THE CHILD OF MÜRINDÜR IS!!" Ignis screamed as he shook his fists. The giant grabbed his mace, and raised it high above him.

"TELL ME, OR YOU DIE!"

"I died a long, long time ago." Ojin knelt to take the blow.

The mace fell fast, and the thunder of its impact shook the dead limbs from the old trees on the far riverbank. The cracking of failed iron echoed through the Valley. Ojin could scarcely breathe as he looked up to see the Princess, standing there holding the mace's spikes with her hands.

"I AM HERE, CRETIN!" She slowly pushed the weapon away from Ojin. "I stand before you as Celeste, daughter of Serena, Child of Mürindür, and steward of life eternal in this realm. You have chosen poorly! YOU WILL DIE THIS DAY!"

Celeste's long hair hovered across her back as if it was weightless, and her eyes became white like her mother's. The wind sped across the river as she commanded lightning above. The River Ebon called out to her. The land was hers to orchestrate.

"Ha!! Child! I can crush you with the mere thought of my club!"

Ignis chuckled, and leaned forward into her. Her feet slid but a few inches as the titan leveled his might. His thick bearded chin smoldered with magma fibers, and they dripped slowly over the road stones held closely to the bridge's steel beams. His legs trembled in futility beneath his animal skin kilt. The titan was no match.

Celeste called out to the Lux above, and lightning baptized her as a waterfall. She drove its power into the mace, and the old relic exploded across the bridge. Ignis was knocked back, covering his eyes from the flailing fragments. When he looked once more, the princess stood with her hands open and low. The Ogres turned to run, and Ignis was irate.

"Go back you fools! Take her down!"

They would not.

She swept her hands skyward; the river swelled, and engulfed them all, stealing hundreds of troops from the bridge never to be seen again. The war mammoths backed away, and formed rank along the tree line.

"You will feel my vengeance on your brow, Princess!" Ignis took a deep breath, belched a stream of fire, and Celeste disappeared into the flame. Nothing more of her remained.

Chapter 35: The Battle for Durdan

Creed ducked as the chains of Asys whipped over his head, and he struck nothing but air, once more, with Üstor. Chaos whirled about them as Bellatorum, Caedere, Luxatio, and Ogres fought one another. The dirt was soft, and tripped one's timid steps as mounds of bodies began to accumulate across the landscape. The archers loosed continuous volleys of slender arrows deep into the middle ranks of Leterum, and they withered from the barrage.

Eva fought toward Creed as quickly as she could. Her sword separated more than heads from the imposing brood. Limbs scattered as she sprinted forward until a large male Caedere with two scythes approached. He was older than the others. Leathered skin, and stitched human hide for robes, he appeared to be an officer for the legion. She swung at him as the others, but was a second behind his moves. He struck fiercely into her shoulder, and with a short roll she minimized the impact, but blood was drawn. He was faster than her and stronger. This was an uneven match. Creed caught a glimpse of it all, and tried to assist, but Asys cut him off with another strike to his chest.

Eva kicked at the Caedere's hoof, and sliced for his ham, but a solid knee caught her under the chin. She fell back dazed, holding her head. Creed could not make it to her side in time. The Caedere officer swung both curved blades to deliver the final blows when a slender note of opposition caught him under the belly, and his dusty entrails slipped out of confinement. He grunted and turned quickly to his left. Varsalsae stood there wiping the juices of his flesh wound from her face.

"You disgust me, Caedere. Perhaps you should do us all a favor and enlighten yourself."

She nodded toward the flaming torches impaled across the slopes. The Caedere commander hissed and growled as Varsalsae looked to Eva.

"Child? You planning to get up, or do I have to manage everything for you?"

Eva leapt to her feet, and together their blades met each strike of the lumbering adversary. He was slowed, but not deterred. Both women took a side, and matched blow for blow his intent. It was far too difficult for both Luxatio, and Creed managed to slide closer to them while deflecting another strike from Asys. He briefly looked up, and saw a vulture with two heads hovering above. It seemed linked to the lumbering, large Caedere officer. Creed rolled for a spear while dodging another kick, and slung it far above in one movement. The spear caught the two headed bird square in the chest. It had little air to cry out, and instead fell deflated into the ground like a fallen limb. The Caedere grabbed his head, and the whispers were pronounced. Angered, he swung haphazardly through the air, driving relentlessly toward Varsalsae and Eva. Without a word, they lunged forward in synchrony, and their blades met within his thorax. In half, his severed portions fell to the damp earth, and the movement of his hands ceased.

Creed continued to deflect the barrage from Asys. Just as each warrior would gain some ground, the other countered, and kept the tide of battle ever swaying. Asys struck to his back when she forced him to turn and address her kick, but even as she felt her hooks slow upon impact, Creed managed to twist ever so slightly resulting in nothing more than a glancing blow. She motioned for distraction, but as her fellow Caedere charged him, Luxatio and Bellatorum alike protected him from them all.

The bulk of the onslaught, however, was pressing further forward toward the walls. There were ravenous creatures as far as Creed could see. His ranks were thinning, and now would be the perfect time to escape, but how? Serena was gone. The plans had changed yet again. If the Bellatorum were to leave, the collapse would be accelerated. He couldn't think for more than a second with the constant attacks from Asys let alone coordinate a retreat. Their momentum was lost despite their efforts. His only option was to disengage, and offer himself up to buy the others time. He looked over and saw Varsalsae.

"Varsalsae! Varsalsae!" She turned quickly, but had to react to another Caedere strike.

"What is it?"

"We're losing!"

"Yes! That much I can see for myself!" she exclaimed.

"Then we must regroup! Get everyone back!"

Asys flipped over Creed's head, and stood between them in an effort to charge Varsalsae. Desperate to save his friend, Creed reached out to grasp her cloak, and pull Asys away from Varsalsae. He felt a sheering pain in his side. He caught the arm of Asys in time, but had given up his position. The Anima turned into him mere inches from his face, and grimaced. Asys pulled her chains, and he felt the pain once more. The monster had hooked him

515

squarely between the bound seams of his armor with jagged spikes. Creed fought to take a breath as he stared at her undulating blindfold. He wasn't afraid. He was angry.

"Jessie, hear me! I will kill you! If you're in there, somewhere, you will pay! YOU WILL DIE!"

Asys grunted, whispering. Creed grasped one of the chains, tore it from his side, and wrapped the links around his forearm. Varsalsae ran toward him as everything slowed in his vision.

Unexpectedly, in a torrent of indignation, a flash of white crashed before him, and as Creed reached out to it, the head turned and roared. Morsu grimaced. He loomed over Asys. She yanked hard on the chains, and Creed yelled, but with one swipe, Morsu ended the torment. The broken chains fell to the feet of the Anima as Morsu's spikes were bristled, and he displayed his full set of teeth as a sign of strength. The dusty air was sucked slightly into his gaping mouth, and then his roar. Mighty. Terrifying. It was his declaration of dominance, and for a moment, the fighting ceased. Morsu was rarely seen outside the Steppes, but he was here now. One by one, his pride landed beside him.

From the walls high above, the archers could see a dozen lions encircle the Anima. They steadied their aim onto her. If she were to step back a few more feet, they could safely launch, but as she turned so did Morsu, his back to Creed at all times, never one to take his eyes from Asys. Creed slowly recovered, and stood. The distant fighting continued, but for those near the pride, there was an uneasy cessation. Asys waited for the opportunity to attack. There was no means of retreat. There was another flash. The Bellator Celeste sent, had arrived.

"Hippocrates, you are needed in Durdan! The Princess is ill, and the child is coming! Ignis approaches, and he brings with him a great army! I can take you there, but we must go now!" Creed held his side and looked about. Celeste was in labor, trapped, and under attack. The diversion was working, but they needed more time. Nothing seemed complete. The lines were fading, and the Capital was mere minutes from falling. He could not leave his Luxatio again. Not here. Not like this.

"I cannot leave. My people will die here on these walls. Have we rescued any of the wounded?"

"Thousands have been moved to Durdan, but we did not expect an attack so soon. We cannot move the others to the Cordis Loci. Many of us are fatigued from the Fuga, and our Queen is missing." The Bellator exclaimed.

"She is with Leterum," Creed replied. Asys moved quickly, and Morsu growled, crouching low. His lions did the same. Any one of them could easily rip the Anima Capere in two, but not without giving of themselves in return. One solid touch from her would guarantee death. They waited for Morsu's command. Varsalsae spoke up.

"We will hold this wall, or we will die trying. The Child of Mürindür is most important! Go!"

"There has to be a better way!" Creed said as the Bellator looked around.

"Do not move, Hippocrates." He was gone in an instant.

Suddenly, so were the others. Bellatorum appeared and then disappeared with dozens of Luxatio and Guardsmen at a time. Then there was a crash. Creed turned, and looked behind him. The three hobgoblin brothers stood facing the south with their backs to Creed and Morsu.

"That was a bit rough," Sylvestrae pointedly proclaimed. The three of them turned abruptly, and looked at the debacle before them. Morsu didn't dare take his eyes off Asys, but Creed smiled slowly. The hobgoblins readied their staves.

"Can you three get all of us out of here?" Creed asked. Bellatorum continued to exit with more soldiers, but they needed a faster means, a more effective means. The brothers looked, and discussed with themselves.

"We were sent to get you. We're not sure we can get the others." A spear flew by as a reminder a war still raged about them.

"No more time. I need you to try," Creed exclaimed.

"We will try," affirmed, Sylvestrae.

Asys made a swing at a nearby Bellator, but as he disappeared with a wounded Guardsman, Morsu swatted her head bluntly, knocking the Anima into the dirt. He crouched as if to finish her. "Morsu!" Creed exclaimed. The lion growled. "Can you take us to Durdan?" He motioned to Varsalsae and Eva. Morsu roared. Creed assumed it was a 'yes'. He looked at the brothers.

"Prepare yourselves, and bring the others to Durdan. We leave now! Ready!" Sylvestrae combined with his brothers a ball of light within the middle of them. He looked to Creed, and said assuredly, "We will get everyone home." Creed turned to the Luxatio.

"Everyone comes home! Spread the word! Fall back! FALL BACK!"

Morsu walked backwards with his pride, providing the bottleneck for everyone to make a hasty retreat within the walls. The Caedere and Ogres continued to charge, but fell beneath the hail of arrows launched from above. Asys was unfazed and walked slowly toward the lion. When the last of the ground troops made it safely, Creed ran toward Morsu, and jumped on his back. They stood before the gates as Creed looked down upon the Anima. He pointed the blue flame of Üstor at her head.

"We will finish this, and you will fall," Asys hissed as she was kept at bay by the large pride.

"Continue the volleys. We all go home! Go, Morsu! GO!" Creed commanded.

The lion roared, and leapt with such force the ground shifted, unsettling Asys as she attempted to strike. She ran for the gateway, and struck something unseen. The brothers had managed to construct a blockade over the gap to buy them time. It wouldn't take long, however, before the horde would tear it down. Asys struck the invisible shield with her swords repeatedly, but to no avail.

In the air, Creed looked to his sides and saw Varsalsae and Eva safely aboard their lionesses. He glanced down one last time, and noted the battlefield was clearing. Soon, the archers disappeared as well, and in one massive emission of blue light, the crowds around the brothers vanished. The Capital had been successfully evacuated. The constant barrage of the Caedere, lead to a breach in the hobgoblins' barrier, however, and as they flew quickly westward, Creed saw the flood of destruction pour forth. The army of the dead tore the remnants of civility to the ground, and as they destroyed everything in their wake, small fires took hold throughout the city. The Capital was lost, and Asys vanished in a black mist.

The lions sped toward Durdan as the oldest city of the Highlands faded away behind them. Creed looked below to see the Road of Borainnos, and the farming villages lain to waste along the way. He saw no sign of an army, and no evidence of refugees. The road had been cleared, and whoever was left, likely hid from the watchful eyes above. As they came toward the City of Durdan, Creed's focus sharpened. He saw a giant, blasting fire upon an unseen target.

When the titan took a breath, the attempted cremation ceased, and from within a silken gown, untouched, his wife unfurled. She held her hands high, and a blue light emitted from her hands, blinding the giant, as ice formed like cobwebs across his sockets. He was as sightless as a Caedere.

"Morsu! Get me down to her! Now!"

Morsu roared, and flew straight to Celeste. They dove, and once he was merely a few feet above the bridge, Creed leapt, and fell into a roll. He looked down to his right to see Ojin attempting to stand, and to his left, Celeste with eyes aglow. He looked up to see the titan, shielding his face, and screaming in anger.

"You she-devil! I will break your damn bones!"

"Ignis," Celeste said, "You're going home!"

"ENOUGH, WOMAN! EYES OR NO, YOU DIE!"

Ignis stumbled forward, and smashed his fists into the nearby Centurion statues. The lanterns fell, and the fiery oil slipped and splashed about the bridge. The stone crumbled, and rolled dangerously close to them all. Creed went to Celeste, but she stopped him and flew quickly as a glimmer of light into the mouth of Ignis as the titan inhaled to spew fire once more. Creed dove and covered Ojin instead, who by now had fallen to his back in pain.

"Ojin! Ojin! Look at me!" The old hobgoblin opened his eyes. His glasses had been shattered, so he squinted slowly. Rocks tumbled around them.

"I'm right here. You don't have to yell. I have big ears," Ojin smirked, and Creed was relieved.

"Let's get you out of here." Creed turned to see the wall of ice.

"How do we get out?"

"We don't. If that wall falls, Ignis and his army will take the souls of Durdan."

"Can you fly?"

"No. I don't think so. I'm too weak. Too tired."

"Then we find another way," Creed replied.

Ignis screamed.

"AHHHHH! GET OUT! GET OUT!"

The titan gripped his skull, and shook his body in agony. The same blue light from Celeste's hands spilled from his nose and corners of his mouth. He clamped his throat, and tried to scream, but a rasp and rattle was all that emerged. Celeste tore through his throat, and fell to her knees. Ignis could only gargle frost and magma from the traumatic hole where his voice box once bellowed.

"We needn't hear from him any longer." Celeste walked toward Ojin. Creed looked up, and Ignis stumbled, reaching blindly for a hand rest as the titan squeezed his neck.

"Ignis is incapacitated. It is time for the people of Durdan to stand for Mürindür." She raised her hands to the wall.

"Celeste, no! Leave it. Acrom isn't finished!" Ojin protested.

"Ojin, Bog and Pax will be fine. I won't let any harm come to them. Now for the wall... AHHHHHHHH!" She fell to her hands and knees.

Morsu and the lionesses landed in front of them as the titan hemorrhaged lava, splattering the surrounding rock. Varsalsae and Eva dismounted in an attempt to stand Ojin up, and place him on a lioness, but he wouldn't move. He merely shook his head. Creed placed his hands on Celeste's shoulders, and could see the pain in her face.

"Ojin, tear this wall down! We need to evacuate you two!" Creed shouted as Celeste breathed deeply, but Ojin was barely able to lift his arm. Xaris, Perrindor, and Bog pounded on the ice wall, but nothing changed. They were isolated. Morsu roared, and Creed turned to him.

"Do not leave her side. Get them to the wall!" Morsu gently clasped his mouth about Celeste's arm, and pulled her away to safety.

The Luxatio assisted Ojin, and the remainder of the pride stood guard behind Creed. He turned toward the titan. The bridge rocked as the giant came forward. Ignis held his hand firmly over his throat, and uttered a gravelly command.

"KILL...THEM.... ALL!" The Ogres, Mael'deua, and war mammoths formed on the ridge behind Ignis.

"Hippocrates?" the titan hissed.

"Ignis."

"Welcome... home. It appears it is time for us to die." Ignis reached for him with his molten rock hands, but missed and broke the stone bridge railing.

"We all have our time," Creed replied.

He struck the spear edge of Üstor into the bridge. Something changed, for the metal on stone rang out loudly as a bell through the valley. A small defect formed in a crooked line toward the titan. "Hippocrates, get back!" Varsalsae yelled, but he stood ready. "AHHHHHHH!" Celeste grabbed her belly, and Ojin moved toward her to hold her hand.

Ignis took a step, and Creed saw the necessity of it all. He crouched, and inhaled deeply. After all the lives, and all the loss, he knew his purpose. He gripped Üstor, and ran full force toward Ignis. His chest heaved, and he felt the flame cover him as light from the dawn's sun. He wasn't afraid. He wasn't in pain. Creed was at peace.

"CREED! NOOOOOO!" Celeste cried as he ran alone toward the inevitable.

He didn't look back, and hoped it would be quick. As Ignis took another large step toward the middle of the bridge, Creed leapt with all his might. He arched his back, and positioned Üstor's blade to the heavens with the spear to the mortar of the construct. As Ignis's foot hit mere inches from his, Creed drove Üstor through the bridge stone, and the rock broke through to its core.

The Apicem Bridge buckled, and Ignis appeared blind and afraid. He had committed too much of his weight toward the castle, and with the gap widened beneath him, the titan fell to his side, head first, to a ravenous River Ebon below. The bridge yawed and snapped from the tension of the iron beams, and Creed felt his feet hover for a moment. His weightlessness was freeing as the horizon flipped on his descent. He watched Ignis fall hard into the frigid waters, and as his beard and fiery breath became immersed in Mürindür's justice, the titan sank as obsidian into the river's depths. Nothing but his fingertips remained, and even then, the river consumed those as well. Creed closed his eyes, and prepared for the cold waters of the Ebon.

Chapter 36: The Gift

H is body lurched suddenly, and Creed looked up to the fallen bridge, realizing the white crested rapids were no longer fast approaching. La-mala had caught him mid-air, and together they rose to the city's side of the bridge. As they ascended, Creed saw nothing more but the reflective undulating riverbanks. La-mala set him down gently beside his wife. He looked to her, and rubbed the lion's neck.

"Thank you, La-mala. Celeste?" The Princess lay down on her side when she saw Creed had survived.

"I can barely move. The pain is rhythmic in my back. He's coming, and there is nothing I can do to stop him."

"He isn't ready," Creed replied.

"I'm having this baby."

"Let's get you inside the gates. Someone! Get this goddamn wall down!" Celeste tried to stand, but fell.

"No! No! He's almost here. I can't! Oh Creed, please. Please don't let him die! We all need him so much. I need him so much."

"SOMEONE GET THIS DAMN WALL DOWN!" Creed felt movement, and looked to see Ojin grabbing his leg.

"I can do this. Stand me."

Creed scooped him up, and held Ojin facing the wall. The hobgoblin made two fists and then crossed them three times in front of his chest. The wall cracked vertically through the middle and split the sides inches apart. The ice fell in small pieces as it melted into puddles, draining slowly to either side of the bridge. Through the wall's defect the archers and Durdan's soldiers could finally see the bridge, and communicated as much to Xaris and Perrindor. A long doting trunk sniffed, searching for Ojin's face, and the hobgoblin reassured the mammoth.

"I'm fine old friend. Just fine. I need rest." Ojin patted his trunk, and Creed lowered him to the ground once more. Ojin stared forward.

"Creed, those Ogres are looking for a way to launch another attack. The war mammoths are waiting, and the Mael'deua are lighting their torches. We need everyone back inside the city walls. No one can pass here."

Ojin coughed twice harshly to clear his lungs. Celeste screamed again. Her robes were bloodied, and she was in labor. Creed knelt beside her, and removed his helm. As he placed his hand on her forehead, he could feel her shake.

"OHHH! This hurts, my love. Something is wrong. I can feel it. Our son is sick." She looked at him with tears.

"Let me look. Morsu, circle us."

Morsu commanded the lionesses to form a circle as Varsalsae and Eva stood watch. Celeste had another, longer contraction. Creed knelt down and pulled her robes above her knees. He could see the dark hair of their son between her thighs. He set Üstor down beside him, and looked at his hands. They were covered in Ogre and Caedere blood. He washed his hands in the melted ice water, and noticed Celeste was shivering in the cold. He had never seen the elements affect her before.

"I need clothes. Robes. Something!" he called out. Varsalsae and Eva removed their robes and threw them to Creed. He rolled one of the robes, and placed it beneath Celeste's head. The other he placed beneath her hips. Ojin slowly removed his, and handed it to Creed. "Use this for the child, my friend." Creed could see Ojin's eyes were sunken, and his breathing was erratic.

"Thank you, Ojin. Rest. I will get all of you out of here." Creed looked to the sky, praying for Serena to arrive, but she was nowhere to be found. The lightning in the distance continued to ignite the darkness.

"I wish we had something warm for our son. It's so damn cold," Creed said as he looked around. There was a commotion of rustling behind the ice wall. The murmurs rose, and then Xaris spoke.

"Hippocrates, we have blankets! We have food and water. Anything you need." Creed could see the shadows moving behind the ice as others continued to pick away.

"How about a basin?"

"Hold on!" Creed waited as Celeste grimaced through another wave of pressure. Morsu stood at her head, and licked her gently. She rubbed his leg.

"Morsu, I love you. Thank you, my kind friend." La-mala lay beside Morsu with her head lowered in concern. Celeste reached over to her paw, and squeezed it firmly.

"Hippocrates, we found a basin!" Xaris shouted.

Bog's trunk could now scarcely reach over the wall, but it was enough to lower the hammered copper bowl, and Creed stood to take it. He went to the ice wall, and collected the trickles of water. The bowl was frigid. He closed his eyes, and slowly a subtle flame emerged from his fingertips. It carried over to his hands, and the water warmed until a fine steam wafted over the brim in the cold night air. He knelt once more and set the basin aside. Celeste was turning red as she tried to muffle the pain.

"Baby, breathe. You have to breathe." She let it out, and exhaled slowly. Creed examined her as their son began to clear his face. His flame dissipated quickly. He cupped the infant gently as Ojin observed.

"One more time, beautiful. You're amazing. You're doing great. One more push, and our son will be here."

Celeste nodded, took a breath, and bore down once more. The child's head cleared, and his neck passed through, wrapped twice by the cord. Creed grasped him, unwound the cord, and pulled slightly to clear the shoulders. He delivered their son into the world of Mürindür. Creed smiled, and Celeste's breathing slowed. She was sweaty but relieved.

"How is he? Does he have your eyes?" she asked. Creed didn't respond.

"What's wrong? What's wrong? Creed, what is happening?" He checked twice, but their son wasn't breathing, and his pulse was faint. The infant's color in the flickering flames of nearby lanterns appeared to be dusky. It wasn't good.

"He isn't breathing! He... he isn't breathing!"

Creed placed his mouth over his son's lips and nostrils, and began to blow air into his lungs. The taste was salty and desperate. The pulse seemed to slow, so Creed went into resuscitation mode. He placed his fingers on the infant's chest, and began compressions. Holding the little one in his left arm, cradled in concern, his hand repeatedly and rapidly pressed the little ribs. His throat was tight, and through his tears he couldn't see a change.

528

"He's dying! Celeste he's dying! I can't... I can't do anything!" He breathed twice more into the tiny lungs. "I don't have anything with me. I need medicines! I need an IV!" Ojin placed his hand on Creed's knee.

"We don't need medicine, my friend. We need Mürindür."

"Get the Queen! Can you get Serena here, Ojin?" Creed begged.

"I can't sense her, and I am very weak. It will only be us I'm afraid."

"She followed Leterum into his keep." Varsalsae replied. Ojin shook his head.

Celeste was pale and weeping as Creed's face was covered in tears. "My mother isn't coming," Celeste replied. "If she went after Leterum, it was with the intent of not coming back. We cannot hope for her to help. We can no longer hope at all."

She cried a bit more as everyone remained quiet. The ice wall permitted a limited view, but the word quickly spread through the ranks that the young infant was dying. Slowly, hundreds then thousands of people knelt to pray quietly. Creed muttered under his breath as he kept count of respirations and compressions. He would rather die than lose his son. His chest was beginning to ache.

"Give him to me," Celeste said. Creed looked up at her, and shook his head.

"No! No! Just give me some time! I need more time! I need something. A tool. Maybe Üstor..."

"My love, give him to me." She reached for their child.

Creed sobbed and reluctantly obliged, placing their son on her chest. When Celeste held him for the first time, she brought the infantile promise close to her face, and kissed his limp head. She smelt him gently, and held his little body close to her. She whispered slowly and repeatedly. The clouds above churned, and lightning struck aberrantly about the woods. Trees burst into flame as the lightning escalated, and a forest fire was birthed into the Ember Wood. The Ogres backed away from the far cliffside. As the umbilical cord began to glow with each word Celeste spoke, the warm, perfusing light, pulsated gently from her into the baby's belly.

"What are you doing, Celeste?" Creed asked. He glanced at Ojin. "What is she doing?" He could see tears streaming down the hobgoblin's face. Morsu moaned quietly. The lion struggled to get closer to his Princess.

"Someone tell me what the fuck is going on!" Creed grabbed Ojin by the collar.

"She is gifting him her immortality, Creed. *Largior Immortalitatis* is a spell, a gift only she can give. The heavens are watching."

"Wait. What? Celeste, no!"

"My love, it is mine to give. Mürindür will perish if he dies, and I do not wish to live to see that day," she replied faintly.

"What does this mean? No! No! *You* dying is not an option! Stop it! STOP! Ojin, make her stop!"

"It has already begun. Her essence, what makes her whole, will now be within your son."

"Is she dying? Are you dying? Celeste, will you die? I don't! I CAN'T!"

Everything had changed. Creed looked at his wife, and ailing child. It was too much. He turned away for but a second, and saw the army across the chasm. The demons paced searching for the means to cross. The dynamic sky appeared as slate through the clouds' vitriol. The sun was set.

Creed regained his composure, and knelt beside her once more. He simply kissed her forehead slowly as he looked in her eyes, stroking her hair. She stopped whispering for a moment to look into his.

"I love you, Creed, Hippocrates of the old Age. One man in a cosmos of uncertainty, and yet I had never felt more certain in my life."

"Please don't do this." He shook his head in disbelief. He could see the blood pooling around her hips as she poured herself into their child.

"We have loved one another longer than any love known, and yet, oddly enough, I find it more endearing now. This must be the taste of a mortal love, a sweetness found only in the inevitability of an end."

"I don't want you to go, Celeste. Not now. Not after all of this. Please just stop. We'll find a way…"

"I don't wish to go, but he must live."

Creed cried and laid his hand on their son's back.

"Love him, Creed. Love him as only a father can." She looked down upon her breast to see that their son was moving ever so slightly.

"I can't do this without you. I just can't."

"You will. I am with you, here, now, and always."

Creed bent over to touch his forehead to her shoulder as his cheek pressed into the soft arm of their son. His chest heaved with sorrow, feeling broken, and helpless. No procedures to be done. No orders to give. All he could do was love her, and hold them both. He draped his arm over them, and prayed. He would gladly give of himself. He would barter with anyone who would listen. He screamed into the darkness.

"LETERUM! LETERUM! TAKE ME! FACE ME!"

Thunder rumbled far from it all.

The others held their heads low, solemnly. Forlorn faces pressed close to the broken ice wall as nothing responded but the wind. It swirled, and leaves rustled beside Creed. He didn't listen for he was too far-gone in his grief.

There was a cackle, and then a flutter. Suddenly, a shutter, and a lancinating pain into his back. His armor had absorbed the impact, but left him bruised and with splinted-breath. Celeste watched in horror, helpless and exposed as Creed turned his head, seeing the Anima before him. The lions roared and formed a wall. Morsu stood over Celeste and the infant. He crouched low to protect them both.

THWACK.

SHWOOSH.

THUNK.

Arrows struck and ricocheted about them, some were close to the edge of the broken bridge, but the Ogre archers across the chasm walked their arrows in until they found their mark. Caedere formed columns hastily in the background with their Mael'deua brethren. An arrow struck Celeste in her calf.

"AHHHHH!"

Creed turned to her, and his heart raced as his body surged with anger. The air exploded about him. Üstor scorched the stone, feeding off its master, as it lay scalding, forcing the lions, Varsalsae, and Eva to pull Ojin and Celeste closer to the ice wall. Men clamored for the Durdan archers to respond, and for those with line of sight, they loosed their counter into the chest of the aggressors. The Ogres launched more volleys in kind. Morsu spread his wings, and sheltered Celeste from the hail of arrows. His roar intensified as the barbs struck him repeatedly, painfully, but he dare not move lest she perish. Celeste could only grab his fur for comfort as she continued to whisper to her child.

Creed, however, became something else. Someone else. His eyes changed color as he witnessed his body morph in the ice reflection. He unclasped his breastplate, allowing it to crash to the rock. His body was aflame as ethereal wings tore from his back fulfilling a purpose long meant to be. He pivoted and walked through the hail of arrows as they disintegrated in his fire. Creed sought the blood of the Anima.

Asys looked upon Creed, and whispered rapidly. He roared as an alpha, and the valley trembled. Üstor flew to his extended and eager hand, and he struck Asys repeatedly as she blocked and dodged what she could. He was stuporous in his rage, and through his foreign eyes he saw the black aura of the Anima before him. He heard voices from the distant Caedere and Mael'deua shouting in a language he finally could comprehend.

"The angel is alive! Kill him! Acrom commands it!" they shouted.
Celeste spoke softly behind him.

"His skin is pink! I can feel his heart beat on my chest, Creed! Creed?" Celeste looked to the side of Morsu's leg, and saw Creed for what he had become. "Ojin! What has happened?"

"I don't know. He's ethereal. I've never seen anything like it." Ojin tried with difficulty to stand. Ernest arms behind him pulled him up through the broken wall, though the ice obstructed further aid. Ojin spoke to Creed.

"Creed! Hippocrates! Listen to me," but Creed only continued to attack Asys.

"Creed your child is alive! Breathe, my friend. Let this go whatever it is that consumes you! It will kill you! COME BACK!"

Ojin stood speechless. His friend was nowhere to be found in the creature of fire and fury. Behind him, the infant's breathing was erratic, but as Celeste continued her incantations, it became rhythmic.

"Please little one, for mommy. Open your eyes. We haven't much time." She looked to Ojin, and touched his arm gently. The time for solemn introspection would have to wait. Celeste spoke bluntly and urgently.

"Ojin, we need to get the baby off this bridge! I need you to take him!"

"I can't. I can barely fly."

"You must find a way. You must care for him. Take him far away. No one must know he is alive. I need all of you to go now!"

"What of you?" Ojin asked.

"I will not make it, but my son must."

"We will go with you, Ojin," Varsalsae said with Eva.

"I cannot do it alone. Perhaps the lions can help us. Morsu. Morsu? You don't look so good my friend. Can you fly?" Morsu weakly raised his wings as La-mala licked the blood from his back.

"I don't think he can make it, Varsalsae."

There was a flash before them, and the three hobgoblin brothers had arrived safely, but late.

"I told you we were lost!" Sylvestrae commented.

"Shut it!" Coliquis replied.

"Enough! Look around. Help us!" Ojin admonished them.
Sylvestrae, Maeylincus, and Coliquis stared at Creed.

"What is he?"

"Never mind that. Quickly! We need the Fuga. Take us back to Cordis Loci!"

Arrows continued to land about them as Celeste spoke gently to her child, lovingly as only a short time would allow. Oerbuel glowed brightly, and its rays sped throughout the sky toward Redemptio.

"I will love you always my little one. Your heart is strong, but you must go. Mürindür needs you. Learn and live. I will be there for you in the stars. I will be there for you in your touch, and in the marvel with which you look upon this world. Now live, my little prayer. Live." She kissed her infant on the lips softly, and held him one last time as her tears rolled gently over the baby's chest. Celeste had become pale, and her hands were trembling from weakness. The baby began to stir.

Creed would push Asys to the edge, and back away. He toyed with her. He wanted to see her suffer. He tore a rib from her side, and as a dagger thrust it into her flank repeatedly. He struck the Anima across the face, and punched through her gut until his fist broke rock. She struck to his brow, and as she missed, she threw an elbow into his neck. Creed spun and returned the favor. Again, and again. He bludgeoned her over and over until the dust spilled from her flesh. She thrust toward his chest with a blade, and he grabbed it fully with his fist, pulling her into him. He wanted to see the fear in her spirit as she died. Asys spoke in the dark tongue of Caedere.

"*This. Is. Your. Time. Join. Leterum.*" Creed looked at the beast kneeling before him. Shadows swirled about her face. Eyes flickered beneath her socket cloth. Creed screamed deeply, otherworldly.

"You have struck the heart of my brothers! You steal the souls of the Endüerduul! I will castigate you in front of your beasts! You will cry out for mercy, but none shall be granted! I will take your head to Acrom, and you will watch me rip his spine from his carcass! The days of Leterum and Acrom are over! Elyptos has returned!"

The storms above sensed an unbecoming. The not too-distant moons surged in radiance as the wind howled across the broken bridge, harsh and unkind. Celeste screamed to Ojin over the tumult. "Ojin, now is the time! You must go. All of you! Please, take care of him. Love him as your own. He is the future of our people."

"I will until the end of my days. I swear to you, Celeste." Ojin kneeled. Morsu was held by two of the brothers and La-mala while Ojin leaned on Sylvestrae.

"If you can, I ask that you take care of Hippocrates too. He will need everything you have to avoid his own eternal damnation." Celeste gripped Ojin's fur tightly.

"I will do my best," the hobgoblin replied.

"Then you must go."

Celeste hugged her infant desperately for the last time, and handed him to Ojin. The hobgoblin looked to Creed as he saw him grasp Asys by the throat. The rage was escalating, and the torrid flash of Üstor was decimating the ice wall. It was time.

"Hold on! Sylvestrae, now!" Ojin commanded. Varsalsae, Eva, the brothers, and the lions along with Morsu were all close to one another. The brothers began the Fuga.

Creed crushed Asys by the throat with his knee on her belly. She hissed and writhed, but he had obtained dominance, and proceeded to torture her with his animosity. The cruelty brought him pleasure. He wished to hurl her into the very earth she had helped to tear apart. He would make her pay for every suffering soul, ripping her heart out as she had done so many times before. He stuck his hand into her chest, and grasped her withered soul.

Celeste looked to her infant, and at that final moment, the baby took a deep breath and cried. The sound was a revival of all that mankind had found respite within. Their son had found his voice, and the series of shrill cries broke through Creed's intoxication. It startled him to a degree, and he staggered while Asys was sluggish from the onslaught. Creed was panting, but despite the heat of battle, and with his fist still in the Anima's chest, he turned briefly to look upon their son with his own eyes. He saw Ojin holding the crying infant while their friends embraced one another. Ojin's eyes met his, and in a flash, they were gone. Everyone had escaped except Celeste. Creed was conflicted, but he finally had the demon within his means. His eyes glowed once more, and he looked back toward Asys.

The air was a torrent of stifling retribution. Celeste crawled onto her sore belly, and pulled herself across the stone as the new fallen rain, washed her blood aside. She stood and cried out for him.
"CREED!"
He turned to look at her, confused with torment.
"*My love, the heart never forgets*," she whispered.

Creed blinked slowly, and he felt his body ease. He coughed repeatedly, and as he lost his ethereal form, he saw Celeste with his

mortal eyes once more. He let go of Asys, and stumbled toward his
bride. His voice became his own.

"Celeste? What's happening to me? Are you okay? Are we okay?"

"We will always be," she replied.

She extended her hands to him. Creed looked for the others, but
they were alone. He walked toward Celeste for an embrace, and
noticed the soft brilliant glow of Oerbuel. He exhaled, exhausted,
but relieved she was still alive. A smile emerged slowly across his
face, but he then saw Celeste's eyes widen with fear.

Asys stood behind him, and drew a sword from her back. Creed
leaned in for his wife, but Celeste stepped aside, and made a fist.
Her cerulean energy encompassed her one last time as thunder
crashed about them. She stood ablaze, and charged Asys. Creed
turned to see the Anima lunge for his chest, but Celeste met her
mid-stride, and grasped her by the throat and arm. Lightning struck
them both, and the two fell from the bridge's ruins. Creed screamed
in a delusional state of shock. The stones crumbled before him as
he sprinted toward the end. Lunging into the night air, he witnessed
his wife and the Anima fade into the Ebon below.

Chapter 37: The Fall

Creed fell into the acrid wash, suffocated by the roiled river water. He was slung into the sharp juncture of an elbow from the sunken Ignis, and spun quickly into the granite riverbank. He fought, flailing, with his arms and legs until his head broke the water's surface. He felt a presence pulling him toward the depths, but with each breath he stole, he fought harder to find an edge to harness. In the dark, he could scarcely see his direction, let alone Celeste, though he wished for nothing more. The river took a quick bend, and Creed fell over the falls into the froth below. His knee hit a boulder briskly, and as he winced from the impact, he thought he saw a glimmer of green light. He swam toward it, but nothing was to be found. The river slowed briefly, and he grasped a felled tree long enough to breathe. The rain was unruly, and although the veil of precipitate obscured his vision, he held onto hope nearly as desperately as he did the rotten limbs.

"CELESTE! CELESTE! ANSWER ME!" No response.

The night became quieter as he looked about. He pulled himself from the water, and as the pain of what was now becoming more of a reality, settled in his bones, his rage dissolved into tears. The mud against his face was indifferent and frigid. He dug into the earth, and bear-crawled up the slope until he reached some dry grass upon which he rolled over to his back and sobbed. Everything had been for nothing.

"CELESTE! PLEASE! CELESTE!"

He yelled so hard he could feel his face engorged with angst as he sat up nauseous with arms raised to the moons. Creed shook his head. Everyone was gone. He couldn't see the city let alone the broken bridge that took everything. The Lion of the Luxatio wished to die. He longed for it. This was too much for his broken soul. Minutes passed, and despite his desire, nothing of the world answered the beggar's plea.

Creed pulled himself up, and attempted to get his bearings. The wind whistled, and before he could respond, his back was hit suddenly as if by a planet. He was hurled toward the river once again as his chest collapsed in a vice. He opened his eyes despite the pain, and looked into the hapless smoke.

Leterum was inches from his face with hands clinched about his heart, and as Creed's back broke through a grove of elder trees, Leterum let him go long enough to shear and bleed throughout the timber. Creed lost his breath, but attempted to stand from his side as he saw Leterum near. He reached for Üstor, but it was lost, somewhere on the distant bridge. He threw his arm up to block the incoming blow, but Leterum beat him with the back of his gauntlet. Creed's blood painted the dry tree bark.

"WHAT HAVE YOU DONE? YOU WORM! MORTAL! FOOL! WHERE IS SHE?"

Leterum drove his silver greaves into Creed's stomach. Even if he had breath to answer, Creed could not. What could Leterum possibly want?

"ANSWER ME, HIPPOCRATES! WHERE IS SHE? WHERE IS MY DAUGHTER?" Creed was gurgling blood as Leterum dispersed his life essence to the soil as salt.

Where is your daughter? Aren't you Death?

"I HEARD THAT MAGGOT!" Leterum struck him again with the back of his hand.

"Ackkkk, gurrrrghhh, maahhhhhffff." Creed was muted in the pain.

"Tell me where she…" As Leterum's eyes became red beneath the smoke, a ball of light exploded into the ground behind him. It was so sudden that he lost his footing on Creed, allowing a gasp of air.

"LETERUM! LET! HIM! GO!" Serena flew toward him restitute.

"HE KILLED HER, SERENA! HE BROKE HER! He infested her with that parasite, and stole her from me! FROM ME!" His voice bellowed deeply in a demonic rhythm.

"We do not know what happened, Leterum, but if you take his soul now, we never will! Let him go!"

"Go to Hell!"

"Gladly!" She summoned her trident, and drove it into Leterum's stomach.

"AWWWRGGHH!"

Leterum grabbed the trident and pulled her close, striking her across the face, and Serena stumbled toward the water. He pulled the trident spikes from his body, and cast the weapon down below in a ravine. He harnessed Creed by the throat, and flew into the air straight toward the moon of the Endüerduul. Creed looked down as the fires and glow of Durdan faded into dots of light. The clouds bowed before Leterum, and they came to a height that made the coastline of Mürindür evident. Leterum looked into his eyes.

"I have *been*, longer than Time! I have molded the events that lead to your creation and demise. I have moved heavens and earths, and here before you I cast a promise! YOU WILL SUFFER! YOU WILL KNOW PAIN!"

"I don't know what you want. I don't know…"

"You will ROT just shy of the Nether, and I will hold you there until the sun rises no more! NOW TELL ME, WHERE IS MY DAUGHTER, HEATHEN?" Creed hung there in his grasp where the air was thin and barren. He was weak, and continued to bleed. His ribs snapped when he inhaled, and his back stiffened.

"Asys. Asys is your daughter?" Creed asked.

"NO! FOOL! YOU KNOW NOTHING!"

"Asys…Asys is… Jessie is… Jessie is Asys," Creed mumbled.

"NOT YOUR WHORE!" Leterum struck him again. "MY DAUGHTER! WHERE IS THE CHILD OF MÜRINDÜR? WHERE IS MY CELESTE?"

Creed was fading quickly, but he heard enough to understand. He reeled from the tunnel vision, and stared into Leterum's face. "Celeste? No. No! NO!" Creed struggled to break free, but Leterum held him steadfast. His eyes filled with tears, but he refused to shed them before Death. Instead, Creed hastened what he felt to be a foregone conclusion.

His wings ripped through his back, and he gained leverage in his ethereal form. Flame arose, and slowly crawled across his flesh. Leterum looked at him within that second, and began to laugh. "The arrogance!" he proclaimed.

Creed struck at the face of his tormentor with a fiery fist, the flame illuminated what hid within the hood, and the smoke helm wafted to reveal a hollowed socket of bone upon which Creed's knuckles landed squarely. The bone shattered. Leterum was shocked enough to lose his grip, and Creed flew high above so quickly, that the falcon had lost his prey. Leterum reared back his shoulders and arms, and cried out. He searched angrily, and found the moonlight cut by movement. As he leapt forward, Serena struck from below, and sent the dark angel into a spin. He righted himself as a fiery sickle grew from his hand.

Creed hovered above in the clouds, looking for the means to strike the very beast that broke their world. His mind raced. *How could Leterum be her father?*

Leterum spoke.

"You first, Serena, and then the vermin. I cannot fathom why you defend the very thing that took her from us!"

"My anger will be dealt swift and sure, but know that he did not take her! You condemned her the day you turned your back on the Endüerduul. You are the executioner of that which you claim to love!"

"Lies! Heresy! I fought to right the wrongs of the rites passed forcibly upon us! I fought to win back our home!"

"You burned that to the ground ages ago, Leterum. When you fall this night, the world will breathe again. You are loathed, not loved, in this or any other realm."

"Then I will create a new realm!"

"Only Life can create, Lord Leterum. All you can do is revel in decay!"

She thrust hail and wind into his face, as lightning struck its way throughout the sky. In the flurry, Leterum dove, and pulled the warm winds of the Transitio into the atmosphere as a sandstorm. The grains stung Serena's eyes as he cast the simoom far, as to blot the moons. Her ice clouds dissipated, and Leterum swung his sickle toward the Queen's neck. Her hands caught the blade, and she stared at the end of the harvest weapon. She appeared weaker to Creed, and he knew he had to respond. Leterum drove the weapon toward her heart, and had he thrust once more, it would have plowed through.

Creed flanked him, and fell furiously with his shoulders into the ribs of Leterum, diverting him aside only to be caught in his grasp yet again. Leterum flashed black flame into Serena's eyes, and accelerated toward the earth. Creed couldn't break free, and he scarcely felt the impact as he imploded, unconscious. When he woke in a crater, Leterum stood over Creed with his sickle rooted beside him in the rock.

"You have caused me pause and consternation for the last time, Hippocrates. I will settle this debt. I see something in you that I hadn't seen before, but now I know why."

Leterum threw his gauntlets to the ground, and pressed his boot to Creed's neck, turning his head forcibly with his toe. "I want to squeeze the life from you with my bare hands. It must be difficult to fail twice in battle, Elyptos! You hide in children now, and for what purpose? Did *you* kill my daughter? Did all those years bound within Acrom's walls finally twist the mind you meagerly possessed? I will find her, but for you the end is the same! There is no miraculous sacrifice here to make, brother. It is merely another soul that has long teetered upon my table. It is over. Luxatio. Elyptos. This chimera of the Endüerduul is no more!"

He choked Creed with both hands, and the man known as Hippocrates faded beneath the night sky. The world grew darker in spite of the streams of fire rolling toward them across the treetops from the Pools of Cordis Loci. The brilliance of the Endüerduul illuminated Creed's wings as Leterum struggled to rip them from his back. The same shimmering forces of the Pools flowed through

Creed's veins, and his voice changed into something deeper, foreboding and ancient.

"Leterum! Savor the bitterness, *brother*, and know that on this day, Elyptos has marked your end!"

Creed's hands grabbed Leterum's exposed forearms, and burned Endüerduulian inscriptions into the dark angel's flesh. Leterum bellowed in anger and angst, but though he tried, he could not free himself. As the waft of fire in the boughs above them dissipated, Creed's grip loosened, and Leterum reached for his scythe. Serena beat him to the weapon, and pulled it away.

Leterum looked into her eyes, smelt the air, and smiled as if he found something. His sickle disappeared in her hands, and he was gone in a cloud of black smoke. Serena stood there alone beside a broken man.

Creed opened his eyes to see trees swaying and seemingly reaching for him. His strength was ebbing, and although he could feel himself moving, he closed his eyes to see his wife once more. As hard as he tried, he couldn't find her face.

Serena had carried him into the Ember Wood, laid him across the ground, and motioned her fingers so that a blanket of warm moss would be against his back. She leaned over and blew gently in his face. He looked at her.

"Hippocrates, it is time."

"Time?" He was confused.

"It is time to go home. What has been done cannot be undone. We may yet see one another again."

"Celeste! I can't leave. I can't leave Celeste!" He tried to sit up.

"She is gone, my son. Mürindür has taken her home."

"No. No. She fell. She simply fell!" Serena shed tears as she held his head.

"Where did she fall?" she asked.

"Beneath the bridge into the Ebon. She fell, and looked at me. She was alive. She…"

"I promise you on my existence. I will look for her until the end of my days. I will search every inch and crevasse this realm provides, but she is not here, not now. You have a purpose still left within you, Hippocrates. I do not know what that may be, but as broken as I am in this moment, I know well enough to send you home."

"This *is* my home," Creed replied.

"Take the light with you, Hippocrates. The world in which you entered has all but run out." She placed her hand on his chest, and pressed firmly. It burned and sent a convulsive shock through him. He felt it again, and again, and again…

§

"CLEAR!"

The nurses moved away, Flannigan charged the defibrillator to 200 joules, and shocked his friend once more. They had been at it for half an hour, and the last two weeks had been touch and go. His heart had stopped once more. Everyone knew this would likely be the last attempt to revive him. Creed hadn't shown any brain activity for the last few days. Flannigan delivered the shock. *THHHUUUMMMMMPPP.*

Creed's chest lurched in the bed. They continued CPR, and the bed creaked from the chest compressions. The room was quiet. At two minutes, someone whispered.

"Pulse check."

They held their efforts, and felt for a pulse. The monitor was silent. The caregivers held their breath. The monitor's green screen faintly displayed a straight and then fine wavy line. Slowly at first, and then with each passing second a blip of energy emerged, erratic, but stubbornly progressive. Creed's pulse was eventually strong enough in Flannigan's fingertips, and the surgeon's face relaxed. The cardiac monitor showed a good pattern, and as it quickened, they continued to bag his lungs forcibly with oxygen. "How many more times are we going to do this?" a nurse asked Flannigan.

"As many times as it takes, and then once more," he replied.

The room slowly emptied, and the respiratory therapist began reconnecting his breathing tube to a ventilator. As she adjusted the tubing, her wrist was grabbed. Shocked, she dropped the syringe in her hand. Creed's grasp was fierce.

"Dr. Flannigan! Dr. Flannigan!"

Flannigan and the ICU nurses ran back into the room. They were shocked. Creed looked at the respiratory therapist, and pushed her hands away. He was disoriented, and angry. He wanted to get back and find his wife, but his hands were tied down, and he felt trapped. Flashes of Mürindür mixed with his surroundings, and the nurses appeared to be Ogres reaching out to him. He began sweating, and pulled against the cloth restraints on the bed rails. The right-sided restraint snapped as the bed rail crashed off its hinges. Although it was ill advised, Creed reached for the breathing tube, and began to pull.

"Creed! Creed! Listen to me! You need it to breathe!"

Flannigan rushed to grab his hands to prevent him from removing it, but despite his efforts, Creed fought him, and the tube was slung to the ground covered in sputum and blood. As he stared at Flannigan, he saw an aura about the surgeon that was perplexing, so he hurriedly reached for the left restraint. When he leaned quickly across the bed, the same searing pain he felt when Asys stabbed him in the flank came rushing back and crippled him. He looked over to see tubes of fluid being sucked from his chest into the plastic canisters on the floor.

Although confused, Creed knew he didn't need the tubes. He didn't need the lines. He needed to be back in Mürindür. He looked about his room as the personnel ran to get more sedation medications, and as he attempted to speak, bloody sputum filled his mouth. Creed started to hyperventilate as images of Leterum hung heavily in the air. He stared at the wall, and within a red lacquered oak frame, the Hippocratic oath was written in calligraphy with the background of a winged caduceus and serpents. Slowly, the words came into focus as he stared at them, and prayed for a way back home. His nurse walked over to one of his IV's, and began to push a white liquid. Creed spoke with a raspy tone.

"No. No more. Let me be." She looked to Flannigan, and he motioned to her to hold the meds. He pulled a chair up beside his patient, and marveled.

"Creed. Can you hear me?"

"Yes. I'm tired. Not stupid." It forced a chuckle from Flannigan. Creed glanced at him, and the aura was gone.

"You are one hard son-of-a-bitch, man. You've been to Hell and back."

"Almost."

Flannigan reached over, and untied the second restraint.

"How do you feel?" the surgeon asked.

"Like someone cut me open, and left the hood up."

"Yeah, something like that. We cracked your chest. That patient almost killed you right there in the ER. The officer shot him four times, and killed him instantly. We managed to get you to the OR, and fix everything we could. You died twice on the OR table."

"I was motivated."

"He hit your lungs, a pulmonary artery, and nicked your heart. You've been here for a couple of weeks, and lost a lot of blood. Wasn't sure you'd wake up." Creed looked slowly to his left and right. He could see the monitors and hear the obtrusive beeping of the alarms. His mind swirled in all that had happened, and his throat was on fire.

"Can I have a drink?"

"Water? How about we just do some ice chips," Flannigan replied.

"How about bourbon?"

"Oh? *Now* you want to drink?"

"I've earned it."

"When we get you on your feet again, I'll be the first to buy you one."

"Deal," Creed replied. Flannigan became somber.

"Creed, I never got to tell you how sorry I was we lost Jessie that night. I really, we really did everything we could. The damage was too extensive."

"It's not your fault. It was hers, and hers alone. Don't put that on yourself."

"I'm sorry for never sitting down with you afterward. It wasn't what you deserved. Those other traumas came in, and I got called to the OR for another code, and things just spun out of control afterward. I came out to the waiting room to talk with you, but you were gone. I needed to tell you something else about that night."

"Like what?"

"She… she was pregnant too. She was about 18 weeks. In all the chaos, I couldn't bring myself to share that with you. Not after seeing you suffer like that. I thought I would disclose it later, but you fell off the radar, stopped going out, and work never seemed to be the right place. I'm sorry. It was going to be a little boy. I just…" Flannigan's voice cracked. The surgeon's tears dotted his scrubs, and he hurriedly wiped them away with his rough hands.

"I'm sorry."

"Don't be."

"I'm usually tougher than this," Flannigan explained.

"We all are at one point or another. After everything we've learned in medicine, we were never taught one very important lesson."

"What's that?"

"How to grieve for our patients," Creed replied.

Creed merely stared at the cross on the wall. His mind wandered for a moment. He wasn't shocked at the news, although the thought hung heavy. Knowing Jessie had become the Anima, it came together in his mind. He choked up, thinking about Celeste, and their little boy. He wanted so desperately to go back to her. Tears rolled over his hospital gown.

"Did you know?" Flannigan asked. Creed blinked a few times.

"I think I did. Something inside, something I've realized very recently made it more likely. She never said anything to me though."

"I'm sorry," Flannigan replied.

"She did it to both of them. People never seem to realize how selfish they are when they do it. They never think about the ones left behind. You would think she would have at least fought harder knowing she had someone else depending on her."

"Maybe she did. Maybe she fought as hard as she could. Jessie was a beautiful person. She was a gentle soul, Creed. She was very kind."

"She was very sick." He looked out the window. "Thank you for telling me. Not sure what it means anymore after everything, but it means something I suppose."

"Well, I wasn't going to let a third soul get away from me." Flannigan patted his forearm.

"That sounds familiar." Creed looked down, and the memory of Leterum's forearms burning, flashed before him. He grimaced as his head ached.

"Do you need anything for pain?"

"Shit man, I just want to wake up." He groaned as he tried to sit up. It was a terrible idea. The room spun like a top.

"Stop. Just lay there. We can work on getting you to the side of the bed tomorrow. Maybe even the chair. I'm shocked you managed to rip the tube out, and you broke the freaking bed! You haven't moved in two weeks. You should be too weak to lift a spoon," Flannigan teased.

"Kudos to the Physical Therapists," Creed smirked.

"Yeah. I guess so. Everyone kept coming up here to see you. Your whole group has been in some constant vigil day and night. I had to kick them out just so we could do procedures and studies. Damn, man. You're lucky to be alive!" Creed looked at him.

"I think you and everyone else had something to do with it. Luck is for the ill-prepared." Flannigan just smiled. All he could do was nod.

The next day was a marathon of visitors and well-wishers. They did get him to the side of the bed, and with a little charm, Creed managed to convince the nurses to set him up in a chair. Everyone came to visit him including his chairman. He was assured that his job was waiting for him as soon as he was ready. Creed wasn't sure he wanted the job let alone wanted to stay, but he kept that to himself. His nurses were phenomenal, and helped him get cleaned up. One of them trimmed his beard. He remembered her from the night Jessie died. She had been kind, and brought him coffee when all he could do was walk in circles.

Creed felt fortunate to be with his work family, but for every second he was alone in his room, his heart and mind raced back to Mürindür. *It* was too real to be gone. *Celeste* was too real to be gone. He couldn't trust anyone with what he had been through, but it was as real as the caduceus before him. Creed stared at it for hours, and would give anything to see her once more, to hold her, and smell the honeysuckle and lavender of her hair. As he thought of Durdan and the fallen bridge, he wondered if Leterum had told the truth, and then he questioned why Death of all things lost what mattered most.

After another week in the ICU, the tubes were pulled from his chest, and he could walk with minimal assistance. The trauma team took him from the ICU to the hospital floor where the healthier patients recuperated, and he was able to get a little more sleep. He continued his therapy, and one morning after a grueling session of resistant bands, a nurse's aide asked him how he was feeling. At first, he thought she meant his body, and the sore muscles. He chuckled.

"Well, it wouldn't hurt if you had a little WD-40."

Creed made the mistake of looking into her eyes. They were similar to Celeste's, and sound faded from his senses. It came from far away, but the meteoric rush of loss, crushed him, and he cried inconsolably. The aide sat him down quickly in a wheelchair, and wheeled him into his room beside the window. He felt embarrassed for losing control, and wouldn't look at her when she brought the charge nurse in to assess him. That afternoon sitting beside him was Mrs. Ceres, his counselor.

"Hello, Creed." He was still processing how quickly she got there.

"Hello." he replied.

"Dr. Rainard told me what happened to you the day you were admitted. I'm sorry. After everything you've been through, and then to be shot. You seem remarkably resilient."

"It happens. Life sucks sometimes, and we have to eat it." Creed cleared his throat.

"Life is also light, optimistic to those willing to look," she assured him.

"I've been looking. Every stone I turn over is filled with insects and venom."

"Who are the stones?" Ceres asked. He smirked. The analysis had begun.

"Milestones, every one of them. I achieve something, I accomplish something, and then it is gone. Taken. Broken. Burned to the ground. I'm done." He fumbled with the frayed thread of his hospital gown seam.

"Done? Done with Life? Done with living?" He looked her in the eye to ensure there was no confusion.

"I'm done. Period. Whatever that means to you." She nodded slowly, and jotted some notes down in her folder.

"You would think you could just remember that. No need to write it down," said Creed.

"I understand you are in a great deal of pain, and under some medications for that. I am just writing my concerns. In fact, we're all concerned."

"Well at least you're concerned. That makes one of us." He turned his head to look at the green live oak tree outside his window. Everything else was brown and wrapped in winter gray.

"I think you would be surprised how many people are concerned."

"I don't think I care," he replied.

"That's the problem, Creed. You've detached yourself from everyone and everything. That is a very lonely place to find yourself. You will end up on an island, and without bridges none of us can save you."

"Funny you mention bridges. They don't always provide the means to salvation that you suggest they would. You know a great deal about many things, but you don't understand what I am going through, or how I feel."

"You survived a horrific event following a horrific series of years and losses. You are not alone. Thousands suffer just like you."

"Just like me? Really? Did they lose a wife and child? Did they see the undead come to claim what meant everything? Did they stare Death in the eye, and challenge him? Did they see a company of men and women that trusted in something significant only to fall and succumb to an impossible nightmare? Did they lose an entire world?"

"Creed, I don't understand. Are these metaphors, or did you dream these events."

"These events happened." Creed rubbed his thighs. He felt like the room was getting warmer.

"You mentioned wife and child. Were you and Jessie married?"

"No."

"Were you married before?"

"No."

"Help me out here. Whom are you referring to?" Mrs. Ceres leaned toward him. Creed hesitated. His palms were sweating.

"It doesn't matter. The world is gone. There is nothing more I can do."

"Some people feel as if their world is ending, Creed."

"No, an entire world. A realm. A civilization of people that are likely obliterated because Death wanted it so." Ceres frowned with concern.

"What kind of world do you feel is lost, Creed?"

"You won't believe me."

"It isn't important whether or not I believe you, but whether or not you understand why we need to work through this. When we dream, our minds try to reconcile thoughts, experiences, or pain. It works through these issues via our subconscious plane, and we often manifest this process through things we believe have meaning. You likely had very vivid dreams while you recovered from your injury. Dreams are just dreams, and nothing more than reflections of our perception of reality."

"It was not a dream. It was not a series of hallucinations. It was real. As real as you are to me right now, the people, the beings, the anguish, the hope. All of it exists, even now. We sit here, and they are fighting for their lives. I can't even get back to them."

"Do you want to go back to them?"

"Yes."

"How does something like that happen?"

"When I die."

"Do you want to die?"

"I am not afraid of it."

Mrs. Ceres spoke with Creed for hours. He outlined the events of Mürindür and its people. He told her about Ojin, Xaris, Serena, Pax, Bog, and although it was painful, and his words were tearful, he spoke lovingly about Celeste. He detailed the complexities of the Luxatio oath, and how he had returned to Mürindür repeatedly his entire existence. He explained how he could never go to the Endüerduul, and how he would never see all those that meant so much to him in all of his lives. Ceres took notes to the extent that her binder was nearly full. She thanked him for his time, and left his room. Once she closed the door, she looked at him from the window. She shook her head.

"How is he doing?" Flannigan asked as he and Rainard stood there. It was the end of the day, and they had met on the elevator to visit Creed. Little did they know that their patient, had opened the door slightly to listen.

"Not good. I suspected some delirium, but this is significant. He is suffering from major depression with psychotic manifestations. He is suicidal, and needs to be on precautions. I can't tell yet if it's his medications, or the time he was in the ICU, but he seems delusional to a degree," Ceres replied.

"He died multiple times. We had him on five drips of medications for weeks. I'm sure if he remembers anything, it was through a fog of sedation and anesthetic."

"Perhaps, Dr. Flannigan. What medications is he on now?" she asked.

"Antibiotics and maintenance fluids, but he has been refusing his pain meds for the last three days."

"Curious. Is he getting out of the room? Going outside?"

"He began walking the day after he extubated himself. I've never seen anything like it," Flannigan noted.

"Why is he refusing pain medications?" she asked.

"He says he doesn't need them anymore, and he wants to go home."

"I've been taking care of his home, and planned on him living with me for a while. Mrs. Ceres, how long do you think it will be before he can be home alone?" Rainard wondered.

"I would recommend he go to an inpatient psychiatric facility once he is released from here."

"A psych hospital? Really?" Flannigan was dismayed.

"He needs therapy. He was already struggling with his issues with Jessie. Then he gets shot, and dies. I would say he has a lot of work to do."

"Just doesn't seem fair," Flannigan replied.

"No, but if we want what is best for him, this is the way to go," she insisted.

"I will ask case management to start looking into placement. My plan was to discharge him after the weekend. Maybe Monday evening or so."

"Well, that should be enough time for them to get things lined out I suppose." Ceres rearranged her notes.

"He is strong. Stronger than anyone else I've ever met. He will get through the counseling, and the therapy, and I look forward to helping him get back on his feet. He's a good physician, Mrs. Ceres. He's done a great deal of good for humanity. Now it's time we pay him back," Rainard insisted.

"Dr. Rainard, I hope he does."

She turned toward the clerk's desk to ask for copies of her notations, and Creed's chart to make her recommendations. Creed closed the door to his room, slowly. Rainard and Flannigan talked in the corner for a few minutes. As they walked toward the desk to speak with Ceres once more, they heard a crash. It sounded like broken glass.

Flannigan ran to the door, and found it barricaded. Creed had taken the chair in the room, and bolstered it under the handle. Flannigan could see the exterior window had been shattered, and the window blinds were slapping the frame from the wind. He didn't see Creed.

"Get this open! Get it open now! Call plant operations! We need to get the door off the hinges!"

Flannigan kept pounding the door with his shoulder. Rainard did the same. Finally, they forced the chair's legs to scuttle across the waxed hospital floor. The door begrudgingly surrendered, and as it flew inward, the doctors could see IV tubing, fluid and blood on the floor beside the bed. The monitor had been disconnected, and the medications wasted away in a puddle as the IV pumps continued to bump and whir. The men ran to the window, and felt the bite of the icy air on their faces. As Flannigan stuck his head out the window, he could see from the third floor view an awning below. Bloody footprints trailed across the awning toward the reflection pool of the hospital's courtyard. Creed was gone.

Chapter 38: The Escape

Creed reached under the window eve, and pulled out the key to his back-patio door. He entered his home shivering, and turned off the alarm. Rubbing his body repeatedly, he walked through the kitchen, down the hall past Jessie's room, and into his bedroom. He checked on his fish assuming they would be dead, but miraculously they were still swimming about in the incandescent light. Someone had apparently been feeding them, and even added some decorations to the otherwise bleak underwater landscape.

He shuffled through the doorway looking into his bathroom mirror, and realized how thick his beard had become. He looked ten years older. There was gray on his chin that he hadn't seen before. Creed stared at the mint green Mercy scrubs, appearing to be the same doctor that had helped so many lives weeks before, but he knew he wasn't. Not anymore. The eyes were recognizable, but little else. The shower curtains had been pulled closed in his absence, which he hated, and with the quick nervous jerk of the plastic, he anticipated an attack. The scorn of the mildew plaster tub was all that he received. His shaking hands turned the knobs slowly, and hot water poured from the shower head above. The steam was welcoming. He took off the dusty scrubs that he had stashed away beneath his hospital bed days before, and frantically scrubbed the oily residue of stagnant sweat, blood, and sleeplessness into the drain. He likely had little time.

Creed knew what Ceres was thinking, but felt it necessary to tell someone here what happened. He couldn't help but feel that the boundaries between the worlds would likely fade soon, and he felt a sense of guilt if he didn't share that with someone. A warning if you will, no matter how insane it may sound to the uninitiated. He wondered why now, of all times, he remembered everything. There was no amnesia about his past lives, his moments in Mürindür, or the pain he still felt about it all. He closed his eyes as he rinsed the soap from his scalp, and thousands of images pummeled his consciousness like hail. Creed bent over in the shower with grief, but attempted to regain his composure beneath the scalding water. He felt paralyzed with the suffocating losses.

An angry voice entered his mind, the same one that got him out of the hospital bed each day, and forced a willingness to heal. He picked at the stitch in his arm, pulled his PICC line, and washed the skin as it slowly leaked venous blood over his feet. He threw the line in the trash, rinsed, and turned the shower off. Toweling himself, he found a bandage to wrap his arm, and went to his closet. He emerged, layered in a t-shirt and flannel button down, with some old blue jeans, and his waterproof Keen hiking boots. His backpack from his last hike in Utah had all the essentials, and he went to the nightstand to get his gun. When he pulled the drawer open, it was still there, his new Colt stainless .45 caliber 1911 pistol. He pushed the release button on the side of the grip, and caught the magazine. It had eight rounds, and once he seated it back in place, he racked the slide, and put a bullet in the chamber. He reached for the second magazine when an image from WWII flashed before him.

He was standing on the beach at the frontline of his platoon. Bullets whizzed past him kicking sand and gravel into the air. He was to advance with his men, but when he turned, he saw everyone dead. He was the last one standing. He looked in his hand, and saw the military issued 1911. The Japanese were charging, and although they didn't see him yet, it wouldn't be long before they caught him. He remembered in the briefings how tortuous the Japanese command was, and the techniques they used on POWs to gain intelligence. He looked at his pistol, and had to make a decision. It was best if it were on his terms. He dropped the thumb safety, and felt his finger slip from the gritty slide to the trigger guard. It needed to be quick. The Japanese soldiers came sprinting over the ridge, and they had the faces of Caedere. They hissed in a foreign tongue, and their hooves dug deeply into the sand. His palms were sweating as he raised the pistol. Then something broke the hallucination of war.

As he stared at the weapon, he heard a faint sound, subtle but familiar. It seemed so out of place on that beach. It continued, and as it resonated across the ocean water, Creed blinked, and found himself in his bedroom again. The Japanese Caedere were gone. He looked at the gun in hand, and saw the safety was off. He exhaled briskly, and set the weapon down with the safety locked back into the slide. The hammer was cocked and waited for a decision. The sound was there again and again, louder and more recognizable. He ventured out of his bedroom, and walked down the hall. The sound was coming from Jessie's room.

It was an infant's cry, and as he approached with the floors creaking, the infant wailed more hurriedly in anticipation. Creed shook his head, and grabbed his ears, hoping to occlude the noxious cries. He knew he was hallucinating. He began to fear what others assumed to be happening in the hospital. His mind was broken.

Creed turned to walk back to his bedroom to gather his things, but the crying was persistent. He covered his ears again and screamed.

"Enough! Enough! Goddamnit! I'm not crazy! SHUT UP! SHUT UP!"

The crying was at an exceedingly high pitch. The further he walked away, the louder it became. Then, a familiar voice.

"Maybe if you opened the door, my friend, the crying would stop."

Ojin?

Creed ran to the door, and swung it open. Sure enough, there stood the elder hobgoblin with Creed's infant in his arms. The child was red faced and his little arms wavered ever so slightly above the fur. They appeared to be real. Creed walked slowly over to them, and touched Ojin. He was shocked when the fur was coarse and moved through his fingers. The hobgoblin had to duck to avoid the ceiling fan.

"Yes. We're real."

Creed cried, and fell into the hobgoblin. He wept upon his chest, and embraced him, never knowing if he'd hear that voice again.

"Now, now, friend. I can't hold both of you. Look at me." Creed looked up.

"How are you, Ojin? I thought you were going to die."

"That makes two of us," Ojin chuckled. "Nothing the good people of Mürindür couldn't help me with. Serena took good care of me, and your son, naturally."

"Please tell me. Did they find Celeste? Did they find her…" Ojin stopped him from asking.

"We've seen no sign of her. It doesn't make any reasonable sense. Serena has searched endlessly, but we haven't given up, and neither should you." The infant cried, and stared at Creed.

"This is your son, the embodiment of your love for Celeste. Take him." Ojin offered up the baby.

Creed looked at him through wet eyes, and took the infant into his hands. The child stopped crying. Little fingers reached and grabbed his dark beard, and pulled a little too hard. Creed jerked his head back, and the infant was left with a fistful of facial hair. "That's a good grip."

"Well he is pretty strong despite not eating. He hasn't in days. This is the first time he stopped crying in nearly a week. I think he has been searching for his parents."

"How are you here?" Creed asked.

"I said we weren't *allowed* to come here, I never said it wasn't possible," Ojin replied.

"What is his name?"

"He doesn't have one. That is something reserved for his father." Ojin patted Creed's shoulder. "You look horrible."

"I feel horrible. The images are all here. Every single one. I remember it all."

"The boundaries are blurred. It will likely get worse. The worlds will no longer have discernable limits, but first this child needs a name. It is very important."

"Ok. I will have to think about it."

"This child is strong, and I suspect a bit of a rebel much like someone else I know. Take that into consideration." Creed brought his son close to his chest and rocked him gently.

The infant nuzzled his face into Creed's neck as they walked out into the hallway, with Ojin following close behind. The bedroom door was open, and Creed saw the gun on the stand. He looked at Ojin, but his friend was tired, and wished to sit on the couch. When he did so, the couch bent in the middle. The creaks gave notice for some casualty springs as the hobgoblin laid his head back. Creed stared at the gun, and thought how close it had been. How little control he had in the moment. He looked into his son's blue eyes, and placed his forehead onto his.

"I will name him James Colton Huntly."

"That's an interesting name."

"I think it fits, and Colton was my name once," referencing the Japanese beach. "Well, when I was a young GI in another life not too long ago, I suppose."

"And James?"

"James. James was my father's name in this life."

"James Colton Huntly it is then."

"What do we do from here?"

"You need to survive. You need to hide your child here on Earth, away from Leterum. *Leterum* will be relentless."

"How are the others?" Creed asked.

"Bog and Pax are at the Pools, and Xaris has taken a band of Luxatio and Bellatorum to fortify Durdan. It will take some time before it is what it once was."

"What about the hobgoblin brothers?"

"Our homeland. They took Morsu there to heal, and before you ask, Morsu is alive and well. He had as much of a trial as you did. I visited only once because I felt it too dangerous to draw Leterum to the island. When your son stopped eating, I knew where we needed to go."

Creed swayed with his son in his arms, and reached gently to stroke the fine hair on his scalp.

"I miss her, Ojin. My heart is just… I feel dead inside. I can't believe she's gone. She was right there, and I was walking toward her, and then it all ended. I did all that I could, Ojin, everything within my power."

"Your power *is* something different, something dangerous, Creed. Do not unleash that here. It will create a conduit for the Undüavalle, and you will bring Leterum and Acrom upon the constructs of this world. You must find a way to temper that within you, while we find a way to rebuild," Ojin explained.

"Where is Serena?"

"She continues to search the world for Celeste. She can do little else. We have met once or twice, but she is consumed with her loss. Leterum continues to reign with a closed fist and vengeful mind. The Queen's people need her, but she is mourning."

"Did she not want my son?" Creed asked.

"She knew as well as I that it would merely make them both targets. Keeping them separate for now is the only way."

"How do I explain this to people? Suddenly I have a baby?"

"You have to leave. I'm sorry, but there is no other way. You will have to find a new life, and settle there," Ojin explained.

"Everything is here for me. I've been here for years. Where will I go?" Creed paced slowly in circles.

"You are Hippocrates. You have traveled the world. You can go wherever you please," Ojin assured him.

"How will we survive? I won't have a job or money to buy things."

"Take this." Ojin handed him a leather pouch of gold coins. They had the American eagle on them.

"What do I do with this? I can't walk into a grocery store and get baby formula with these things. Where did you get them?"

"We stopped by a military installation."

"You stole these?"

"Man has many artificial means of purchasing. These are just symbols. You give them worth, but in Mürindür they mean very little."

"When was the last time you were here on Earth for more than a few minutes?" Creed asked.

"A handful of centuries after the Cataclysm."

"Yeah. Things are a little different now. Did they get you on camera?"

"I don't suspect so. Remember," he snapped his fingers and enacted the Penumbra. "Hobgoblins have observed humans for millennia." The doorbell rang.

"Shit!" Creed exclaimed.

"We need to go!" Ojin jumped up from the couch, and grabbed his staff. They would have to leap in the Fuga.

"Can you do the Fuga here?"

"Maybe. Grab your things. Hurry. We haven't much time."

Whoever was at the door, they began to pound loudly. Creed rushed to the bedroom, and looked at the gun. He laid the baby on the bed, and racked the slide to remove the bullet. He placed it back in the magazine, and stowed the pistol in his backpack. Once he pulled the shoulder straps over, he grabbed James, and went to the living room. He reached for Ojin's cloak.

"Hang on to your baby. We won't be going far," the hobgoblin explained.

In a flash, they were gone.

Flannigan and Rainard kicked the door down. They went through the whole house. Flannigan found the bloodied bandages and PICC line in the shower.

"Well he was definitely here. There is still steam on the bathroom mirror."

"We'll find him. I just hope it's before he hurts himself." They looked at one another as Rainard called the police. Creed's face would soon be all over the news.

§

They landed on the hilltop overlooking a dense evergreen forest in the mountains similar to the world they left behind. The air was crisp and clean. Ojin looked down at his two wards. He felt that, for now, they would be safe.

"This is a place that I saw on our way to you. It is small, and a good region to raise a son. It reminds me of the Highlands." Ojin motioned below the ridge with his large arms.

"We need a home, Ojin. I need a job."

"Then find those things. Whatever you do, you two must survive. No matter what."

"When will we see you again?" Creed asked.

"I don't know, my friend. I must go back, and work on our defenses. Now that I don't have the child, I can move about more freely. Leterum is pushing his forces to the east, and the remaining regions of Mürindür are in danger."

"I just don't know where to begin."

"Begin with a name. Your name."

Ojin stepped back, and the Fuga blinded them momentarily. James Colton Huntly cried for a moment as Creed consoled him.

"I know. I miss him already, too." The infant fussed a bit more.

"I bet you're hungry. We'll get a plan together tonight. I have some money in my backpack. Got my wallet and I.D. Guess I'll need to ditch that while we're at it. Begin with a name... a name. Hmmm. I need a new one. What do you think, bud? Hmmm? Should I go with Hippocrates?" James sneezed in his face. "Ha. Good enough. Nope. That won't work. I'll sleep on it." The wind howled around them, and the air moved the infant's hair like duckling feathers. Creed wrapped him up tighter within the linens Ojin brought.

"We need to get going, but where? Ojin was a little too optimistic about my navigation abilities."

They stood there as small cars drove, weaving around the foothills below, on a dark highway a few hundred yards away. He looked to either horizon hesitantly when he noticed a faint glimmer in the stars. It flickered briefly, but was hard to miss. He smiled, teared up, and hugged his son.

"I think I found the way."

They traveled down the dim gravel trail, toward the blacktop road. Creed took a deep breath and sighed, knowing that hope likely lie within the beams of a faint green beacon in the distance, as a promise yawned, nestled in his arms.

Glossary

Acrom- The first fallen angel. He has been likened to many symbols of doom and destruction, but most of all he feeds off of fear and hatred. He has been imprisoned twice before since the Dawn of Time.

Ashi- A great mountain of the Highlands. It has many secrets and connections to other realms. Once a great symbol of prosperity and pride, it has become a dark labyrinth of restless spirits and trolls drunken with greed.

Bellatorum- Queen Serena's loyal warriors. They have existed since the stars were born across the galaxies. Bellatorum souls are derived from the initial fire bursts once a star comes into its own.

Caedere (Latin "to kill or cut down")- The Children of Leterum. They arrive as Vagus in the Dunes of Transitio, and are transformed into Death's version of angels. They have ashen wings which prevent full flight, and are forever bound to vultures and Leterum for sight and sense.

Capital of Guillarne- Capital of Mürindür and located in the heart of the Highlands. Located strategically to facilitate peace throughout the land.

Celeste- The Princess of Mürindür. She is the daughter of Queen Serena, wife of Creed, and mother to their unborn son. She was born shortly before the origin of man.

Durdan- The City of Durdan is a fortress city across the River Ebon, and holds the western front of the Highlands secure. The city is populated with a hearty people, proud to live on the edge, and survive the onslaught of the Ember Wood.

Ejiciam- The spear used to wound and drive Acrom from the Endüerduul for eternity. It is powerful and feared, lost somewhere in the realm.

Elyptos- Serena's greatest General. He was mortally wounded at the conclusion of the Cataclysm while dueling Leterum for the sake of his soldiers and Queen. He sacrificed his life to imbue the gates with power, enough to imprison Acrom for millennia.

Ember Wood- A dark forest with roots that reach deep into the magma pools beneath Mürindür's western mountain range. Trees have been known to spontaneously catch aflame, and the ground at times becomes excessively warm.

Endüerduul- Paradise for all those deemed worthy whether it be life on Earth alone, or through purpose on the plains of Mürindür. Immortals come from the Endüerduul, and some remained to rule the ways of the Cosmos. Those Immortals that chose to leave for Mürindür and the mortal plane are highly regarded. Serena was crowned Queen of Mürindür by the Council of the Endüerduul, and she is in frequent counsel with the Oracle of the Pools of Cordis Loci. It is seen as the white moon in the sky of Mürindür.

Festorbius- A special bread made of slow rising yeast, dried fruits and nuts harvested from the Groves. The grain is harvested by farmers in the Fields of Effugere.

Fuga (Latin "flight")- The method of flight for all Immortals, dark and light alike. Some creatures of the Lux can learn the magic spell as well, such as imps and hobgoblins.

Leterum (derived from Letum, the personification of Death)- He is one of the greatest angels to have ever been created. Until the time of the Cataclysm, he had been highly revered in the Cosmos, and by all in the Endüerduul. He began to question the motives of those in high command, and felt he was best to decide all things for mortals. Though his role was as a steward for humanity, it morphed into a hunger for power as his prominence peaked during the great Egyptian dynasties where Death was worshipped as most supreme.

Lux (Latin for light)- The power of good and harmony in the Cosmos. It serves to direct, protect, and nurture the evolution of life. Those that serve the Lux are rewarded with peace in the Endüerduul.

Luxatio (Latin for dislocated)- A selfless band of warriors, mortals that have chosen to forever forfeit their right to the Endüerduul (dislocated fragments of light) in order to serve mankind. They return to Earth in each new life as stewards of the Lux, and return to Mürindür when it is time. They are the most powerful of mortals in the Cosmos, and have been pivotal in each significant historical moment of man.

Mael'deua- Dark, horned crimson demons that serve in the Onyx Order as the infantry of Acrom. They were imprisoned during the Cataclysm with their master. Now that the gates have been broken, they have found their way into Mürindür.

Mebum- A Highland medicinal drink of glacier water and nectar from fruit blossoms in the Groves.

Mürindür- The intermediary land created to bridge Earth to the Endüerduul and the Undüavalle. It became the realm for all magical creatures and beasts once the Cataclysm had concluded. Creatures of myth and legend all now reside within the confines of Mürindür.

Oerbuel- A beautiful green emerald cradled within gold leaves. Forged and crafted in the Endüerduul with the light of the first star, Oerbuel has always served as a symbol of hope. It can harness, protect, and even project light regardless of how deep the darkness may be. It is the wedding gift Creed offered to Celeste.

Ojin- An elder hobgoblin, and best friend of Creed. He has fought alongside Serena and served the Lux for thousands of years. He was there at the time of the Cataclysm, and still has a tendency to return to Earth for visits and observations. He is a wise scholar, and powerful in the ways of magic.

Ostiarius Chamber- A Chamber manned by a cyclops to assess all newly fallen souls. If the soul is not meant yet for Mürindür, it is sent back to Earth, and not allowed to pass.

Penumbra- A magical spell cast by hobgoblins to obscure light and perception. It facilitates invisibility, but consumes the magical powers of the hobgoblin, casting the protection over time.

Pools of Cordis Loci (Latin for "the heart of")- The heart of the Endüerduul cast upon the ground of Mürindür's mountain range. It serves as a portal, Oracle, medicine, and waters consumed during sacred rituals. It reflects the purest intent of the Endüerduul.

Serena- Queen of Mürindür and goddess of Life. She is the balance to Leterum, and when focused, she is the most powerful of all the Immortals not living in the Endüerduul. She is the mother of Celeste

572

whom she named after the heavens. She imprisoned Acrom the second time, but at a great cost.

Silva Luctus (Latin for forest mourning)- The forest is made of alder trees which have become the final resting place of Caedere granted peace and forgiveness with their last breath. The Caedere's soul becomes clean within the tree, and rests as it shares its knowledge of existence with the Rock of Soliloquy through its roots. If struck by lightning or lit aflame, the Caedere soul arises, redeemed to be accepted by the Endüerduul.

Titans- Giants born at the time of Immortals, and scattered through the Cosmos. Ignis is one such titan imprisoned with Acrom at the time of the Cataclysm. They serve their respective masters.

Undüavalle- Eternal damnation. Torturous and unkind, this is the realm of Acrom and the old gods that have fallen out of grace with the Lux. Those deemed most vile on Earth go straight to the underworld where they become slaves and servants of Acrom. It is the home of many dark creatures, demons, and is seen as the red moon in Mürindür's sky.

Üstor- A powerful relic weapon crafted in the halls of the Endüerduul solely for Elyptos. It harnesses the power of the wielder, and beyond immense heat and destructive capabilities, the glaive has certain magical properties in the healing arts.

Vagus (Latin for wanderer)- The Lost Ones. These are the souls that fall in the Dunes of Transitio confused, deranged, and likely did not perish well. Most died at their own hands either through intentional or indirect means. They were granted the power of free will, but suffered from variants of mental illness, and have forever been condemned as a result. It is Creed's intent to find the means to prove that all of humanity deserves a chance at peace and paradise. The Vagus are captured closest to Leterum's Keep, and they are converted into Caedere or sacrificed to Acrom.

Volantum Leonarum (Latin for winged lion)- The winged lions of the Northern Steppes (Praedorum Steppes) have been the apex predators of Mürindür since light first struck the mountain tops. It is said they flew directly from the Endüerduul when asked to serve the Lux as stewards of all animals and beasts within the realm. They battled Acrom when he first fell as they remembered his lust for power and enjoyment in cruelty. Each alpha of the Leonarum is colored white, and Morsu is the third alpha of his kind.

Welfalon- Well fallen souls that arrive in the Dunes of Transitio closest to the Keep of Redemptio. They are not sick or delirious like the Vagus, and they quickly assimilate into the ways of Mürindür. They are fed and clothed in Redemptio, taught their purpose in existence, and directed on a path to follow toward the Endüerduul.

www.ingramcontent.com/pod-product-compliance
Lightning Source LLC
Chambersburg PA
CBHW020623020726
47494CB00001B/17